IT'S NOT THE END OF THE WORLD

IT'S NOT THE END OF THE WORLD

a novel

JONATHAN PARKS-RAMAGE

BLOOMSBURY PUBLISHING

NEW YORK · LONDON · OXFORD · NEW DELHI · SYDNEY

BLOOMSBURY PUBLISHING
Bloomsbury Publishing Inc.
1359 Broadway, New York, NY 10018, USA
50 Bedford Square, London,. WC1B 3DP, UK
Bloomsbury Publishing Ireland Limited, 29 Earlsfort Terrace, Dublin 2, D02 AY28, Ireland

BLOOMSBURY, BLOOMSBURY PUBLISHING, and the Diana logo are trademarks of
Bloomsbury Publishing Plc

First published in the United States 2025

ISBN: HB: 978-1-63973-614-0; eBook: 978-1-63973-615-7

Library of Congress Cataloging-in-Publication Data is available

2 4 6 8 10 9 7 5 3 1

Typeset by Westchester Publishing Services
Printed in the United States by Lakeside Book Company

Bloomsbury books may be purchased for business or promotional use. For information
on bulk purchases please contact Macmillan Corporate and Premium Sales Department at
specialmarkets@macmillan.com.

For product safety–related questions contact productsafety@bloomsbury.com.

I believe the children are our future.

—WHITNEY HOUSTON, "GREATEST LOVE OF ALL"

Can the future stop being a fantasy of heterosexual reproduction?

—JOSÉ ESTEBAN MUÑOZ, *CRUISING UTOPIA:*
THE THEN AND THERE OF QUEER FUTURITY

CONCEPTION

2044

PROLOGUE

8 hours, 34 minutes

Larvae seethed inside the butchered chest cavity of her daughter's cat; the tender white bodies glistened as they feasted on black lungs, driven by a primordial instinct to destroy the very carcass that served as their birthplace. Jenna recoiled at the mess they'd made of their home, not that *she* was in a position to judge anyone's real estate situation. Jenna surveyed her worthless property; the corpse of Chairman Meow resonated with cryptic symbolism, joining the grim vignettes that dotted her backyard like grisly hieroglyphs: the charred lavender bush, the burnt-roofless backhouse, the fire pit abandoned for its redundancy.

A haze of smoke threatened to ruin another day. Ash blanketed her drained pool. The hot tub bubbled inexplicably; Jenna hadn't turned it on in over a year, not since they'd decided to bleed their Olympic-sized money monster. Still, Jenna clung to the hot tub with an irrational sentimentality; surely, they could afford to keep the smaller body of water, if for no other reason than to preserve the delusion that they'd return to their abandoned backyard in some utopian future, when the fires subsided and the smoke dispersed and they were once again free to squeeze a swim cap on their daughter's recently fused skull and watch her splash and giggle and squeal against a sky so bright it could convince them all that blue was the color of hope.

The stench of death invaded her nostrils. She backed away from the cat's body; her bare foot sank into a small puddle. She turned. It was a leak. Coming from the hot tub. The water had created a muddy rivulet that was, unfortunately, not deep enough to drown oneself in, something Jenna would rather do than explain the concept of death to her sweet baby girl and contend with the ensuing breakdown once Willow learned her beloved pet had been ripped in half by, well, by what exactly? Jenna walked along the trickling streamlet like a crime scene investigator sent to solve a Lilliputian murder; the river's baby banks offered nothing in the way of explanation, only a riparian battlefield littered with headless Barbies. Their gruesome fates were the result of a tantrum Willow had thrown on a rare clear day last month when Mommy demanded that her daughter come back inside because the Air Quality Index had returned to its hazardous status quo, and yes, Mommy knew that Willow's outside time was agonizingly brief these days, that Willow was mad because she wanted to swim but couldn't because Mommy and Daddy drained the pool, and oh, the pool, the pool, it always came back to that fucking pool, what an idiotic move that had been, a three-hundred-thousand-dollar investment meant to increase their property value, a decision born out of logic that—ten years later—no longer held weight, much like the toppled support beams of the thatched canopy that had once covered their outdoor dining area and its eighteenth-century farmhouse table. It was a French antique their designer had found at a Moroccan flea market and shipped back at great expense because it would be the perfect addition to their "design story," a narrative that reached an improbably dystopian conclusion when the gorgeous backyard tableau was reduced to a charred skeleton by the ruthless fire that had laid waste to Burbank last year. That fire—beautiful, terrifying, over-the-top. Something out of a TV apocalypse, like one of the shows she'd written scripts for in the 2030s, before the work dried up faster than the Los Angeles Aqueduct and she found herself in a professional drought. Her agents couldn't even score her a job in children's television, the place TV writers go to die, which made Jenna worry that the money in her bank account was a nonrenewable resource, a considerable concern since Cord was a stay-at-home dad and the majority of their wealth was tied up in a house they couldn't fucking sell.

It had been on the market for over a year. Untouched, unwanted. No one even bothered to insult them with a lowball offer, something to scoff at—*when I entered the market, this property was worth $2.7 million*—but then accept, because what choice did she have in 2044, when so many Los Angeles homes were being abandoned, written off, left to burn? But Jenna was determined to sell. For her family. They couldn't afford to withdraw from the housing market with zero return on their investment. They couldn't take that financial hit. Abandoning this house would mean abandoning Los Angeles, the lifestyle they'd built, and the future they expected for themselves, for Willow. Really, this was all about Willow. Jenna's three-year-old miracle, with light-blue eyes and blonde hair so soft there were times it felt like the locks might evaporate from between Jenna's fingers as she stroked her child's head.

Then again, what was so important about Los Angeles? Why was Jenna clinging to this city for her daughter, when Willow could be just as happy somewhere else, somewhere safe from climate change and the now-seasonless threat of wildfire? Let the banal charm of some third-tier suburb lobotomize their weary minds; let the endangered chirping of Midwestern songbirds drown out the hum of dread festering in their skulls; let Walmart bestow upon them its bounty of built-to-break products manufactured by wage slaves and destined for ocean trash futures; let them embrace the bottomless promise of the Olive Garden breadstick bowl until death delivered them from the burning planet.

She sighed. Looked back. The cat returned her stare; maggots danced in its eyes.

That was it. They would leave. For Willow.

A simple decision, one she'd fought for years. It brought a relief so profound she couldn't believe she'd waited this long to make it. Things had become too difficult to sustain in Los Angeles. Hope was reserved for the wealthy. They were no longer wealthy. They'd leave. *Escape* was a better word, really.

Thank God, she thought. *We'll escape.*

This is when the pink haze first appeared. It drifted over the dead palm trees that bordered Jenna's scorched yard. A ghostly, cotton candy floss. Just a small puff at first, like something expelled from the sneeze of a cartoon dragon. The strange mist descended, billowing exponentially; it enveloped the landscape in a candescent fuchsia smog reminiscent of those increasingly magnificent Los Angeles sunsets, with their toxic aerosol-tinted clouds sinking into the rising ocean. But there was no sun above their bungalow that day. Just the thickening smoke with its shocking hue.

Pink. Willow's favorite color.

Jenna had the sudden urge to wake her daughter. Bring her outside to see the magical fog enveloping their property, likely a beautiful byproduct of the fires consuming the forests that bordered Burbank, the danger that would force them into yet another evacuation. Their final evacuation. Before they left for good. Jenna took one last breath and marveled at the beauty that was possible amidst collapse.

*

Fifteen minutes later, the world had ended for Jenna and her family.

The house was silent. Smoke filled the kitchen, drifted in through open patio doors. The scene had the stillness of a diorama, an outline of domesticity barely visible through the blushing fog. The suggestion of cabinetry. The surprise of a marble island. The edge of a breakfast nook. A single white foot, bare against the hardwood, calloused at the heel. A Santa Ana gust pushed through the French doors. The smoke shifted, cleared. The foot was connected to a leg, which was connected to a torso, which was bent at the middle, splayed on a small oval table. Cord. His bowl of cereal. Cap'n Crunch—Willow's favorite, Cord's guilty pleasure. An abandoned spoon. A splatter of milk. Then the splatter of Cord's skull. An explosion of bone and blood and tendon. Smeared onto the white tabletop. Teeth protruded from the gore like gravestones.

The family room. Overturned. Furniture poked through the haze at impossible angles. Couch legs tilted heavenward. A felled lamp flickered on the ground. A coffee table leaned against the wall. Jenna knelt on the banquette by the bay windows. Her head had been thrust through a glass pane, her neck impaled on a thick shard, her pale face frozen in agony. A tiny cliff of glass jutted from her left eye. She wept blood.

Willow. The child's room was neat, orderly, just like she liked it. Her outfit for school had been laid out on the bed. A dress the same color as the smoke. Mommy had picked it out, like always. Willow's bed was tightly made. Hospital corners. Her head rested on a pillow among the row of her favorite stuffed animals: a frog in a crown, a love-worn teddy, a cow in high heels.

Her body lay across the room.

Fifteen minutes was all it took. But what happened in those fifteen minutes, like so much of what happens within a family, was known only to its members.

GESTATION

2044

ONE

6 hours, 32 minutes

I cannot *believe* that Jenna still hasn't RSVP'd to our baby shower." Mason invaded his lover's office, only to be confronted by a horrific sight: an iced latte, violently sweating through its glass, threatening to stain the un-coastered wooden expanse of the fourteen-thousand-dollar gold-plated ponderosa stump that served as Yunho's desk. Mason picked up Yunho's well-worn copy of *The Origins of Totalitarianism*—research for a film the couple hoped would help them recoup the considerable cost of the day's impending affair—and placed the book under the dangerously perspiring coffee. This was not the crisis Hannah Arendt had intended to dispel with her text, but it was a crisis nonetheless. He repressed his impulse to confront Yunho about the nearly ruined furniture; this was not a battle worth waging on a day they needed to be allies. "This is *insane*."

"Honey, if she hasn't RSVP'd at this point, she's not coming."

"I mean, I bought Willow the entire Prada baby collection for *her* shower."

"Which was probably the last time you spoke to Jenna. Who cares if she doesn't come?"

"It's the principle. If I'm forced to buy your unborn child designer clothing, I will absolutely seek revenge by inviting you to *my* baby shower."

"Oh, stop." Yunho delivered a weary eye roll. Neither of them had slept the previous night. There was the anxiety of the impending shower, and the perpetual fact that Yunho never slept when revising a script, a character trait Mason had begrudgingly accepted after fourteen years of sleeping next to each other. Yunho had tried Xanax, melatonin, meditation, but his insomnia could not even be tamed by BenzOh, the most powerful amygdala-tranquilizing app on his iOS Cerebrum. Compounding Mason's frustrations with this bout of restlessness was the script in question: Yunho's reboot of *Reds*, Warren Beatty's epic portrayal of the radical leftist John Reed and his involvement in the October Revolution. Mason wished Yunho would *drop* the doomed project; it would never get financed, not after the public thrashing Yunho had received at the hands of the House Anti-American Speech Committee for the script's communist themes. But a "no" only served to trigger Yunho's rageful defiance. Mason had begged Yunho to reboot something innocuous instead, *Jem and the Holograms* perhaps, something that didn't jangle the alarm bells of federal government fascists eager to annihilate the couple through bureaucratic, legal, and financial torture.

"Fine, I'll drop it." Mason proffered a capitulatory grin. "I'm sorry for being so cranky." He could never stay mad at his lover for long. The formidable power of Yunho's cuteness could neutralize any domestic fracas; anger was no match for the adorable curve of his pouting lips; hatred could not withstand the loving gaze of his tender brown eyes; bitterness cowered before the majestic architecture of his cheekbones. His six-foot physique was built for javelin throwing, backup dancing, dragon slaying—that he utilized all that muscle for a craft as delicate as writing never ceased to disarm Mason. But Yunho was a director; he created illusions for a living, valued aesthetics over function, and as such his muscles worked only in service of his image: Yunho Kim, acclaimed filmmaker, with a body far hotter than the demands of his profession dictated. But beneath Yunho's curated exterior was Mason's tender, big-footed, beauty-seeking giant, and Mason loved the way his own five-foot-ten, former-twink frame nestled perfectly in Yunho's embrace. "Let me in," Mason cooed in the voice they used when seeking comfort in the arms of the other after some stupid spat. "I'm sorry, my angel."

"It's okay, my love." Yunho welcomed Mason into his lap, kissing his cheek. "But I will say, this Jenna thing is a symptom of a larger problem I've had with this event to begin with."

"I know."

"I thought we agreed our shower would be free of toxic heteronormativity."

"That plan went out the window when my mother booked the stork-costumed synchronized swimmers."

"Storks don't even swim. They *wade*."

"Why did we allow my mother to help plan this?"

"Because the other option was allowing her to murder us."

The terrifying math of their baby shower: One hundred guests. Two event planners. A ten-piece orchestra. Five caterers. A twenty-person waitstaff. Six bartenders. Two florists. One invitation designer. Three DJs. Fifteen carpenters to install a dance floor on the lawn. And eight synchronized fucking swimmers, hired by Mason's mother. A grand total of one hundred thousand dollars. A sum ten times what they spent on their wedding: a courthouse elopement free from the machinations of the wedding industrial complex, followed by a fifteen-person dinner. Mason's mother had been invited a week before the wedding, filling her with furious disappointment (though she tried to mask it with a failed performance of normalcy, which had the heartbreaking side effect of underscoring her limited skills as a professional actress). Mason felt immeasurable guilt—she'd expected to be involved with the wedding planning. She believed it was owed to her, the way so much of her son's life was owed to her after years of single parenting and poverty, all so that Mason could eventually have the life of abundance he now led.

"Sweetie." Yunho clenched his jaw. "You're paying her mortgage. I don't think you also need to take on her desire for synchronized swimmers at *our* baby shower."

"But she *has* been helpful. She's spearheaded planning while *you've* been working—"

"I'm working so we can afford this—"

"Oh, please. *Reds* is gonna ruin us financially—"

"Who are you throwing this baby shower for? Us? Or your mother?"

It was a fair point. When Samantha had been excluded from wedding planning, it caused such a horrific fight that Mason felt he had no choice but to involve her in the planning of the next heteronormative ritual expected of him. Mason had insisted to a skeptical Yunho that he too wanted this baby shower; Mason *did* love a party, and their wedding *had* felt a little understated. It had been Yunho who'd insisted on the humble affair, who hated the pomp and environmentally ruinous circumstance of wasteful American weddings, who felt that February of 2032 was a strange and desperate time for two queer men to pledge allegiance to the institution of marriage, when the Senate was on the verge of codifying a federal gay-marriage ban made possible by the Supreme Court's obliteration of *Obergefell v. Hodges*, thereby, as Yunho asserted, "exposing the anti-queer roots of an institution that was never interested in changing to meet the needs of queer and trans people, only in forcing upon them assimilation to a cis-patriarchal tradition designed to beat the American family into capitalist submission."

Still, could Mason be blamed for wanting a *little* more romance?

And so, twelve years after their modest wedding, Yunho capitulated to a larger baby shower (though he had no idea how large it would become, how far Samantha Daunt would push her matriarchal influence). Yunho's only stipulation was that he be removed from the planning, a condition to which Mason initially agreed, but eventually defaulted on. It was difficult for Mason not to take personal offense at Yunho's absence from planning. Eventually, the shower preparation became so fraught Yunho agreed to handle only one symbolic task, to show his support for the man he'd called his husband before the State stripped away that title and its accompanying benefits.

"Did you confirm with the rain people?" Mason asked.

"I talked to them on Tuesday."

"So you didn't confirm."

"I confirmed on Tuesday, honey."

"But it's now Saturday and our event is in six hours, and you didn't confirm *today*."

"Okay, I will call the rain people again."

"Thank you." An expectant pause. Mason stared at Yunho.

"Oh, you want me to do this right now?"

"I know how you get when you're working."

"I will get to it—"

"Honey," Mason's voice was tinged with warning. "I need to head to the studio to save my work from impending incineration. Then I'm picking up the cake, the flowers, *and* our surrogate. I'm asking you to do *one* thing, which will take five minutes while I spend the next six hours of my life pulling our baby shower out of my ass."

"Calling now!" Yunho lifted his arms in surrender.

"Thank you." Mason stood from Yunho's lap.

"Hey." Yunho grabbed Mason's hand. "I love you." Yunho's tender smile—so beautiful, so delicate. So powerful because of its fragility. A reminder that even the strongest bonds were destructible, that their life was something they'd built together, something that had nearly collapsed under the awful weight of the past year. *Tend to me*, Yunho's eyes said. *Tend to us.*

Mason felt the sudden urge to cancel the shower. "I love you."

"We're having a baby."

"We're having a baby," Mason echoed as he donned his gas mask.

*

They were running out of money.

It's just one bad year, Mason thought as he tightened his Gucci gas mask and walked toward the garage, through the blanket of smoke smothering his backyard. *Plenty of rich people have suffered worse and survived.* He attempted to breathe normally, but he never could in this fucking mask. It looked cool and cost a shit ton but didn't work like it was supposed to. *Unless we don't. Unless the year we have a child is the year that begins our descent into bankruptcy, divorce, and the destruction of our nascent family.* An army of gas-masked laborers trudged through lush grass, leaving boot prints in Mason's irresponsibly watered lawn. He wove through their ranks as they hauled boxes, installed cocktail tables, hammered a massive dance floor into the soil. *But no, it's just one bad year.* The sight of the workers reminded him of the salaries he couldn't afford to pay them. *But why did the bad year have to be* this *year?*

"Mason!" a familiar female voice called. "Mason, wait!" He turned to look at his mother, but all he could see was her mortgage. The mortgage he'd been paying for the past four years, just one of the many expenses that contributed to his increasingly impossible overhead.

"Hi, Mom."

"Honey, have you confirmed with the rain people?" Samantha ran through the haze, her gas mask muffling her question. "The smoke is awful. We can't throw this party without WeatherMod and—"

"Yes, Mom. Yunho's taking care of it."

"Okay, because if he's busy, I can take on—"

"I *said* he's got it," Mason snapped. "You're doing *more* than enough."

Samantha's eyes watered in her mask. Steam rapidly fogged the plastic eye lenses, obscuring his mother's face, but he could tell from her shudders that she was crying.

"Mom—I'm sorry, I'm just stressed."

"Sweetie, I understand. This is such a big day for our family. And I'm only trying . . . to help . . ." She sobbed harder.

Mason put his arm around her shoulders. "And I'm grateful for you, Mom. It's gonna be a beautiful day," he insisted, even as he assessed the stagnant smoke lingering above their pool.

They'd almost canceled the shower. The Angeles National Forest was a sea of flame, lapping at the northernmost border of Burbank. It had started two days prior, prompting Yunho and Mason to debate the moral implications of their impending celebration. Was it in bad form to persist with a frivolous party when L.A. County was yet again on fire, when a thick layer of smoke had descended, when even at nine A.M. that morning the sun had been unable to shine through the haze? But they decided to persevere, in part because they couldn't afford to cancel—their vendor deposits were nonrefundable. Besides, this is why they—like so many other wealthy Californians—booked the boutique climate-engineering service Weather-Mod to clear whatever fatal miasma hovered in their backyard. Finally, Mason realized with a pang of sentimental dread, this was perhaps the last event they'd ever host at their $10.8 million, six-bedroom, Spanish colonial home, with its grand stucco arches, immaculate terra-cotta roof, and grove of purple-budded jacarandas that lined the driveway and still elicited tears of gratitude from Mason whenever he steered his Tesla into the comforting womb of their four-car garage.

Yunho wanted to sell it.

They needed to sell *something*. Their liquid assets were evaporating with terrifying speed, and now that the House Anti-American Speech Committee had successfully sued Yunho, there was a $3.9 million judicial lien on their home. This only increased Yunho's desire to offload the estate before weekly wildfires torpedoed property values any further. Plus, they had the ranch in Montana. They could move there, Yunho argued, and follow the wave of celebrity climate migration. Yes, they'd be forced to contend with the permanently installed Republican supermajority in the state's legislature, but they knew friends who'd moved there and reported that the vibes were more libertarian than authoritarian. Though Montana officials *had* outlawed queer adoption and surrogacy, they'd not yet criminalized existing gay parents who moved *to* Montana from out of state. If you managed to not do something stupid like protest the state's lack of free elections, then you could enjoy the disaster-lite climate of its majestic wilderness in peace.

But Mason was insistent on remaining in Los Angeles. While Yunho could work from anywhere (traveling when a shoot required it), Mason's art warehouse was in Burbank, and it would be costly to move the studio, complete with staff, equipment, and massive installations-in-progress. He needed to be in Los Angeles for work. *And for your mother,* Yunho had once snapped.

"It seems like just yesterday I was taking you to the Fosters Freeze on Glenoaks for ice-cream dinner," Samantha declared wistfully.

"I can't believe you let me eat banana splits instead of actual food."

"Well, sometimes Mommy didn't have room in the budget for dinner *and* dessert."

"Do you remember that poor waiter who was forced to wear the Little Foster costume?"

"That human-sized ice-cream cone was more of a father to you than your actual dad."

"I was a Little Foster Child."

"Oh, honey." Peals of muffled laughter emanated from his mother's gas mask. She threw her arms around her son. The familiar warmth of her body kindled Mason's nostalgia for the summer of 2021, when the oppressive pandemic distance learning of eighth grade had concluded and he was free to spend his days with Mom. Even though her "audition drought" meant near-nightly ice-cream dinners, Mason didn't mind that they were broke, because his mother was his best friend and he loved wrapping one arm around her waist while they sat at the iron picnic tables and ate their desserts, brains freezing in unison. Though the days were hot, nights in the Valley were cool that summer. When Mason looked back, he sometimes felt that he might never be as happy as he'd been then, back when there was still a fire "season," before the blazes became a perennial crisis due to environmental destruction sanctioned by politicians who had obliterated American democracy, before climate migration forced millions from the state where he was born, the state where he now wished to raise his own child against his better judgment. He felt tied to this land by history, by family, by love, and by the fact that Joni Mitchell could still bring him to tears with her vow to California, that she was coming home, that she'd even kiss a Sunset pig for the chance.

"It's going to be an amazing day," Mason promised, wondering what Joni would think of the ash that frosted the jacarandas in his driveway. Would she still feel the pull of this once-great state or would she run to where life was better, greener, where the air was easier to breathe, and write her songs there, in Montana, maybe? After all, it's hard to sing in a gas mask.

"I love you so much, sweetie." His mother's voice made his heart seize. Mason couldn't leave. Not yet. "Love you too, Mom."

But how could he raise a child in a city on fire?

*

John Mayer appeared on his Tesla's video console. The aging musician played the opening chords to his oldie "Your Body Is a Wonderland." The melody was the same, but the lyrics had been altered: *Your body is a signature. Your chip is installed, just use your mind.*

The video cut to a scene of John Mayer at a coffee shop. The barista handed him two paper cups. Mayer glanced at the attention-sensing interface of the credit card reader; the word APPROVED appeared on the screen. He bounded out of the shop and into a sunny street. *With iOS Cerebrum, your Apple Wallet lives right up here*, he said and tapped his finger against his temple. *Leave your hands free for the things that truly count.* The musician winked as a beautiful woman bounded into his arms. He handed her the coffee and kissed her cheek. *And try our ad-free premium subscription, starting at just $7.99 a month.*

The video ended. Siri's voice rattled his car's speakers. *Subscribe today?*

"No!" Mason shouted. Yunho constantly implored him to *just subscribe to premium*, to put an end to the advertising his body's internal operating system forced him to sit through.

I've noticed your body has failed to perform its usual morning bowel movement.

"Thanks for reminding me," Mason groaned.

You're welcome. MiraLAX is the doctor-recommended brand for gentle relief from constipation. Would you like me to order a bottle now?

"No."

Additionally, I noticed a spike in your blood pressure last night around eight thirty-seven P.M. Was this caused by anxiety due to your upcoming baby shower, scheduled for four P.M. this afternoon? Your conversation circled this topic at dinner with your mother, Samantha Daunt, and your domestic partner, Yunho Kim, as you consumed five glasses of wine. High levels of alcohol in your system disrupted your REM cycles. May I suggest—

"*Shut up!*" Sometimes, Mason regretted his ten-thousand-dollar decision to install a Brain Computer Interface. When the quarter-sized BCI had been drilled into his skull, when microelectrodes thinner than human hair had been threaded into his brain, when, after his recovery, he was able to sync his mind with all his devices, yes, life got more convenient. But corporations now had access to his brain waves. Whatever. It was nice when you had a hangover. Mason glanced at his Tesla's attention-sensing console and turned on the seat-warming feature with his mind. Thermal leather seared his skin, quelling the ache in his muscles. "Just drive."

Putting the car into autopilot. By the way, I'm happy for you. Today's baby shower is a major milestone.

"Thank you." Mason, vulnerable from the hangover, felt suddenly moved. "We've been through so much this year. It'll be nice to celebrate." Though he was stressed, a part of him enjoyed the minor drama of an impending party: the list of errands, the weight of the flowers in his arms, the joy of seeing the cake before anyone else, and throughout it all, the wistful Dallowayian dread that accompanied the preparation for an important celebration, with its cast of characters from every era of his life, all colliding to commemorate this one milestone, this marking of time that, like all markings of time, carried with it the subtext of death. These celebrations felt like a surreal time warp, an acknowledgment that the past was the present was the future. Nothing was new. Family was eternal. History controlled fate.

Control. The thing Mason always wanted, but rarely had. He certainly didn't have it when it came to his future and his finances and the thought of bringing a child into the mess of his life, not to mention the greater mess of the planet, with its floods and fires and prisons and myriad of oppressive forces bolstered by a neoliberalism that benefited a cabal of autocrats and trillionaires; everywhere he turned there was more evidence that the long arc of the moral universe no longer bent toward justice but had adopted a curvature that favored the dominance of a predatory global capitalism determined to annihilate all life on Earth.

How was his kid supposed to cope with any of *that*?

A shameful thought percolated in Mason's mind: hopefully their privilege would protect their family. But who knew how long that would last? Who knew if they would continue to be rich enough to remain on the right side of the chasmic class divide? And forget the big picture, how the fuck were they going to afford $100,000 for private preschool when they were spending *over* $100,000 on a baby shower, and they owed the government $3.9 million?

Still, the shower felt essential. It came back to control. Mason couldn't control his baby's *future*, but he could control his baby's *shower*. And weren't they kind of the same thing? Didn't the shower represent the future? The impressed coos from attendees would amount to a prophecy—*look at this gorgeous event, this kid is in good hands, what a bright future lies ahead.* Mason nursed this delusion with increasing intensity, until finally it felt like the baby shower was of life-and-death importance, because wasn't that what they were *really* celebrating, the transition into an era where every decision *was* life-and-death—*you'll suffocate the baby if you hold it like that, you fucking idiot*—where the fragile mortality of their delicate child would only draw attention to the inevitability of their own deaths? Yes, this party *mattered.*

Besides, he wasn't about to trust anyone else with the fucking flowers.

Siri pulled the Tesla out of the driveway. A newscaster's voice filled the car. "*. . . Smoke continues to blanket Los Angeles County. But in a strange development, certain pockets of the haze have taken on a pinkish-red tint. Scientists are baffled by this unusual coloration. As of now, calm wind conditions have prevented the pink smoke from spreading out of Burbank. Officials urged residents to leave the area, but stopped short of a mandatory evacuation—*"

Mason shut it off. He'd be in Burbank soon enough.

TWO

5 hours, 52 minutes

I'm quitting, darling." Mahmood's melodic British accent made a song of his resignation. Mason stood with his now-former COO in the loading dock of their Burbank warehouse, watching as five gas-masked art handlers loaded a massive marble penis into the gaping mouth of a moving truck. Beyond the vehicle, there was only the dense haze, so thick it had darkened from pink to red. Like a mist of blood, as if somewhere above a giant's throat had been slit.

"But . . . I need you." Mason's respirator muffled his retort.

"I'm terribly sorry, dear." Only Mahmood's eyes were visible through his gas mask, but even his partially obscured expression betrayed a definitive sadness. "I'm happy to stay on in an advisory capacity. But in terms of the day-to-day, you'll need to look for someone else."

"But why?"

Mahmood rubbed his belly. "I'm pregnant again."

"Oh my god, congrats!"

"Thank you. I worry the decision to have a third child is a sign of mental illness."

"I thought the extra pounds meant that you were just embracing your identity as a bear."

"First of all, I am *far* too petite and adorable to be a bear." Mahmood set his thick arms akimbo. "If anything, I identify as a *koala* bear." Indeed, there was something appealingly marsupial about his round face, stocky frame, and plump thighs that moved with an unhurried confidence. The weight gain was recent, brought on by his last two pregnancies, and it suited Mahmood, as if his frame had always been destined for more meat. When Mason first met him during their art school days at RISD, Mahmood was still in his twink phase, and he'd never seemed at home in his rail-thin body. His movements had been jittery, clumsy as a plastic skeleton clattering in a Halloween breeze. However, that jumpiness may have had more to do with the ghoulish amounts of cocaine he and Mason consumed during the brief period they fucked freshman year before being confronted with the unfortunate sexual math problem that terminated the relationships of so many queers before them: Two bottoms do not equal a top.

"Admit it—this is just your way of stealing my baby shower's thunder."

"*Stealing* your baby shower's thunder would be the only way I could afford WeatherMod." Mahmood rubbed Mason's back. "But I wouldn't dream of it. You know how happy I am for you two."

"Fuck." Panic mixed with despair as a strange heat blossomed in Mason's ears. "I don't know what I'm gonna do without you."

"You'll be fine. Oh, and I got you an I'm-quitting-don't-hate-me present." Mahmood crossed to the far wall of the warehouse, where a large canvas hung, covered in a white sheet. "Which is also my baby shower gift." Mahmood ripped off the cloth.

"*Fuck You Faggot Fucker*," Mason said in astonishment, not as a slur, but as a recitation of the title of the piece of art that miraculously hung in front of him. "Is this real?"

"I wouldn't buy you fake art, darling. I'm not a monster."

"This must have cost you a fortune."

"It wasn't cheap. But it also wasn't as expensive as it deserves to be. Unsurprisingly, our modern authoritarian market doesn't value an artist and AIDS activist who accurately denounced America as a racist, capitalist, anti-queer 'killing machine.'"

"It's stunning." Mason had only seen it once in person, as a child, when his mother brought him to *History Keeps Me Awake at Night*, the Whitney's 2018 David Wojnarowicz retrospective. Mason remembered little about that New York trip, but he did remember this four-foot-by-four-foot collage, a stencil of two shirtless men kissing in a body of water; the image was superimposed on a deconstructed and reconfigured map of the world; photos of naked men floated in each corner of the piece. Something had stirred in Mason when he saw it, an emergent understanding of who he was, as if the strange map charted a distant queer utopia that Mason knew he must one day inhabit. It filled him with longing; it gave him his first erection. This led to a lifelong obsession, shared by no one he knew until he roomed with Mahmood in the RISD dorms. "Our favorite Wojnarowicz," Mason said. "You have no idea how much this means—"

"Yes, I do."

Was it strange that, as a college freshman, Mason felt nostalgia for an era he'd never inhabited? That he longed to be a queer artist during the AIDS crisis, to experience the righteous fury that fueled Wojnarowicz, to know what it felt like to fight for the lives of everyone you loved? There was something bracingly ungentrified about the pre-assimilationist queer politics of the time. There was hope, beneath the rage, that queer people could build something better.

Mason found it difficult to hold on to hope. He'd watched American "democracy" crumble over the course of his adolescence. By the time he reached his senior year at RISD, he'd already witnessed years of anti-queer and anti-trans legislation, he'd witnessed racist gerrymandering become increasingly aggressive, he'd witnessed local election boards seized by conservative activists successfully overturn legitimate election results, he'd witnessed the subsequent protests get crushed by police violence, he'd witnessed feckless Democrats cling to power by making empty promises to take action, and he'd watched as evangelicals created the Christo-fascist utopia of their white supremacist dreams. It was in this context that Mason first felt he could make a difference with his art, could rebel against the rising tide of oppression and religious bigotry, and so, for his RISD thesis show, he created a virtual reality installation entitled *Jesus Is Fucked*, a digital landscape in which the Stations of the Cross were turned into hard-core queer BDSM scenes where one's avatar could literally fuck a sub/bottom Jesus. As a bonus, you could give Mary an abortion for Christmas. Once news of this project entered the national discourse, it marked Mason as a target for right-wing moral outrage and cemented his reputation as an art star even before his graduation.

"My dads pitched in too," Mahmood confessed with a grin. "They say, 'Happy baby shower,' by the way."

"That's so sweet."

"I'll have one of the handlers deliver it to your place."

"Thank you."

"And of course, even though I'm leaving, my fathers' gallery will still represent you."

Mahmood had attended RISD to satisfy his fathers. The couple co-owned Khan & Bhutto—a global art gallery with outposts in Los Angeles, New York, London, and Karachi—and wished to see their son continue the family legacy by becoming an artist. But Mahmood was too easily bored to focus on one project for any real length of time; he found the quick-fire pace of sales more to his liking. So, after college, his fathers hired him as a dealer for Khan & Bhutto's L.A. location. Mahmood made Mason his first client. Mason had moved to Los Angeles instead of the more traditional art capital of New York because of his mother—she'd developed chronic fatigue syndrome after his graduation. Mason, in uncharitable moments of frustration, wondered if this was a ploy to keep her son locked in a codependent dynamic. Still, he took care of her rent when flare-ups of fatigue prevented her from auditioning. It was a small price to pay as Mason's bank account swelled under Mahmood's representation. He successfully exploited his client's reputation as an enfant terrible to great financial gain. Soon, it was trips to Art Basel, to Frieze, exhibitions at the Whitney, private dinners with billionaires, with trillionaires.

But in 2036, when the Republican supermajority in Washington estab-lished the House Anti-American Speech Committee, a fear began to fester in Mason's heart. A fear that the committee would charge him with crimes of artistic sedition, that he'd be summoned to D.C. for a public flogging where he'd be forced to answer for his early radical work and admit to being a communist or socialist or anarchist. Not willing to risk this career-obliterating fate, Mason's started making more "mature" work: giant mean-ingless sculptures for Parisian bank lobbies and Wall Street hedge funds and British countryside estates, prints for Moschino handbags, paintings that could be mass-produced by artificially intelligent robots. Ironically, as Mason drained his work of the radical politics that made him famous, he became even *more* successful. Eventually, he and Mahmood launched the Daunt Factory. Mason was CEO, Mahmood COO. They bought the Burbank ware-house, staffed it with ten assistants, and developed a client list that included some of the world's wealthiest individuals and largest corporations.

"You know I love you."

"I love you too." The sadness Mason felt at Mahmood's resignation was unbearable; Mahmood was the last link to the artist Mason used to be, back when he wanted to tear the world apart.

"And I love what we built. But I need to focus on Daniel and the babies right now. Also, I must admit that this"—Mahmood gestured to the smoke—"is giving me second thoughts about raising my family in L.A."

"I understand." And of course he understood. Los Angeles was oppres-sive. But Mason was stuck here, with this warehouse and his backup storage space downtown, a storage space he'd been forced to rent when the *last* fire threatened to consume his Burbank studio. Now here he was, once again emptying out all the sculptures and paintings and partially constructed installations from his Burbank studio and moving them downtown to save them from the blaze. It was such a waste. Yes, they'd started out with some-thing queer and punk, but what had it grown into? A global business. He was a professional billionaire cocksucker. Or at least he used to be. Busi-ness had been slow recently, the Daunt Factory was operating at a loss, the market was moving on to sexier pastures, newer artists, and now, when he most needed money, it seemed everyone had lost interest. Well, almost everyone.

"Make sure they stop at the Sullivan estate *before* they go downtown to storage."

"I can't believe the Dark Empress wants her sculpture delivered *today.*"

"I can." Mason sighed.

"Why don't you head out, darling? You have a baby shower to prepare for."

*

The crimson haze had thickened. He could barely see three feet in front of the car. Siri auto-enabled the high beams. Petals of pink ash fell onto his windshield, like it was raining burnt azaleas. "Siri—call Becky's Buttercream Palace."

Sure. Calling now.

"Hello, Becky's Buttercream Palace?"

"Hi, just wanted to say I'm on my way to pick up a cake despite current, uh, conditions."

"We're closing early today, sir. Because of the fires. I'm about to head out."

"Can you just . . . wait?"

"*Wait?* Have you looked out your window—"

"I'm literally around the corner . . ." The smoke parted. "*FUCK—*"

A body appeared. Lying on the road.

"Sir? I don't appreciate that use of language—"

He hung up. "*FUCK.*" Siri slammed the breaks.

Silence. Mason looked down. A mangled face met his gaze. One eye had been gouged out, cheeks shellacked with blood and vomit. Its left arm—a shredded stump. Bicep tendons sagged like wet party streamers. A clavicle jutted from the slop of muddled sinew. Its shirt had been torn off; its heaving chest was julienned like steak tartare. Still-breathing steak tartare.

It was alive.

The figure writhed in the glare of Mason's headlights. A streak of shit seeped from the body as it moved, smearing the pavement. Its one eye widened in terror while the ghost of its gouged twin caused the muscles of its empty socket to pulse. The bloody hole belched pus; viscous bacteria streamed down its left cheekbone. The thing's ear had been hacked off—all that remained was a skinned circle of white fat around a gaping orifice; it frothed with yellow discharge. A destroyed gas mask dangled from its neck, hanging by tattered straps. It opened its mouth but failed to scream—a seizure took hold of its body; its mauled limbs thrashed against asphalt, swashing in the brown-red puddle of its own waste.

Finally, it settled. Cracked its butchered lips. Howled. Its throat seized from the scream.

I detect an obstacle in front of us. Shall I investigate another route—

"*Shut up!*" Mason froze in the driver's seat. He felt a wetness beneath him. Smelled something sour. He'd fucking pissed himself.

The thing floundered, pumped its legs, and pushed across the pavement, sluglike.

But its speed was astonishing.

Mason grabbed his gas mask, slapped it on, and opened the door. He got out but kept his keys in the car, the high beams on. He lingered by his Tesla like it could somehow protect him.

The figure vanished into the smoke.

"Hey!" Mason called out. Nothing. A truck roared by, materializing out of the thick haze. He jumped aside, then called out again. "Hey, I . . . I wanna help you. But I can't see where you went? So, if you just come back, I'll get you to a hospital . . ."

Silence again. Mason ventured deeper into the haze, in the direction the body had slithered. His car gradually disappeared behind him, becoming a muted glow behind a curtain of red smoke. A gust of wind chilled his damp back. Then, a rustle.

He wheeled around; his entire body tensed. Sweat fogged the interior of his gas mask.

It was nothing. No one. He felt the urge to rush home, into his lover's arms, call off the shower, and somehow reverse the hellish hours, days, and months that led him to this moment.

Why, oh why, did they ever decide to have a child?

THREE

18 months, 16 days, 3 hours, 49 minutes

Yunho's right testicle was pregnant with cancer; it hung lower than the left, weighted by a tumor that grew within his scrotum like a hostile alien fetus. "Get this *out* of me," he moaned.

"It's bigger than it was yesterday." Mason cupped the malignant growth in his hand; it was the size of a golf ball. He sat on the edge of their claw-foot tub; Yunho stood naked in front of him, backlit by a halo of sunlight. "But it'll all be over after tomorrow."

"I'm worried about the recovery."

"If you're still struggling, we don't have to go to Gabriel's party next week—"

"I refuse to miss it. I'm missing *everything* in my life but my endless doctor's appointments. I just want to go back to my normal existence for *one moment* and attend a kid's stupid birthday and eat a dumb cupcake and forget that my fucking balls are trying to kill me." Yunho sighed and stroked the red welt where yesterday a rookie nurse botched the venipuncture for an IV line containing contrast dye that would highlight his insides during his CT scan and illuminate whether the cancer had spread. "I'm sorry."

"It's okay." The CT scan proved inconclusive; the imaging highlighted the mesenteric lymph nodes in his abdomen, though just barely. The doctor said the results were worrisome, but it didn't necessarily mean the cancer had spread. It also didn't mean it *hadn't* spread. They'd proceed with the radical orchiectomy to remove the cancerous testicle, and then, a week after surgery, they'd test the tumor markers in Yunho's blood levels. If they were still elevated, it would mean death had a lease on his guts. But for now, they could only wait and let dread fester.

"I just want this to be over."

"It will be soon."

"But . . . you don't . . . know that." Yunho sobbed so hard it frightened Mason. Tears flooded Yunho's face; his eyes were empty, mind lost. Mason stood, wrestling his lover into an urgent embrace. Yunho steadied, returned from whatever psychic abyss he'd visited. Mason wet a washcloth and cleaned his lover's face. They kissed carefully, as if Yunho's skull might shatter from the pressure. Mason stroked his back; Yunho suffered a series of small hiccups.

Then, quiet. Yunho's naked cock pressed against Mason's thigh. It swelled, stiffened.

Mason took it in his hands. Yunho winced. "You okay?" Mason whispered.

"Yeah." He licked Mason's ear. Yunho took the head of Mason's cock, stroked it gently. Precum blossomed from the tip. Yunho brushed the white sap with his finger, then stuck it in Mason's mouth. Mason lapped at his own precum, opened his throat. Yunho pushed his finger deeper inside; his lover's uvula pulsed against his knuckle.

Mason gagged. Yunho pulled out. Slapped Mason's face, pried open his jaw. Spat inside. "Get on the fucking floor." He threw Mason to the ground. Mason's knees hit cold terra-cotta tile. Yunho grabbed the back of Mason's skull and forced his cock deep into Mason's throat. Mason's neck spasmed as he gagged. But Yunho didn't release his grip on Mason's head; he just impaled it harder. Spit erupted from Mason's mouth, dripped down Yunho's swollen sac. He could taste Yunho's precum; he was desperate to drink it. Yunho's pulsing cock teased the entrance to Mason's esophagus. He relaxed. Opened up. Let Yunho in. Tears coursed down Mason's face as he looked up. A dark power lit Yunho's eye. "You want my cock, boy?"

Mason moaned, mouth full.

"I can't hear you, boy." Yunho kicked Mason off his cock. Mason gasped for air, fell onto the floor. Yunho straddled his neck. "I *said* do you want my fucking cock?" Before Mason could answer, Yunho thrust his dick back inside Mason's mouth. Yunho jackhammered Mason's throat, pounding his head against the floor. He slapped Mason's cock-plugged face, hitting him again and again, until his cheeks were hot, red, aching. "Tell me you're just a hole."

Yunho ripped his cock out of Mason's throat. "I'm just a hole, sir," Mason choked.

Yunho rammed his erection back inside Mason's mouth. Mason gagged; his entire body heaved, retched. "That's a good boy. Now, say it again: You're just a worthless fucking hole."

Yunho pulled out again; precum splattered Mason's face. "I'm a worth-less fucking hole—" Yunho shut Mason up with his cock. It throbbed in Mason's throat, busted; semen bubbled inside his mouth, coating his tongue. Yunho pulled out, smeared cum across Mason's lips. Mason tugged at his cock; ejaculate geysered to his mouth and mixed with Yunho's. Yunho tongued the sap from Mason's lips. Grinned. "Wow."

"Fuck, that was hot."

"I have to say, cancer has done wonders for our sex life."

"You should get it more often."

"I don't know about that." Yunho laughed grimly as he turned on the shower. Ever since Yunho's diagnosis, they'd been fucking like they might never fuck again. Why did that turn Mason on so much? Perhaps it was a way to eroticize death and thereby sublimate the fear of it, to manage the terror that pulsed through their relationship as they confronted the fact that Yunho could be ripped from this Earth by the very organ that was supposed to *create* life. At Yunho's suggestion, Mason imagined himself as just a hole, a grave for sperm, a place for life to die. It was fucking for the sake of fucking, fucking divorced from reproductive futurity, fucking as oblitera-tion, fucking as the irreparable loss of presence. Fucking as the death instinct.

Which was why Mason was taken aback when, minutes later, Yunho emerged from the shower with a bashful smile and said, "They asked me if I wanna freeze my sperm."

"Who is 'they'?"

"My doctors. There's a chance that removing my testicle could make me infertile."

"There's still plenty of cum on my face. Should we run to the sperm bank?"

"I'm serious, Mason." Yunho snapped a towel from the rack.

"I . . . it was a joke."

"Well, I don't feel like joking—this is our future."

"I'm sorry. I mean, this is just a little bit out of the blue."

"It's not—we've talked about kids before."

"Yes, *theoretically*. But we never talked about having them, like, *tomorrow*."

"I never said I wanted to have them *tomorrow*. I'm having *surgery* tomorrow."

"Oh my god, I didn't *literally* mean tomorrow, honey."

Yunho began to sob. "I . . . I . . ."

"Hey, I'm sorry. I didn't mean to upset you." Mason pulled Yunho into a ferocious embrace. "I was just taken aback. I think freezing your sperm is a good idea. Because I *do* want children." Mason was unsure if this was true, but when faced with the mortality of the man he loved, what else could he do but say: *Yes, we'll rebel against death by creating new life.*

"I . . . I didn't mean to pressure you to have kids."

"I know, I know." Mason stroked his lover's back.

"We can just freeze the sperm . . . and decide later."

"Okay," Mason murmured. A zygote of fear blossomed in his belly.

FOUR

5 hours, 6 minutes

M ason stood at the counter of Becky's Buttercream Palace, smelling like piss. The eponymous Becky, an anorexic blonde woman in her thirties, wrinkled her nose as she hoisted a massive cake box onto the counter. "You're lucky I'm passionate about my cakes." Her ghost-white arms trembled under its weight, looking like they might snap. "Next time you might wanna use friendlier language."

"I'm sorry. I was . . ." He trailed off as a flash of the mutilated body replayed in his mind.

Becky stared at him, waiting. When it became clear he had no idea how to finish his sentence, she pressed on. "It's fine. We *were* about to close. But we don't want you having a cake-free baby shower," she said with terse irony. "I hope the party isn't here in Burbank."

"No. Los Feliz."

"Lucky. Fires won't reach you. Not today, anyway. But still, *the smoke.* So nasty."

"We have WeatherMod coming. It was the only option if we were still gonna do the party . . ."

"Well, the 'only option' if you're rich," she said with a tight little smile.

"Thanks for the cake." Mason ignored the barb. "How much do I owe you?"

"Don't you think it's just a way of forgetting?"

"Excuse me?"

"Weather modification. A way of forgetting what's happening to us. Addressing the symptom, but not the cause. You pay some fancy company to launch a bunch of chemical compounds into the air, which creates artificial rainfall, which clears the smoke over your mansion, which allows you to have your party in peace and sunshine and forget about the rest of us struggling to breathe, running home from work, not sure if our houses will be still be standing when we get there because we didn't get to leave our jobs as early as we wanted because some *asshole* needed his fucking cake for his goddamn baby shower."

"I'm . . ." Mason stammered. "I'm sorry."

"I don't want your apology." She sighed, suddenly deflated. "Just give me my money."

*

He kept calling Yunho, but it went straight to voicemail every time. He tried texting. No response. The cake box bounced in the Tesla's back seat, buckled in like a fussy toddler. Mason glanced at it, terrified the thousand-dollar three-tier confection would slip from its restraints and splatter on the floor. Where the hell was Yunho? Still writing, no doubt. Obsessively revising the doomed *Reds* reboot. When he got like this, a grenade could detonate their backyard sauna and he wouldn't take his eyes off his laptop. Mason respected Yunho's right to work without interruption but sometimes there were emergencies, like today, when Mason had almost run over that, that *thing* in the middle of the road, that human-gore-slug that summoned a scream from the depths of hell and directed it at Mason's Tesla before vanishing into the blood-colored smoke enveloping fucking Burbank. He *needed* to talk to Yunho.

Suddenly, Mason's phone rang. "Yunho?" he gasped, picking up before Siri could announce the caller.

"Hi, this is Steph, from WeatherMod?" Her voice echoed from the car's speakers.

"Oh. Hi, Steph. Not a great time. Didn't my husband call you earlier today?"

"No, I wish that *the* Yunho Kim called me. I'm *such* a fan."

He forgot to confirm, Mason thought, grinding his teeth. "Is everything set for the party?"

"Oh, *definitely*. You're confirmed for our four-hour Cloudburst Package. That includes the pre-party rainstorm with high winds. The smoke should clear for about two hours, at which point we'll do another mid-party downpour. Our guys have tents ready to keep everything dry. And that should keep you smoke-free for—"

"We don't need to go over the package again. Just wanted to confirm. Thanks!"

Mason hung up the phone. The Tesla slowed to a stop. A procession of taillights appeared in the windshield. Bumper-to-bumper vehicles crawled down the highway like segments of a metal centipede. Evacuation traffic. Mason inched past the Hollywood Bowl; down here, the smoke was thinner, higher, it hadn't yet descended to street level. It was still a natural gray color. Now that he'd escaped the pink cloud stifling the Valley, the memory of the body on the road began to fade. Surely, he couldn't be blamed for moving on. He'd gotten out of his car and really searched for that *thing*. But it had vanished. Even if he'd called an ambulance, there would've been nobody to collect, living or otherwise. Also, he'd be stuck with an ambulance bill, which was *not* a line item on their baby shower budget. Calling 911 would've been a waste of money and time when he had neither to spare, when he was already late to pick up the flowers, and now there was this fucking traffic, this honking and braking and screaming gridlock.

Past Hollywood and Highland, the cars cleared. Mason sighed.

A text binged onto the Tesla's screen.

Siri dictated: *Message from Patrick Sullivan.* "Come now. It's an emergency."

FIVE

5 hours, 2 minutes

**FBI COUNTERTERRORISM DIVISION——NATIONAL
THREAT CENTER SECTION CLASSIFIED:
SUSPICIOUS ACTIVITY REPORT——SEIZED EMAIL**

From: Claudia Jackson <claudiajackson@gmail.com>

To: <DSS2044@gmail.com>

My dear sweet someone,

I want to tell you about a dream I had . . .

I was lying in a burned-out basement, looking up at a bright sky. There was nothing between me and the world above; whatever building had once stood upon this now blackened foundation had been obliterated by fire. I turned to my right and saw a pile of ash, still glowing with the warm embers of the structure that had perished while I'd been unconscious and suddenly—staring at this devastation—I was seized by joy.

Yes, joy. Everything was gone, but I knew that somehow, somewhere, there was still something left for me. For us. The borders of the basement created a cement frame, and the blue of the sky filled it, and this beautiful picture led me to believe something great lay beyond these ruins now that the fire was over. I wanted to climb out of the basement and face the dawn. A feeling swelled inside me, awakened by the fresh warm air; every time I filled my lungs this feeling got stronger, but strangely, I couldn't name it.

I turned and saw my wheelchair. It too had survived the fire. I crawled over, and my arms were so strong, my whole body was filled with purpose and *this feeling*—I still couldn't name it but the feeling was connected to the intuition that once I got out of this basement everything would make sense, I would learn everything I needed, I would meet other people and listen when they told me what they needed to survive, and we would create a small and beautiful and ungoverned society, freed from the false promises of representative "democracy," a lie so many people still believe, even though it's clear we live in a failed State, that *every* State throughout history has been a failure to the people oppressed within its borders because the State is wedded to capital, protects the ruling elite, and must always exploit, imprison, and kill an underclass.

This is why we must dismantle the State, burn it down, until we're left with nothing but its razed and blackened foundation, the surface upon which we will build something new, and that beautiful, blackened foundation will be something like that burned-out basement in which I lay in my dream.

I wanted you to be there. But I was all alone in the basement. I didn't know how to escape. I wheeled my chair along the perimeter. The walls were ten feet high. There was no staircase. No ramp. No way up and out and into the bright blue day. I screamed for you. Screamed as loud as my lungs would let me. Once again, that *feeling* swelled within me, and gave me the *strength* to scream louder, and as I heard my voice echo in search of you, I realized what that feeling was.

Love.

It was the love I felt for you. I prayed this love would be enough. Enough to free me. To free you. To free us all. But I never found out. That's when I woke up.

It's strange to think you occupy such a huge space in my heart and mind, when I haven't even met you yet. I suppose that's why I keep writing these letters; I need an outlet for all this love, a place to put the hope I feel when I think of what we will create together.

Because I have a plan. It's already in motion. I'm doing it all for you.

Yours forever,
Claudia

SIX

4 hours, 34 minutes

I just don't know *where* to put the sculpture," Patrick moaned, surveying the visibly annoyed art movers as they dragged the ten-foot marble penis from one side of his ostentatious foyer to the other. "I'm afraid it's just a little too much . . . penis for the entryway."

"Frankly, I agree. And I made the thing."

"You're *hilarious*." Patrick issued a grinless cackle. Though he was capable of laughter, smiling had been taken off the menu long ago by his overworked plastic surgeon. Patrick's botched mirth was disconcerting to witness; the lack of coordination between what was on his face and what came out of it lent him a sinister unreality. He was somewhere between forty-eight and sixty-seven years old. His smooth, malfunctioning features combined with a steroid-juiced body made him seem like an evil, short-circuiting cyborg whose inability to mimic anthropoid social cues made it impossible to conceal his secret agenda to exterminate the human race. "Thank you for coming at the last minute. I was *so desperate*."

Of course, there was no "emergency." Or rather, there was a complete nonemergency that qualified as one for Patrick Sullivan. This was typical behavior for the billionaire entrepreneur who Mason and Mahmood had dubbed the Dark Empress. Everything was an emergency to Patrick, even though his wealth removed the threat of most *actual* emergencies that non-billionaires experienced. With no frame of reference for real-life danger, Patrick created crises where none existed to sublimate the screaming existential dread that one experienced when all threats (except the guarantee of an open grave) had been erased. For him, the death drive manifested in a million little bullshit "emergencies" that were not remotely serious, yet he demanded his friends (who were all, without exception, his employees) treat them with extreme urgency.

"I just don't know what to *do with it*." Patrick's mouth collapsed into a sad pile of lip filler. Tears pooled in their ducts. "I didn't spend two hundred thousand dollars on a marble penis just so it could sit in storage with the rest of the art that I hate." He collapsed into Mason's arms, weeping softly.

"We'll find another space." Mason massaged Patrick's neck, a tactic that typically dispelled a Dark Empress meltdown. "Your compound is palatial."

"It *is* . . . an entire . . . city block," Patrick gulped as his sobs subsided.

Patrick was as pitiful as he was violently wealthy. His parents were millionaire evangelical oil tycoons in Texas who'd taken their son to court for sodomy and won; Patrick had been sentenced to six months in one of the state's conversion therapy internment camps that cropped up in the early 2030s; he'd emerged traumatized, furious, gayer-than-ever yet determined to beat his parents at their own game. He launched a press tour to lie and claim conversion therapy worked; his well-publicized "transformation" became "proof" the state's internment camps were a success, a fact that endeared him to GOP leaders and conservative magnates who opened doors for him within global business, enabling him to surpass his parents' pathetic millions and deliver a "fuck you" to Mommy and Daddy from the billionaire's club.

His breakthrough came when he bought NuGrow Industrial, a startup that produced agricultural chemicals to service "emerging markets in global agriculture," aka nations formerly inhospitable to crops due to subarctic climates but that, thanks to global warming, were increasing their capacity to produce food. NuGrow's main target was Russia, and in 2034,

Patrick cut a major deal with Russian kleptocrats to become a main supplier of agricultural chemicals for the country's farms. Other larger multinationals were skeptical—their own experts insisted NuGrow's investment in a projected "Russian farming boom" was twenty years premature and thus doomed to fail. But, after five years of losses, Patrick's bet paid off and climate change—outpacing scientific forecasts with ease—delivered a fertile-for-farming Russian landscape (not to mention a robust workforce of Chinese climate refugees, who were forced to settle in areas most susceptible to carcinogenic pesticide runoff). Russia became the largest producer of food in the world, tilting the global power scales in its favor and leaving the United States with little trade leverage due to increasing domestic food scarcity, particularly after the MegaDust Bowl ravaged American farms in 2041. With a stronghold on Russian agriculture, NuGrow's valuation skyrocketed faster than the temperatures in newly verdant Siberia, and Patrick became a billionaire. NuGrow's PR team touted a vague "mission of sustainable global stewardship." But behind the scenes, Patrick struck another deal with Russian kleptocrats to ensure NuGrow experienced no environmental regulation on their products. Why, when NuGrow and Russia had experienced a massive business boom due to climate change, would they wish to curb its spread?

"Maybe I need to ship it to my Moscow compound." Patrick sighed, wiping his tears.

"We'll find someplace here. I'll chat with your interior designer."

"You're so good to me." Patrick tackled Mason into a hug. Mason winced. The man had billions of dollars but zero real friends, a fact Mason exploited six months earlier when they'd met at Art Basel Hialeah (the Floridian city closest to the art fair's former Miami headquarters, which were now underwater along with the rest of Miami Beach). Patrick had recently moved to Los Angeles to launch the latest NuGrow outpost and was desperate for art to fill his new estate and friends to fill his social calendar. Mason flirted, fawned, nearly broke Florida's "child protection" law against homosexual public affection to endear himself to someone who could infuse the Daunt Factory with direly needed capital. "I'm lucky to live so close to my artist."

It wasn't the first time Patrick referred to Mason as "my artist." Every time he did, Mason disassociated just the tiniest bit. But before he could fully leave his body, Mason was confronted with a rare sight: the sun. Warm beams poured through the skylight above them. *Sunlight*, Mason thought. *What a luxury*. Patrick was one of the few Americans wealthy enough to purchase round-the-clock weather modification. Not even the largest corporate farms, desperate for water during the MegaDust Bowl, considered this type of geoengineering a justifiable expense. The rain a costly WeatherMod Cloudburst yielded was insufficient to extinguish a wildfire or irrigate a factory farm. But Patrick had no problem burning money. Sunlight was his kink. "I must say, I'm jealous . . ." Mason motioned to the radiance spilling from the skylight.

"Sexy, isn't it?" He slapped Mason's ass. "I couldn't live in Los Angeles without it."

"I just came from Burbank and it's like another *planet* over there—"

"*Burbank?*" Patrick jumped backward. "Please tell me you wore your gas mask."

"Of course. The air is filled with—"

"Pink smoke," Patrick interrupted. "I'll send you articles on this. Octo-Liberals are—"

"Patrick—it's best for us to steer clear of politics."

"—attempting population control through poisonous, pink, bio-engineered smoke. All morning, I've been in touch with the Anti-OL guy who's aggregated info on this." Patrick was a man who could, in one moment, extemporaneously lecture on Milton Friedman's economic theories with such brilliance that he could convince a communist that the only social responsibility of a business *was* to increase its profits, while in the next moment, he could undermine all credibility by offering up the most unhinged conspiracy theory to explain why a third term for the current president was a dire necessity because the Democratic presidential nominee (a candidacy that was always more a symbolic protest of the authoritarian Republican supermajority than a genuine attempt to win, which was an impossibility for any "Puppet Dem" due to the stranglehold the GOP held on election boards in perma-red states that were once electoral battle-grounds) was secretly an octopus-human hybrid with an agenda to sell white children into sexual slavery to finance propaganda about the myth of climate change. But the Democratic nominee wasn't the only "Octo-Liberal." Conspiracy theorists had fabulated an entire "Octo-Force" of alleged "OLs," political archvillains that gained cultural prominence when Warner Bros.—seeking to curry favor with the House Anti-American Speech Committee and avoid hefty "seditious content" fines—produced *Tentacles*, a film starring Chris Pratt as a grizzled marine biologist determined to murder a secret cabal of octopus-human hybrids bioengineered by evil communist scientists to destroy the Republican Party. It was the first major studio film to directly peddle a conspiracy theory to the masses (and eventually helped Chris Pratt win his campaign for California governor during the 2042 recall). And it worked. The Anti-OL Caucus gained a real presence in Washington, thanks to the $97 million Patrick spent backing a multitude of Anti-OL Senate and House candidates.

"The smoke is an Octo-Liberal plot—"

"Patrick—*stop!*" Mason snapped. Patrick looked at him in astonishment; no one ever told Patrick Sullivan to stop anything. "Sorry. It's just been a stressful day."

"That's okay," Patrick muttered.

"I have so many errands to run for the baby shower . . ." Mason immediately regretted the slip.

"You're having a baby shower?" Patrick's face twitched into a failed imitation of hurt.

Nausea overwhelmed Mason's senses. There was only one way out. "You didn't get your invitation? It must've gotten lost in the mail," Mason lied. Fortunately, the GOP's systematic defunding of the U.S. Postal Service made this historically flimsy excuse a modern likelihood.

"No one uses the USPS anymore," Patrick chided. "What time should I be there?"

*

Why the fuck had he agreed to buy the flowers himself? The party planners had secured the small arrangements for the standing tables that would
be peppered throughout the lawn, but Mason had insisted that only he
could properly oversee the massive arrangement that would stand on the
gift table. *I'm a sculptor*, he'd harrumphed to Angelica, their perpetually
taxed party-planner. *I'm very sensitive to the relationship between objects
and space.*

"I heard it was bobcats," a woman whispered behind him in line, as he
waited for the florist to finish the arrangement. "Something in the pink
smoke triggers hormones in their brain? Almost like rabies? They come
down from the mountains and attack anything that moves."

"No, the bobcat thing is a conspiracy," the other woman countered. "I
heard it debunked on NPR. They're saying it's possible chemical warfare,
maybe from North Korea—"

"You listen to NPR *once* and suddenly you're an expert on bobcats *and*
red smoke?"

"It's *pink* smoke. And I'm not saying I'm an expert, I'm just trying—"

"*To shut me down as usual.* Mindy says this is a central motif in our—"

"Don't bring our couple's therapist into this stupid bobcat debate—"

"And here's your arrangement," the florist chirped, emerging from the
back room. Mason stopped listening to the warring lesbians and took in
the stunning burst of white lilies. The bouquet brimmed with life, beauty,
hope, and love. He started crying. "Sir? Is everything okay?"

"Sorry, yes. It's just that . . . I'm having a baby."

SEVEN

18 months, 9 days, 1 hour, 28 minutes

They walked into Gabriel's third birthday party a week after Yunho's surgery. The cancer had been successfully removed; Yunho was still limping from the procedure. Mason slowed his gait to match his lover's. They clenched their hands together, like Yunho might ascend into heaven if either man loosened his grip. The subject of children had not been raised since the eve of Yunho's radical orchiectomy; they'd had bountiful post-operative anxieties to keep them occupied without heaping procreation onto the pile of mortal dread. Yet now, faced with the adorable chaos of Daniel and Mahmood's backyard, it was impossible not to think about kids. They were everywhere. But rather than address the tiny elephants stampeding their hosts' Astroturfed lawn, they broke apart, nervously disappearing into opposite ends of the party, hiding from each other behind clusters of helium balloons.

"You okay?" Daniel approached, wielding an umbrellaed tiki drink with his hirsute paw. Daniel's journey into bear-land had coincided with his partner's; he gained baby weight in solidarity with Mahmood. But if Mahmood had turned into an adorable koala, Daniel had gone full grizzly. His once-muscular body now ballooned with fat; his neck was the thickness of a baby cedar stump. Though his physical presence may have been as intimidating as a pro wrestler's, Daniel was the gentlest individual Mason had ever met. "Looks like you need to be tiki'ed."

"Thank you." Mason accepted the cocktail. "It's been a tough week." Daniel had been Yunho's friend first; in fact, it was Daniel and Mahmood who introduced Mason to Yunho on a group vacation to Provincetown all those years ago. Daniel was an L.A. native; his parents were Korean immigrants who'd paid for his medical school (they would not, under any circumstances, fund Daniel's true dream of film school) with earnings from the Del Taco franchise they owned.

"I know how much you guys have been through. You truly didn't need to come."

"Trust me, we did. Yunho's desperate to pretend he never had cancer."

"I know. He's been bugging me to start that new *Reds* script. But I told him, 'You can't walk yet—Warren Beatty's ghost can wait.'" Yunho was an addict who had replaced alcohol with work, to the same self-destructive effect, and his $20 million deal with Disney was up for renewal, which only heightened his anxiety. Yunho had been signed to the pact after sweeping the Oscars with *March First Movement*, a historical romance between two queer revolutionaries during the Korean Independence Movement. Yunho was branded as the last great hope for cinema, an auteur who resisted Hollywood's Morality Code and produced astutely leftist films in an industry that favored action movies carrying authoritarian propaganda. But upon signing his Disney pact, Yunho faced resistance to his ideas; even films he pushed to production were shelved, because Mickey Mouse feared political persecution. This censorship activated a furious rebellion within Yunho, which is how he conceived of the *Reds* reboot: It was a Hollywood classic starring Warren Beatty, one of the straightest, whitest men in film history, and Yunho hoped this would distract the studio from the film's depiction of an anarcho-socialist labor revolution in America. "I also made him promise he wouldn't touch any other projects either."

"Thank you. He's afraid Disney might cancel his overall deal."

"Well, I told him they weren't gonna end it because he got *cancer* and had to take time off." Daniel had survived his own professional burnout, which is why Yunho trusted him in this realm. For years, Daniel was an overworked member of the Norma Collective, an underground organization of doctors who risked criminal prosecution to provide abortions in a country that had federally outlawed the practice. His selflessness had a dark side; when faced with the bottomless abyss of trauma created by draconian antiabortion laws, Daniel jumped into the darkness, plummeting endlessly, as if he alone could provide pregnant Americans with the care they needed. This led to a breakdown; Yunho suggested he take time away from work. To rest. Rethink his priorities. Yunho thought Daniel's experience in the Norma Collective might make for a compelling film. Though it took some convincing (and a promise that identifying details of former colleagues would be fictionalized), he agreed to Yunho's pitch. But Disney killed the project after nine torturous years of development; they feared the subject matter would alarm the Anti-American Speech Committee. Still, Yunho had been impressed by Daniel's talent, and offered as consolation the opportunity to collaborate on the script for the *Reds* reboot.

"Darling, you made it!" Mahmood cried as he swam through the sea of Disney princesses hired for the party. He paused momentarily to kiss Gabriel, the youthful honoree, on the head. Gabriel's long black hair fluttered in the breeze as they ran from their dad's embrace and jumped on the back of a haggard-looking Ursula, already drooping under the weight of her tentacles.

"Ursula is an inspired choice for a princess party," Mason observed. "Usually, the villains don't make an appearance."

"It was the only way to inject a little queerness into the proceedings," Daniel said grimly.

"Invite a fat gay witch to fuck things up?"

"Precisely," Mahmood said. "Also, we hired a trans Elsa."

"It's the age-old question of: What to do when your child, who you're attempting to raise in a gender-neutral way, wants to throw a themed party that replicates the toxic cis-heteronormative dynamics present in most Disney princess movies?"

"Well, clearly my lover is enjoying your selection of Disney characters in his own way." Mason pointed across the lawn, where Yunho stood flirting with Prince Eric.

"I wouldn't be mad if you two stole a prince from our party." Mahmood grinned.

"That prince is probably an aspiring actor. And there's nothing less sexy than bringing a résumé to a threesome." Yunho and Mason had an open relationship. They'd started dating just after Yunho had gotten sober, and for years, Mason was the sole sexual partner with whom Yunho had experienced a healthier, sober sex life. Yunho wanted to expand his whoreish repertoire now that sex wasn't tainted by shame and substances. Who was Mason to deny the man he loved this healing? Besides, it wasn't like Mason *didn't* want to fuck other people.

"I'm jealous. Daniel here is so tragically *monogamous*." Mahmood rolled his eyes.

"That's not true. I'm *open* to being open, I'm just a little busy with our two children. I don't have time to hunt for random ass."

Mason hesitated. "Do you ever regret having kids?"

"Not for a single fucking second," Mahmood insisted.

"Those kids are our whole life."

The miracles of parenthood, the jokes about the sacrificed sex life, blah, blah, blah. Part of Mason's reservations about parenthood were aesthetic; new parents always employed the same tired clichés to describe their experience. Was there no room for innovation? Then again, even if there were universal truths about child-rearing, Mahmood and Daniel could hardly be accused of pursuing a "normative" path toward parenting. Fortunately, California had not outlawed pregnancy for trans and gender nonconforming individuals, like Texas, for example, where pregnant trans people could be classified as sex offenders and thrown into prison, where the babies they birthed could be kidnapped by the state and thrust into foster care. But even in California, the gendered nature of the birth industrial complex made it difficult to find medical providers willing to affirm Mahmood's gender identity, not to mention the challenges of discovering prenatal classes and meetups that didn't cling to the ludicrous idea that pregnancy was some divine right belonging to women alone.

"Daddies—look at me!" Auden, their six-year-old, ran over with a plastic sword, slicing the air as he barreled across the lawn. "Uncle Mason—you look too!"

"Great job, Auden!" Mason yelled. He watched Mahmood and Daniel watch Auden. Mason was determined to detect some secret regret in their body language. He wanted confirmation that he was right to ignore the nagging paternal impulse hovering in his thoughts. But only love emanated from his best friends as they watched their son skip across the lawn.

"Oh shit. Auden—put down that cup!" Mahmood yelled as he and Daniel bounded toward their boy, who'd swiped a tiki drink from the bar. *"That's grown-up juice!"* Auden rapidly lifted the cup to his mouth, downing the forbidden liquid before his parents could stop him.

Mason turned from the chaos and caught Yunho's gaze in the crowd. Opportunistic Prince Eric was gone; off to find another director to flirt with, no doubt. Yunho was now crouched in the sandbox with Gabriel, playing with building blocks. Mason approached, smiling.

"A house, a house!" the child cried.

"You wanna build a house?" Yunho asked, stacking the blocks. "There's your house!"

Gabriel frowned, unsatisfied, pointing at the newly constructed home. "Tell a story!"

"You want a story about your house?"

Gabriel nodded, eyes widening in anticipation. Gabriel was never content to mindlessly fiddle with toys; they needed story to fuel their play. The child's ravenous imagination was a refreshing contrast to their brother's boneheaded antics. Despite Daniel and Mahmood's gender-neutral parenting efforts, Auden had self-selected a toxic cishet male identity; he was a bully who pushed femme kids into puddles. But Gabriel was a beautiful rarity, a child whose imagination danced out of step with established social scripts.

"Once upon a time, a child named Gabriel lived in a beautiful, refurbished Craftsman in Echo Park with their parents and their brother—"

"And a dragon!" Gabriel demanded.

"—and their pet dragon, Dennis," Yunho amended. "Dennis was a nice dragon, a vegan who never killed people and only ate pomegranates—"

"—and poop!" Gabriel screamed, then burst into shrieking giggles.

"—and poop." Yunho laughed, then looked at Mason. "You wanna take it from here? This transgressive territory seems more in keeping with your aesthetic."

Mason sat in the sandbox, and kissed Gabriel's cheek. The child beamed, thrilled to have *two* storytellers. "Well, as you mentioned, Gabriel, Dennis the dragon had an insatiable appetite for poop." Another delighted squeal from Gabriel. "So, one day, Dennis opened a restaurant serving the poop-pomegranate cuisine favored by modern dragons in Los Angeles. He threw an opening-night party and his whole family came, including Gabriel, Auden, and their daddies—"

"You a daddy?" Gabriel asked, pointing to Yunho, eyes filled with wonder.

"I'm not anyone's daddy." Yunho looked at Mason, his gaze softening. "Not yet at least."

Yunho gently caressed the child's silken hair. There was an instinctual tenderness in the gesture that made Mason recall the moment in the recovery room after Yunho's cancer surgery when Mason made a similar gesture, stroking Yunho's sweat-crusted mane. *You need to pee before we can release you*, said the nurse, a challenge that was surprisingly hard to meet. Yunho could barely walk due to the pain, but he shuffled back and forth to the bathroom, clinging to Mason, unable to make himself go. Both were humbled by Yunho's momentary disability, a reminder everyone becomes disabled if they live long enough, which begged the question: Who would take care of them when they were older, incapacitated, incontinent?

Mason had been thankful that Yunho's parents' recovery room drive-by had been brief, curtailed by their usual discomfort in Mason's presence;

he was a physical manifestation of their son's homosexuality and its direct opposition to the teachings of the Korean Baptist Church in San Jose to which they belonged. They comforted their son in Korean and said nothing to Mason. Then they left, offering Mason the same cold smiles they'd given the nurse. Yunho burst into tears. Mason cradled him, debating whether to call his own mother into the recovery room; she'd shown up uninvited, riding her emotional steamroller, determined to give herself a starring role in this crisis. She was standing by in the waiting room "just in case anyone needs me." Mason had been surprised when Yunho invited her into the recovery room; he longed for a parental figure who was accepting even if she was overbearing. But Yunho regretted his decision the minute she arrived weeping, possessed by a hysteria that somehow made Yunho's cancer about *her*. Yunho asked that she leave and, when she was gone, whispered: *Promise we'll never act like our parents. Promise we'll be different when it's our turn.* When Yunho said "our turn," Mason felt punch-drunk from the impact of those two words. He wanted the love he shared with Yunho to extend beyond their bodies, to be transferred to a child; their personal histories would become less painful if they created a new kind of family, an evolved family, *their* family.

Yunho beamed as Gabriel kissed his cheek. Yes, there was enough love to go around, in fact it could be *multiplied* by a child; seeing that infinite generosity burgeon within Yunho increased Mason's ardor in turn. What bullshit the rest of it was, how sad that their lives were focused on work, money, and fame, egocentric activities that distanced them from the selfless desire to care for another human being. The look in Yunho's eyes as he held Gabriel was all that mattered. A look that said: *I will save the rapidly dying world for you, my sweet, gentle creature.*

"Let's have a baby," Yunho gasped suddenly. His eyes widened, as if he'd been surprised by his own statement. Gabriel hummed to themself, playing with the blocks, oblivious.

"Okay." Mason took a deep breath. "Okay, yes."

"Yes?" Yunho echoed, a tentative ecstasy spreading across his face.

"Yes!" Mason cried, swept up in adrenaline.

"More story!" Gabriel insisted, annoyed by the conversation happening above their head.

"Okay, my little dictator." Yunho snuggled Gabriel as they giggled. "So, the dragon—"

"Fire!"

"There's a fire?"

"Dragon breathes fire. House on fire!"

"That's not nice. I don't think—"

"*House on fire!*" Gabriel yelled, furious that their storytellers were no longer responsive to their demands. Partygoers shot concerned stares toward the sandbox. "*Dragon breathes fire!*"

"What if they—"

"*FIRE, FIRE, FIRE!*" Gabriel's face reddened; spittle foamed from their lips.

"Gabriel, please—

"*House on fire!*" the child screamed. "*Everybody dies!*"

EIGHT

3 hours, 56 minutes

He needed Vex.

Broken blacktop stretched out in front of Mason. A thick layer of ash coated the dead landscape. His every footstep released a charred cloud. He knew this road so well. The cluster of dead trees. The burnt and blackened shell of that house. The faded billboard, meant to look forgotten, though it never was. Today—an advertisement for WeatherMod. Mason thrust his binoculars to his face. There, at the bottom of a sloping valley: the memory of a city. Ruins waiting for future civilization.

No one could know that Mason was here. Especially not Yunho.

He shifted his focus to the road ahead and saw the gas station. No matter how many times he visited, his pulse still sped at the sight of those two rusted pumps and the small service shed. He glimpsed a rustle of movement through its grime-coated windows. *Was that Vex?*

Mason ran toward the building. Pounded on the door. It swung open.

But it was just SoftBoi34. His seven-foot-two frame loomed in the entrance; he was bulky, with a menacing frown designed to scare off trolls who wanted to attack their community. "Hi, Mason," SoftBoi34 intoned.

"Is Vex here?"

"Yes. But he's increased his session price. It's four hundred and fifty now."

"That's fine," Mason said, guilt churning in his gut. Another expense he couldn't afford.

"Fantastic." SoftBoi34 motioned to the station's pitch-black interior. "Come with me."

*

The room was empty, except for one red bulb that cast a dark glow across the concrete interior. Mason prayed Vex would appear soon. But Mason knew he'd wait as long as necessary, even if it meant being late to his own party. Vex was the only one who could cure his dread.

Suddenly, Vex appeared. In a corner, in the shadows. Mason's cock stiffened. Vex stepped into the light. He grinned, flashing blood-coated fangs. A long coarse tongue whipped from between his teeth, wiping his wet maw. His gray fur took on a fuchsia tint under the red bulb. His eyes were blazing white. "Strip!" Vex shouted. Mason's limbs weakened; he did as he was commanded. "Get on your knees."

Mason hit the ground. Vex circled, prowled; tendons in his haunches bulged with every step. His torso was that of a human bodybuilder's; it rippled with swollen, steroidal muscle. A thin layer of fur sprouted across his entire form, highlighting contours of sinew. And between his legs: that foot-long cock with its glorious network of veins, the type of cock Mason had first seen in wolf-kink CGI porn (which led him into the sprawling universe of wolf-kink literature), never imagining he could experience it for himself. It was a cock Mason worshipped in secret visits to virtual reality, a cock that haunted his dreams, the last thing he saw before waking up every morning, next to Yunho, who had no idea Mason possessed a parallel digital life that occupied an alarming amount of space in his psyche. Ironically, it was Yunho who'd awakened this kinky impulse during the violent fuck-spree into which they'd sublimated their mortal fear in the weeks leading up to Yunho's cancer surgery. But after the successful operation, Yunho had zero interest in anything but the most vanilla sex. Mason worried a return to BDSM would trigger Yunho, remind him of his encounter with death, and so Mason never brought it up. Instead, he sought erotic obliteration from lupine sex workers in the nether regions of virtual reality.

Vex slapped him across the face with his cock. The force of the blow triggered his iOS Cerebrum's advanced haptic technology and sent a wave of divine pain surging across his skull. "Lie down, bitch," Vex snarled. Mason scuttled, beetle-like, onto his back.

Mason was canisexual, though he was terrified to admit this to anyone, especially Yunho. How to explain his sexual attraction to half-canine/half-human avatars and, more specifically, Vex, the gray wolf muscle god who was the only entity that could make Mason cum? Yunho and Mason had only discussed the bounds of their open relationship within actual reality. Never had they broached the gray area of hiring VR sex workers, though Mason suspected Yunho wouldn't approve. It wasn't just that Yunho (like many others in the wake of the news stories that had exposed their community) made the occasional derogatory joke about canisexuals. What worried Mason was the fact that sessions with Vex were brutal, transcendent, almost spiritual. Sex never felt like this with Yunho.

"What brings you crawling in here today?" A coil of rope appeared in Vex's hand.

"My . . . baby shower."

"Your *baby shower*?"

"Yes."

"You're having a baby shower *today*? In L.A.? You're more disgusting than I thought."

"Yes, I am, sir. With a hundred guests."

"*One hundred guests?* Put your arms and legs in the air." Vex hog-tied Mason.

"I would do anything for you, sir."

"No, you wouldn't."

CRACK. Vex whipped Mason's bound body. Mason's iOS Cerebrum was synced with his state-of-the-art ThrashJacket™ to ensure authentic haptic violence. Real agony. *CRACK*. Vex flogged him again. Nine cords seared Mason's back. *CRACK*. Another lash. Blood vessels burst beneath his flesh. *CRACK*. "*Yes, I would!*" Mason screamed.

"*Stop lying, you little shit.*" *CRACK*. "Do you know that my species is extinct? That the gray wolf is gone from this Earth? Did you do anything to save us?"

". . . no."

"So, then you *wouldn't* do anything for me. In fact, you *didn't* do anything for me."

CRACK. Another howl from Mason. "I'm sorry, sir."

"Sorry? Your pathetic apology is worthless. What did you do when politicians lifted protections on the Arctic National Wildlife Refuge?"

". . . nothing," Mason moaned. *CRACK*.

"And what did you do when BP began offshore drilling in the Arctic, which led to a catastrophic oil well eruption that caused the extinction of my species and made Deepwater Horizon seem cute?"

" . . . *nothing.*" *CRACK*.

"And now you wanna bring a *child* into the world? The world you *refuse* to protect?"

"*I'm sorry.*" *CRACK*. "*FUCK.*"

". . . And not only that, but you're *celebrating* this terrible decision with a one-hundred-person baby shower that will produce sixty-two tons of carbon dioxide? You might as well just burn *sixty-five thousand pounds of fucking coal.*" *CRACK*.

"*I'm sorry,*" Mason cried, tears and snot pooling inside his VR mask. *CRACK*. His back was numb. His spine was brittle. "*What should I do?*"

"*Figure it out yourself, slug.* You're really going to employ a sex worker to take on the emotional labor of laundering your guilt about climate change?"

"*We have solar power!*"

"*FUCK YOUR SOLAR POWER!*"

CRACK. CRACK. CRACK. Mason screamed and shuddered as cum shot from his dick.

Everything went white. An alarm wailed. Something was wrong.

*

Mason took off his VR headset. The rush of his orgasm mixed with vertigo; his omnidirectional treadmill had been deactivated, leaving him swooning and destabilized. His BDSM ThrashJacket released, "untying" Mason from the restraints that Vex had placed on him.

The alarm continued to blare. He squinted in the harsh fluorescence of his room, a small white box that matched the others in this VR hotel. Patrons could check in for an hour or a week or even sign up for a long-term residency in which they relocated permanently to virtual reality.

"Attention customers, this facility is being evacuated. We have powered down your headsets and request that everyone calmly make their way to the exits."

Mason burst from his room to discover the narrow hallway jammed with dazed patrons, disoriented by sudden confrontation with the physical world. Mason pressed into a pungent crush of bodies. Their smell mixed with his own; sour panic seeped from his pores as he pushed down the corridor with the rest of the clawing mob. Someone grabbed his wrist. Someone punched his raw and battered back.

Humanity was hard for Mason to stomach after visits to virtual reality; there was a comforting level of detachment Mason attained during his trips to *The Road*, just one of the "gated dystopias" that Cyclops VR added to their portfolio during the virtual reality boom of the late 2030s. Cyclops VR had succeeded where other metaverse ventures had failed, due to their ability to render a stunningly realistic 3D universe, while creating affordable devices to be consumed on a mass scale. However, users willing to pay exorbitant fees could unlock their choice of any "gated dystopia," virtual worlds based on intellectual property such as *Mad Max* or *The Handmaid's Tale*, allowing the wealthy to participate in thrilling post-apocalyptic fantasies.

The Road's virtual universe was modeled after the reboot film adaptation of Cormac McCarthy's novel, produced in 2040. Users could play in a designed story experience that took them through the events of the film, or explore the landscape independently, or even rent private plots of virtual land to form their own communities. The latter option led to controversy, when Cyclops discovered racist hackers had circumvented the company's hateful conduct policy to hold white supremacist rallies in private community spaces. But when Cyclops attempted to oust the white supremacists, Republican lawmakers became incensed on behalf of their furious supporters. The Senate passed the "Freedom to Virtually Assemble" bill, designed to "protect free speech" across the metaverse. But, as usual, when they said "free speech" they *meant* "white supremacy," which is why they were shocked when people other than racists embraced the bill's titular freedom, and an influx of kinky queer communities arose within previously sex-policed virtual arenas. Lawmakers were now scrambling to draft a new Anti-Perversion Bill, which would make illegal any virtual queer sex, targeting the canisexual community in particular for BDSM "climate-guilt play" that "was essentially bestiality."

"Out of my way." A tall, muscular gay man pushed past Mason. A possibility sent adrenaline coursing through Mason's system.

"Vex?" Mason shouted into the chaos. "Vex?" Nothing. The man didn't turn, just shoved his way to the front of the fleeing throng. The Anti-Perversion Bill loomed in Mason's mind; Mason was driven to find Vex in real life in case their virtual one was destroyed. It was foolish to hope that the human behind Vex's avatar was in the same VR hotel (or even the same country), but Mason was desperate. The humiliation he experienced in Vex's lair was a life source. Each whip was punishment, each spasm of pain was penance, and for the length of an orgasm, Mason's mind was wiped clean. Nothingness reigned.

"*Vex!*" Mason yelled again.

"*Shut up.*" A woman shoved him backward. He lost his footing, crumpled to the ground. He attempted to stand; the panicked mob knocked him down. The alarm wailed louder. The crowd grew violent. Feet trampled his back, stomped breath from his body. The pain was unrelenting, transcendent. For a moment before he lost consciousness, he almost forgot his ever-festering dread, almost achieved that blissful nothing he chased like a junkie's dragon.

*

He awoke with a gasp. A pocket of pain ballooned in his chest. A pair of fists pounded his rib cage. Three men stood above him. Fluorescent light crowned their skulls. The glare made their faces difficult to discern. "Can you tell me where you are?" one of them asked.

"*The Road . . .*" Mason slurred.

"The . . . what?"

Mason's focus sharpened. EMT lanyards dangled from the men's necks. The hallway was now empty, except for Mason's saviors. "Sorry. I meant to say, 'I'm at a VR hotel.'"

"And what day is it?"

Panic seized Mason's chest. "*My baby shower.*"

*

"Siri—take me to Astrid's house."

You're running one hour behind—

"*I know that.*" His Tesla crawled out of the VR hotel's parking lot. Pink fog hovered in the air. *Fuck—it's made it over the hill,* Mason thought.

You have five missed calls, Siri nagged. *All from Astrid Nilsson.*

"Shit—call her back." The phone rang as the car creeped toward the ticket booth at the edge of the lot. The structure was abandoned, the gate open. The Tesla arrived at the road; even though they were on autopilot, Mason checked both lanes. Empty. Through the smoke, just north of the parking lot: an armored truck. Blocking the road. Uniformed men flanked the vehicle.

The FBI.

The Tesla turned left, going south on Vine. The phone kept ringing. Then, Astrid's voice filled the car: "Mason—we were worried about you!"

"I . . ." Mason couldn't tell her the truth, couldn't divulge his canisexual habit and its accompanying climate-guilt play, which was designed, in part, to rid him of the ambivalence he felt about the life forming in Astrid's womb. His child. "I . . . got in an accident."

"Oh my god—are you okay?"

Mason looked in his rearview mirror. There, in the thickening pink haze, stood the line of FBI agents, all in gas masks, distant enough to appear like toy soldiers. Suddenly, one hit the pavement. A dark figure climbed on top of him. Tore at his neck. The others drew their guns.

"I'm fine." Bile burned in Mason's throat. "I'm fine."

NINE

2 hours, 48 minutes

Mason rang the buzzer and longed for a lobotomy; how else to forget the trauma that rose out of their decision to engage Astrid as their surrogate? The misery lived on in his muscles—Mason clutched his shoulder, hammering out a knot in his back that never unhitched, only tightened, as it now did while he waited outside the glass door of Astrid's smoke-sealed portico.

Technically, it was Yunho and Mason's smoke-sealed portico. They'd been the ones to pay twenty thousand dollars for its permanent installation, even though they were merely renting the property on which it was built. *A small price to pay for peace of mind*, Yunho had insisted. Mason was endlessly frustrated by his lover's hypocritical excess; Yunho claimed to be the frugal half of their partnership, but he was happy to part with wild sums of cash in the name of surrogacy.

The portico entryway slid open. Mason stepped inside, bringing a cloud of haze with him into the tall glass booth that enclosed the front door of the home. Smog swirled inside the structure, like candle smoke trapped in an upside-down drinking glass. "Please wait for Air Quality Index reading," the system demanded. "Current portico AQI: 317. Air quality: Hazardous. Stand by for purification." The industrial air purifier rumbled to life. *We can't have Astrid inhaling smoke*, Yunho had argued to justify the system's price tag. *Do you want her to suffer preterm labor? Gestational diabetes? Do you know what a* risk *it is to have a baby in California?* "Adjusted portico AQI: 25. Air quality: Good. You may enter the building."

Mason walked into the home they'd rented for Astrid at ten thousand dollars a month. Another of Yunho's small prices to pay. "Mason! My beautiful Mason," Astrid cried from the black marble island that divided the kitchen and living room in a masterfully designed, minimalist interior. She swept him into a hug; her very pregnant belly swelled between them. She carried the weight of a child effortlessly, the extra load anchoring her somehow, giving her divine purpose as she moved through the world. "Are you okay?"

"I'm fine," Mason said and took off his gas mask.

"Your eye! Oh, that's an awful bruise. Come sit, baby." Astrid had a habit of calling everyone *baby* in a manner that both infantilized and sexualized them simultaneously; the disconcerting tonal blend did little to ease Mason's jangled spirit. He settled on the couch reluctantly; they were already running late. "I'll find something for that."

Mason's phone buzzed. The caller ID read: MOM. He pressed decline. Another shower-planning "emergency," no doubt. He barely possessed the fortitude to erect a pretense of normality with Astrid and couldn't bear the thought of storm-chasing his mother's ever-strengthening panic tornado.

"Here," Astrid said as she hauled her pregnant girth onto the couch and handed him a brick of frozen peas. "To stop the swelling." She stroked his hair. He lifted the bag to his face; a merciful numbness prickled his cheek. "Feel better?" He did, slightly, though he was disturbed by the fact cheap frozen peas in "butter" sauce (which likely contained all sorts of baby-killing chemicals) had somehow made their way into Astrid's freezer when he was paying a prenatal nutritionist two thousand dollars a week to cook Astrid a custom meal program.

"Frozen peas? Where did you get these?"

"The . . . grocery store?" Astrid blushed; a perfect burst of freckles dappled the suddenly scarlet canvas of her cheeks. Her pale skin needed no makeup, her wild strawberry mane needed no combing—some primordial inner light provided a splendor no cosmetics could mimic. She wore a floral-print Chloé maxi dress, a gift from Yunho that had been tailored to her pregnant body yet still seemed ill-fitting, like the meticulously crafted garment was a bourgeois imposition on the effortlessness of her natural beauty. "Now, tell me what happened, baby."

"Um, just a fender bender," Mason lied. "This guy stopped in traffic, I slammed into him and my face, like, hit my steering wheel."

"I'm so glad you're okay. Shit is crazy out there today. I almost wondered if . . ."

". . . we should've canceled the shower?"

"No! I mean, you've got so much planned, and we'll be safe with WeatherMod—"

"I saw the FBI."

"*The FBI?*"

"In Hollywood. Just . . . blocking the road."

"Well, that's not good. Maybe you *should* cancel."

"No, it'll be fine." Mason's phone vibrated again: MOM. He pressed decline. "My mom would *kill* me if we canceled. Plus, guests are already on their way, so we really should get going."

"Give me just a moment." Astrid rose from her seat. Mason stiffened. In Astrid's dreamy world, a "moment" was an ever-expandable unit of time that could be filled with all sorts of esoteric dalliances. "I need to find that little fan I carry around . . ." She tiptoed through the kitchen gingerly, like she was afraid she might break something if she moved too freely. Mason felt annoyed by this tentativeness, which was reflective of a larger failure on Astrid's part to adapt to her newly luxurious surroundings; sure, Astrid had *been* poor, but she no longer *was* poor, and the fearful naive gaze with which she navigated this caste ascendency always elicited within Mason a pang of class guilt that he reflexively converted into anger, which was followed by shame, because how could he feel anything but profound gratitude toward this poor twenty-six-year-old who'd uprooted her life to give them a child? Then again, it wasn't that simple. That's how the arrangement started, but it had curdled into something agonizing and broken, something they were desperately attempting to reconstruct after the chaos of the past six months.

Mason's jugular vein pounded against the snarled musculature of his tweaked neck. "And is Claudia almost ready?"

"She's . . ." Worry somersaulted across Astrid's features. "She's not coming."

TEN

2 hours, 21 minutes

**FBI COUNTERTERRORISM DIVISION——NATIONAL
THREAT CENTER SECTION CLASSIFIED:
SUSPICIOUS ACTIVITY REPORT——SEIZED EMAIL**

From: Claudia Jackson <claudiajackson@gmail.com>

To: <DSS2044@gmail.com>

My dear sweet someone,

To think, it'll be years before you see any of these letters. If
you see them at all. But it feels important to have some record
of what we're doing, the mission that remains a secret to all
but a precious few. We need documentation of our history.
Evidence of our efforts to build a better future. Still, I often
wonder if I'm focusing on the future to avoid the present realities of my life.

My life—whatever that is right now. It feels like a broken thing. I never imagined myself in L.A. But Astrid moved and I had no choice. Pregnancy is one of the most traumatic things you can do to your body, so I wanted to support her. I had no other purpose. The Anarchist Cutie Club had disbanded; it was just me and Grey squatting in that Shreveport warehouse, mourning the death of our community, exhausted by the never-ending project of abolition and mutual aid in a country hellbent on the opposite. What could I do except move to L.A. to be with the woman I love? She says that surrogacy "is her calling," but I don't think I believe her. I know what she's been through. I know what she wants.

But she's too poor to support you on her own. She's too poor to have a child.

Or, at least, that's what people in Mason and Yunho's income bracket believe. You shouldn't have a child if you "can't afford it." Which begs the question: Who *can* afford it?

Astrid sobs at the slightest provocation. "Just hormones," she says. They're "making her crazy." But I say America is making her crazy. A land where she worked three minimum wage jobs and could barely support herself, let alone a child. Decades of bipartisan neoliberalism ensured there was no way out of the crushing poverty she'd been born into, except then, miraculously, there was: Mason and Yunho came riding into her life with bags of cash, all she had to do was bear them a child, these two rich men who could afford to dream the dream she couldn't.

She's tried to be a good employee. But sometimes being a good employee is bad for you. And I've seen the trauma she's endured. The horror we've both been through. It feels like we landed in Los

Angeles and stepped into quicksand. We're stuck in this pit with these men and the harder we fight, the deeper we're pulled into the muck, and right now we're up to our necks, and all we can do is scream at each other as quicksand tickles our chins. I can't believe we're supposed to hand you over to Mason. You don't belong to him, children shouldn't "belong" to anyone, yet Mason acts like he "owns" you. At least Yunho is sympathetic to our concerns. He hasn't told Mason about our talks, our plan, the vision that, yes, started with me, but when I look at Yunho I can see this idea blossoming in his mind; he seems lighter, like he's being lifted out of the quicksand, and it's that way with Astrid too, her eyes brighten when we discuss it, and I'm reminded of why I love her so deeply.

And you. I already love you so much. We all do. It's strange, the way my heart bursts and breaks for you, the mysterious beautiful being I have yet to meet. Your birth is so close, and every day that passes fills me with a greater determination to see our plan brought to fruition.

But any hope is undercut by encroaching fear. Mason has a sense of ownership over you. I worry nothing will change this. I can present our vision for your future, I can tell Mason how love guides us, and because we love you, and love him, something must change, if we stay in the quicksand we'll die, so let's take a risk, save ourselves, bet on love, and trust the rest will work out. I can say all of this, but I know he'll hear only one thing: We want to kidnap his child.

Yours forever,
Claudia

ELEVEN

2 hours, 16 minutes

H oney, what are you talking about? I'm still coming." The bedroom door burst open. Claudia was an expert in the art of the entrance; her presence was so electric it was essential to appreciate it without the distraction of lesser arrivals. Today, she sported blue box braids that flowed from her scalp in a neon waterfall. She wore a tight red Margiela dress wrapped in sheer black tulle, another gift insisted upon by Yunho. She did a small spin in her wheelchair, allowing her braids to float from the force of self-generated momentum. Her muscular arms flexed as she gripped her hand-rims and came to a stop, smiling. "It takes time to get this gorgeous."

But her buoyancy felt forced, manic, the tone of her cheer off-key. Mason looked beneath her glittered lids—were her eyes bloodshot? Astrid and Claudia exchanged a coded look Mason couldn't decipher. His nerves twanged; Mason prayed for no surprises, but worried that God was too preoccupied with her current catastrophic reckoning to heed his invocation. "Let's go. It's baby shower time," he said with the feigned joy of a beleaguered party-bus driver.

*

His Tesla crossed Franklin, traveling northeast on Los Feliz Boulevard. Just as the vehicle came to the bend before Oxford, it pulled to a stop. More fucking traffic. A swarm of taillights blinked ahead. Cars accumulated behind. Mason felt trapped. The Tesla inched forward. Rounded the bend.

Then, an awful sight.

A wall of pink smog, stretching infinitely toward the sky. Billowing. Volcanic. Opaque. Its toxic depths, a mystery. The fortresslike cloud advanced imperceptibly, maintaining an illusion of stillness, of permanent stasis; but it was always moving, pushed incrementally forward by persistent winds. Mason took a breath and closed his eyes; when he opened them again, the pink mass was half a car closer. And yet, because of the smoke's illusory inertia, it seemed as if it had always been where it was, that Mason could not trust his own perception of its movement. It eroded his confidence in his own sense of reality and led to the vertiginous arrival of a fresh delusion—utterly absurd to Mason's rational mind and yet impossible for him to dismiss due to the way his gut churned in response to it—the feeling that the Earth was flat and the cloud concealed its end and just within its dark billows the planet's crust crumbled and dropped off into something worse than nothing, an eternal void through which their Tesla would plummet without end, and death would never relieve them of their miserable, unstoppable descent.

"*Fuck.*" Mason pounded his steering wheel. Claudia sighed from the back seat.

"It's okay, baby," Astrid insisted unconvincingly. She sat shotgun, repeatedly smoothing her dress over her belly, an anxious tic. "I'm sure it's just an accident. We're almost there."

It was true—they were less than a mile from Mason and Yunho's house, with an hour to spare. But they were stuck—cars behind, cars in front. Claustrophobia shortened Mason's breath; if the pink smoke weren't such a terrifying enigma, they could've gotten out, grabbed Claudia's wheelchair from the trunk, and trekked the remaining distance back to Mason's beautiful home where WeatherMod would already be clearing the air. "You're right," Mason said, desperately playing into Astrid's charade of normalcy. "Probably just an accident."

"I heard on the radio that some people think the smoke is a nerve agent dispersed by an Anti-OL militia," Astrid said. "Like chemical warfare. To kill liberal Californians."

"It's funny you should mention Anti-OL. Because I was with Patrick Sullivan earlier today . . ." At Mason's mention of Patrick, Astrid recoiled. She and Claudia had made their anti-Patrick position very clear, but Patrick was also indirectly paying for Astrid's pregnancy chef, so Mason felt Astrid could unwrinkle her nose at least a *little*. ". . . and he said the opposite was true. That it was Octo-Liberals attempting to wipe out Anti-OL militias secretly stationed in Burbank."

"And you believe that?" Claudia asked, horrified.

"Oh god, no. Patrick is a psycho." In the rearview, he caught Claudia mid-eye-roll. "But I also doubt this is an Anti-OL job. That pink smoke is so widespread. It seems unlikely any human force is behind it?"

"I dunno," Claudia said. "I think those Anti-OL fuckers are capable of some crazy shit. And your billionaire daddy is just making things worse. Patrick Sullivan basically abolished federal laws preventing private paramilitary activity . . ."

"You can't blame Patrick. That was the Supreme Court—"

"But he funded the massive movement that led to that decision," Astrid interjected.

"Well, it's up to the states now and at least California still outlaws citizen militias—"

"Oh, but you *know* there are underground militias in L.A. County," Claudia retorted. "White supremacists with guns need *somewhere* to go after retiring from the police—"

"I'm on your side, Claudia! All I'm saying is that Patrick is just as clueless as the rest of us about the pink smoke and we're all trying to figure this out—"

"Letting him off the hook, as usual—"

"*I'm not defending Patrick—*"

"Really? Because it sure *sounds* like you are—"

"*I am not—*"

"*Then what are you doing?*"

"*I guess I'm defending myself!*"

The three sat in tense silence. A gust of wind rattled the car. Suddenly, the wall of pink smog was upon them. Slowly, it enveloped the vehicle, and they were unable to see farther than a foot in any direction, as if they were in a plane speeding through a fuchsia storm cloud.

Astrid sighed. "Should we just tell him now?"

"Tell me what?"

"Yunho said he wanted to be there as well," Claudia insisted.

"*Tell me what?*"

SLAM. A human body hit the windshield with violent force; its intestines splattered against the glass like a dead insect's entrails. Steam escaped from a gaping stomach laceration and fogged their view. The passengers screamed. The body slid downward, leaving a ruby blur of organ slime on the windshield. Its jaw had been ripped off, its mandible reduced to jagged splinters. Blood bubbled from its open neck—an exposed thyroid pumped under the crimson deluge. Then, the thing's arm twitched. Its shredded eyelids fluttered. The arm spasmed with increasing intensity, as if electrocuted by some unseen shockwave. The thing's gaze became lucid, alive. It pounded the windshield. It wanted to get inside. Mason slammed the horn. It blared, long and loud, underscoring their screams.

SLAM. The thing's palm hit the glass. Mason whipped his head to the left, to the right. Concrete barriers on both sides. *SLAM.* In front of him, a car. Behind him, a car. Nowhere to turn. *SLAM.* "*Everyone get your gas masks!*" Mason yelled, slapping his own onto his face.

SLAM. The windshield cracked.

SLAM. An arm broke through.

Some animal compulsion overtook Mason's musculature. He moved without thinking, ripped off his seat belt and threw his body over Astrid's pregnant belly. Wet fingers clawed at Mason's neck, caught a patch of curls, and yanked. He screamed as hair and skin detached from his scalp. Blood blossomed from the ravaged follicles and spilled down the top of his gas mask, streaking the protective glass of his eye goggles. His mind told him he should run, save himself, and leave them behind. But a deeper instinct demanded he stay and use his own body as a shield. He wanted to call this instinct love, but it was more urgent than any love he'd felt before, heavier, a devastating weight on his heart. He would sacrifice his life for the child growing within Astrid's belly. *His* child. He would die for his child.

He would kill for his child.

TWELVE

12 months, 2 hours, 14 minutes

M ason felt dizzy at the sight of her. Speechless. They'd found her in just fifteen days. It took another twenty to get her to Los Angeles. The agency said she had a concern. About the process. Or the terms. Or something. The agency said not to worry—it could be sorted out in person. The train was moving. The velocity was unbearable. Mason couldn't imagine his life with a child. But he also couldn't imagine his life *without* one. She smiled. Her dimples triggered a panic attack. The room spun. Mason clutched the conference table. She seemed even younger in person. Was she *too* young? Could they trust her? *What did she need to discuss?*

"Astrid! It's so wonderful to meet you in person!" Yunho exclaimed. The men rushed toward Astrid, through a space more appropriate for foreign policy deliberation than a surrogacy discussion. A solemn conference table stretched above black marble flooring; thirty ergonomic chairs lined its perimeter. A war room. Crystal vases bursting with snapdragons were installed at two-foot increments along the table to dispel the militaristic vibes and create an atmosphere of corporately sanitized fecundity, which was enhanced by a wall mural featuring a diverse array of pregnant women bursting from the blooms of various flowers. An overwrought cursive logo snaked across the painting: FUTURE GENERATIONS. Floor-to-ceiling windows framed an epic view of downtown Los Angeles that felt predatory; from this vantage it was almost impossible *not* to plot the corporate takeover of all those distant gleaming buildings and the businesses within. Indeed, this is the vibe that the Chinese conglomerate that owned this global surrogacy firm was aiming for, not only to inspire executives during discussions of mergers, but also to assure any wary would-be parents concerned about bringing an expensively produced newborn into the burning world that the neoliberal weight of global capital was behind their decision and would ensure their child avoided whatever terrible fate would befall those poor souls who could not afford a seat at the Future Generations conference table.

"My favorite daddies." Astrid gave a tentative laugh, scooping Mason and Yunho into a group hug. The sudden penguin huddle felt overly familiar, but Mason was grateful for the immediate intimacy. Though they'd talked for hours via multiple virtual interviews, Mason was inexplicably nervous in her real-life presence. Why did he feel—what? Unqualified? Unworthy?

Brecklyn, the Future Generations representative assigned to their case, looked on in robotic mirth. With her severe bob, porcelain skin, and tailored skirt suit, she had all the neutered beauty of a stock photo model in a sexual harassment training brochure. "Isn't this beautiful," Brecklyn cooed in a voice suited to GPS narration. "Now, shall we get started?"

"There's one thing I want to bring up first," Astrid said. "In the interest of being transparent. I feel like you guys should know why I want to do this." Mason was intimidated by the urgency in her voice. *Her* reasons for doing this were not something with which he had expected to contend.

"Of course." This was it. Mason's anxiety spiked. "You can tell us anything."

His name was Chet. He worked at the same Walmart Astrid did. He wasn't important to the story though, Astrid insisted. She was pansexual; cishet men were her least favorite fucks, but occasionally she felt an urge for toxic cock. So she'd fucked Chet in a regrettable moment of twenty-one-year-old horniness and gotten pregnant with a child he insisted wasn't his. Chet's denial filled her with rage, but she repressed it, not wanting to erupt during a shift at the superstore and lose one of the three jobs she needed to survive in Shreveport while caring for her dying mother.

The weeks passed—fifteen to be precise—as she debated what to do. Her biggest problem: She lived in Shreveport. Not only was abortion a federal crime, but Louisiana and the states that bordered it had enacted laws that allowed prosecutors to charge any woman who tried to terminate her pregnancy with attempted murder. If Astrid wanted to get an abortion, she would need to drive nine hundred miles to the closest underground Norma Collective clinic in Colorado Springs. (She didn't have money to fly, nor did she wish to create incriminating travel documents.) If she was caught, she'd be charged with crossing state lines with the intent to murder a fetus, elevating her offense to a federal crime (though thankfully, she was too poor to afford an iOS Cerebrum, so there would be no AppleBody Data to subpoena as proof of abortion). Complicating matters was the fact she'd always dreamed of having a baby. But not right now. Not with Chet. Not when she had three jobs. Not when her mother had cancer. Not when every day the stress weighed on her like a medieval torture press.

She broke down to her best friend, Claudia, the founder of a local queer art group Astrid attended in her very limited free time. That's how important the group was—Astrid was willing to sacrifice rare hours that could be spent sleeping to connect to this beautiful community, one where she could share the paintings she made, quiet domestic scenes of queers in love. Without this vital creative outlet, she would've succumbed to the obliterating numbness of a life spent working under the dull fluorescent lights of Walmart and the liquor store and the movie theater concession stand. This art group also had a social justice mission—Astrid was weirdly elusive about the details here, but Mason gleaned that part of their activism involved transporting women to and from underground abortions. With Claudia by her side, Astrid drove fifteen hours in one day, desperate to miss as little work as possible. Astrid couldn't afford this trip, but she also couldn't afford a baby. Finally, they arrived in Colorado Springs. They spent the night at a shitty motel, woke up and ate greasy eggs at a diner, and pretended to be brave.

But when it came time for the abortion, Astrid couldn't go through with it. She sat by herself in the clinic and wept. Claudia wasn't allowed to know the location—Norma Collective rules—so she waited back at the motel. An overworked nurse watched Astrid with as much pity as she could muster. *I've always wanted a child*, Astrid sobbed. The nurse understood. Still, Astrid felt like a failure to herself, to Claudia (though Claudia insisted she was supportive of Astrid's decision), and to the cause of reproductive rights.

She returned to Shreveport. Her pregnancy advanced. Then, the unimaginable happened: Walmart shifted to the AI-powered cashier-free model that revolutionized the retail sector. The fully automated "smart store" tracked items shoppers put into their carts, eliminated the need for human employees, and saved the mega-retailer hundreds of millions in labor costs. Astrid barely got by on the three jobs she had; the loss of income was devastating and confirmed that a baby was not an option for someone like her, someone who subsisted on stolen popcorn from the concession stand at the AMC where she worked in one of her remaining two jobs.

She found an adoption agency. The agency found a wealthy infertile Louisiana couple. She went through with the pregnancy. And she was glad she did. She loved being pregnant, all that hope and promise blossoming within. Her mother, in the days before her death, remarked that she felt confident leaving this Earth because her daughter had found her divine purpose.

Astrid no longer felt like a failure. With the money the agency paid her, she was able to avoid getting a third job (at least for a few months), which opened space in her life to make more art and forge deeper friendships. She and Claudia began dating, bonded by their journey. It didn't bother her that the adoptive parents didn't want her to have a relationship with her child (though they did let her stop by for an hour on Christmas Eve the first year). No longer did she feel saddened by the fact she'd been unable to keep this child; instead, she felt joy. She'd found her calling. She was born to create life for others. "Which is why I want to be a surrogate. A child is the greatest gift you can give someone. And I want to give that gift to you two," she concluded with a smile as she wiped her cheeks, drying tears that had flowed in the wake of her utterance of the phrase *Christmas Eve.* Mason chose to believe these were tears of joy. *She said this is her calling,* he assured himself. "It's just important for you to know how much this means to me."

"And we can assure you, it means just as much to us," Yunho said.

But did it? Mason wondered. *Did it mean as much to them as it did to Astrid?* Something about her blind faith in these two men she'd met only three times made Mason feel like an impostor. Did they deserve this beautiful act of generosity? Of course, Astrid was also getting something out of this—a modest amount of cold, hard cash. Plus, they'd pay for her relocation to California, due to federal laws that criminalized interstate surrogacy and adoption for queer and trans couples. Still, what was money, when compared to a miracle?

"A beautiful story," Brecklyn said, eager to end the human-emotions portion of the meeting. "Was there anything else you needed to discuss?"

"I think that does it for me," Astrid said.

"Us too," Yunho chirped. "We're so excited!" Astrid squealed and hugged the men.

"There's a car waiting for you outside," Brecklyn said to Astrid. "I just have a few things to tie up here with the boys."

Mason had the impulse to grab Astrid's arm and stop her from leaving. He wanted her to tell him that he and Yunho were making the right decision, that they'd be good parents, that they deserved this child. But he didn't stop her, of course. Then, Astrid was gone, leaving the men to make their final decisions about her pregnancy.

THIRTEEN

2 hours, 9 minutes

There were so many things that could go wrong during a pregnancy, yet for all his catastrophizing about birth complications, nothing prepared Mason for the dead-eyed pack of mutilated bodies that was swarming his Tesla. Two of them hit the windshield, piling on top of the body already there, pummeling it to death. Another slammed into the right side of the car. Another vaulted onto the roof. They writhed like a mess of worms forced from the dirt by rain.

They greased the windows with their mucilage. Brick-red secretions swirled on the surface of the glass. They rocked the car. They kicked the doors. Their arteries hemorrhaged into the fissures of the fractured glass, spinning webs of blood across the windshield. Mason clutched Astrid's stomach and prepared for death. A wave of horrific relief cleansed his panicked mind; there was nothing more to worry about, this was the end. He would go out protecting the life inside Astrid and he would probably fail, but the small hope he might prevent his child's death made him clutch Astrid's belly with lunatic purpose. *Just make it quick*, he prayed. *Let's go*. He repeated that phrase in his mind—*let's go, let's go*—until he realized it wasn't his voice he was hearing, but Claudia's. "*Let's go!*" she screamed, crouching on the floor in the back seat. Above her, the window was close to shattering. "*Let's go!*"

"Go where?" Mason moaned into Astrid's stomach.

"*To your motherfucking baby shower, bitch.*" Claudia punched the back of Mason's seat. "Listen to me. These things are attacking the *right* side of the car. You have a clear shot at the trunk from the driver's side. So you're gonna run to the trunk and grab my wheelchair. Astrid will crawl out the driver's side door. Then, we run."

The bodies on the windshield convulsed. *CRACK.* One of them rammed its head through the hole in the glass, thrashed its skull against the jagged perimeter. Bloodied glass rained down. "But—"

"*Pop the trunk, Mason.*" *CRACK.* Shards of bone jutted from the thing's forehead. Its detached nose dangled from a string of cartilage. "*Pop the fucking trunk.*" Mason did as he was told. "Now *go.*" He tightened the straps on his gas mask. *CRACK.* The thing snapped at Mason; broken molars flew from its mouth. "*GO!*" she screamed.

And Mason was gone, slamming the door behind him. He crouched in the pink smoke, looked up at the rocking metal cage he'd just escaped. The things seemed singularly fixated on his Tesla, as if their human consciousness had been overtaken by dumb animal instinct that prevented them from dividing their focus. He squinted through the haze at the besieged intersection, suffering the symphony of horns and screams and bursting tires. One by one, cars were toppled by those disgusting creatures, those, well, not *zombies*—zombies weren't real, and besides, zombies were *drained* of life, whereas these things seemed to possess *more* life, *more* strength, a superhuman drive for destruction unfettered by whatever brutal maiming had turned their bodies into half-butchered beasts.

He crawled through shattered glass, toward the trunk. A freshly amputated finger pointed to the ravaged body from which it had been severed. Human slop bubbled from the cadaver's gored stomach, forming the lake of blood through which Mason slid. He choked back vomit. His mask fogged with sweat. He looked up. Through the condensation he spotted the open trunk.

He sprung to his feet. Flinched.

But those things were gone. They'd given up, their mission thwarted by the car's resilient exterior. He hunched slightly behind the open trunk, watching as a final straggler furiously limped in the direction of the next car. Its left foot had been severed at the ankle, but still it powered forward, slamming its grisly stump against the pavement.

Mason shuddered, shifting his attention to the trunk. The wheelchair. Mason hauled it to the pavement. He scanned the compartment for anything that could be used as a weapon. Two eyes flashed at him from a dark corner.

He froze, looked closer.

It was just a child. A girl. No more than four years old. Scared and coiled in the shadows.

"Hey, sweetie," Mason cooed. "Are you okay?" The girl said nothing, just slid forward shyly. She wore a tattered Minnie Mouse T-shirt. The cartoon's smile was crusted in a layer of dried blood. "How did you get back here? Do you know where your mommy is?" She inched closer, right to the edge of the trunk. Her pupils were dilated black saucers. Her lips curled inward; she chewed on her frown. "We're gonna get you help, okay?"

She jumped. Like a flying rodent—fast, light, vicious.

She seemed rabid, unconcerned with her own life, stricken by a suicidal hunger for destruction. She landed on his torso, wrapped her legs around his waist. She clawed at his chest with ratlike fervor. Her tiny nails sunk into his flesh. He attempted to push the child off, but she climbed farther up his body. She wrapped her small legs around his neck; they were impossibly strong, two baby pythons. Her fingers raked the back of his skull. Her torso pressed against his gas mask, blocking the air filters, stopping the flow of oxygen. Mason attempted to rip her body off his face. But the more he pulled, the tighter she constricted. He wheezed, fought for breath. His vision blurred. The last thing he felt were his knees hitting the pavement. A shattering pain. Then he was out. Just another body on the pavement.

The child didn't let go. She clutched him harder.

FOURTEEN

1 hour, 43 minutes

Solid black. Forward motion. A jagged heaving momentum.

Then: gradual wakefulness. Consciousness crept in before the dark lifted. Memories or nightmares evaporated before Mason could grasp them. Dull panic spiraled in the void.

A cool film of sweat beaded his face. Something constricted his skull—a gas mask. He was wearing a gas mask. Right. And his legs—they ached. A wetness at the kneecap. A pulsing, a gradual seeping. Blood.

His eyes opened. Smashed asphalt. A road. Pink smoke. He lifted his neck. His spine twinged in protest. His vision dipped to black. Then, an explosion of white. Lilies. A bouquet. A woman. Pregnant. Her floral dress, ripped. Her profile was obscured by her gas mask. *Astrid*, he realized. *My bouquet. My baby shower.*

Below him: Claudia. He was sitting in Claudia's lap. She wheeled them across asphalt; braids of sinew swelled with every pump of her arms. "Uh . . . uh . . ." Words failed to formulate.

"Is he awake?" Claudia gripped her hand-rims. The chair slowed to a stop.

"*Oh fuck.*" Sudden agony coursed through Mason. "*Fuck, fuck, fuck.*"

"What's wrong?" Astrid rushed to his side.

"My . . . knee. *Fuck.*" It was the right kneecap. Something inside felt shattered.

"I can't carry him much longer." Claudia looked to Astrid.

"I can push you both—"

"You *can't*. You could go into preterm labor or—"

"I think . . . I can get up. It's just the right knee," Mason grunted.

"Does it feel broken?" Astrid held out her free hand, cradling the bouquet in the other.

"I don't know." Mason grabbed onto Astrid and lifted himself off Claudia. "*Fuck.*"

"Keep the weight on your left leg as much as possible," Claudia coached. Mason stood, breathing through the pain. "Can you walk?"

"I think I can limp." Panic seized Mason's chest. "*The little girl,*" he gasped. "What happened to that little girl?"

Astrid's eyes watered. "She's . . . she's . . ."

"She's gone," Claudia said flatly. "Astrid got out of the car and found her wrapped around your head . . . she had no pulse."

"Fuck . . ."

"I . . . I . . ." Astrid burst into sobs.

"All we can do is push forward." Claudia wheeled to her lover and stroked her back. "We can't break down."

"Where are we?" Mason squinted at his companions through the thickening pink smoke.

"Still on Los Feliz Boulevard."

"But closer to your place," Astrid insisted. "Give me your arm." Mason slung himself around Astrid. They formed one lurching entity, feet stumbling forward in painful syncopation. The fog gradually thinned, revealing the road he traveled daily. Adrenalized hope numbed his pain; they were less than a mile from home. They turned the corner. Mason stepped into something slick and warm. He looked down—it was an exploded poodle, intestines scattered across the pavement like piñata loot.

He looked up again. The smoke parted.

An unholy tangle of vehicles emerged from behind the pink gauze of dispersing vapors. There was something almost cubist about the horrific abstraction of the scene—the intersection was a surreal jumble of steel and rubber and fire and flesh. They circled the pileup cautiously. A T-bone collision boasted three accordioned sedans as its fiery spine. A legless torso slumped through the shattered windshield of a truck. Mutilated body parts lined the perimeter of the accident, mashed together at inhuman angles. The open doors of an overturned ambulance framed a mess of corpses crushed by medical equipment. A fire had turned the front carriage into an oven; a flame-retardant seat belt kept the driver's charred skeleton hanging in place.

"*Freeze!*" A white man in a gas mask emerged from behind the ambulance. He wore a blue jacket, the letters FBI emblazoned across his heart. He held a gun in his trembling hands. His panicked gaze kept shifting to the horror all around. "*Hands in the air!*"

"Officer, please—" Mason begged.

"*Shut the fuck up!*" the man yelled. "*Shut the fuck up unless I ask you a fucking question. Got it?*" The three nodded. "Now tell me: What the fuck happened?"

"We didn't do anything," Astrid pleaded. "We only just got here ourselves—"

"*Don't lie. You're the only ones alive. So tell me what happened and . . . and . . .*" A fit of hyperventilation racked the man's thick frame—a panic attack. He fell to his knees; his spine spasmed with each throttled breath. He slapped his gas mask as if retaliating against a strangler.

"Are you okay?" Astrid's empathy knew no bounds, *And bounds are definitely called for in this particular fucking case*, Mason reflected as, to his horror, Astrid shimmied Mason's arm off her shoulders. "Here, lean on Claudia's wheelchair," she whispered to Mason.

"*What are you doing? He said not to move—*"

"He's clearly in trouble—"

Gunfire erupted. Mason dropped to his busted knees, screaming. He whipped his head to Astrid, who crouched beside him. Safe. Thank God. The officer had only fired into the air.

"I told you . . . don't . . . fucking move." The man's breathing steadied as he rose to his feet. His smoking Glock seemed to dispel his panic, as if inflicting violence restored some sense of order within him. "Give me your identification."

Astrid slapped the pockets on her dress. "I . . . I don't have mine . . ."

". . . neither do I." A panicked whisper from Mason. "I left it in the car . . ."

"I do." Claudia dug her ID from the pouch on her wheelchair.

"Throw it to me."

Claudia tossed it as far as she could. It plummeted to the ground like a sick bird. The man kept his gun cocked, and stooped to pick up the ID. "Claudia Jackson," he read with unnerved recognition, as if she were some mythical being brought to terrifying life. He cocked his gun at Astrid and Mason. "*You two—on the ground.*" They wormed onto the pavement as he forced handcuffs onto them. "And you . . ." He grunted at Claudia, threading handcuffs through the spokes on her left wheel and shackling her wrists. She struggled with her restraints; a patch of bruises flowered beneath the steel. "It's nice to finally meet you."

FIFTEEN

10 months, 1 hour, 27 minutes

" 'M omma—where were you when you learned I was a "terrorist?"
Did you believe in the FBI's violent classification of my life? Will
you ever speak to me again? I worry your silence is an answer. Especially
since all I'd known prior to this silence was your fierce, suffocating love.

" 'My coming into the world traumatized you. Destroyed your marriage.
My father left when he learned his child had cerebral palsy, the minute he
understood what it meant to fight for someone whose body was born at war
with a world that refused to accommodate their existence.

" 'I was all you had left to love. You worked so hard to ensure I'd be as
able-bodied as possible, which meant endless doctor's appointments, physical therapy, and brutal surgeries. I screamed and cried but let me be clear,
Momma: I'm grateful for every surgery you put me through, especially
when so many disabled people don't have access to healthcare and are left
at the mercy of a society that scorns and criminalizes disabled bodies. But
your love felt like pain. Because instead of fighting to change *the world*, you
were fighting to change *me*.

" 'It felt like *I* was the problem. Like you were frustrated at *me* when
doctors told you I'd be unable to walk. Like you were angry with *me* every
time we encountered another medical or bureaucratic obstacle. My resentment mixed with the raging hormones of my teen years. I channeled my

pain into art. I dove into the DIY punk scene, which bubbled up in Shreveport when poor artists got pushed out of New Orleans by the rising ocean. I found two disabled friends, Grey and Keisha, and we started a noise band named LOMAX!!!, a reference to Brad Lomax, whom we called our sexy disabled Black Panther daddy. We couldn't really play instruments, but that wasn't the point; the point was to scream, to reject harmony, to create noise that defied society's expectations of what the world should sound like.

"'You hated it. Worried about me every time we played some fire-trap punk club. But my most significant rebellion was sparked by the prospect of college. You pushed me to apply to public policy programs. You worked at LSU's Public Policy Research Lab and wanted me to follow in your footsteps and learn the machinery of policy so I could fight authoritarianism and ensure the future of the American state. But I believed the American state was inherently rotten and inequitable, that the only thing to do was abolish it. I started reading Marquis Bey, William C. Anderson, Lorenzo Kom'boa Ervin, Lucy Parsons; their words made sense in a way nothing else did. I'd found a new language, a new love: anarchism. You humored me at first, your little radical, but you still expected me to "be realistic" and engage in the battle you'd fought your entire career: to change the American state from within. The more you pushed, the more I rebelled. *Why can't we just fight about boys?* you always said, exasperated by our shouting matches. Finally, at eighteen, I left home to squat in an abandoned Shreveport warehouse with my LOMAX!!! bandmates and start the Anarchist Cutie Club.

"'You were furious. You stopped returning my calls. We became strangers. I threw myself into work. When you're trying to remake the world, there's much to be done; we wanted to abolish the State, the prison industrial complex, and capitalism. We dreamed of an ungoverned society based on models of Black and queer kinship, mutual aid, and direct democracy. Sure, our twenty-person art collective didn't bring down the U.S. government, but we *did* create a self-sustaining anarchist community that operated *outside* the State. I didn't need our family anymore. I'd found a new kinship unit. I was grateful for our estrangement. It led me toward utopia.

"'Except. Sometimes I longed for your embrace. Sometimes I wanted my momma. Like when I discovered the FBI had been surveilling me. It was 2039. I was twenty-four years old. An anonymous source leaked FBI documents online, revealing I was on a list of "terrorists" for surveillance, labeled "Black Identity Artists with Extremist Agendas." The ACC's art was inextricable from our activism—we protested police, transported people to criminal abortions, helped trans children secure illegal medical treatment—so it made sense they'd targeted us. From COINTELPRO to the Patriot Act, the FBI has always spied on activists and anarchists, on Blacks and queers and Muslims and anyone who challenges the white supremacist, cis-heteropatriarchal foundations of our country. Still, I wasn't prepared for the terror I felt upon discovering that they'd tracked me for five years, watched me even as I slept in Astrid's arms, noting every time I stirred in the night.

"'The terror was so great that I called you, Momma, desperate to hear your voice on the phone. I tried again and again. You never picked up.

"'I love you, Momma. We don't need to be a family. But can we be a part of something bigger? This book is for you, for us, for everyone on Earth. How can we work toward a horizon of universal care? How can we better love one another?'" Claudia concluded, looking up from her memoir and at the crowd assembled before her at Skylight Books. Everyone applauded. The space was packed; air-conditioning was no match for the teeming hive. Yunho, Daniel, Mahmood, and Astrid seemed unfazed, but Mason could barely focus on the reading. *The Anarchist Cutie Club*, Claudia's memoir, had become a grassroots publishing success, a rare victory for a small press outside the larger corporate publishers (who rejected her manuscript because it defied their new Decency Mandates). The book release coincided with Claudia's move to L.A., and her publisher scheduled an event in their author's new city.

The applause subsided. "Just a footnote: The FBI never successfully put together a case against me. Now, through my writing, I've wrested my story from the government's hands."

Mason looked to Astrid, who stared at her lover with an uncharacteristically hardened expression that communicated a near-violent devotion. Panic twisted Mason's gut upon seeing the rage in Astrid's eyes—he realized he didn't *really* know her, this near-stranger for whom they'd rented a $10,000-a-month home, who'd just received a costly IVF treatment, and a private chef, and a weekly allowance of $1,000 (under the table, as Future Generations forbade bonuses). Astrid was the most significant investment the couple had ever made beyond their real estate portfolio. Most people didn't "do" surrogacy in this extravagant manner, most people couldn't afford the baseline $250,000 Future Generations charged. But Yunho would allegedly shoot his *Reds* reboot soon, for which he'd likely receive a $5 million directing fee; still, Mason felt nervous about spending money that wasn't in the bank, especially when he was struggling to move product in an art market losing interest in his work. They were betting big on Astrid, gambling more than they could afford, all because of their passionate *need* for a child. Which is why, when looking at Astrid's strange expression in Skylight Books, Mason became frightened she was hiding something; why had she concealed her involvement with the Anarchist Cutie Club, which she'd initially framed as a vague "art group"? In *theory* Mason found the ACC's activities noble, but in *practice* he was paying too much money for this surrogacy to have it surveilled by the FBI. He worried the agency would now track *his* movements, that this unjust web of surveillance would ensnare his new family.

Mason's cheeks flushed; he couldn't tell whether his body's temperature spike was due to panic or the sweltering crucible of the bookstore. Claudia continued to speak, but he wasn't listening. He needed to escape. He pushed through the pungent throng and burst onto the street.

"Mason—are you okay?" Yunho called, following Mason out.

"Sorry, it was too hot in there."

"I thought I was gonna pass out." Yunho palmed sweat from his brow. "But Claudia is a *star*. I wonder if anyone's optioned the TV rights—"

"*Are we making a mistake?*" Mason blurted out.

Yunho's eyebrows arched like two threatened cats. "What are you talking about?"

"With . . . this surrogacy thing . . ."

"You're a little *late* to the party with these concerns," Yunho snapped.

". . . not in general, but with Astrid. I *want* a kid. But given her history . . ." Mason trailed off, silenced by the sight of Astrid emerging from the store, along with the rest of the exiting crowd. Yunho's eyes burned with furious disbelief.

"My sweet boys." Astrid glided up to them. "Let's lead the charge to the afterparty!"

*

"I'm surprised you two never considered adoption," Mahmood pondered, sipping his drink.

"We wanted a kid that felt like *ours*." Yunho looked at Mason with unconcealed hurt. Astrid carpooled with them to Akbar, so the men had been unable to speak openly; instead, unbearable tension swirled between them like a banshee whose screams only they could hear. "We thought surrogacy would be easier, which is laughable in retrospect. There's nothing easy about an endless process that involves my frozen sperm, hundreds of thousands of dollars, eggs donated by Mason's insufferably heterosexual cousin—"

"It's not *my* fault I'm related to straight people."

"—and Astrid as a surrogate." Yunho gored Mason's heart with another sharp stare. Suddenly, screams pierced the dance music pumping through the packed gay bar. Claudia had arrived; she wheeled in with a lapful of flowers, followed by Grey, her fellow ACC founder. People took photos, applauded; Astrid rushed up to Claudia and kissed her on the cheek. The men turned to take in the scene. "I'm gonna go chat with Astrid." Yunho excused himself.

Mason stepped away from Mahmood. "Yunho, stop. We need to talk—"

"Can't hear you!" He sauntered vengefully in Astrid's direction. Mason disengaged from Yunho's provocations and attempted to flag down the lethargic bear slinging drinks.

Suddenly, Claudia appeared at his side. "Mind grabbing me a gin and tonic?"

"It would be my honor. You were amazing tonight."

"Thank you."

"How's the house?" Mason said as pleasantly as possible given the anxiety he felt concerning the cost of the rental. His attempts to make eye contact with the bartender were unsuccessful; his fearful gaze shifted to the jukebox beyond, where Yunho stood in serious conversation with Astrid. *What are they talking about?*

"It pains my anarchist soul to admit this, but it beats squatting in an abandoned warehouse in Shreveport."

"But you were doing something so valuable there, surely it was worth it."

"You should tell my mother that." Some obscure agitation flickered in her eyes. He didn't know her well enough to divine her moods—their interactions were limited to one "family" dinner upon her recent arrival in Los Angeles. "I do miss the ACC sometimes. The purpose I felt. The people we helped. But the lifestyle was unsustainable. You get older and no longer have the energy to host ketamine art raves, then wake up in the morning to smuggle someone across state lines and become an accomplice to the federal crime of abortion."

"I get it."

Claudia laughed incredulously. "Do you?"

"I used to make art that . . . meant something," Mason muttered sadly, surprising himself with his own admission. Before he could elaborate, Astrid bounded up, dragging Yunho.

"Hi, baby." She kissed Claudia. "Are we getting drinks?"

"Attempting," Mason said, making concerned eye contact with Yunho. The weight of unresolved tension pressed on his rib cage. "But first, I need to steal Yunho—"

"Wait! I have something to tell you both. I . . ." Astrid paused dramatically. Mason's pulse sped; he looked to Yunho, who still withheld his gaze. ". . . I'm pregnant."

"Wait—for real?" Yunho clutched Astrid's hands.

"Yes, I'm pregnant!" Astrid dug a pink stick from her purse. "I know we were supposed to wait until the fertility clinic, but I couldn't resist, so I did an at-home test and . . . it's positive."

"You're pregnant," Mason repeated, stunned, desperate for his lover to just *look* at him.

"You're pregnant!" Yunho shouted, embraced Astrid, then kissed Claudia's cheek. Finally, he turned to Mason and whispered in a voice aching to reconcile: "We're pregnant."

*

Later, Diana Ross seduced the dance floor. *Upside down, boy you turn me . . .* Bodies undulated to the beat. *Inside out and . . .* Yunho rocked Mason in his arms. *Round and round . . .* The deluge of feeling left Mason relating literally to the song; he felt inside out, like his organs were exposed, like any passerby could pluck his beating heart right out of his chest. He kissed Yunho, searching for forgiveness with his tongue. Yunho pulled back, mouthed *I love you* and *we're pregnant,* and Mason felt a joy so profound it overpowered whatever cowardly fears had gripped him outside the bookstore. He turned to Astrid, who gave Claudia a lap dance in the middle of the floor; her red mane whipped through the air, licking her lover's body like a flame. The temperature in the room rose, but Mason welcomed the warmth, the crush of bodies. He felt comforted, cocooned. He broke a sweat; his body felt loose, sensual. He felt loved. He felt hope. He felt like a father. He could overcome any obstacle through the power of his newfound happiness; the strength he derived from this elation would protect his family, and that *did* include Astrid and Claudia. Yes, this love was great enough to revive Mason's imagination, to instill within him the creativity to fight the world's evils—through art, through activism, hell, through anarchy even. *If there's a cure for this, I don't want it,* Diana moaned. *Sweet, sweet, sweet, sweet love.* The force of his happiness hit him like a hurricane gust; he threw his arms around his lover and held on for dear life.

SIXTEEN

1 hour, 6 minutes

The man's boot was untied; tattered laces burst from the leather tongue like strands of solid spit. The shoe was all Mason could see; the eye holes in his gas mask limited his range of vision. He didn't dare move his head; that would get him shot. He remained facedown, handcuffed; his body pulsed against the pavement—a chunk of asphalt bore into his stomach.

"*What happened here?*" the FBI agent shouted.

"We told you," Mason pleaded. "We don't know—"

The man fired a shot into the air. "*Don't fucking lie.*"

"Please, just uncuff us."

"*I'm not uncuffing shit until—*"

A hulking figure materialized in the smoke. It was three hundred pounds, hurtling through space toward the agent. He didn't have an instant to dodge or run—there was just a sudden crushing weight upon him. He crumpled like a cardboard cutout in a trash compactor. His legs snapped, buckled in the wrong direction at the kneecap. The knob-ends of his femurs burst through the skin. The agent's screams echoed across the devastated intersection.

"*What . . . is that thing?*" Astrid rolled to her side, sobbing in fear.

"*We have to get out of here.*" Claudia slammed her handcuffs against the spokes of the wheel they were entangled within. Mason moaned on the pavement.

The figure appeared to be a man, though its face had been shredded into featurelessness; mere suggestions of facial topography surfaced in a sea of red muck. Like some kid's shitty Play-Doh sculpture. The whites of its eyes popped against the crimson mess. The thing straddled the agent's torso, clawing at his chest. It ripped at the agent with the ease of a child attacking a present on Christmas morning. Shreds of clothing flew skyward—bits of jacket, scraps of bulletproof vest. The agent screamed again. Flesh joined the spray of fabric.

"Your gun!" Mason shouted to the man. "*Get your gun.*" The agent's head flopped to the right. His fingers crawled toward the gun. Then, it was in his grasp.

A shot fired. The bullet went straight through the thing's skull, bursting its left eye like a swollen summer grape. But rather than kill it, the injury only revived some primal anger. It howled in agony. It picked up the agent's head and slammed it against the road, slammed it until his skull shattered like a bowl of soup; blood and brain and bone exploded onto the pavement. Even then, it didn't stop; it pounded the agent's rib cage with its fists, until gradually the thing began to lose consciousness, and rolled off the headless corpse, shuddering.

Mason choked back vomit, not wanting it to fill his gas mask. Astrid wretched beside him. Claudia screamed into the haze. Silence fell. Behind them, an errant squeal emanated from the totaled ambulance, the siren's throttled swan song. "Astrid," Claudia said, her voice weak.

Astrid slowly lifted her head; her gas mask was streaked with dirt and blood. "Uh . . . huh?"

Claudia nodded toward the agent's corpse. "He has the keys to our cuffs on his belt . . ."

"Okay," Astrid said, regaining her focus.

". . . And you're closest to his body." Astrid turned from Claudia and looked toward the agent. Between her and the felled officer lay the hulking carcass of that thing. "So here's what you're gonna do. Are you listening, Astrid?"

"Yes."

"You're gonna wriggle on your side and push yourself *very carefully* over that . . . *thing's* body. Then you're gonna thrust yourself on top of the agent and grab his keys."

"I . . . I could also go," Mason interjected.

"*Astrid is going*," Claudia snapped. "You've already fucked up enough today."

"Okay." Astrid's handcuffs clattered as she wriggled onto her side, propelling herself across the pavement by pumping her legs. Her thin dress shredded more with every push; her flesh scraped against the pavement. A muffled groan escaped through the filters in her gas mask.

She thrust herself up against the thing, over the mountain of its belly, and landed on the other side, flopping in a puddle of the agent's brains. She wretched at the gore spilling from his neck. "The keys are clipped to his belt!" she yelled out, pushing her body onto his torso. She lay face up and wriggled to align her cuffed hands with his belt loop. She yanked at the keychain. "I can't . . . get it . . . off." She tugged and wrenched, frustration mounting until finally, she threw the full weight of her body into one violent pull. The belt loop snapped. "*I got them*," she cried.

A hand grabbed her ankle.

Astrid screamed. The thing lurched to its knees, grabbed Astrid's other foot, and dragged her across the asphalt. Mason howled. Claudia rocked in her wheelchair, trying to break out of her handcuffs; the chair toppled, her body smashed against the pavement, and there was a crack as her arms twisted like the limbs of a mangled Barbie. Another scream—Astrid. The thing was now on top of her, straddling her body. It clutched her masked face in its hands.

Then, it spoke. "Melanie," it moaned—the voice sounded male. "*Melanie*."

Astrid trembled in his grip. He brought his face close to hers. His features were stripped of skin, just sinew stretched over bone, like a diagram of the muscular system in a doctor's office. Scraps of flesh dangled from his cheek bones. A hunk of jowl dripped onto her gas mask. The bullet had opened a dark, wet cavity in his head, right where his eye should've been. Heat emanated from the hole; it gaped like a second mouth.

"Please," Astrid whispered. "Please . . . let me go."

His one eye widened. He gasped, as if waking from a nightmare. "*Melanie*," he said, urgent and confused. "*Melanie*."

"I'm not . . . Who's Melanie?" Astrid begged. "You're confused."

"Oh god, Melanie," the man groaned. "I . . . I'm so thirsty." He clutched her head tighter.

"*Please, I'm not Melanie.*"

But he was somewhere else, his gaze distant. He looked through Astrid, like she was a window into some awful hellscape that only he could see; every raw wet muscle on his face cramped in terror. "What happened, Melanie?"

"*Let her go!*" Claudia screamed.

But her objection didn't register; the man was in another world. He stroked Astrid's hair with a strange tenderness. "Melanie . . . I thought you were dead . . ." Moisture pooled in his one remaining eye, something like teardrops but not. A pus-like substance. The viscous saltiness mixed with blood and slid down the exposed muscles of his face. The hole where his other eye should've been spasmed with grief. ". . . but you're right here with me."

"No . . . I'm not—"

"Let's go back . . . to Positano," he begged. "The kids . . ." He burped up blood. ". . . the kids need to see the Amalfi . . . Coast . . ." Astrid headbutted him, but he grabbed her neck and pinned it to the ground. ". . . or we get your mom . . . to watch them . . ." He nestled his skinned face into Astrid's chest, smearing bloody fat across her breast. ". . . and we can go alone . . . and make love . . . like we did on our honeymoon . . ." He kissed her gas mask, slobbering blood into the air filters. ". . . and make another baby . . . because you're the best . . ." He grabbed her head. ". . . mommy . . ." He pressed his hands into her skull like he was trying to pop a balloon; Astrid screamed. "... in the whole ..."

"*Let her go!*" Mason shouted.

"... wide ..." The man pushed into her temples harder.

"*Fucking stop!*" Claudia howled.

"... world." An animal wail erupted from Astrid's throat; the man howled with her, as if they were part of the same pack of dying wolves. Still, he didn't release her skull. Suddenly, his one eye widened; some private horror played out in the back of his brain. He collapsed on top of Astrid; his body trembled with sobs. "I ... love you ..."

Then, he was silent. His massive hands dropped from Astrid's face. They twitched on the pavement, curling up like two murdered tarantulas. She wriggled out from under his body, slapping his girth off her. She rested for a moment, face up on the pavement.

He was dead at last.

She still had the keys in her grasp.

"Astrid—are you okay?"

But Astrid didn't answer. She looked up at the sky and burst into manic laughter. "*Positano!*" she screamed, and her fit of hysteria crescendoed into something awful—a mirthless, violent, and uncontrollable wailing. "*Positano!*"

SEVENTEEN

9 months, 2 days, 58 minutes

The fresh cranberry sauce was a controversial luxury to include on their Day of Mourning table; Mason worried it was callous to consume the delicacy when salt water from sea level rise had flooded Cape Cod's famed cranberry bogs and led to the near extinction of the fruit. But just because locals could no longer afford the berries, didn't mean he too should be forced to give them up, right? Besides, he and Yunho were *almost* locals; they spent two months each summer at their Provincetown home, nestled in the hilly woodlands north of Bradford Street. They'd bought it ten years ago, before the ocean consumed most of the Provincetown peninsula, decimating $100 million in tourist revenue, and turning the gay destination into a ravaged near-Atlantis.

"Are we on a island?" Gabriel asked.

"*An* island," Mahmood corrected his child.

"Yes, we come here every Thanksg—sorry, Day of Mourning—remember?" Daniel said.

"No . . ."

"Well, Provincetown wasn't always an island, which is maybe why you don't remember." Mason smiled at Gabriel. "It used to be the tip of a peninsula." Mason flexed his arm to make the shape of Cape Cod. "And

Provincetown was right here." Mason tapped the knuckle on his closed fist. "But now, North Truro is underwater"—he slashed at his wrist to delineate the town's demise—"and Provincetown is an island."

"But why?" Auden chimed in.

"Capitalism." Mason shrugged.

"Yuck," Auden spat after tasting the cranberry sauce.

"My thoughts exactly." Yunho laughed, as he ruffled the child's hair.

"We have freshly carved turkey coming in hot." Claudia held the dish as Astrid pushed her into the room. Claudia placed the golden carcass at the head of the rustic dining table, made by local artisans out of reclaimed timber from centuries-old sailing ships. The room's vaulted roof resembled the hull of an upturned boat—dark support beams contrasted the white wooden ceiling. An eighteenth-century iron chandelier hung from the rafters, mounted on a block-and-tackle system. The turkey completed the problematic tableau of their feast, calling to mind a traditional Thanksgiving aesthetic mere miles from the Wampanoag lands that English settlers stole to create the colony of Plymouth. "But I'm not sure why we're doing this," Claudia added. "You can call it 'Day of Mourning' but we're still celebrating genocide with turkey."

"Well, it's illegal *not* to celebrate it," Mason replied. The Senate recently removed environmental protections preventing pipelines from being built on Indigenous lands so fossil fuel companies could continue to speed the melting of polar ice until the land that was stolen in 1620 was underwater, finally completing a centuries-long ouroboros of colonialism. In an evil twist, there was a clause buried in the bill that made it a crime to protest Thanksgiving.

"Oh god," Daniel groaned. "Should we just trash the whole meal?"

"Absolutely not," Claudia said with a sly smile. "My turkey is fucking delicious."

Everyone laughed and settled into dinner. But a strange sadness lingered in Claudia's eyes. Though she conversed with the rest of them, her gaze kept drifting to the window, as if the horizon presented some unattainable utopia she'd rather inhabit. Mason looked through the pane himself, hoping to discern where that might be. Outside, the tide gained ground, each wave as searching and insistent as a snake's flickering tongue.

*

There, in the distance: the belfry. Small waves lapped at the barnacle-crusted bell within; it swung tunelessly, its submerged clapper silenced by salt water. Even still, phantom peals reverberated in Mason's memory. "We're almost there!" Mason yelled over the roar of their pontoon's motor. Yunho lay across the boat floor, looking resplendent in a Speedo, allowing the sun to broil his skin. Astrid wore a diaphanous long-sleeved maxi dress to protect her fair complexion. She held her billowing sun hat in place, smiling. It was a worrisome eighty degrees at eight thirty A.M. on a November morning in Massachusetts, but what could they do except enjoy the beautiful day? Daniel, Mahmood, and Claudia had declined the excursion, preferring to nurse hangovers in the air-conditioned house while sedating Gabriel and Auden with VR playtime. Mason was secretly delighted; to share this moment with Astrid alone felt like a necessary intimacy, a way to draw her and their child deeper into "the story of Yunho and Mason."

Mason cut the motor and allowed their pontoon to drift the final yards to the belfry. He dropped anchor and looked back toward his passengers. "You two ready?"

"I think so." Yunho scratched his stomach, yawned, then stood and opened the hatch with snorkeling gear. He shared a tender look with Mason.

"This is so sweet to invite me out here." Astrid shimmied out of her dress and took a wet suit from Yunho. "To see where you two first met."

They jumped into the water. Its rippling surface refracted sunlight onto their wet suits; they glimmered like mermaids with cleaved tails. From behind a curtain of seaweed, it appeared: the Provincetown Library. The building, once white, was now covered in undulating sea moss, as if it had sprouted green hair. The structure was remarkably well preserved, with the pitched roof intact, though the windows had been shattered by various bits of ocean trash over the years. Ribbons of eelgrass sprung from the land where the lawn used to be; a family of horseshoe crabs crawled through the brown blades, guided by whatever superior instincts led their species to survive 480 million years. Mason watched their jagged shells traverse the terrain where he and Yunho had their first conversation on August 13, 2030, a date he'd never forget.

They both hated parades. But they'd been forced to attend Provincetown's Carnival Parade, a situation over which they commiserated while seeking refuge on the library lawn, far from the plague of drunken gay men on the front lines of the procession, screaming for float-flung beads and lube as if they were catching a supply drop from a war zone helicopter. Yunho was fresh from a flight; he was showrunning the second season of *The Dispossessed*, his hit television adaptation of Ursula K. Le Guin's novel. The production schedule had shifted two days, delaying his arrival to the vacation Daniel and Mahmood had planned.

"Stepping off a flight and into a parade is a hell I don't wish upon my worst gay enemy."

"He's probably already here."

"Why do so many people enjoy parades?" Yunho sighed. "I lack the gene that makes me wanna spiral into a k-hole amidst thousands of screaming strangers."

"I also lack that gene. I guess that makes us twins."

"How unfortunate." Mischief danced across Yunho's face. "That means we can't fuck."

Mason laughed, blushing. Sexual tension is essential to any gay vacation, and Mason quietly thanked Daniel and Mahmood for curating the invitees to their Provincetown rental according to this rule. "I loved *The Dispossessed* by the way," Mason said. "The guy who plays Shevek—*so* hot. Broker peace with those space anarchists, daddy."

"Gay men are so base." Yunho laughed and quickly the conversation gained the giddy momentum of two people who shared the same sense of humor and cultural shorthand; they started with their love for Le Guin, then moved to Samuel Delany—both adored *The Motion of Light in Water*, and discussing New York in the sixties led them to Warhol, who brought them to the eighties and Mason's beloved Wojnarowicz, and no one could discuss Wojnarowicz without mentioning Peter Hujar, or Sarah Schulman's works grappling with AIDS, and oh, what about her cameo in *The Watermelon Woman*, Cheryl Dunye's New Queer Cinema classic, and, well, what exploration of that filmmaking era would be complete without Gregg Araki and his Teen Apocalypse trilogy, which "pushed the boundaries of queer cinema and—" Suddenly, a white man in a pink thong puked in front of them.

"Someone disagrees with your take." Yunho smiled grimly.

"Is this our sign to run screaming? We could grab lunch somewhere."

"Oh, are you asking me on a date?"

"*No.*" Mason's blushing cheeks undermined his assertion. "Maybe," he added shyly.

"I don't do rice queens."

Mason laughed. "I promise that's not what this is."

"A lot of white boys have promised me a lot of things. And it's never worked out well."

"Well, those white boys can go fuck themselves."

Yunho grinned. "Let's be friends. That's better. Besides, I prefer having friends who are in love with me."

Mason let out a shocked laugh. "I never said I was in love with you."

"You will be." And Yunho was right. Mason fell in love with Yunho over the course of one sexually tense yet maddeningly platonic year, twelve months of dinners and drag shows and parties where they mixed friend groups, and their social circle morphed with the speed possible only in that heady era of your twenties where selfhoods shift with electrifying momentum. Soon, both Yunho and Mason experienced career breakthroughs; Yunho secured financing for his sophomore film, and Mason had his first gallery show. It felt like they were riding the same wave of success; their perspectives became deeply embedded in each other's work. An aesthetic understanding pulsed between them, as urgent as life itself.

During that year of yearning and friendship, Mason and Yunho shared their histories with each other. Yunho was born in Seoul, to a father who was co-CEO of Samsung's electronics division, and a mother who presided over their palatial Gangnam home and raised her boy in the church. Early in Yunho's childhood, his father secured a hard-won transfer to Samsung's Silicon Valley headquarters and the family moved to San Jose. There, Yunho's private school education was marred by racist and homophobic taunts, but he was too scared to tell his parents he was failing to adapt to the American life his father had worked so hard to attain.

The one place that offered respite: the Korean Baptist Church. Communing with other Koreans brought comforting memories of Seoul. But when Yunho felt an erotic pull toward the man who led the youth group, church became the source of a new shame: The Bible said he was going to hell. He felt unbearably lonely. His shame calcified into anger, and workouts transformed his body into a fortress of muscle, a first defense against the hatred of the world.

For college, Yunho attended the Korean Academy of Film Arts; this disappointed his father, who valorized American success. But Yunho felt there was something unresolved within him that could be fixed only by a return to Seoul. He found healing through the creation of *March First Movement*, his thesis film, which imagined a love affair between two secretly queer activists in the Korean Independence Movement. The lovers befriend a white American missionary who joins the resistance effort leading up the March First Movement of 1919, though the missionary betrays the men upon discovering they're gay; ironically, both men are expelled from a Korean nationalist movement by a white American missionary. The film gave Yunho a vessel to explore his own struggles against racism, homophobia, and the colonialism that created the conservative Protestant culture of Korea to which his parents subscribed. The accolades, the Oscars, the $20 million deal with Disney, all of it was diminished by the fact his parents pretended the film didn't exist. He knew why—it was his method of coming out to them.

Yunho moved to Los Angeles in the wake of his film's success. But even though his parents were a forty-minute plane ride away in San Jose, they never visited. Never called. Their absence felt like a death. Yunho began to drink. Heavily. Blackouts eradicated the pain. So did K, G, LSD, and whatever else could destroy the body he spent so much time building up, because his body was the site of his shame. Sex was another method of destruction. Every time he got wasted, Yunho ventured into the racist-infested waters of Grindr. Why? Maybe it was the intoxicating tyranny of the white muscle gay aesthetic, maybe his father's obsession with American success had infected his erotic subconscious, maybe he felt a self-destructive assimilationist urge. Regardless, he powered through a string of bad white boyfriends; they took him on trips to Mykonos, Puerto Vallarta, Fire Island—gay vacations filled with sun, sand, and racist microaggressions.

Then, Yunho got sober. From substances and white boys. He went to therapy. He found supportive friends, who included Daniel and Mahmood. Things felt good; even if he didn't have his parents, he had a life in Los Angeles that had taken shape after an anxious, wasted beginning.

Which is when he met Mason. In those early days of sobriety. Despite Yunho's rule about white boys, the two men were drawn to each other with an almost supernatural force. Nothing felt more vital than those heady and hungry conversations that lasted until three A.M., where each learned the contours of the other's existence. "Love" was the only name Mason could think of for this divine work. It lasted a year before they consummated their bond. Then, the work deepened; their romance became a beautiful collaboration that was not without conflict but made them better humans than they ever thought possible.

Now, fourteen years later, Mason swam through the drowned landscape of their earliest memory; he watched Astrid float above that fateful street corner and felt as if she was joining the project of his romance with Yunho. He wanted to tell Astrid he loved her, though his snorkel prevented him, so he simply watched as she followed Yunho toward the sunken library. Mason imagined a day when the water would recede, and the building would gleam in the sun, and all that drowned knowledge would come to light. As books dried in the breeze, they'd laugh, cradling their newborn, amazed they ever believed the world was ending.

*

"I don't have a *purpose* anymore." Claudia's voice echoed through the house and into the mudroom, where Mason slid out of his flip-flops. Yunho and Astrid were still unloading the car. "When we moved to L.A., the Anarchist Cutie Club fizzled out, and I thought a new city would inspire me. But the more time I spend there, the more I'm like, *what am I doing with my life?*"

"I completely understand," Daniel said. "When I quit the Norma Collective, I had this year of total burnout—"

"We're back!" Mason tentatively waltzed into the room.

Claudia turned from Daniel and Mahmood. "How was snorkeling?"

"Beautiful." An understatement, but how else to explain the divinity of their day?

"Well, *we* did absolutely nothing," Mahmood proclaimed. "And it was glorious."

Mason looked at Claudia; the residue of frustration lingered on her face. He couldn't bear the thought that Astrid's surrogacy was a source of stress, that this miracle unmoored Claudia. He wanted her to share the joy he felt. But before he could say anything, his phone vibrated. His mother. "Sorry, guys—have to take this." She'd spent the holiday in the Long Beach nursing home where her own ailing mother resided. He didn't want to engage in an endless phone call (the only kind his mother knew how to have), yet he felt guilty for not talking with her yet. "Hi, Mom." All he heard were sobs on the other end. "*Mom?*"

"He's . . . dead."

"Who's dead?"

"Your father."

*

It was as if a rug he never knew he'd been standing on had been yanked out from under him; shock intensified the terror as he plummeted. The lie that his father meant nothing to him had become easier to believe as the years stretched on. The last time he'd seen his father was from his vantage point in a McDonald's ball pit, on his eighth birthday. Mason had squeezed a red ball, slick with some other kid's fry grease, and cried as his mother pushed his father out of the party, screaming about his endless infidelities. At first, Mason believed his mother had forced his father out of their lives, but eventually, he came to understand that dad had been happy to jump from their home like it was nothing more than a McDonald's bounce house.

The years passed. Mason told himself it was impossible to miss someone you could barely remember, and he believed this until he got the call about his father's death. Everyone comforted him in its wake, but he didn't cry, he just felt numbness and some mounting chaos swirling around him, as if he were in the eye of a hurricane, waiting to be ripped from Earth.

Later that evening, he and Yunho helped Daniel and Mahmood tuck in Gabriel and Auden. On this vacation, the children had developed a cute habit of demanding that "*all* our daddies tuck us in," implying Mason and Yunho had been magically granted paternity. The men laughed when the children said this, but also felt moved by the idea that a father could be anyone with enough love in his heart. So all their daddies tucked them in, and Mason's tears finally flowed, and he vowed he'd be a better father than the man who abandoned him; he wouldn't deny his or *any* child the love they deserved.

He watched Daniel and Mahmood kiss their children good night; seeing them perform the role of "father" triggered a strange longing within Mason, and a surprising eroticism. Mahmood turned off the lights and closed the door. The grown-ups walked down the hall and the conversation drifted to how Mason was coping with his father's death. Mason said he was *hanging in there* but neglected to mention his growing erection. He couldn't explain it, or maybe he could, maybe his father's passing elicited some Freudian yearning, maybe Mason wanted to be cared for by Daniel and Mahmood in the way he was never cared for by his own father, but he didn't want to *fuck* his father, which made the erection confusing. Still, this eroticism lured him into Mahmood and Daniel's bedroom where he continued talking about his father, and soon he was weeping. Mahmood rushed to his side. Mason sobbed in his arms. Settled. Some long-buried instinct surfaced, an erotic remainder from their college romance, and Mason pressed his forehead against Mahmood's. They kissed. It felt like a dream— impossible and urgent. They broke apart and looked to Daniel and Yunho, who stood opposite, shocked and swept up in sexual momentum. Daniel grabbed Yunho and kissed him, slamming the door shut. Clothes fell to the floor. They swapped partners. Mahmood got onto the bed, down on all fours. Yunho slipped inside him. Mahmood released a sharp groan, then eased back onto Yunho's cock. Yunho slapped Mahmood's ass cheeks. Fucked him harder. Daniel threw Mason onto his back and stretched Mason's hole—one finger, then two, and Mason gasped and suddenly Daniel's cock was inside him. Mahmood—with Yunho still fucking him— inched toward Mason on the bed, until Mason and Mahmood's mouths aligned for an upside-down kiss. Mahmood tongued Mason's open mouth. Mahmood was dripping wet; he palmed some of his own honey, then thrust sticky fingers between Mason's lips, pushing deep inside his throat. Mason wanted every hole plugged; his voice vibrated against Mahmood's fingers as he moaned for Daniel to fuck him harder. Yunho and Daniel reached out and grasped hands, forming a bridge over their bottoms. Yunho whispered something in Korean and Daniel responded. They kissed, and Mason suddenly felt guilty he'd never learned Yunho's mother tongue, insecure that Daniel could give Yunho something Mason could not. But wasn't this the reason they opened their relationship? Because it was absurd to think one man could give you everything you need? Mason let go of his anxiety; there was enough love to go around, this foursome would strengthen his connection with the men who'd share this journey of fatherhood. Weren't they lucky to have four fathers instead of two, or one, or none? Daniel slapped Mason. *Where'd you go, boy?* he demanded. *I'm right here, daddy,* Mason moaned. Daniel thrusted harder. Mason's legs went numb; a head rush flooded his vision with purple amoebas. He departed his body; his stomach plummeted as if he was ascending to heaven or falling to hell, wherever his father happened to reside. But before they could reunite,

Mason orgasmed and came back to his body, enmeshed with three other postcoital fathers, sweaty, ecstatic, exhausted, and confident the love they shared had deepened forever.

*

It was impossible to sleep late with Gabriel and Auden in the house. They bounded down the creaky corridors at seven A.M., screaming and laughing. Gradually the grown-ups roused and joined the children in the kitchen. Daniel scrambled some eggs with leftover Gruyère from last night's cheese plate, and Claudia whipped up her grandmother's drop biscuits (the secret was full-fat mayonnaise). Yunho crisped the bacon, and the kitchen filled with the smell of butter and baking. The meal was a family effort, though this time it wasn't connected to centuries of oppression like their Thanksgiving feast; this morning the food felt like freedom, cooked by a new kind of family, one invested in creating something beautiful, something that nourished everyone.

They took their plates to the porch. Astrid and Claudia cozied on the wicker love seat, with Gabriel and Auden between them. Daniel sat on the porch railing and flung his arm around Yunho; Mahmood reclined in the rocking chair with Mason at his feet. They settled into contended silence as they ate; it felt like they were the only people on Earth.

"Is it already one forty-five?" Claudia frowned at the brass porthole clock hanging above her.

"Oh no, sorry." Mason laughed. "That clock is always stuck—it's a busted antique."

"Well, at least it's gorgeous." Claudia licked the last bit of egg from her fork.

They settled into a deeper silence. The broken clock failed to tick. All they heard were frustrated waves unable to satiate their hunger for stolen land because the tides needed time to do their work and here on the porch it was one forty-five forever, and love was eternal, and night would never fall.

EIGHTEEN

47 minutes

U nlocked handcuffs. Wet pavement. Claudia writhed in pain, but her dislocated arm remained dead still, like an anchor preventing her body from levitating into the afterlife. Astrid kneeled on the asphalt and pulled at Claudia's arm; her humerus bulged from her shoulder. Then, a pop—bone snapping back into place. Claudia screamed.

"Are you okay, baby?" Astrid scanned the horizon for further danger.

"Let's just . . ." Claudia's gas mask amplified her labored breathing. ". . . keep pushing." They were a half mile away. So close. Mason summoned the strength to limp without assistance as Astrid pushed her lover's wheelchair forward. Claudia cradled her injured shoulder. Miraculously, the bouquet sat in her lap, the lilies bedraggled but still beautiful. They'd survived.

Ahead, at the Hillhurst intersection: hope.

The pink tint dissipated from the haze. Moving headlights pierced through gray smoke. Traffic. Glorious, awful, everyday Los Angeles traffic. A barricade diverted cars from the pileup on Los Feliz Boulevard. They turned either left or right at the intersection; each headlight flash brought Mason a rush of relief. He'd expected a shell of a city, a zombified landscape. But no. The dull march of Los Angeles gridlock persisted. Maybe the accident was a fluke. A pocket of contained madness. "We're *almost* there."

"Yes." Claudia gritted her teeth. The flowers bounced in her lap.

But Astrid remained silent as they arrived at the intersection, her focus fixed. Mason followed her gaze across the street to a homeless shelter, set up in the husk of an abandoned strip mall. It was an increasingly common occurrence in Los Angeles. Constant fires forced businesses to flee the city, along with those wealthy enough to settle elsewhere. People who couldn't afford to leave often couldn't afford to stay either; whatever jobs hadn't vanished along with brick-and-mortar businesses had been automated (DoorDash's delivery bots, McDonald's cashier-and-cook-free "smart restaurants"). The unhoused population skyrocketed. Activists led a campaign that diverted funds from the L.A. police budget to convert the city's many vacated strip malls into housing for the poor. But these facilities became immediately overrun, and tent cities spilled into their parking lots.

Mason squinted at the encampment across the street. It had been destroyed. Shredded tents. Toppled shopping carts. A mass of bodies lay slaughtered in the lot, piled atop one another, entrails tangled. All the windows in the strip mall had been shattered.

"Fuck." Astrid staggered backward. "What's that?"

A hobbling silhouette emerged from some long-abandoned seafood shack, backlit by a neon boat that had shipwrecked upon the sidewalk. The signage flickered, sending shocks of blue backlight pulsing across the man's lurching body; Mason discerned the outline of a gas mask. The figure fell to his knees. "*Help me!*" he bellowed across the intersection.

"He needs us." Astrid rubbed her chest as if the pain of this stumbling stranger had somehow manifested in her own heart.

"*Astrid.*" Mason wanted to shake her. "Sometimes your empathy verges on suicidal."

"We can't just *leave* him." Claudia slapped the crosswalk button. "He's in trouble."

"*So are we,*" Mason replied. "And finally, when we're less than a mile from safety—"

"You don't *know* your house will be safe—"

"*Yes, I do,*" Mason snapped. "My house *will* be safe. It's where this fucking nightmare will finally *end,* and we'll get on with our lives and pretend *none of this shit ever happened.*"

Claudia slapped the button again. "Okay, while *you* live in denial, we'll live in *reality* and help someone in need—"

"*Oh my god!*" Mason screamed. "*You could die out here!* And you'll risk the life of *my* child, which shouldn't come as a surprise since . . ." Mason trailed off, regretting his slip.

"Wow, Mason," Claudia said, stunned. "You're really gonna go there?"

A pang of remorse constricted Mason's heart. "I'm sorry, I—"

"I thought we moved past this," Astrid interrupted, coldly. The walk signal blinked white. She pushed Claudia into the crosswalk, leaving Mason behind. "But I guess not."

They didn't look back.

NINETEEN

8 months, 5 days, 3 hours, 38 minutes

Sita needed the money. For her two children, ages three and five. She'd left them in Namjung, a Nepali village two thousand kilometers from her small bed in the dormitory in Anand, Gujarat, where she now failed to fall asleep. She tried to conjure their faces as she tossed in overly starched sheets; Lakshmi with her plump cheeks and long eyelashes, Jalesh with his small fists that balled tightly when he was excited. But thoughts of her children failed to pacify her; they only increased her worry. The more she tried to envision them, the fuzzier her recollection became, until she feared she was forgetting what her children looked like, and that they in turn would forget their mother altogether, that she'd return to Nepal in nine months to discover blank stares in her children's eyes. Her husband barely had time to care for them; his brutal days were occupied with the impossibilities of farming the dead soil of Namjung. The fields had turned to dust; rain rarely fell and when it did, it came in violent sheets that obliterated whatever fragile crops had busted through the desiccated ground. Displacement was on the horizon. But could her family survive the dangerous and illegal journey into Russia, where her cousin (who'd already fled there) promised lush soil and a booming farming industry? The question triggered her anxiety, so Sita turned her thoughts to the baby in her womb and the seven thousand U.S. dollars she'd been promised for its delivery, or rather, the five thousand she'd get after paying the recruiter his cut. It wasn't a lot of money, but it was enough to fund a move to Russia. That money could save her family.

Sita felt uniquely qualified for surrogacy; she'd always been an excellent mother. Well, not that she was a *mother* in this case. The doctors told her to think of herself as a *vessel*; the *mother* was an infertile woman in Norway, a woman she'd never meet per this woman's requests. It was better this way, painful but made less so by the anonymity of the transaction and swiftness of the child's removal. *It's almost like it was never inside you*, her doctor said during orientation. *Then you get an empowering opportunity to change your life.*

So why couldn't she breathe? Why did her chest tighten as she tried to drift to sleep? Maybe it had something to do with the dormitory. The beds were lined up in a long, rectangular room she shared with seven other surrogates. The walls were bleach white and bare; a mere three feet separated one bed from the next and the woman to her right snored. It was identical to the other rooms in their dormitory; just one building in the corporate park that constituted the Indian flagship of the Future Generations global surrogacy network. The complex boasted medical facilities, luxury suites for visiting clients, and separate dormitories for the janitors, cleaners, and cooks. Manual laborers were required to live on campus. Doctors and senior executives were not; they lived in spacious homes miles from the Gujarat compound.

To avoid clutter, surrogates were allowed very few personal items; matching maternity uniforms were supplied by Future Generations. Each meal shift was fifteen minutes. No visitors were allowed. The place ran with the efficiency of a military base. Babies were all delivered via C-sections conducted by artificially intelligent machines. Cesarians were scheduled for the earliest possible date to reduce the time surrogates were under Future Generations' care, thereby optimizing the company's expense-to-profit ratio.

That night, Sita snuck out of the dormitory. She needed air. As she sat on the pavement, she felt a hand on her back.

Can't sleep? It was Vimal. Big as a house, her belly was busting out of her starched white uniform. Sita threw her arms around her friend. They'd first met on a night when neither could sleep; Vimal had also made the long trek from Nepal and the women bonded over a longing for their homeland. Now their rendezvous were tradition; they'd escape their claustrophobic dorms and meet in the late evening quiet, when streetlights cast an orange glow over the towering white buildings.

Don't leave me, Sita said, eyes wet with tears. *I will miss you.*

I will miss you too. Vimal rubbed Sita's back. *But you'll be out of here soon.*

Are you nervous for tomorrow?

No! Vimal let out a sharp chuckle. *I am excited to no longer be the size of a cow.* The women laughed; the sounds of their joy echoed defiantly across the compound.

Vimal was gone in the morning.

But soon, rumors began circulating in the dormitories. There were whispers that she had died during childbirth. A malfunction had occurred with the AI birthing technology; the cesarean machine failed to stitch Vimal's incision properly. She bled to death on the table.

The child survived.

Fury fomented among the surrogates; they feared for their own lives. Management addressed Vimal's death, insisting they bore no responsibility. Pregnancy was always a risk, they reminded their surrogates. Birth was a life-and-death business.

But the surrogates had lost trust in Future Generations. Sita was the most enraged; her friend's life was so cruelly wasted, and she was terrified her own might end before she saw her children again. Soon, her sleepless nights were spent meeting in secret with a surrogate who'd been a farm unionizer. They made plans for a surrogates' union, folding in their fellow workers. Sita organized a walkout; she secured buckets of red paint from a disgruntled repairman and splashed each woman's white uniform with a murderous spatter of crimson. The women lay themselves on the road outside their dormitory. The demonstration attracted international press.

Sita secured a meeting with the head doctor of Future Generations Gujarat.

After tense pleasantries, Sita broached the issue. *I'd like to discuss our demands—*

That's not why we're here today, the doctor interrupted. *I'm here to discuss your pregnancy. And to remind you of your contract: Payment is conditional upon successful birth. If, God forbid, you were to expire during childbirth, that would be a breach of contract. And if you don't survive the birth, there's no one to remit payment to.*

But . . . my family.

Future Generations didn't sign a contract with your family. So if you wish to be paid, I suggest you do everything within your power to ensure a successful birth. For example, I recommend you cease any strenuous activities. Like that demonstration the other day.

Is that a threat?

Of course not. I'm simply advising you about a potential risk to your pregnancy. Though we care deeply for our surrogates, our primary concern is for their babies. Let me remind you, Vimal's child survived.

What are you saying—

You're expendable, Sita. All surrogates are expendable.

". . . and that's where the recording ends," Astrid said, pressing Pause on the subtitled video that had been secretly recorded by Sita. Claudia held her partner's hand. Above them, a hummingbird labored over the bougainvillea in Mason and Yunho's meticulously landscaped backyard. A sprinkler's wet shudders echoed in the distance.

"That's . . . that's awful," Yunho stuttered, shocked by the story he'd just been told, and the accompanying video. "What should we do?"

"Well, we've been in touch with Sita and other organizers about . . ." Astrid hesitated. ". . . how to apply pressure to Future Generations on a global scale."

"So some sort of protest?" Yunho asked.

"Yes," Astrid replied. "We want a standard, universal wage for surrogacy. Livable conditions in Future Generations dormitories. Life insurance.

An end to exploitative contracts. And the right to pre-negotiate with clients about having a relationship with the child after birth."

"We've been very fair to you on all those fronts—" Mason insisted.

"This isn't about you or Yunho." Claudia smiled. "This is about the bigger picture."

"I get it. Future Generations is an evil global corporation. But I think we as *individuals* have gone above and beyond to provide you with a *more* than adequate living situation—"

"*Mason, stop,*" Yunho snapped. "They're not attacking *us*. If we're engaged with a company that's committing, you know, *human rights violations*, I think we as clients should stand with the workers and support their fight for humane conditions."

An agitated hush fell over the backyard. The sprinkler ticked incessantly, marking time with each wasteful spurt. Mason's thoughts drifted to that perfect Provincetown breakfast, when their bellies were full, their hearts content, and it felt like they'd achieved the impossible: a happy family. Guilt softened his voice. "I'm sorry. Tell us what we need to do."

"Well, as an alliance of workers with a unique power over the means of production, we've determined that the greatest leverage we possess is our control over the product itself."

"You mean . . . the child?" Mason asked, astonished.

Astrid hesitated, her eyes glistening. "Yes."

"You mean *our* child?" Yunho shook his head in disbelief.

"What do you plan to do to *our child*?" Mason demanded.

Tears flowed down Astrid's face. "We're not doing anything yet—"

"*Why are you crying, Astrid?*" Mason interrupted, his voice raising.

"*Mason, stop!*" Yunho shouted. "Let's *listen* to what she has to say."

Astrid slapped moisture from her cheeks. "Our global workers' collective has decided to join together and . . ." Astrid paused. ". . . threaten abortion."

Mason jumped to his feet. "*No!*" he screamed. "*No fucking way are you aborting our child.*" Mason stormed off, hiking up the incline to the house.

"*And abortion's a crime, by the way. So good fucking luck.*" He burst into their kitchen, fury pumping in his veins.

Suddenly, Yunho was there too. "Mason—calm down—"

"Please, don't tell me you plan to abort our child because of . . . of . . . *class guilt.*"

"I *don't* want to abort our child. I just . . . this clearly . . . means a lot to her and—"

A horrific realization crossed Mason's mind. "Are you having second thoughts?"

Yunho swallowed, pausing for a second too long. "I—"

"Oh my god, you *are*. You're having second thoughts—"

"Don't be ridiculous."

"And this is the way out. I can't *believe* this. After how *hard* you pushed for a kid—"

"*Mason, just shut up!*" Silence fell. The men caught their breath in opposite corners of the kitchen, like two punch-drunk boxers. Astrid and Claudia appeared in the doorway.

"I . . . I'm sorry." Astrid sniffled. "I hate that it's come to this."

"It's . . . it's okay." Yunho hesitated. "I think Mason and I just need a little time to wrap our heads around this."

"And, of course, I don't *want* to abort this child either," she insisted. "I'm praying we won't need to go to that extreme. We're hopeful that Future Generations will come around."

"But if they don't . . ."

Astrid's tearful gaze hardened. "I'm prepared to do whatever is necessary."

TWENTY

33 minutes

Mason limped north on Hillhurst. Two lanes of gridlock, separated by a dead grass divider. He looked up at the sky, through the skeleton of a gnarled oak. The smoke was gray, not pink. And it was lifting. The haze was just a shade lighter, but it *was* lighter, the smoke *had* to be dissipating, this city *needed* to breathe again. He marched onward, refusing to let the pain stop him, refusing to let his busted knee be the thing that stood between him and what came next.

The part where they picked up the pieces.

The party where they picked up the pieces.

Yunho was waiting. One kiss and the awful day would be erased. Yes, this smoke was clearing. Or was it? Just ahead—a darker patch. A grounded cloud. Suspended above the divider. And was it just a little pink? Mason ran to inspect the smoke—ignoring the agony slicing through his leg. He staggered through traffic, until he was standing on the divider, amid the cloud. But once inside, he lost perspective. It seemed thicker. Then thinner. Then gray. Black. Pink. Sweat pooled inside his gas mask. His lungs seized. He released a scream, a prayer that burned his throat. He needed a sign. Some hope.

And then he saw it: the sun. He stood. Crossed the street. Right on Inverness.

Blue-white sky. Cotton clouds. No smoke.

Mason ripped off his gas mask. His skin burned where the straps had been. Dried sweat caked the perimeter of his face. He threw the gas mask to the ground. *Fuck that piece of shit.* It landed on someone's irresponsibly green lawn. Mason leaned against a lime tree, sucked in the sweet fragrance of its white blossoms, inhaled the tang of the rotted fruit at its base. A sprinkler shuddered to life. The spray beckoned him. Mason laid on the grass, desperate for baptism. Let the water wash it all away—the grime and vomit and ash and blood. He closed his eyes. Let the mist purify him. He would be clean of his past. Clean of memory. Ready to start life anew.

BOOM! A sonic blast jolted him awake, rattling his rib cage. It sounded like war.

BOOM! Mason scanned the sky for an answer. Clouds began to darken.

BOOM! Rain. Just a drizzle at first, no heavier than the mist of the sprinklers.

And then, a downpour. Sheets of precipitation fell from the sky. A warm waterfall. Soaking Mason. Cleansing Mason. Suddenly, he realized: All this rain was just for him. He'd purchased it with his own Amex.

For his baby shower.

BOOM! Mason shot up from the lawn. Ran uphill, through the pain in his knee, against the flow of rainfall rushing down the sidewalk. Ran past a gated driveway, its collection of Bentleys safe behind bars. Ran until he saw the white truck with the WeatherMod logo: a giant globe where the continents were stamped with the company's name.

He stopped running. This must've been the second downpour, the one they scheduled for the middle of the party. Orange roadblocks obstructed the right lane of traffic. Behind them—the WeatherMod "cloud-seeder." The fifteen-foot steel tube pointed skyward, propped up by metal scaffolding, like a military-grade rocket launcher. Two technicians flanked the machine; the women wore clear rain ponchos, Kevlar vests underneath, gas masks, and noise protection earmuffs. One of them had a bright-pink mane.

BOOM! The cloud-seeder launched a white projectile—a salt-and-mineral hygroscopic bomb, geoengineered to accelerate the production of water molecules in clouds. It sped through the atmosphere, until it vanished into the dark folds of a looming nimbostratus. *BOOM!* A second explosion emanated from inside the cloud; this one was distant, like the echo of thunder. Detonation. Silence. Then, another cloudburst. The pink-haired woman screamed, "*Yes, bitch!*" Her shouts broke through the noise of the downpour. "*Make it rain!*"

Sudden pain surged back into Mason's knee, but he didn't give a shit. Not now.

It was time to party.

*

"I'm sorry, sir. I don't have your name on the list." The bouncer frowned at his clipboard, treating Mason like some homeless grifter who was trying to infiltrate a world beyond his reach.

"That's because this is *my* party. I'm not *on* the list, I *made* the list."

The bouncer narrowed his eyes, sizing up Mason's haggard appearance. The gash on his cheek, the tattered clothing, the aroma of piss—none of it was helping Mason prove he was the owner of the estate behind the ten-foot hedge wall. "I have a hard time believing that."

"*Are you kidding me?*" Mason shouted. "*I am literally the person paying your salary!*"

"Sir, I'll be forced to call security—"

"*Please call security, so they can tell you this is my fucking party—*"

The bouncer spoke into his walkie. "I need backup at the entrance—"

Mason grabbed the walkie from the bouncer's hand and threw it onto the sidewalk. "*Fuck you! This is my baby shower—*" Two hulking security-ogres burst out of the gates and seized Mason. "*Let me go!*" Through the open doors, he saw a glimpse of someone who could save him. "*MOM!*" He sucked unpolluted air into his lungs and had to admit—even as the guards dragged him screaming past his neighbors' mansions—it felt incredible to breathe easy once again. "*MOM, HELP!*"

TWENTY-ONE

7 months, 14 days, 8 hours, 22 minutes

A strid sat at a table outside Intelligentsia Coffee. Sun baked the red terra-cotta building. She tore at a croissant but didn't eat it; she just piled shredded bits on the tabletop. Once she'd destroyed the pastry, she returned to the mound and tore the scraps into even smaller pieces. The table rocked as she worked, its legs unable to find their footing on the uneven sidewalk.

A wealthy white couple ambled past her, pushing a colossal tank of a stroller. The child within was so dwarfed by the militaristic apparatus that it was difficult to discern its swaddled face. Suddenly, Astrid's elbow slipped, and the table jolted, launching croissant fragments into the stroller. The couple jumped in surprise, then laughed and brushed the greasy bits from their child's blanket. Miraculously, the child did not cry. A good-natured exchange occurred between the two parties, filled with gracious gesticulating and laughter. Eventually, Astrid's distracted face indicated that the discussion had reached a natural end point.

But the couple didn't leave. They gestured to a pair of unoccupied chairs at a neighboring table, as if to suggest they might pull up a seat. Astrid shook her head in polite protest, but the couple ignored her. They dragged chairs over to Astrid, who winced at the sound of metal legs dragging against concrete. The couple pulled their stroller closer.

Their baby wasn't real—it was a doll.

Astrid's body stiffened. She listened intently as the couple spoke for about five minutes. Then they stopped. Astrid responded, her head hung low. The man dug into the baby doll's blankets and pulled out a small, portable safe. Astrid placed her phone and purse inside. The man locked the safe and placed it back in the stroller.

A white, windowless van pulled up. Its license plates had been removed. Astrid and the couple ran to the vehicle. The back doors flung open. The couple threw the stroller inside. Astrid leapt into the vehicle and the couple followed, slamming the doors behind them. It sped off.

Mason and Yunho and Claudia watched from their vantage point across the street. They sat in Mason's Tesla, silent. They'd been warned not to follow the vehicle. It took all Mason's strength not to tear after the van like some movie vigilante saving his pregnant wife from villainous abductors. But, of course, this was part of the abortion plan they'd discussed with anonymous Norma Collective avatars in their hyper-encrypted virtual meeting room. Astrid would be driven blindfolded to an undisclosed location, where she'd receive an illegal abortion from a team of masked doctors and nurses. Because she was in her second trimester, the collective needed to keep her for two days. She wouldn't be permitted to contact anyone from the outside. The first day, cervical softening and dilating would be performed with small dilating sticks called laminaria, which would stay in her cervix overnight to prepare her body for surgery.

She'd then sleep at the facility; the Norma Collective realized it was stressful to be unable to see loved ones, but the doctors and nurses couldn't risk being discovered by the authorities, which could lead to felony charges of murder and conspiracy to commit abortion. The next day, she'd go into surgery. Anesthesia would be delivered intravenously; doctors then used a small suction tube to empty the uterus. The fetus would be cremated, as Astrid had elected for this option during her initial consult. Astrid would stay in a recovery room for two hours, where nurses would monitor her. Then, she'd be placed back in the white van, blindfolded, and dropped at a random location. Loved ones received a call notifying them of this location an hour before the drop.

Daniel would perform the procedure. Despite his insistence that his employment with the Norma Collective had ceased years prior (something all Norma doctors told loved ones about their work—if they told them at all—to avoid implicating family and friends in a federal crime), everyone instinctively understood it would be Daniel at the operating table. The giveaway: the tension that radiated from Daniel toward Yunho, Mason, Astrid, Claudia, and Mahmood during an excruciating pre-abortion luncheon at the Kim-Daunt estate, one final meal to say goodbye to the fetus in Astrid's womb or, rather, to *not* say goodbye, to *not* say anything incriminating, to pretend this was just another blissful California afternoon and not the day before Mason's best friend would destroy Mason's dreams of fatherhood. It had to appear as though Astrid made this decision on her own. Even a brief mention of the plan could be used as evidence in an abortion trial, should they receive FBI-issued subpoenas for iOS Cerebrum audio records (the AI software recorded its user's conversations, a fact that led Mason and Yunho to hire a security firm to erase incriminating audio files and metadata). Mason's anger roiled as everyone made small talk about the potato salad Daniel had brought, he'd used *horseradish* and *didn't the horseradish add a nice kick* and Mason thought he might murder Daniel if he said *horseradish* one more fucking time.

Astrid got in the white van. For two days they waited. Then, they got the call. They picked Astrid up on the seventh level of the parking garage at The Grove shopping center. Her face was crusted with dried tears. She held an urn. A *turquoise* urn. A hideous urn that triggered Mason's rage. *How ugly*, he thought. *I invested three hundred thousand dollars in my dream of having a family and all I got was this lousy urn.* Yunho jumped out of the Tesla and helped Claudia into her wheelchair. They rushed to Astrid and enveloped her in a warm embrace. Mason remained in the car, trying to regulate his breath. Getting oxygen to his brain—that was a task that could distract him. Because what he really wanted was to leap from the car and pummel their three faces into the pavement. This rage, this wasn't like Mason, he wasn't a violent person, and yet he couldn't deny the violence that swelled within him. He'd tapped into some dark corner of his soul he'd kept hidden from himself, and so this violent fury was accompanied by a wave of dysphoria that led him to question if he even really knew himself, and this only increased his anger, his feeling that had this abortion never taken place, he would've been able to keep believing that he was not the type of person who would exit his Tesla and shove his lover off the woman who'd carried their child, a child that had been reduced to ashes in an urn that Mason wrenched from her grasp as he screamed, "*What the fuck is this?*"

"*Mason—stop.*" Yunho pushed himself between Mason and Astrid.

"A *turquoise* urn? It's not even *ceramic*, it's *plastic!*"

"*It's . . . all they had!*" Astrid shouted back, eyes wide as if she was in an incomprehensible dream, forced to surrender to its bizarre logic. Mason raised the urn in the air, but couldn't bring himself to slam it to the pavement, couldn't bear to see his child's remains scattered outside an elevator to the Cheesecake Factory, and suddenly, reality rushed in, and shame robbed him of his strength, and he lowered the urn and gripped it against his chest and crouched on the ground and muttered *I'm sorry* over and over again, unsure of who the phrase was directed toward, only sure that sorrow was called for. Astrid kneeled on the ground next to him and said, "If it makes you feel better, I thought it was ugly too." She relieved the tension with a smile Mason didn't deserve, a smile that must have cost her dearly. "But we can get a new one, if you like."

The gentle whir of the Tesla's motor underscored the awful silence of the ride home. Mason sat in the front seat. He cradled the urn like the baby it would've been, had the world not been such a terrible place.

TWENTY-TWO

18 minutes

Y ou know, I played a nurse on *Grey's Anatomy* once." Samantha
wrapped Mason's knee in a thick bandage. "It's how I paid for your
preschool." She constricted his leg with greater force. He frowned. *Does she
honestly expect me to thank her for preschool right now?* "I was trying to
graduate from those one-episode arcs and take on meatier recurring
roles, but I also wanted the best for you. So I did that quick stint on *Grey's*
and also played a cop who got exploded after four lines on *911* and
voilà—preschool!"

"Thank you?"

"Oh, honey, you don't have to thank me for *preschool*," she insisted
unconvincingly. "Anyway, I had to bandage this person's knee over and over
again on the set of *Grey's*. Never really forgot it." She finished and assessed
her work. "That feel a little better?"

"Yes," Mason said. He *did* feel better. Sunlight flooded into the bathroom
through the arching window positioned above the porcelain bathtub where
his mother sat. Mason faced her, perched on the toilet seat, fresh from a
warm shower, swathed in a towel. Cold tile stung his bare feet. A pleasant
shiver rippled up his back. He closed his eyes for a moment. When he
opened them again, he was overwhelmed. It had been weeks since he'd
seen this room filled with natural light. Dust swirled in the glow, haloing

Samantha's concerned expression. His annoyance was erased by sudden gratitude for his beautiful mother, his elegant home, his blessed life, and the gorgeous rush of dopamine triggered by the rare occurrence of sunlight on his skin.

Mason burst into sobs. His mother rushed to his side. "Oh, sweetie, the *day* you've had." She stroked his hair. "You know, I don't think anyone saw me whisk you in here. You don't have to go out there. In fact . . ." Samantha paused and then, with Herculean effort, uttered a question that took at least three years off her life. "Do you want me to send everyone home?"

"*No*," Mason gasped, jolting out of her embrace. "*Please* keep them here. I just want things to go back to normal. *I wanna forget all the shit I've been through today! I need this party! Okay?*" A frown distorted his mother's face. Mason realized he was shouting. "I'm sorry, I—"

"You don't have to apologize, honey." She swept him into a ferocious hug.

"Okay, Mom."

"We're gonna have this party and it's gonna be great." She stroked her son's back.

"It's gonna be great," Mason echoed.

"That's my baby boy."

"I . . . I need to talk to Yunho."

"You will, you will." Samantha suddenly stopped caressing her son. "Mason . . ."

"Yes?"

"Where are Astrid and Claudia?"

TWENTY-THREE

6 months, 16 days, 4 hours, 12 minutes

The Escalade lurched forward, struggling over humps of unpaved earth. Mason peered through his window at the abandoned dirt plot formerly known as Skid Nation, the largest settlement of unhoused people in the country. A week prior, everyone had been rounded up and cleared from the site because Disney had purchased the lot to build an event space for a pre-Oscars party celebrating *End Times*, their dystopian award season frontrunner. Executives had scouted many locations, determined to find a milieu that evoked, as the invitation insisted, "a fun apocalyptic setting to honor the spirit of *End Times* and all its talented nominees." The structure was a glowing beacon in a pitch-black expanse of rubble, enclosed by electric fencing, and patrolled by an army of policemen who ensured that those without legal claim to the land would not return.

"I know you didn't want to come." Yunho squeezed Mason's hand. The Oscar party had been on the calendar long before Astrid's abortion; Yunho's $20 million deal with Disney was up for renewal, and since award season events were just office parties with better fashion, he needed to show face and beg Mickey Mouse for more money. "I didn't either."

"Maybe it'll be a good distraction." Mason looked through the rear windshield at the Escalade following their own. "But was it the best idea to invite Astrid and Claudia?"

"We all deserve a night out," Yunho insisted. "To forget the hell we've been through."

That she put us through, Mason thought. *That you agreed to.*

The Escalade came to a stop. They exited the vehicle. Yunho's publicist waited in the dirt path that led to the red carpet; her stiletto heels sunk into soil, forcing her to do an awkward jig. "Yunho! Mason!" She waved eagerly. She spotted Astrid and Claudia disembarking the other Escalade. "And . . ." She glanced at her clipboard. "Astrid and Claudia!"

"We're just gonna make a quick cameo." Yunho clenched his jaw.

"Of course. Is everyone going to make a red-carpet appearance?" She asked this in a manner that made it clear that everyone should *not* make a red-carpet appearance.

"We'll just head inside and catch up with you boys there," Astrid murmured.

"*Great.*" The publicist dragged the men toward a blazing, halogen-lit oasis amidst the dark and devastated lot. A desperate horde of celebrities bottlenecked the entrance to the red carpet, conspiring in the shadows with their publicists about strategies for skipping the line.

A gunshot rang out. A scream.

But it was from the outer banks of the lot, beyond the electric fence. Nobody important.

Mason did not walk down the red carpet so much as float above it, disconnected from his body by a dissociative rage. Photographers called their names, but all Mason could hear was the furious echo of his inner monologue. *Did Astrid even want to help us?* Mason spat during one of his fights with Yunho. *Or did she and Claudia just want a free mansion in L.A.?* Yunho had been horrified. *How can you say that?* Yunho shouted back. *She loves us. And you've seen how this has devastated her too.* But a darkness in Yunho's eyes betrayed his doubt. Mason felt vicious satisfaction. He wanted to believe the worst—that Astrid and Claudia were evil manipulators— because then he had somewhere to put his anguish. It was easier to rage at these two women than a global corporation that remained indifferent to the protests of its American surrogates, the majority of whom crumbled under Future Generations' union-busting measures or coercion from parents-to-be who threatened litigious retaliation if their surrogates obtained illegal abortions. In the end, Astrid's solidarity with her abused Gujarati counterparts made no difference, and she fell into a deep depression. *We can try for another baby, without Future Generations*, Astrid told the couple while she cried in Yunho's arms; Mason resented that he was forced to deal with *her* grief. *I still want to carry a child for you. We're family.* Mason sensed that Astrid agreed to attend this party out of a desperation to prove her loyalty. So, rather than address the festering tension, rather than admit their queer family was imploding, Mason and Yunho and Claudia and Astrid clung to a bullshit veneer of normalcy and attended a fucking Oscar party.

"Sir?" Suddenly, Mason was in the glittered crush of the soiree, with no memory of how he got there. Yunho stood next to him, scanning the sea of people like a suicidal bridge jumper. The room had been designed to mimic the futuristic set of *End Times*, in which the climate-ravaged planet is taken over by an Amazon-like corporate entity that enslaves the world's poor to toil in its factories, until the workers rise up and attack their bosses. Replicas of the factory sets featured conveyor belts that moved swag bags through the party. The waitstaff were dressed in the same uniforms as the workers in the film. "Toxic Waste?" A server proffered a tray of neon-green cocktails, each in a glass resembling a radioactive waste bin. "It's our specialty drink."

"Sure." Mason grabbed two, suddenly, deeply saddened. Regret and shame gripped his heart; he'd been so cruel and petulant and resistant to Astrid's desire to show solidarity with workers in Gujarat. As much as he hated the abortion, it was an action imbued with more integrity than anyone in this room possessed. What were they doing at this rich clown gang bang? Where a bunch of self-satisfied actors, directors, and executives patted themselves on the back for their superficial allegiance to a vague idea of anti-capitalist uprising while eating gourmet catering at a party hosted by one of the largest corporations on Earth, which had erected an entire *building* to host just *one* party that displaced and jailed hundreds of unhoused people? And he had the nerve to assume the worst about Astrid, just to protect his sense of entitlement to a child? He needed to find her. And Claudia. To apologize. A breathless panic built in his chest. "Yunho, I . . . I need to find Astrid and Claudia and we need to leave."

"Honey, you're freaking me out. What's—"

"Vegan slider?" a waiter interrupted. "They're sustainable—"

"No thanks," Yunho snapped and turned back to Mason. "Now what is going on?"

"I . . . I'm realizing I've been a total bitch and I need to *apologize* to Astrid and Claudia—"

"Mason. We've been on this roller coaster for the past month. We all need a rest," Yunho murmured, trying to calm his lover. "Besides, we *just* got here. I have to say some hellos."

"Toxic Waste?" Another fucking waiter.

"*No thanks!*" Mason barked, then turned to Yunho. "The fact that you want to stick around at this bullshit event is just *wild* to me, when we are dealing with a *crisis* in our family!"

"You can't ghost a party when there's a twenty-million-dollar price tag on your head."

"Our child was just aborted. *This party does not fucking matter!*"

"*Yes, it does!*"

"*How can you say that?*"

"*Because I was just subpoenaed by the Anti-American Speech Committee!*"

A rush of vertigo. Mason gripped a cocktail table. "Wait, what?"

"It happened yesterday. They seized the script for the *Reds* reboot. They say I'm making communist propaganda. They're investigating my entire body of work for seditious material . . ."

"Vegan slider?"

". . . and so, I *do* have to be at this party. So I can do damage control with the studio, so they don't blacklist me and refuse to renew the deal that funds our life and the extremely expensive endeavor of surrogacy, which we will now be doing for a *second* time."

"Honey . . . I'm so sorry. I mean, I can pick up the slack—"

"Your art studio has been operating at a loss for the past two years."

"We're just in a dip right now but—"

"Delusion doesn't pay the bills, Mason."

"Toxic Waste?"

"Actually, I *will* take one of those." Yunho grabbed a cocktail.

Panic shot down Mason's spine. "Babe, you haven't had a drink since—"

"And *you're* one to talk?" Yunho shot an accusatory stare toward Mason's hands, each of which held a tiny drum of Toxic Waste.

"Yunho!" A heavily botoxed woman grabbed Yunho's arm.

"Haylin—*so good* to see you . . ." Yunho followed her deeper into the party. Mason watched, stunned. Yunho eyed his drink like it was a grenade that might detonate in his hand. He slammed it back, downed the entire thing without taking a breath, and Haylin looked alarmed, but clearly she had some vested interest in talking to him, some amount of money was at stake, so she pretended nothing had happened as Yunho grabbed another drink and they carried on, probably talking about Yunho's deal or her deal or someone else's deal. Every time Yunho sipped his cocktail he shot a look toward his lover, a *fuck you* stare, and Mason knew not to interrupt this conversation, Mason *couldn't* interrupt this conversation because he was frozen, experiencing an internal collapse so total he feared it would lead to an external one. He clutched the bar and suppressed a panic attack; the news of the subpoena was too much to bear, *not this, not now,* not when they'd already suffered unbearable loss, not when they'd just started to sift through the rubble of their decimated identities. This was no state in which to appear before the Anti-American Speech Committee, they needed to be strong, to present a united front, not that it mattered whether they were strong or weak, united or torn apart and blasted into tiny pieces, because it always went the same way with the AASC, a subpoena would lead to a hearing, then a DOJ investigation, and, finally, Yunho would be indicted. There was nothing to do but surrender to ruination.

He sucked down his cocktail. Ordered another. And another. And another. A compulsive itch crawled across his flesh. He wanted Vex. He needed his lupine master. The bitter relief of his whip. The brutal weight of his cock. The little death only Vex could induce, the brief merciful oblivion where the force of a single orgasm obliterated all thought and it wouldn't matter that his child was dead, his partner was drinking, and the government was watching.

He slipped out of the party.

*

But when he got to *The Road*, Vex was unavailable. Mason ripped off his VR helmet. He was terrified to be home alone, wasted, with dark convictions fomenting in his mind. He poured a gin and tonic. Downed it. Stumbled to the fire pit. Cranked the gas. Pushed the lever past the safety stop. A wall of flame rose. The beauty of fossil fuels. Mason reclined on a patio chair. He peered into his glass; the frozen cubes had fused together, forming one melting ice cap. He gave it an anxious shake and threw back the tasteless dregs. It was his second drink since arriving home. Without Yunho. All he could do was wait and drink. His pulse hammered in his ears.

"*Mason . . .*"

It was Yunho. On the other side of the fire pit. Mason squinted. The heat from the flames distorted Yunho's silhouette. His image rippled like a mirage. Yunho smiled; or the waves of warmth pushed his lips upward. He was a memory brought to life. The wall of flame was a portal to the past and on the other side it was the afternoon of Gabriel's birthday party, and Yunho sat in the sandbox with the child in his lap, and they played with blocks and told a story about dragons and the moment was so perfect and tender. How could they experience the divinity of Gabriel's love and come to any other conclusion than the one they'd arrived at that day, when Yunho gasped and said, *Let's have a baby*?

Yunho turned off the flames. In his arms—the urn. Mason began to cry. Yunho rushed to his lover. Cradled Mason against his chest. Mason caught his breath. "I'm sorry," he whispered.

"The abortion was hard for me too, you know." Yunho stared at the extinguished fire pit. "I pretended it wasn't because I wanted to support Astrid, but if I'm being honest it felt like . . ."

". . . Like a death?"

"Like a death." This acknowledgment created a space between the two men, something like the void Mason yearned for whenever he let his canine daddy cockslap him into oblivion, yet the nothingness he felt now with Yunho was more liberating than a Vex orgasm; this was the real deal, not a little death but the big one, the infinite abyss. Mason met Yunho in the boundless dark, and they plummeted together, their physical bodies sat facing each other on stupid patio furniture, but Mason could tell from Yunho's desperate stare that his mind was also hurtling toward the same dark conclusion, the same premature ending, where they'd let go of the physical world. But before they reached that magnificent threshold, Yunho grabbed Mason, and that one action brought them crashing back to the feeble earthly realities they'd spent a lifetime constructing, and Yunho ripped the lid off the urn, and ash ejaculated from the hole, and the child's remains scattered across the soil like dead seed. No hope for a garden here.

"I love you, Mason."

"I love you too." Yes, the script still worked. The story held.

"But babe?"

"Yeah?"

"I . . ." Yunho fingered the rim of the urn. "I . . . did something bad."

TWENTY-FOUR

10 minutes

M om—it's beautiful."

"It's all for you, my sweet baby boy."

Mason took in the sweeping expanse of his home's ground story. The floor-to-ceiling glass walls that surrounded the living space had been retracted to allow for a seamless indoor–outdoor flow; the party spilled into the blooming slope of their backyard, which led to an infinity pool that overlooked Mason's very own chunk of begrimed skyline. The palatial kitchen thrummed with life, with people, with gloriously insipid chatter. The vast marble island boasted a lavish catering spread—cheese boards and caviar and crudités and mini-cheesecakes molded into storks. Small floral arrangements floated throughout—little bursts of vivid ranunculus. The crowd spilled into the adjacent living room, enjoying the view from the tufted expanse of a handsome beige sofa. His mother pointed toward an outdoor table, brimming with an embarrassment of presents. "The only thing missing is the centerpiece for the gift table. The bouquet that you were going to pick up . . ."

"Astrid has it."

His mother frowned. "And you don't think we should send someone to look for them—"

"She's coming, Mom." A manic violence flattened his tone. "We're not sending someone back out into that mess." But, Mason realized, his outburst was inspired by more than a desire to avoid subjecting someone to the danger outside their weather-modified bubble. Mason simply didn't want Astrid or Claudia there. He wanted to enjoy his party without having to contend with the reality the women represented, the reminder of all the torture he'd endured both today and during the mess of months that preceded this party. He didn't even want to find Yunho, didn't want to explain or confront or relive the trauma he'd just been through by recounting the terror to his husband.

He just wanted to have fun.

"But Mason, I think we should . . ." His mother's voice faded; he pushed into the crowd, leaving her trapped behind a wall of guests. He quickened his pace, as if reality was a murderer in pursuit, attempting to bludgeon him with the weight of bitter memories.

TWENTY-FIVE

6 months, 1 day, 2 hours, 9 minutes

Who'd like to start?" Cove asked. They sat in a black Saarinen Womb Chair, dressed in a navy slim-cut suit. Shaved head. They held a notepad in their lap.

Mason, Yunho, Claudia, and Astrid squirmed silently in the minimalist office, Claudia in her wheelchair, the rest on a chic midcentury sofa so low to the ground that one did not *sit* on it so much as *slide* into a nearly supine position that sent immediate shockwaves of pain through one's lower back. The piece was selected with a sadistic disregard for function; Mason already distrusted the person who'd chosen it. Just like he distrusted this whole situation.

"I . . . I can," Yunho offered.

"All right," Cove replied. "What happened that night?"

"It started when I relapsed. I was going through this unbearable amount of stress. The subpoena, our financial situation, the . . . grief I felt after . . ." Yunho's sobs strangled his words.

Astrid stroked his back. "It's okay, baby." She looked to Cove. "I think what Yunho's trying to say, is that the abortion was so hard for all of us. Part of what happened that night was, like, this collective mourning."

The word *mourning* triggered a sense of loss in Mason that manifested physically; grief burned through his veins like venom, his temperature rose, nausea roiled his gut, and suddenly he was shouting. "*Oh, fuck you, Astrid.* You really want me to believe you're mourning the loss of the child that *you* aborted?"

"*Do you think any of this is easy for me?*" Astrid shouted.

"Mason, I thought we put this *behind us,*" Yunho snapped. "I thought you wanted to *apologize.*"

"I knew this was a terrible idea." Claudia sighed.

"I want to return to something Astrid said." Cove paused, inserting a calming quiet into the conversation. "What did you mean, when you said that night felt like a 'collective mourning'?"

"Well . . . it was so intense. We went through this trauma and then suddenly we were all going to this Oscar party. I don't think any of us wanted to go, but Yunho *had* to, so we went to support him. Also, none of us wanted to be alone. Because we'd all experienced this terrible loss. But it was surreal and awful to be somewhere so frivolous while I was feeling such profound grief. And regret. Because it was all for nothing—my solidarity with the Indian surrogates was fruitless. But you have to believe me"—she turned to Mason and Yunho with a pleading look— "I felt like I had no choice. You guys have never been poor—broke at times, maybe—but not *truly* poor, like born-into-it poor. And when I see someone who has it worse than I did, I feel this *need* to help, no matter the cost. But I've learned this self-sacrificing impulse can hurt me. Like it has here. Since my abortion, I've realized that I *did* feel a bond with the being that had been growing inside me, or at least the *idea* of this being and how it would connect me to Mason and Yunho—two men I love—and how Claudia and I could possibly have a role in this child's life.

"I was thinking about all this at the party, and I began to panic. I'd made a mistake. My identity was falling apart in real time. I needed to leave. We went to find Yunho and Mason. But Mason had already left. And Yunho was drunk. And I know he doesn't drink. But I was also drunk and so was Claudia and it felt like, well, if there was ever a night to cut someone some slack it would be that night. I held Yunho in the middle of the party, and he cried. Claudia said we should leave but Yunho said he wasn't ready to go home. So we went to my place instead.

"We took the Escalade and Yunho cried the entire ride and the alcohol was really hitting me now and I blacked out and suddenly we were in my bedroom. I didn't know how we got there. I was laying in Claudia's lap, and Yunho was laying in mine. We were, like, this sad chain of humans. I looked down at Yunho and stroked his hair.

"He stopped crying. Caught his breath. Looked up. His eyelashes were clumped together by tears. I saw the emptiness in his eyes. It matched the emptiness in my own. In Claudia's. We shared a death. It had created a hole inside all of us. A hole I wanted to fill. A hole Yunho wanted to fill. A hole Claudia wanted to fill. Sex seemed like the way to make that happen. I don't remember much of that night. But I remember when it was done. Me and Claudia and Yunho were lying in bed, soaked in sweat. And I just started laughing. Then Yunho started laughing. Then Claudia. It was so absurd, so beautiful, all of us tangled together, fucking our way out of hell."

Another silence. Claudia stared out the window. Yunho picked lint off the sofa. Mason turned to Cove. A victorious gleam lit his stare. Here, in front of a neutral third party, Mason would be vindicated; Yunho would be chastised; someone would finally sit them down and say, *This has gone too far.* "So, Cove, now I hope you can see the insanity I've been dealing with."

"I'm going to ask you to refrain from that sort of judgment—"

"Mason—I . . . I promise this wasn't some kinky sex thing, it was like, like, *mourning.*"

That *word* again. "Enough with the fucking *mourning*, Astrid—"

"Mason please, let's not resort to that language," Cove said.

"What are we even doing here? You're a couple's therapist, not a quadruple's therapist."

"My specialty is *family* therapy and the four of you have created a family unit here, albeit one that may be regarded as non-normative by some."

"I'd say we're massively more fucked up than your average family."

"I wouldn't," Cove said. "I've seen families with far more toxic dynamics than yours, due to any number of issues. I'd say you should—"

"My husband fucked our surrogate and her girlfriend. How many ways do we need to say it to make you understand that this is completely hopeless?"

"Mason, why does this upset you so much?"

"Um, I think that's fairly obvious."

"I don't. You have an open relationship. And according to what you told me in our initial consultation, this is a carte blanche to have sex with anyone."

"Anyone but Astrid and Claudia."

"But did you ever articulate this to Yunho?"

"Well, no . . ."

"And *why not* Astrid and Claudia? Why does the fact that Yunho had sex with them upset you so much?"

"It just makes me feel . . ."

"Left out?" Cove asked. Shock forced the air from Mason's lungs. Like he'd been punched. Then, he was crying. "Mason," Cove continued gently. "Is it possible you're not really angry about the sex, but that this act of mourning occurred without you?"

"I . . ." Mason gasped. "I . . . yes." Yunho grabbed Mason with primal intensity, like they were standing in the shadow of a tsunami and the only thing that could save Mason from being swept away was the anchor of Yunho's embrace. Mason surrendered to the warmth of his lover's body, realizing this intense love was the reason there was still hope for their strange queer family. They could survive this moment, even succeed *because* of it. They'd endured this pain together, and pain led to growth, transformation.

"Mason—we've had an important realization here today. I'm happy you were vulnerable enough to answer my question. I think this is a good place to wrap things—"

"Wait—" Astrid gripped the arm of the sofa. "I wanted to say one more thing."

"Okay," Cove allowed.

"Yunho, Mason. I wanted to let you know . . ." She took a breath. "I'm pregnant."

TWENTY-SIX

7 minutes

Mason was stung by the weird feeling that his party did not need him. It had commenced without him. It could continue without him. It could finish without him. There were people they'd paid to clean up. Mason could walk out the door, back into the smoke, and no one would notice; yes, perhaps a few guests would ask about his whereabouts, his closer friends might do a little hunting, but eventually they would encounter another acquaintance and get pulled into small talk or a casual flirtation or a networking opportunity and even Yunho would not be able to resist the centripetal force of the party. It suddenly seemed strange to Mason that he at one time felt this party would be of great consequence—a return to order after all the chaos, an assertion of his identity as a *father*—when in actuality it was of no consequence whatsoever. This party meant nothing; a party couldn't *mean* any one thing, the meaning of a party was diffuse, as varied as the number of guests, there was no singular takeaway, no moral of the story, everyone who attended walked away with a different sense of what it *meant* to be there, something debated in many car rides to many homes; and if this baby shower failed to properly cohere into some sort of meaning upon which Mason could build his identity, then what was the point of any of it? What were any of them doing here? Who was Mason?

"Mason!"

"Patrick! Glad you could make it." Mason felt estranged from reality, as if he was reciting lines in a nightmare, unable to control his speech. "Enjoying the party?"

"Yes." Patrick hugged Mason. "It means so much that you invited me here today."

"Oh, it's nothing, really . . ." Really, it *was* nothing, all of it, nothing.

Patrick's lip quivered. "You don't understand. I don't see my own family. Ever. They hate me. So it means a lot that you've brought me into *your* family. You're like a brother to—"

"*Mason!*" Mahmood shouted, barging his way into the conversation, dragging Gabriel by the hand. "Jesus Christ, we've been worried about you. Where have you been?"

"We got . . . tied up." A flash of Astrid's pregnant body getting dragged across the pavement by that, that, *thing*.

"Where's the baby?" Gabriel demanded, looking up at their father.

"I told you, love. The baby isn't here yet. It's still in Astrid's tummy."

"Where's Astrid?" Gabriel pouted.

"Where *is* Astrid?" Mahmood shifted his focus to Mason. "And Claudia?"

Mason's throat felt parched. He coughed, stalling for time. Mercifully, Patrick interrupted. "Good to see you, Mahmood. Thank you for delivering my sculpture toda—"

"Where are they, Mason?" Mahmood said, ignoring Patrick.

"I'm sure they're here somewhere . . ." Mason lied; he wasn't sure of that, he wasn't sure of anything except his desire to escape this conversation and the reality it represented and, like a genie with a bad sense of humor, the party granted his wish in the form of dancing synchronized swimmers that split this discussion in two. Mahmood attempted to shout across the conga line of storks, but not a single scream could overpower the noise. The swimmers danced toward the pool, their movements synced to the thumping bass line blasting across the backyard. Their costumes were uncanny, too realistically birdlike. Disgusting. Real feathers sprouted from their chests, blinding white, bristling in the wind. Their heads jerked and bobbed in perfect imitation of avian movement; each sported a headpiece with a gigantic orange beak, its texture too coarse, too bone-like to be fake. They were stolen mandibles, ripped from living birds; atop each poached bill, two dead eyes glistened. Something about the realness of the storks made Mason feel fake, as if *he* were the one in costume; he swooned, staggered backward. He was no one, nothing.

"*Mason*," Yunho's voice called to a person who no longer existed. Mason turned to face his lover, feeling like the rind of an orange that had been pieced together to resemble its former shape; yes, Mason's pulp had been sucked out, his guts ripped from their epidermal encasement, and all that remained was a Frankensteined layer of skin that might fall away at any minute, revealing the hollow truth of Mason's gutted soul: He was incapable of feeling anything, of doing anything other than trying to keep his husk patched in place; this was what love looked like for Mason now, this was all he had left to give, an illusion of the person he used to be, the person Yunho used to love, but to conjure this person required strength that Mason couldn't sustain and if he'd still had a heart it would've broken when Yunho slammed him into a naive embrace and said, "*Where have you been?*"

Sudden exhaustion overwhelmed Mason. He didn't want to talk. He wanted to fall asleep. Right there on the lawn. "I . . . I . . . ." That familiar tenderness appeared in Yunho's eyes. That look that said: *Tend to me. Tend to us.* But before Mason was forced to fabricate a comforting phrase his dead self would've uttered, Yunho pointed to something.

It was Astrid. Looking haunted, haggard.

She was alone.

But she had the bouquet.

TWENTY-SEVEN

5 months, 23 days, 8 hours, 4 minutes

T here were to be no surprises that day, or, at least, they *expected* no surprises, for Mason and Yunho had seen this drama play out on television many times before. It was disturbing to watch someone get judicially gangbanged by the team of paranoid commie-hunters that was the Anti-American Speech Committee, but nothing compared to the terror of being called before the committee yourself, knowing that the script was set, as predictable as a police procedural in which the bad guy was always caught. It was this terror that beat within Yunho's heart as he and Mason and Mahmood and Daniel and Astrid and Claudia stormed down the halls of the Rayburn House Office Building, halls like intestines, labyrinthine tripe, filthy with the residue of all the shitty injustice the building had pumped through its system over the years. The grime-caked halls lacked the grandeur Mason expected of such a storied American institution, which was disappointing because if they were to be dramatically summoned before the United States government for a trial that would paint them as public villains for the rest of their lives, then certainly they deserved a sufficiently grand locale, a setting appropriate for the climax of some future biopic, produced when the tides of American authoritarianism turned and freedom of expression was a thing again and people looked back on this era and sang the songs of heroes wrongly persecuted by the Anti-American

Speech Committee. But Mason's biopic dreams withered as he and his sad family marched through the dingy innards of Rayburn and ended up in a holding room with wall-to-wall carpeting that looked like it had not been vacuumed since McCarthy died in 1957. Busted folding chairs sat next to a rickety card table littered with four tiny water bottles and seven snack-sized bags of Cool Ranch Doritos. Mason was so starving and nervous that he demolished packet after packet, consuming them like a bastard Sesame Street puppet whose raison d'être was to count packets of flavored tortilla chips as he slammed them down his felt gullet. He wished he'd eaten back in the private jet, but the flight was too turbulent, he'd been so nauseous he didn't even touch his filet. They were running frighteningly low on liquid assets and Mason had almost picked a fight with Yunho about the expense of the jet but then thought better of it. Yunho deserved a break, deserved the jet; they *all* deserved the jet after the hell they'd been through, not that Astrid or Claudia needed to be there, but Astrid was pregnant again and Yunho wanted her in his sight at all times, to protect the baby at all costs, not that he articulated this, not that any of them had time to unpack the ramifications of this new pregnancy amidst the drama of preparing for their battle with the AASC.

First, the committee called Daniel into the hearing room. Everyone else watched from the screen in the holding area as Daniel sat at a wooden table facing three rows of foul hobgoblins wearing congressman costumes. They grilled Daniel about the *Reds* reboot he was co-writing with Yunho. The committee's Chair-Goblin accused Daniel of creating communist propaganda, because the script was sympathetic to the radical American journalist John Reed, who covered the October Revolution and supported the Soviet takeover of Russia. Daniel defended himself, explaining that the film also followed Reed as he became disillusioned with the Revolution because of its descent into totalitarianism and therefore *Reds* couldn't be viewed as communist propaganda because it illustrated the potential for fascism to foment among the left and foreshadowed the decades of oppression that would take place within the Soviet Union, at which point another congress-goblin interjected to characterize Daniel's critique of the Soviet Union as a veiled attack on Putin ("that wonderful ally to the United States") and his successful military project of reuniting all former states of the Soviet Union under the great democratic banner of Russia. Daniel stammered, insisting Russia wasn't a democracy, but the congressgoblin accused Daniel of spreading anti-Russian propaganda and concluded that this was evidence of his guilt. The floor was then handed to the Democrats, and the committee's ranking minority goblin pitched a few softballs designed to provide left-leaning citizens assurance that there were members of the Democratic party still fighting authoritarianism (even though these Democrats held no real power). He concluded with a bloodless monologue about freedom of speech while everyone in the courtroom just stared at the clock.

Then, Yunho was called in. The hearing room fell silent—this was the big climax. Yunho was asked about the *Reds* reboot, though these questions were just goblin wrist warm-ups for the flogging that followed, in which every film or television show Yunho had ever produced was twisted into evidence of his diabolical plot to destroy America, and truthfully, his work *did* often critique the power structures of the ruling elite, from the anarchist themes of *The Dispossessed* to the anti-colonialist sentiment of *March First Movement* and everything in between. Yunho was then forced to disavow his life's work in front of the committee and the country. Mason could tell this was the most painful part for Yunho, to say all those years of labor and love meant nothing, that he'd been wrong about everything he'd ever created. But he had no choice, to say otherwise would've meant incarceration. Yunho disavowed and disavowed, until finally it was time for blessed softballs from the Demgoblins. His shoulders relaxed. Now, someone would at least pretend to care about justice. He faced the Democrat and waited for easy questions to wash over him like a healing balm, but, in the first surprise of a day in which there were to be no surprises, the Democrat asked Yunho about his relationship to Astrid and Claudia.

Everyone in the holding room jolted in their seats. Mason froze, a Dorito bag covering his fist like a mitten, and watched his lover admit that Astrid was his surrogate and Claudia was her girlfriend, but he didn't see how this related to the concerns of this committee. The Democrat asked if Yunho realized that Astrid and Claudia were anarchists, and Yunho stammered and pretended to have no idea. The more the Democrat pressed, the more Yunho was forced to disavow the women he loved, women who listened to the proceedings as if they were listening to their own death sentences.

Yunho returned to the holding room with the devastated expression of someone who'd just had their insides scooped out in front of the entire nation. In the end, Mason was the only one spared because his recent artworks were so morally vacant, so apolitical, so meaningless that there was nothing for the committee to pick apart. He became the sole member of their family to emerge from the hearing unscathed.

The AASC hit Yunho with penalties he couldn't pay. A $3.9 million judicial lien was placed on their home. Meanwhile, Disney declined to renew his $20 million overall deal; Yunho suspected he'd been secretly placed on the New Blacklist. His agents dropped him, studios refused to work with him. His career was over, presenting a serious existential threat to his nascent family: Astrid and Claudia couldn't garner the capital to maintain their lifestyle, and even if they could've, there was no way for them to do so now that they too had been slandered by the AASC. The pressure fell to Mason to earn amounts of money he hadn't earned in years. Mahmood was sympathetic to Mason's plight because Daniel had been blacklisted too. Mahmood also became a sole breadwinner, which is how he and Mason found themselves at the convention center for Art Basel Hialeah, with a gallery booth overlooking the ocean. If you squinted you could see the ruins of Miami Beach far in the distance, waves lapping against the eighth and ninth floors of abandoned luxury buildings. Mason was in the middle of a trance, watching these monoliths refuse to fall, when Patrick Sullivan walked into his booth and into his life, with a grin on his face that told the world he was a man who got what he wanted, and what he wanted was Mason, and the way he'd get Mason was by buying artwork today and promising to buy more later, promising to commission sculptures for NuGrow factories in Sochi and Austin and Los Angeles, and Patrick's art adviser broke off to discuss details with Mahmood, and Patrick and Mason were left alone, and Patrick invited Mason to drinks at his hotel later that night, and of course Mason went, he had to, and of course Mason fucked Patrick, he had to, and Patrick got what he wanted and Mason got what he needed, which was just enough money to delay the imminent implosion of his entire fucking life.

TWENTY-EIGHT

5 minutes

FBI COUNTERTERRORISM DIVISION—NATIONAL THREAT CENTER SECTION CLASSIFIED: SUSPICIOUS ACTIVITY REPORT

[*Conversation recorded via roving bug installed on Frank Hanson's phone*]

FRANK HANSON: . . . . That sounds beautiful, Claudia. I've been trying to do something sorta like that at the shelter before . . . today . . . [*crying*] I made . . . good friends there . . . and they're all gone . . .

CLAUDIA JACKSON: Frank—I'm so, so sorry. Come here, I got you.

FH: [*catching his breath*] I don't want . . . to keep you . . . from your party.

CJ: [*laughs*] Oh, Jesus. That's the last thing on my mind.

FH: But Astrid . . . ?

CJ: It's probably a good idea to have someone go ahead and keep the peace.

FH: Because of what you're gonna do?

CJ: Well, what we *want* to do. But we have to get Mason on board. And she's better at placating Mason, which I don't have patience for. But I don't wanna do this without him. Despite all the shit we've been through I guess a part of me loves him? Or, at least, a part of me understands that Yunho loves him and I love Yunho and I want Yunho to come with us. I need Yunho for this to work, so I guess wanting and needing and love are all tangled up and somehow Mason is the knot at the center of that tangle. And—

FH: Wait—Claudia, look—

CJ: Fuck, fuck, fuck.

FH: LET'S GO—

[Recording ends.]

TWENTY-NINE

2 minutes

The bouquet. The one Mason bought this morning. He couldn't believe Astrid still had it. She set the flowers down on the outdoor gift table, gently, like the bundle was an infant she'd saved in a military raid.

Mason burst into tears. The flowers had survived. They'd all survived. And now they were here, surrounded by beauty, and the most beautiful thing of all was that bouquet, the hope it represented. Why keep that fragile cluster of flowers amidst all the devastation unless you believed in a future where splendor and grace and love would once again be possible? Just moments before, Mason had contended with an existential void so powerful it sucked every fragment of his shattered identity into its boundless nothing. But now, the bouquet. It felt imbued with magic, like some talisman needed to lift the curse of Mason's crisis and reunite the splinters of his selfhood until they coalesced into the familiar shape of his soul. Thank God—he was back to himself, back *in* himself, back in his body. The sun struck his skin; serotonin hummed in his bloodstream. It had all worked out. This party was proof. The beginning of the happy ending. Surrounded by friends. By family. By Daniel. By Mahmood. By Yunho. By Astrid.

And Claudia, well, surely Claudia was on her way.

Yes, it had all worked out. Their money problems were, well, not solved exactly, but on their way to resolution. Right now, there was a desperate billionaire yelling something unintelligible at Mason across a conga line of well-salaried storks—and Mason took comfort in the need in Patrick's eyes, knew that Patrick would continue to hire Mason to make more hideous sculptures for various factory lobbies and grand foyers across the globe. Patrick's interest in Mason's art would correct its marketplace value, and soon Mason's stock would soar again, and the parties would never stop, and their newborn would want for nothing.

Suddenly, Claudia arrived.

She was pushed by the homeless man, the one from the intersection where Mason had abandoned Astrid and Claudia. The man was shirtless, his thin torso caked with grime. An open wound stretched across his abdomen, glistening in the sunlight. He wore tattered *Looney Tunes* boxers; Bugs Bunny's smiling mouth was severed at the jaw, revealing the man's tattooed thigh. His face was hidden behind a battered gas mask, and it was the gas mask that pissed Mason off the most; not only had Claudia brought some nearly naked homeless man to *his* party, but now this man was wearing a mask when he didn't *need* to, when Mason had spent an exorbitant amount of money to ensure *no one* would have to wear a fucking gas mask at his party so they could all *forget* the horrific realities that lay beyond the walls of his estate.

How did he even get in? Fury tightened Mason's chest. *I didn't give Astrid or Claudia a plus-one.* There was a feral quality to the homeless man's gait. Who was to say he wouldn't rob or rape their guests? *"Claudia, who is this?"* Mason shouted, storming across the lawn.

Claudia ignored him. *"Everyone inside!"* Her voice was pure panic. *"The smoke is coming!"*

THIRTY

1 minute

A stampede ensued just as a crest of pink smoke materialized behind the jacarandas. Steph, the WeatherMod publicist, did her best to hand out WeatherMod-branded emergency gas masks, but there was no time to don them, so she gave up and dropped them in a pile on the ground and joined the crowd pushing toward the smoke-sealed house. The bottom floor's automated window-walls were closing; a nervous caterer stood by the control panel, slamming buttons repeatedly. Glass inched forward as guests bottlenecked into the ever-narrowing entrance to the kitchen, clawing their way toward safety.

Mason was trapped at the back of the panicked mob, clutching Yunho's hand. He looked over his shoulder. The cloud expanded, obscuring the horizon. The billowing mass advanced; its pace was slow, menacing, steady as some mythical death ship. It overtook the jacarandas. The dance floor. The pool.

Mason and Yunho pressed closer to the house, shoving human storks out of their way. Behind them: Patrick. The billionaire yelled to Mason, but his words were drowned by the screams of the crowd. Mason whipped his head toward the house. Inside: Astrid, Claudia, and the homeless man. If that homeless man survived and Mason did not, Mason would be furious, well, he wouldn't be furious because he'd be dead, but his fucking ghost would haunt this property with a goddamn vengeance and *why the fuck is "I Gotta Feeling" playing?* Mason looked to the DJ booth as its sole occupant leapt into the stream of bodies, abandoning his station, unconcerned with the maddening irony of the Black Eyed Peas' insistence that *tonight's gonna be a good night* despite horrific evidence to the contrary. Mason wailed, and dropped to his knees in surrender because this was it, who the fuck cared anymore, the smoke had found them all at last.

A hand gripped his forearm. Yanked him up. Nearly dislocated his shoulder. Yunho pushed Mason into the herd, into the house, into the throng of bodies sweating in the kitchen.

Mason was safe.

But then, through the window, he saw something outside that made his heart sink: the bouquet. Just sitting on the gift table. About to be ruined by smoke. Something broke inside Mason. *Not the bouquet. Not now. Not with everything it represented.* He had to save it. It was such a stupid thought. But though Mason understood intellectually that his attachment to the bouquet was sentimental idiocy, it was as if he couldn't control his own body, couldn't control his legs as they propelled him forward, couldn't control his arms as he pushed through the house, the crowd, the door.

Then, he was back outside.

Only a few straggling storks and Patrick remained on the lawn. Patrick was bent over, picking up a discarded gas mask that Steph had abandoned on the ground. "What are you doing back out here?" Patrick attempted to push a gas mask into Mason's arms. "Put this on in case we can't get inside—" Mason spat in Patrick's face. Kept moving. All he wanted was his precious bouquet. All he wanted was hope.

Then, he had it. Right there in his grasp. A beautiful burst of lilies.

Suddenly, they disappeared behind a rose-colored haze.

Mason gasped.

His lungs filled with pink smoke.

THIRTY-ONE

0 minutes

Sharp points, like small nails, filled his lungs. With each inhalation they stabbed his organs anew. Sliced their spongy tissue. He couldn't see inside his body, but after a few agonizing breaths he was certain his lungs were just strips of shredded meat dangling from his trachea; each gasp sent them shuddering like paper streamers in the wind. Panic joined the pain in his chest, and he could barely breathe. His gasps grew smaller and smaller and suddenly his head was shaking and his eyes rolled back and he lost control of his body and tumbled to the ground and convulsed against the earth. Hot liquid surged up his throat, out his mouth, and he puked up his own lacerated lungs, yes, bronchial nuggets coated his lips, and his seizure gained galvanic autonomy, like some lightning god was throttling his body, slamming his head into the pile of slop that had exploded from his mouth.

Then, it stopped. Everything stopped. His body stopped seizing. His lungs. His lungs weren't shredded. They were still inside his chest, still capable of doing their job. *In, out. In, out.* He lifted his head from the pool of his own sickness. Reason came rushing back. Of course, his lungs weren't shredded. How could he have ever believed there were small nails inside him, ripping away at his organs? And yet, he *had* believed it. Literal nails. Reality really was that mutable, moldable, like putty that dissolved if you played with it too long.

He stood. In the distance, through the fog of pink smoke, he could make out a structure. His glass-walled home. The entire party stared back at him, through the glass walls. They looked frozen. An exhibit in a wax museum, *ha, ha*. His house was a wax museum, *ha, ha*. He started laughing, laughing at the thought of his house as a wax museum. He knew it wasn't *that* funny, but the laughing became a strange tic, a spasm he couldn't stop, and the people inside the wax museum kept frowning as he laughed even harder until a sudden longing stopped him. He wanted to be back inside his house. But he couldn't move his legs. He looked down at his feet. Two lead stumps. He looked up.

He couldn't see the people in the house. Or rather, he could, but they were out of focus. Fuzzy. Their forms bled together. Bled into the house. Bled into the lawn. Bled into the pink smoke. The whole scene became a wavy wrecked watercolor, something a kid had poured juice on. Colors swirled together, the sky melted, the ground surged, shapes collided and fused until he faced an infinite and scrambled panorama that contained the entirety of the universe, and he was alone, on the outside, one panicked speck pitted against a blurred mass of all matter.

Terror raged through him.

Then, the scene faded, losing its color, its vibrancy. *Am I going blind?* His vision started sparkling with pinpoints of white light, as if some microscopic parasite was punching holes into the backs of his corneas. Punch, punch. White, white. Punch, punch. White, white.

Then it was all a white void.

He screamed. Felt a warmth in his groin. A warmth that emanated from his cock. Had he pissed himself? The warmth spread into his abdomen. It wasn't piss. What was it? The warmth worked its way through his veins, his lungs, his neck, became an excruciating heat, flushed his face, spread down through his arms, into his palms. His fingernails felt like chunks of hot steel. He ripped them off. Nail by nail. The pain was a distraction. From the heat. The burning. His body was burning from the inside out. His blood was hot oil. He screamed and flailed. Pain surged through his system, pain but also power, an adrenalized fury. A hunger for violence.

All he could see was white.

Then, he caught a flash of something. A streak of red, slicing through the white void.

He wheeled around. It disappeared. Then, another streak of red. It vanished almost as soon as it appeared. Something was out there. Moving. A threat. His rage now had an object. The red streak danced closer, then vanished. Something was connected to the streak. A person. An animal. A threat. Another streak appeared. Now there were two. Twin comets, leaving scarlet trails in the whiteness. Two threats. Every movement could destroy him. He had to destroy them first. Save his life. Erase the red. Restore pure whiteness. Righteousness fortified his fury, a knowledge that violence was necessary to preserve the purity of the void, the great white nothing that was his only safety, his whole world.

A red streak came dangerously close. Disappeared. But he sensed there was something directly in front of him. He could smell it. He could smell a body. And hear a muffled voice. Like someone was talking underwater. The voice drifted closer. Became louder. A threat.

He pounced. Pinned it to the ground. A deluge of red streaks striped his vision as the thing struggled beneath him. It wanted to destroy him. But he was stronger. He would win. Mason straddled the warm body. It writhed beneath him. Screamed. Slapped. He punched and punched its face. Adrenaline seared through him. Adrenaline like he'd never felt. Adrenaline that strengthened his hands as they pressed into the delicate flesh of what felt like a throat, and his fingers broke through. It was as easy as piercing a ripe peach. He dug in and found a pit, a small mass of cartilage, an Adam's apple, and he crushed it in his fist then ripped the cavity wider and shoved his hand deep inside the neck, down into the chest cavity, dug until he felt a wet sponge, a blood-soaked bag. He ripped out the lung and shoved it in his mouth, felt the gristle between his teeth, felt more alive than ever.

Mason was safe at last. No more threats. Just a comforting sea of white.

BIRTH

2044

THIRTY-TWO

S mash, smash. Blue fingers. Smash, smash. Blue hands.

Gabriel loved to eat blueberries. Sometimes Gabriel would smash the fruit and then lick their hands because it was fun. Sometimes Gabriel pretended they were a cow that loved blueberries because Gabriel also loved their cow. Actually, it wasn't *their* cow, they didn't own it, no one owned the animals on the Ranch. Or no, that wasn't right. *Everyone* owned the animals on the Ranch. Gabriel didn't mind sharing, but sometimes they wanted a cow to themselves because cows were cute, and Gabriel was four years old, which was old enough to take care of an animal if someone would just give them a *chance*. Gabriel plopped too many blueberries in their mouth, looked at Astrid, chewed like a cow, and said, "Look, I'm a cow!"

"Wow, I didn't know cows ate blueberries." Astrid poked Gabriel's nose and laughed.

Gabriel loved sitting in Astrid's lap while she worked the register at the Community Commissary. The store smelled good. Like fruit and earth and sweet sweat. The air was warm and wet and so thick you could almost eat it. But Gabriel wanted to eat blueberries, *all* the blueberries, so many boxes of blueberries piled in big crates, next to piles of apricots and snap peas and bright-red tomatoes. A fridge hummed in the corner, keeping the cheese and milk cold. Flowers spilled from big silver buckets. Gabriel felt happy in the store. Proud. All these things came from their home. The Ranch. And all the people Gabriel loved helped grow these things. Gabriel loved everyone at the Ranch, but they especially loved Astrid, who hugged Gabriel tighter than all their other Guardians combined.

"Yes, cows *love* blueberries," Gabriel said.

"Well, I love *you*."

"What happened to the baby in your tummy?" Astrid used to have a baby in her tummy. But now there was no bump. And the baby was in the Nursery.

"Well, I gave birth, and the baby came out."

"Like how Guardian Mahmood gave birth to me? Back when we lived in L.A.?"

"Yes, just like how he gave birth. And how he's going to give birth again soon!"

"So where's your baby now?"

"Well, it's not 'my' baby. People aren't property. They don't belong to anyone."

"But where is it?"

"The baby is with the other babies on the Ranch. With the Nurses."

"What's the baby's name?"

"We named them Fennel. You were at the naming ceremony, remember?" Gabriel did remember, they just wanted to hear Astrid tell the story again. All six Care Pods came together for a party. They ate cake and named the baby. But Gabriel forgot the name because it sounded funny. "I think it's a pretty name."

"I guess it's pretty," Gabriel said. "But don't you want to see Fennel?"

"But I'll see Fennel all the time. Because the whole Ranch will take care of the baby, just like everyone takes care of you."

"But I have my Guardians."

"And so will this baby. When they're old enough to choose their Care Pod, they'll leave the Nurses and pick who they want to live with. They might even choose us!"

"You don't wanna be a Nurse? Even though you were pregnant?"

Astrid sighed and made a sad face. "I was a Nurse once. Back when I lived on the Outside."

"They have Nurses on the Outside?"

"Well, not quite. They call them surrogates. And they aren't valued like we value—"

"Excuse me." A woman stomped up to the register. An Outside Person. A customer. The person had white skin like Astrid. "I don't understand this sign." The person pointed to the sign that hung above the fridge: ALL PRICES ARE SUGGESTIONS, PAY WHAT YOU CAN.

"Anyone can take what they need, regardless of what they can afford. If we're coming into this town and we can eat but others can't, we aren't genuinely supporting the community."

"So what should I pay for this loaf of bread?"

"Well, can you afford five dollars?"

"*Of course.*"

"Then, I'd suggest you pay five dollars." Astrid smiled. "But it's up to you."

"So I could just *steal* this loaf of bread right now if I wanted."

"It wouldn't be stealing. You're free to take the loaf without charge."

"This is *insane!*" the woman shouted. "What kind of business are you all running? Joanie told me there was something weird happening up here. And she was right—this is some *crazy shit.*"

Gabriel covered their ears. "My Guardians say we don't need to shout to communicate."

The person frowned at Gabriel. "Your Guardians? What is this little girl talking about?"

"I'm not a girl."

"Sorry, boy."

"I'm not a boy either." Gabriel shrugged.

The person's eyes got big and angry. Gabriel felt nervous. Astrid whispered into their hair. "Sweetie, why don't you go count blueberry baskets for me? That's always really helpful."

"I can count to twenty," Gabriel said proudly, then jumped from Astrid's lap and walked to the blueberries. Gabriel started counting the small green boxes. *One, two, three . . .* But they couldn't concentrate. The mean woman was shouting now. Yelling at Astrid. Gabriel was scared. They wanted to run. Hide. They snuck out the screen door in the back. The springs groaned.

Gabriel ran through the tall grasses behind the Commissary, letting their fingers hit the stalks. They ran through the gardens, where Chef Alvaro was picking tomatoes. He gave Gabriel a funny look, but Gabriel didn't stop. They ran past the field where the cows grazed. Past the barn, the greenhouse. Finally, they got to the wooden fence. Climbed it. Saw the road. Empty. Exciting. Gabriel wasn't allowed to be on the other side of the fence. On the Outside. Alone.

Something shiny appeared in the distance. A red car.

It got closer. Bigger. Gabriel knew they should run back to the Ranch, back to their Care Pod. But the car was pretty. It slowed to a stop. There was a man inside. His skin was pasty, like the bread dough Chef Alvaro made on Sundays. The man smiled and rolled down his window.

Claudia always told them that if there wasn't a grown-up around, they shouldn't talk to people from the Outside. Because some of those people were not nice. But this man seemed nice. Gabriel walked closer to the car. The man said, "Hey there, little boy."

"I'm not a boy."

"Of course you aren't." He smiled. Gabriel's tummy got upset. They didn't like talking to this man anymore. "What're you people doing with this land up here?" Gabriel didn't say anything. The man tried a different question. "Who's your mommy? Can I talk to her?"

"I have five Guardians." Gabriel was proud of their Care Pod. Some people on the Outside just got one mommy or daddy but Gabriel had five Guardians and got so much extra love because of it. But the man wasn't impressed. He looked mad. Gabriel felt scared.

"What are they teaching you kids up there?" the man said. Gabriel didn't say anything. In the back seat, a weird machine started to move. It was shaped like a dog skeleton. But it was made of metal. "A whole load of nonsense, that's what I'm guessing. You people just march into *our* neck of the woods and do your weird cult shit. And the people who've *lived here forever* are just supposed to put up with it. When you're up here, with all your land, *building* God knows what, *planning* God knows what, *thinking you can just run shit on your own—*"

"Excuse me, is there a problem?" Astrid was out of breath. She'd been running. Searching for Gabriel. They hid in the folds of her skirt where the man couldn't see.

"No problem at all," the man said. "Just having a chat with your boy about what's going on at this ranch. You people love your little fucking secrets—"

"*Just leave!*" Astrid yelled. Gabriel heard an engine. Smelled gas. The car drove off.

"You scared me, Gabriel." Astrid lifted them up. "You can't run off like that."

"I won't ever again, I promise." Gabriel threw their arms around Astrid's neck and didn't let go until they were back at the Commissary.

THIRTY-THREE

The Safe Futures™ Smart Home Surveillance System is the most advanced residential security system in the world. Of particular interest to California users is the "Fire-Looter" feature—the cameras detect smoke and engage a thermal lens feature, tracking intruders who would otherwise be obscured by smoke. Heat controls the color palette. The hotter the object, the whiter it becomes. The surrounding environment is rendered in shades of gray and black.

In the video, a body stands motionless. Mason. His figure glows white against the black expanse of his lawn. When viewed on a laptop, Mason's outline is no bigger than a fingernail.

There is no audio.

Mason seems to be in a trance. There is a gray cluster of something in his fist. The flowers. Mason lets them go. They drop to the ground. Mason does not move.

On the left side of the screen, synchronized swimmers push their way inside the mansion. Their blazing-white bodies jumble together as they fight for safety. Another bright spot lingers behind them, wearing a gas mask: Patrick.

Patrick hesitates then moves slightly toward Mason. Mason drops to the ground. Seizures rack his body. Patrick freezes on the black lawn. Suddenly, a streak of white stretches from inside the house to where Patrick stands. Fast as lightning. It settles, takes shape: Yunho.

Yunho pauses next to Patrick. The men consider Mason, who has stopped shaking. Mason rises to his feet. Yunho and Patrick approach carefully—two lion tamers with an untrained cub. Is Patrick's mouth moving? It's difficult to tell. But his head bobs as he gets closer, with Yunho trailing behind. They stop, five feet in front of Mason.

They pause.

Mason leaps forward and tackles Patrick. Yunho jumps into the fray. Their silhouettes blend, becoming one ball of white light, an amoeba of heat. Suddenly, a figure leaps back. Runs toward the house. The white flash is so rapid it's impossible to determine who's behind the blur.

On the lawn, the amoeba settles. Its edges become distinct: Mason straddles a body. Digs his fist into its throat. Its face has been battered to a pulp.

*

"This is bad for us." Renata spoke slowly, dramatically, stretching her statement with the extortionate conviction of someone who knows they're being paid $450 an hour. Renata's physique was a study in the combined effect of American Spirits and exercise bulimia; nicotine-strangled blood vessels were unable to properly oxygenate her skin, resulting in wrinkles desperate for fatty filling that her aerobically desiccated face couldn't supply. Her nickname among the queer and trans Hollywood elite whom she defended in high-profile criminal cases was "Skeletor," a reference to her resemblance to the bad guy in the 2039 *He-Man* reboot. "Really fucking bad." Renata paced the open-plan kitchen in Mason's depressing rental home, a relic from the 2020s, when all those hideous "modern farmhouses" afflicted Los Angeles in a plague of gentrification. The corners the architect had cut now crumbled: cheap black latticework on the windows peeled, laminate flooring sagged. Renata returned to the weathered kitchen island where her laptop sat, open to the video, frozen in its final frame: Mason's white silhouette straddling a mutilated body.

"I knew getting that security system was a mistake."

". . . So was killing Patrick Sullivan with your bare hands."

Mason had very limited memory of that afternoon. All he was left with were flashes of white. Resurgences of bodily heat. Night terrors. Compromised lung capacity. He'd been hooked up to oxygen in the hospital for ten days after the incident. His room had been monitored by law enforcement. No visitors allowed. Not even Yunho. Not that Yunho tried to visit. Not that Mason knew where Yunho was. Or Daniel. Or Mahmood. Or Claudia. Or Astrid.

Or his child. The child that would be born by now.

Mason wept. "I didn't mean . . . to kill . . . anyone."

"I know." She handed him a tissue. "Let's save those tears for the witness stand, okay?"

"Just tell me, am I fucked?" Mason blew his nose, issuing a vuvuzelan honk.

"I'm gonna be honest—we face a tough road ahead. That video will be shown at the trial and that video is bad. Very bad. Plus, the state is pissed off. There's a government-wide vendetta against you because Patrick's death has threatened NuGrow's deal with the state." Patrick's latest agrochemical miracle—the ability to render crops drought-proof *and* flame-retardant—was seen by Governor Chris Pratt as the agriculture industry's Last Great Hope in California. Already, NuGrow had built factories across the state as a part of a $150 million government contract. But the second phase of the deal wasn't complete; officials were drafting a complex arrangement with NuGrow that would give the state a vast quantity of this agrochemical to supply to farmers at low cost as a way of incentivizing them to reestablish farms in California, resuscitating the state's tanking economy. Patrick's death halted negotiations as NuGrow reeled from the loss of their CEO. The governor was furious, and Mason was cast as scapegoat.

"Did we get anywhere with reducing the charges?"

"First-degree murder is sticking. They're uninterested in a plea deal. They want to take this to trial. They want someone to blame in splashy press conferences. They want you to be the big bad villain that killed this man and ruined California's future."

"*But I wasn't in my right mind.* You *know* this, Renata. That pink smoke . . . fucked me up. I couldn't control my own actions."

"Sadly, until there's empirical scientific data detailing precisely how this pink smoke 'fucked you up,' we're screwed. Experts still have no idea what we're dealing with. And with no answers, there's no hope of getting a sexy scientist to bat her eyelashes on the witness stand and tell us how the smoke caused you to go temporarily insane and kill the governor's biggest donor at your goddamn fucking baby shower . . ." The rest of Renata's statement was drowned out by the sound of a siren ringing in Mason's skull, followed by the usual announcement blasted across his thoughts by Ankl, the house arrest security app installed on his iOS Cerebrum by the state for $175 dollars a week, a sum Mason had been forced to pay for the past five months: *ATTENTION MASON DAUNT: YOU ARE UNDER HOUSE ARREST. DO NOT LEAVE PREAPPROVED GPS LOCATIONS UNDER ANY CIRCUM-STANCE. IF YOU DO, YOU WILL BE ARRESTED FOR VIOLATION OF PAROLE.* The message repeated and was followed by a full minute of deafening sirens only Mason could hear. This cycle repeated hourly, no matter the time of day, even if Mason was sleeping, which he rarely did due to the constant interruption.

Finally, the alarms ceased. "Sorry, Ankl again."

"I figured." Back in 2040, the California Supreme Court delivered a win for criminal justice advocates when the judges abolished pretrial detention and cash bail, except in the most extreme cases. In place of bail, the state mandated other forms of pretrial monitoring—check-ins with case managers, treatment at rehab facilities, and electronic monitoring. It was the latter form that the bail industry latched onto, pairing with Silicon Valley investors to create new technology for pretrial surveillance: apps that could be installed into any iOS Cerebrum by the government, so a criminal's pretrial movements could be tracked via the Apple chip embedded in their body. The fight criminal justice advocates now faced was the abolition of invasive surveillance techniques, a difficult task when Apple was funding corporate lobbyists to protect the bail-cum-surveillance industry.

"It's cruel. I'd rather be in jail than be subjected to this relentless monitoring happening *inside* my brain while locked in my fucking house, waiting for a trial the state keeps pushing."

"As far as house arrests go, you're wildly fortunate to have a twenty-five-hundred-square-foot home—"

"Just tell me I'm not going to prison, Renata." Mason suppressed a surge of nausea.

"I can promise you I'll fight these charges with every weapon in my dyke bitch arsenal." Renata slammed her laptop shut. "But *no one* can promise that you won't end up in prison."

THIRTY-FOUR

**FIVE MONTHS AFTER DISASTER, SCIENTISTS BAFFLED
BY TOXIC PINK SMOKE**

Scientists still lack a concrete explanation for the mysterious
clouds of toxic pink smoke that caused mass devastation in Los
Angeles County five months ago. Both the federal government and
the state of California have poured millions into an investigation
that has engaged the country's top experts, yet failed to provide
answers to a fearful nation.

Meanwhile, thousands have fled California in the biggest
exodus the state has ever seen. Though the pink smoke has dissipated, memories of the terror it brought—and the fifteen thousand lives the chaos claimed in just five days—remain lodged in
the minds of many. "I'm going back home to Iowa," says Angel
Price, thirty-seven, a former Westlake resident. "I lost some of my
closest friends. I don't want to be in L.A. for another round of
White Death."

"White Death" is the colloquial term locals use to describe the horrific experience of those who inhale the toxic pink smoke. Victims suffer from a temporary blindness in which their entire field of vision turns white. "It was like being trapped in a cloud," says Glenda Lake, forty-three, who remains hospitalized with complications from White Death; of the estimated 4,500 individuals exposed to the smoke, only 34 survivors remain. "I couldn't control my mind or body. I had these wild violent urges. I felt like I was going insane."

The legal system is struggling with how to deal with survivors of White Death, all of whom have killed multiple individuals in what appear to be psychotic reactions to the toxic smoke. Charges range from second-degree manslaughter to first-degree murder, with little guidance from the state as to how those charges were decided, or why there is such a range in their severity. "No one should be charged with murder, when it's clear that inhaling this toxic smoke leads to temporary psychosis," says Sheila Millet, a criminal defense lawyer. "White Death patients are victims themselves—of a terrorist attack or militia plot or whatever force created this toxic smoke. We don't know what happened and the state's already charging people with murder? It's absolutely unjust."

Doctors have also failed to arrive at definitive conclusions when assessing the medical impact of the toxic smoke. Part of the problem lies in the limited pool of survivors available to study. Most are under house arrest as part of ongoing murder and manslaughter investigations, and the state has made access difficult for doctors who wish to monitor these survivors. "We've determined that exposure to this toxic smoke can cause hallucinations, temporary blindness, paranoia, violent behavior, overproduction of adrenaline, seizures, and tachycardia," asserts Dr. Sophie Adler, director of clinical research at Keck School of Medicine at USC. "Those are just short-term effects. Long-term effects are still being studied, but many survivors report flashbacks, lung damage, and chronic constipation, among other debilitating conditions." Some researchers have suggested the body's reaction to the smoke resembles reactions to the designer drug "synthetic cathinones," otherwise known by its street name: "bath salts." But experts agree this is an anecdotal comparison. While side effects may be similar, chemical analyses have failed to make any linkage to synthetic cathinones . . .

*

Read the newspaper. That was a trick the grown-ups liked. Gabriel couldn't read all the big words in the newspaper, but they could look at the pictures and make up their own stories and the grown-ups would laugh. Gabriel grabbed the newspaper off the carpet; there was a photo of pink smoke on the front page. They ran up to the bed where Astrid and Daniel were talking. "I can read the newspaper."

"Not now, sweetie," Daniel said. Gabriel wanted to cry because they wanted to read the newspaper to their dad—no, they couldn't call Daniel *Dad* anymore, they had to say *Guardian* now. Everything was different on the Ranch. Anyway, Gabriel wanted to get all the attention before Auden came home from school, because once he did, everyone would pay attention to *him* because he was a loud boy who caused problems.

Gabriel didn't have to go to school today because they saw that scary man. Astrid closed the Commissary early, so she could watch Gabriel. Gabriel adored being home alone with the grown-ups, getting all the love and not having to share it. They had to share everything else on the Ranch. Even their house. The house was a mansion, and all the people Gabriel knew in L.A. who lived in mansions didn't have to share them with anyone. So it was weird to share this mansion with thirty-two people; some of the people were from L.A., but some of the people were Claudia's friends from Louisiana. Gabriel lived with their Care Pod in the northeast wing of the house. That's what Yunho called it—a *wing*. It had tall ceilings, and you could see all the wooden beams that held the house up like bones. Gabriel shared a room with their brother. Daniel and Mahmood were down the hall. Next to their room was where Astrid and Claudia and Yunho slept.

Thrum, thrum. The sound of the dryer going, in the distance. Mahmood was doing laundry. When he was done, he always brought out a warm towel and wrapped it around Gabriel and said, *You get an extra warm hug today.* Gabriel would giggle and scream and say the towel was too hot even though it wasn't, it was just warm enough.

"It was a threat," Astrid whispered to Daniel on the bed, while Gabriel played with the newspaper on the carpet. Blah, blah, boring grown-ups. "The locals are starting to notice us."

"I was afraid of this," Daniel replied.

"Well, we all were. But if they'd just take two seconds to get to know us, they'd see—"

"That man wasn't interested in understanding our community. *Murdering* us, maybe."

"Daniel, come on. Let's not overreact."

"I'm not. People are catching wind of what we're doing, and they don't like it."

Mahmood walked into the room, holding a hamper of laundry against his pregnant belly. "And may I remind us: The militia presence in this state is second only to Idaho. Which is why Claudia wanted to introduce a Defense Clause into the Articles of Community . . ."

"Let's not resuscitate *that* dead horse," Daniel said.

Gabriel ran up to Mahmood and tugged at his shirt. "Can I have a towel hug?"

But Mahmood ignored Gabriel, and just started folding the clothes like Gabriel wasn't even there. "Well, I think it might be wise to have that discussion again."

Gabriel flopped onto the carpet. They wanted to cry. No towel hug. No one wanted to hear them read the newspaper. So they'd read the newspaper by themself. The picture on the front page showed a cloud of pink smoke hanging above a dead body. It reminded Gabriel of the first time they saw someone die. They still had nightmares about that baby shower. Seeing Uncle Mason kill that man. After the ambulances came, Gabriel went home with their dads and Auden. Nobody left their house for a week. There were so many sirens and explosions. One day, a man came up to their door and screamed and hammered his head through the window. He bled everywhere. Stopped moving. Died. Pink smoke came inside, through the smashed glass. Everyone put on their gas masks. Their dads made them pack their suitcases. They got in the car and drove to Astrid and Claudia's house. Their dads said they'd be safe there—Astrid and Claudia had *smoke sealing and security*. Gabriel did feel safer; there weren't scary sounds at night. But it was still hard to sleep because the grown-ups stayed up late talking. Sometimes Yunho would come over, sometimes other people Gabriel didn't recognize. They always talked in serious whispers. Then one day Gabriel had to pack their suitcases again. The grown-ups said they were going to a better place. A safer place. Called Montana. Gabriel was scared to go, but also scared to stay. Everyone got into the car. They drove out of Los Angeles. Along the way, as they passed Elysian Park, right by Gabriel's favorite swing set, Gabriel saw a dead body on the road.

Now, seeing the picture of the dead body in the newspaper, it reminded Gabriel of their last day in L.A. Gabriel pointed to the picture and looked up at the grown-ups who were still talking but Gabriel wanted them to *pay attention*, so Gabriel said, "That's my friend."

Astrid frowned. "Are you making up stories about pictures in the paper again?"

"No. That's my friend, and he's dead."

"I think we've had enough newspaper for today," Mahmood said.

Gabriel frowned. "Is the pink smoke gonna get us here?"

"No, baby. You're always safe with us." Astrid kissed Gabriel's forehead.

"Everything is better here," Gabriel said. "Because 'we've got love for everyone.'" *We've got love for everyone.* The Ranch motto. Gabriel said it whenever they felt anxious. Because saying it felt good. It made everyone else feel good too. It reminded them of why the Ranch in Montana was the best place on Earth.

"Yes, we've got love for everyone," Daniel said. "I just worry that everyone doesn't have love for us."

Ding! The sound of the hallway elevator. Claudia wheeled into the room with Auden.

"You're home late," Mahmood said. "Did school go long?"

"I . . . I can't find Yunho." Claudia looked worried.

Auden sat down next to Gabriel on the rug. "I saw a scary man today," Gabriel whispered to their brother. Auden shrugged. "That's why I didn't have to go to school."

"What do you mean you can't find Yunho?" Daniel asked.

"He was supposed to help with a filmmaking project for class. But he never showed up."

"I'm sure he's fine," Daniel said, "I saw him leave the house this afternoon."

"We looked for him after school," Claudia said. "Scoured the whole Ranch. He isn't here."

Maybe Auden would play newspaper with them. Gabriel pushed the paper toward their brother. "My friend in this picture is dead." Auden just shrugged again. Why was everyone ignoring Gabriel? Gabriel got mad and ran back to their Guardians because *they just wanted someone to pay attention.* "My friend in this picture is dead," Gabriel said to the grown-ups.

"*Enough with the newspaper,*" Mahmood snapped. "Yunho is missing."

"*He's dead!*" Gabriel yelled. They had everyone's attention now.

"*Stop it.*" Mahmood snatched their arm. "That's awful to say. Yunho's *not* dead."

"But how do you know?"

"We just do," Daniel insisted. But Gabriel could tell their dad was lying.

THIRTY-FIVE

FBI COUNTERTERRORISM DIVISION——NATIONAL THREAT CENTER SECTION CLASSIFIED: **SUSPICIOUS ACTIVITY REPORT——SEIZED EMAIL**

From: Claudia Jackson <claudiajackson@gmail.com>

To: <DSS2044@gmail.com>

My dear sweet someone,

You have a name now: Fennel. You were just an idea for so long, a figment of my imagination, one that imbued me with life and purpose. Now, you're a real person. An astonishing beauty. It's fitting that the founding of our community coincided with your birth. You've been my motivation from the start, what kept me pushing even as Yunho fell apart after the baby shower. It wasn't safe in Los Angeles. We needed to get out. We had a plan; we'd been discussing it with Yunho for months. We'd drafted community bylaws, and a list of interested parties. So we propped Yunho up, then pulled the trigger.

Yunho's spirit lifted the minute he arrived in Montana. He had room to breathe, space from those horrific memories. His face when you were born, Fennel—I'd never seen a happier man! He held you in his arms like the warmth of your body was the answer to a question he'd been asking his whole life.

And now, he's vanished. People are worried he's been abducted by local militia. Murdered. I can't fathom life without him. The agony of his loss would be unbearable. And I'm terrified his death would trigger a greater collapse. None of us are on the deed to this house. Yunho never updated his will. Mason inherits everything if Yunho dies. What would happen to us then? Would Mason allow us to stay? Or would we be left without a home?

Everyone looks to me for answers, but I have none. Some days I worry this community is only as strong as I am. Yes, we're all creating this utopia, every decision has been determined through democratic consensus, and physical labor is evenly distributed. But it's the spiritual labor I take on alone. It's too much to bear. Sometimes I wonder if true anarchy is possible, if even the most egalitarian communities foist greater responsibility on one individual who becomes the unofficial leader in a setting in which there is to be no hierarchy.

Fennel—you're asleep in the Nursery as I write this. It'll be years before you read these letters. So why continue to write? Perhaps to reconnect to the idea of you, that hope you instilled within me. Because I'm overwhelmed by an amorphous dread, the witchy sense that Yunho's disappearance set something into motion, something unknowable yet imminent, something irreversible and deadly.

Yours forever,
Claudia

THIRTY-SIX

H e held his cock in his right hand, the plastic sample cup in his left. The piss would not come. He looked in the mirror; a lizard looked back. Scales of psoriasis crusted his cheeks. His eyelids drooped with saurian languor, as if he were a sunbathing Gila monster waiting on a rock for warmth to wake its gelid veins. Yes, his blood was sorbet. He needed to figure out the fucking thermostat in his rental. The HVAC turned into a yeti at night, issuing thunderous polar burps that igloofied his bedroom and made sleep an impossible task. Insomnia rendered reality evanescent. Increasingly, Mason felt as if he were trapped in some virtual game-scape specifically designed to torture gay men who'd murdered billionaires. Rest came in half hour snatches between Ankl alarms. And that was only if he could trick his body into relaxation—a rare occurrence. Over the past six months, his exhaustion had become an all-consuming deadness that intensified with every excruciating breath he sucked into his damaged lungs. *Why can't I piss?* He picked up the glass of water that had been placed on the sink as extra fuel for the drug test. His charges were unrelated to any drug crime, yet the state wouldn't rest until his body was violated in every legal way possible. He brought the glass to his lips, but as he did, he felt it: a window for sleep. A miracle. He let the glass slip from his hand. Shatter on the ground.

Everything went black.

He woke up on the floor. His parole officer loomed above. His mother crouched next to him, a familiar expression on her face, one that broadcasted an intense need for comfort because nothing brought her greater pain than her son's distress. Yet paradoxically, the only person who could quell this pain was her son, the person in need of comfort himself. "Mason—are you all right?"

"I'm . . . just . . . tired."

"Let's get you a cold brew, honey," she said.

"*I want to fucking sleep, Mom,*" Mason snapped. "That's *all* I want. All I *have* wanted for the past five months. So why on Earth would you think it's a good idea to offer me a *cold brew*?"

Samantha burst into sobs, her classic deflection. "Because . . . you love . . . Starbucks."

*

"Sweetie, we need to talk about our living arrangement." Samantha eyed her son warily. Mason stared down at his cold brew. They sat on the couch that came with the rental, some West Elm artifact with fossils of ancient ass-prints depressed into its tattered cushions. "While I'm happy to help with your medical recovery and house arrest and be on call twenty-four-seven, I don't think it's healthy for us to live together. I need my own home."

"I know, Mom."

"When you sold my house, a part of me died." Her lifelong parade of parental martyrdom had led to this one great sacrifice: the moment she'd relinquished her home to—once again, as she'd done throughout Mason's fatherless childhood—care for her son when no one else would. Yunho, Daniel, Mahmood, Claudia, Astrid—they had all vanished, as if they'd been denizens of a dream that dissipated when Mason woke from his brief coma in the wake of White Death.

Familial guilt left Mason weepy. "I'm . . . I'm sorry, Mom. I needed the money. Renata isn't cheap. And Yunho just pulled the rug out from under me." Their Los Feliz home had disappeared. Poof. Presto. Abraca-fucking-dabra. A shitty magic trick Yunho had pulled while Mason was on life support, sucking oxygen from a mask, fighting for survival in his hospital bed. A police officer his only companion.

Yunho hadn't so much as texted to let Mason know he sold their house, choosing instead to maintain the impenetrable rampart of silence he'd erected in the aftermath of the baby shower. Mason found out through *Dirt*—the celebrity real estate gossip site—during his daily Google search for news of Yunho's whereabouts. Yunho had sold the house to the only bidder, a developer buying up luxury real estate for bargain prices to convert the properties into "apocalypse rentals"—high-security homes where the world's wealthiest individuals could safely stay if business forced them to visit the newly dangerous Los Angeles. Technically, as the article pointed out with dishy malice, Yunho could do whatever he liked with the property, as the deed was in his name alone. The money from the sale was enough to pay off the federal lien on the home imposed by the Anti-American Speech Committee, and even make a small profit.

Yunho had also drained their joint bank accounts and liquidated their investment portfolios. Thankfully, Mason still had his own account with the money left over from Patrick's latest sculpture purchase. (Why, oh why, did he kill the last person on Earth interested in buying his art?) But he needed to refill the coffers—fast. Selling his mother's home had been the only way. He'd suffered a $1 million loss—it sold for a pathetic $150,000. Still, Mason was lucky it sold at all. White Death brought an astonishing crash in the Los Angeles housing market. People were fleeing in record numbers; anyone rich enough to buy a home didn't want to live in L.A. and those who had no choice but to stay—the unhoused, the impoverished—couldn't afford these homes even at their apocalyptic price points. In the wealth gap lay a sea of empty houses. *When do buildings officially become ruins?* It was a question Mason often considered when staring out his window at the vacant apartment complex across the street, its abandoned parking lot now home to a churlish horde of pregnant raccoons who acted, rightfully, as if they owned the place.

"Mason, I'm sensitive to your money problems. But I've become accustomed to a certain lifestyle. And I deserve to maintain that lifestyle, especially when I'm doing *so* much for you—"

"I can't afford to buy you another house—"

"But you *can* afford to at least *rent* me a space where I can pretend to have some semblance of an identity outside of caring for my son."

"Fine, Mom." The only answer that would end this hell. "We'll figure it out."

A bell pealed in his brain. Mason winced—a reflex. But it wasn't the Ankl system. Siri's dulcet voice echoed in his skull: *Notification from Cyclops VR. VexTheDestroyer says: "Hey, slug. Get your ass into my dungeon. You've been bad."* A surge of endorphins swamped his brain, an analgesic to the painful sight of his mother scrubbing last night's lasagna from her helpless son's baking dish. Yes, he was trapped, doomed to repeat the same day, with its alarm bells and parole officers and exhaustion and heartbreak and the suffocating love of Samantha Daunt. But there was a way out. A world beyond reality.

I have been bad, Mason replied. *I'm coming to receive my punishment, sir.*

*

But once in the dungeon—under the familiar red bulb, tied to that chair, his cheek aching from the aftershock of Vex's cockslap, his ears ringing from epithets screamed by his lupine master, his throat sore from moaning, *Yes, I killed a man, yes, I deserve death*—something broke inside Mason. "*Penguin!*" he screamed. "*Penguin!*"

"Penguin?" Vex blinked in surprise; his eyelids shuttered like the leaves of a Venus flytrap.

"Penguin." Mason had never utilized their safe word before. It felt cathartic to conjure security with just two syllables; the ease of it, when so much of Mason's life was a daily battle to buttress the jokers that held his house of cards in place. He could relax here in his dungeon master's arms, a virtual reality away from the banal agonies of real life. "Please, I'm . . . not doing well. I just need someone to talk to."

"Okay." Kindness crept into Vex's tone. "What do you want to talk about?"

Loneliness. That's what Mason wanted to talk about. The unbearable desolation that occurs when everyone you love evaporates overnight. The voracious grief that eats you from the inside like a parasitic alien hungry for your heart—the best bag of meat. But before Mason could open his mouth, the Ankl alarm wailed in his mind. *"I just want my husband back!"* Mason screamed over the siren only he could hear. *"Where is my fucking husband?"*

THIRTY-SEVEN

Yunho was dead.

Why else would he leave all the people he loved? He wouldn't. Unless he was dead. Gabriel cried all night in their bed, the bottom bunk. Auden got the top bunk because he was older. Auden pretended he didn't hear Gabriel crying, so they cried louder and kicked the underneath part of Auden's mattress. Auden told them to *shut up*, but Gabriel couldn't stop crying. *Everyone should cry!* Gabriel screamed at their brother. *Yunho is dead!* And then Daniel came in and told Gabriel to *calm down*, because *Yunho isn't dead, the whole community is going to search for him tomorrow, and we're going to find him. But first we need to rest up, my crazy angel.* Daniel rubbed Gabriel's back with his big warm hand until they fell asleep.

Then it was morning. Mahmood said he'd stay at home with Gabriel while everyone else went out to look for Yunho. *You're too young to go searching for him, darling.* But Gabriel didn't want to be left out. If anyone could find Yunho it was Gabriel because they played hide-and-seek all the time and Gabriel knew where Yunho liked to hide in the woods. Also, Gabriel loved Yunho more than anything, and if you loved someone enough you could always find them.

"I wanna go with the grown-ups to look." Gabriel stomped their feet.

"But you're not a grown-up."

"*I wanna look, I wanna look!*"

"We're not doing anything except giving you a time-out if you start screaming like that."

"Please, please, please!"

"Just stop, Gabriel!" Mahmood hit the frame of the bunk bed. Gabriel stopped. Waited. Mahmood looked like he might fall asleep right there. He sighed. "We can look for Yunho."

"Yes, yes, yes!"

"But no running into the woods," Mahmood warned. "You're not getting lost out there."

*

People poured out of the house. It was barely dawn. The clouds were black and purple, big bruises in the sky. Gabriel looked back toward their home. It was lit up, glowing in the dark, as big as a castle. The walls were made of big stones stacked on top of each other. The roof had lots of sharp peaks. Chimneys popped up through the shingles. Then, Gabriel's favorite part: a giant princess tower. Where Gabriel looked for dragons.

But today they were looking for Yunho.

They walked in one big pack down the dirt road. All six Care Pods. Thirty-two people. Gabriel was scared. Everybody was quiet. They kicked up clouds of dust. Gabriel's white sneakers turned brown. *Crunch, crunch.* Footsteps on dirt. The sound of everyone joining together. *We've got love for everyone*, Gabriel thought. *And that love will help us find Yunho.*

Gabriel felt braver with every step. The path was lined with brown grass and scraggly shrubs. Flat land stretched out all around them. They passed the Community School, a big boxy trailer on stilts. They passed the Greenhouse; lush branches pressed against the fogged glass. They passed the farm, where everybody grew crops to sell in the Commissary. A sprinkler sprayed water over dirt beds. They passed the chicken coop and the barn where the baby cows slept. They passed the Infirmary. It was in a tent-thing called a *yurt*. That's the funny word Yunho used. *The yurt is temporary until we get enough money to build a permanent doctor's office*, Yunho had explained to Gabriel. *But why do we have to build a doctor's office?* Gabriel asked. *So we can give free healthcare to everyone on the Ranch*, Yunho said. *But what about people from the Outside?* Gabriel had asked. *They can also come to us for free medical care*, Yunho replied. *Because everyone deserves to be healthy, no matter who they are.*

Gabriel and Mahmood came to the end of the path where the flatlands turned into forest. The group stopped. Daniel started yelling orders. Everyone needed to pair up and stay with their search partners. Comb the woods. They needed to be careful. They didn't know what they would find.

"This is where we stop, sweetie." Mahmood crouched and looked Gabriel in the eyes. "I said no woods, remember?" Gabriel didn't respond. They looked into the thick tangle of trees. So dark it was almost night inside.

"Let's go back." Mahmood stretched out his hand.

Gabriel ran into the forest.

*

"Gabriel, come back here right now!"

But Gabriel couldn't stop. Not until they found Yunho. They sprinted deeper into the woods. It got darker, colder. The air filled with mosquitoes. The ground turned to mud. Their legs burned. Their heart pumped. They pushed harder. *"Yunho!"* Gabriel yelled. *"Yunho!"*

"Gabriel, stop!" Something snapped. Mahmood screamed. *"Fuck! My leg . . ."*

Gabriel looked to see if Mahmood was okay, but the treetops blocked the light. He was a dark shape on the ground, rocking back and forth. Moaning. But Gabriel couldn't turn back. They were so close; they just knew it. They charged forward, marching through a stream.

Suddenly, they stopped.

The smell was horrible. Like rotten meat. Gabriel felt sick, scared. They looked back but couldn't remember which way they came. They listened but couldn't hear Mahmood's voice. Then came the flies—a buzzing cloud that mixed with the mosquitoes. Gabriel inhaled a mouthful of small bodies. The bugs crunched between their teeth. They vomited onto the ground.

Which is when they saw it.

A pink-white ribbon. Gabriel crouched to get a better look. No, it wasn't a ribbon. It was an intestine. Chef Alvaro had taught Gabriel about intestines when he made *tripas tacos* one time. *We eat every part of an animal,* he'd told Gabriel. *Even the guts.* The intestine stretched on for yards. Gabriel followed it, their hand clamped over their mouth and nose. Fear bubbled in their stomach. Then, in the distance, in the dark, they spotted something huge lying on the forest floor. A shadowy lump. Something dead. Rotten.

A body.

Gabriel wanted to turn back. But it was too late. They needed to know. A breeze shook the branches above. Sunlight sliced through, just long enough for Gabriel to see a face.

THIRTY-EIGHT

Mason stood on the deck of the Red Inn; his fog of exhaustion dimmed the ocean view, or maybe he just needed to recalibrate his color settings. A CGI shimmer rippled across the water's programmed crests. An artificial zephyr lapped at his skin, eliciting rare pleasure; it had been worth fifty dollars per liter for canned sea breeze from the Cyclops VR Authentic Experience Store. The haze of his fatigue thickened; his mind couldn't bear the cognitive dissonance required to hold space for both virtual and actual reality. Context collapsed. Los Angeles was erased from his mind, and he was really, truly, standing on the deck of his favorite restaurant in Provincetown, where he and Yunho had shared so many twilight dinners.

He'd escaped house arrest. It had been worth every devastating dollar he'd spent (twenty-five thousand, to be exact) to install a VR room in his own home, complete with the latest Sensory Enhancement technology. He'd even splurged on a Food & Drink Printer, should he choose to order a meal or cocktail during his virtual travels.

A waiter approached. "Can I get you anything, sir?"

"Negroni, please," Mason replied. Seconds later, he held the cocktail in his hand. He took a long sip and looked out over the water. Drowsy nostalgia transported him to the dream of his past. The Red Inn was where Yunho had proposed to Mason; after years of debating whether they should get married, whether they would capitulate to the heteronormative ritual of romantic ownership designed to render their union legible by the state and merge their assets, sentimentality got the best of Yunho. That night, on the deck of the Red Inn, with the moonlit ocean undulating in the distance, Yunho had pulled out a ring box and Mason's heart leapt and all the cultural conditioning he'd absorbed over the years overpowered any queer ideological posturing. For a moment, the box and the ring and Yunho's nervous smile filled him with more happiness than he could bear, and so when Yunho finally asked, *Will you marry me even though we both have legitimate reservations about the institution?* Mason laughed, then cried, then said, *Yes, yes, yes.*

"Will another guest be joining you, sir?" the waiter asked.

"Yes, he should be here soon." Mason had asked Vex to meet him in the virtual facsimile of Provincetown, part of Cyclops VR's "Lost Coast" Collection. These digital landscapes were re-creations of seaside locales that had been destroyed by flooding: Provincetown, Miami, Maui, et al. Each was frozen in perfect detail, down to specific businesses, landmarks, and natural wonders. Now that they'd abandoned sadomasochistic rituals, Mason longed for a different setting for his encounters with Vex. Mason's actual reality had turned into an excruciatingly mundane and gradual apocalypse, so the dystopian thrills of *The Road* ceased to hold their appeal. Mason wanted an escape.

Vex appeared on the dock. His hirsute and muscular torso had been stuffed into a tight blue button-down. Tan khakis hugged his supernaturally thick ass with breathtaking force. His tentative smile apologized for the murderous incisors within. The business-wolf attire was almost comic, yet Mason knew better than to laugh. Vex had donned the conservative getup to avoid scornful stares from vanilla neoliberal fags with anticanisexual prejudices. As in its pre-climate-disaster form, the virtual Provincetown was primarily a destination for wealthy white gay centrists.

Vex pulled up two deck chairs. They sat. Mason's heart was a hummingbird. Where to start? Most of their previous conversations had concerned the ways in which Vex planned to destroy Mason's worthless slug life. Small talk felt awkward. "Hi," Vex said.

"What's up, bud?" Mason affected a masculine and porny tone, which he immediately regretted. Thankfully, the server appeared before Mason embarrassed himself further.

"Anything to drink for you?" The waiter looked around the deck, anxiously assessing if the presence of a wolf-human hybrid had irked any patrons.

"No thanks." Vex shrunk under the waiter's rude stare. The waiter sashayed off. Vex turned to Mason mischievously. "Besides, I'm already a little tipsy."

"Well, I'd better catch up then." Mason chugged his drink, and some magical combination of Adderall, alcohol, and adrenaline awakened his body for a brief, exhilarating moment. Vex was here. Not as a dom, but as a friend. Mason's only friend. But he was *paying* Vex to be his friend. Did money make this friendship false? Mason's exhausted mind once again failed to hold two conflicting ideas. The truth collapsed into something easier to believe: Vex *was* Mason's friend. Maybe they'd become boyfriends. Not that anyone could replace Yunho, the man whose absence burned into him like a branding iron that never lifted.

"You come here often?" Vex asked.

"My husband proposed to me here." Emotion bubbled in Mason's throat. "I miss him."

Vex was silent. His eyes rolled back. His neck bobbed. His jaw went slack. Vex was more than tipsy, he was blackout drunk. Regret and anger surged within Mason; he was paying Vex an exorbitant rate when he should've put that money toward his defense. *This is fucking pathetic,* Mason thought. *All I wanted was the weakest simulacra of emotional connection and this sex worker shows up wasted?*

"I said"—Mason slapped Vex's arm to wake him—"that I miss my husband."

To Mason's surprise, Vex burst into tears. "I . . . I'm sorry."

Guilt constricted Mason's gut. It was not this poor sex worker's fault that Mason's life was in shambles. "Please, don't cry." Mason rubbed his back. "I shouldn't have snapped."

But Vex was inconsolable, on a wasted crying jag that logic could not penetrate. "I'm . . . so . . . sorry." Vex spat the words between sobs. "Mason . . ."

"Yes?"

"Mason . . . it's me." Vex's avatar flickered. He became a silhouette of gray static.

Then, suddenly: Yunho appeared in his place.

"Stop fucking with me." Mason's voice trembled with terror. "Who the fuck are you?"

"It's Yunho."

"Don't fuck with me."

"I'm . . . I'm not, I swear."

"*I said, don't fucking fuck with me!*" Mason screamed and slapped the power button on his VR mask. His field of vision went black. "*Fuck.*" He caught his breath in the darkness.

THIRTY-NINE

S ally's eyes. Gabriel kept remembering Sally's eyes. Those big dark circles. Like black grapes. Flies had landed on them. But Sally didn't blink. Her lids were frozen open. Dead. Like the rest of her. Her body had been cut open; you could see her purple heart, her ribs, her intestines, those pink ribbons that spilled from her guts and created the trail Gabriel had followed through the woods on the morning they went searching for Yunho but found Sally instead. Murdered. The grown-ups made Gabriel promise they wouldn't tell the other children. *We don't want to scare any of your friends*, Mahmood had said. That made Gabriel angry. Someone had killed Gabriel's favorite cow. Why was it a secret?

*

"Does anyone know who this is?" Claudia sat behind her desk, holding a photo of an ugly old white man. Behind her was a chalkboard that said: U.S. HISTORY. The classroom was one long white rectangle with a gray carpet floor and a bunch of desks lined up in neat rows. "Ronald Reagan!" Auden shouted.

"And who was Ronald Reagan?"

"A murderer!"

"That's right, Auden. What else?"

"A president?" Sophie spoke up. Gabriel liked her. She was seven. Claudia said that soon the kids would be divided into grades like at their old school, but right now they were mixing the ages because their community was still small, and they needed more "resources" to make the school bigger. But Gabriel liked being with older kids. And Gabriel liked Sophie. Even if Sophie didn't know the truth. Didn't know that someone killed Sally.

"That's right, Sophie. And who did President Reagan murder?"

"People with AIDS and HIV."

"And how did he murder them?"

"He didn't help them get better."

"Correct. For years, he refused to acknowledge a public health crisis that was killing a whole generation of queer and gender nonconforming people. The fact that AIDS remains a global epidemic to this day can be traced back to the murderous neglect of Ronald Reagan."

"If Ronald Reagan was a murderer, why didn't he get put in jail?" Sophie asked.

"That's a great question. Does anyone have an idea?"

"Because he was rich?" Auden said. "And powerful?"

"And white," Felix said. Felix was six. They were in a Care Pod with Grey and two other grown-ups that used to be in a band with Claudia back in Louisiana.

"Those are all right answers. It's also because the government doesn't criminalize all harm. It's legal to murder people through policy, for politicians to introduce legislation they *know* will result in death. Meanwhile, the prison industrial complex creates an illusion of 'justice,' while in reality offering only state-sanctioned violence against Black and brown people, the poor, the disabled, women, and queer and trans people."

"Is this why we're abolitionists?"

"Yes, Sophie. Because we know prisons and policing don't keep us safe. Safety comes from creating a society where *all* people have the resources they need to survive. Everyone deserves housing, food, education, mental health resources, and a supportive community. That's what we offer on the Ranch. And this is where our abolitionist agenda intersects with anarchism. It's our goal to create a self-governing community that exists in revolutionary opposition to the U.S. State. To us, revolution doesn't mean a violent takeover of existing power structures only to replace them with equally oppressive hierarchies. Our revolution comes through defection from our authoritarian nation—and creating our own stateless utopia outside of it. A community freed from capitalism and engaged in mutual aid through consensus-based decision-making. A community ruled by love, not terror. Because we've got what?"

"*We've got love for everyone,*" the class responded in unison. Except for Gabriel. They didn't see the point of school. Someone had killed Sally. How could they pretend anything else mattered? After Gabriel found her body, they went to see Dr. Cove. Gabriel didn't understand why they had to go to the Infirmary if they weren't sick, but Mahmood explained that Dr. Cove was a doctor for your feelings. So Gabriel talked about how they felt: sad and scared. It helped a little. But Gabriel also wanted to talk about Sally now. In class.

Claudia frowned. "Gabriel, is everything okay?"

"No. It's not. Because someone killed Sally."

"Gabriel, I thought we said we weren't gonna talk about Sally in school."

"*Well, I want to!*"

"Someone killed Sally?" Sophie's lip shook. Her eyes watered.

"*Yes! And I bet they killed Yunho too!*"

"*That's enough, Gabriel!*" Claudia shouted. Then silence. The kids looked down at their desks. Sophie started crying. This was proof: Claudia was scared too. Why else would she scream like that? "I'm sorry, I didn't mean to yell—"

A knock on the door. Astrid poked her head in. "Claudia—can I talk to you?"

"Can it wait?"

"It can't," Astrid said. Claudia wheeled into the hallway and closed the door.

Minutes later, class was dismissed.

*

Astrid brought them to lunch even though it was too early. The class filed into the Main Hall, Gabriel's favorite room. It was beautiful, a big wooden circle. Around the edges, there were staircases that led to different wings of the house. A stone fireplace stretched all the way up to the ceiling. Three long tables stood in the center of the space. The sound of chairs scraping the floor echoed across the hall as the kids took their seats. Astrid smiled as she watched Gabriel settle. But her smile seemed fake. "What's wrong?" Gabriel asked.

"Nothing's wrong. The grown-ups just need to talk about something important. And now you get early lunch! Chef Alvaro is cooking up something yummy. Just sit tight, okay?"

Astrid left. Gabriel knew she was hiding something. Something bad. Gabriel stared down at the table. If you looked closely, you could see dark-brown squiggles inside the wood. Daniel called the squiggles "knots" but to Gabriel they looked like drawings. Sometimes Gabriel saw pictures in the squiggles and made up stories about them. Just like they made up stories about photos in the newspaper. Gabriel liked making up stories when they felt confused or upset. Telling stories gave them a sense of control. They could create a whole world and know all the answers about everything that happened inside it.

Gabriel poked Sophie and pointed to a squiggle on the table. "Do you see this?"

"It's just wood." Sophie wasn't impressed.

"No, look inside the wood."

"It's, like, a squiggly line."

"No, it's not." Gabriel pointed again. "It's a picture of a dragon."

Sophie's eyes got big. "Oh, it *is* a dragon."

"Dragons are my favorite animal. I loved them even when I was little."

"But dragons are mean."

"No, they're not. They're the nicest animal in the world and people just get scared of them because dragons breathe fire. So people make up scary lies about dragons and attack them. The dragons only fight back because they're scared. But a dragon would never hurt anyone unless that person hurt them first."

"Wow, I didn't know that."

A woman sat down across from them. A grown-up. She looked tired. She had on a dress with pretty flowers. But it had holes in it. "Your dress has holes in it," Gabriel said to her.

The woman jumped a little in her seat. Then she laughed. "I guess it does."

"Be nice to her," Sophie whispered. "She's from the Outside." The grown-ups said they wanted to make friends with people from the Outside even though most people on the Outside didn't want to be friends with them. But this woman seemed nice.

A kid ran up to the woman and climbed into her lap. "This is Ricky," the woman said. "He's a little shy." Ricky buried his head into the woman's chest, then peeked his eyes out.

"I'm Gabriel and this is Sophie," Gabriel announced. "Do you wanna be friends?"

"Okay," Ricky whispered.

"We've got love for everyone." Gabriel felt happy because they loved making new friends. The Ranch welcomed anyone from the Outside to join them for any meal in the Main Hall, or in the Infirmary for free health-care, or at school if they didn't have one of their own. Not a lot of Outsiders were interested in coming to the Ranch, though. That's why, one time, Gabriel helped Astrid hang signs in the Outside town that told people about how the Ranch would feed anyone for free. While they were hanging the signs, Astrid told Gabriel about the Black Panthers and how they had a free breakfast program for kids in their neighborhoods because no kid should be hungry, and the Black Panthers knew it was important for their communities to take care of each other because the government started a racist war against Black people and tried to kill them and put them in prisons. Gabriel thought it was wrong that the government tried to starve and murder people. That's why Gabriel was happy their community gave people free meals. "Do you know about the Black Panthers, Ricky?" Gabriel asked.

"Ricky's not old enough for that movie," the woman said. The woman didn't understand Gabriel. Sometimes when Gabriel talked with people from the Outside, it felt like they were speaking a different language. "And I don't think you are either."

Suddenly, Gabriel heard something. Shouting. Coming from outside.

"What's that?" The woman looked scared.

"I don't know." Gabriel was also scared. "But Astrid says that nothing bad happened."

"What do you mean 'nothing bad happened'?" The woman stood. Ricky started crying.

A thought turned Gabriel's skin to goosebumps. "Did you kill Sally?"

"What?" The woman's face turned pale. "Someone here got killed?"

"Sally was my friend and—"

"*We're leaving.*" The woman dragged Ricky across the room like a doll and pushed him out the door. She didn't close it behind her.

"*I can't fucking take this anymore, Astrid!*" A voice from outside. Screaming.

Then, Yunho walked in.

"*Yunho!*" Gabriel rushed to hug him and kiss him and ask him why he was gone for so long. But then Gabriel stopped and ran back to their seat. Scared. Yunho was walking funny. Zigzags. His face was red. He looked sick. He tripped and fell onto the floor.

Astrid ran inside. Bent over him. "Yunho, *please.* Let's go to your room—"

"Don't-fucking-tell-*me*-where-to-go." Yunho's words sounded jammed together. "*I own all of this.*" Yunho tried to stand up, but he fell again, and Astrid tried to help. "*Get off me!*" He kicked Astrid. She tripped backward and hit her head against the wall. She fell to the ground, landed on her wrist, and screamed.

"Leave . . . me . . . alone." Yunho's eyelids drooped. He fell asleep on the ground.

Gabriel was scared to look at Yunho or Astrid. So Gabriel looked down at the table. At the knot in the wood. The squiggle. The dragon. The dragon was real. It would protect them. It would come to life. It would untangle itself from the knot, lift itself from the table, and let Gabriel hop on its beautiful back. Gabriel would touch its shiny blue scales. Gabriel would wrap their arms around the dragon's thick, warm neck. The dragon would fly them up to the sky and they would get lost in the clouds. They wouldn't come back down until everyone loved each other again.

FORTY

TRANSCRIPT: COMMUNITY ACCOUNTABILITY CIRCLE

CLAUDIA: I'd like to open this accountability circle with a reminder of our intentions today. Our small bubble here operates outside of society, conducting an ever-evolving experiment in abolition and anarchism. But even as we create a peaceful community, it's inevitable that harmful behavior will still occur. In these moments, we're truly tested. As abolitionists, we refuse to engage the criminal "justice" system to address harm within our community. No matter how angry we may be, we can't surrender to the horrors of the prison industrial complex. This is why we've created our own accountability process, which we'll be using for the first time today.

So, let's begin. Yunho—you disappeared for seven days. No one knew where you were, or if you were safe. Our community loves you and we were very concerned. Your Care Pod was particularly anxious during your absence; the children in your care were confused and agitated.

Yesterday, you returned. You had relapsed. You were blackout drunk. Belligerent. Astrid and I confronted you. We asked you to remove yourself from shared community spaces, because you were a danger to yourself and others. We asked you to go to your room and sleep. We said we'd address this when you were sober. You became irate. You started screaming. The encounter spilled into the Main Hall. You fell onto the floor. Astrid attempted to help you up. You kicked her. She stumbled backward. She hit her head and got a gash on her temple. She fell on her wrist—it fractured. You passed out on the floor and had to be physically removed by Daniel and Mahmood. You were taken to bed, where you were monitored by Daniel to ensure you didn't wake up and harm another community member or yourself.

Earlier this morning, we held a separate healing circle with Astrid to hear how this incident of assault affected her. Because he is the perpetrator of this harm, Yunho was not present. Together, we created a path toward accountability that we'll share with Yunho. But first, let's hear from Astrid.

ASTRID: Thank you. First, I wanna say that . . . I . . . [*A pause. Astrid starts crying.*]

DANIEL: It's okay. [*Daniel puts his arm around Astrid.*]

ASTRID: . . . I love you, Yunho. Which is why this is so hard. Because we share so much history. I've carried a child for you. We *founded* this community together when our lives in Los Angeles fell apart. I trusted you deeply. I never once doubted our love. Until yesterday.

Yes, I have a broken wrist and a cut on my forehead. That's okay—my injuries will heal. But I don't know if I'll ever heal from the breach of trust that occurred when you became violent. Someone I viewed as a source of safety became a source of harm. I don't think you intended to hurt me. I think you just wanted an outlet for all the hurt you felt inside yourself.

But I need to know what that hurt is. I need to understand the root of your behavior. And I need to know that you understand it too, so you can address the underlying issues here. This can't happen again. Because if it does, that's the end of our relationship.

Tell us what happened during the last week. Tell us what's happening inside you. Because even if I struggle to forgive you—and I may struggle for a while—I want to at least understand.

YUNHO: Thank you, Astrid. First, I want to apologize to you, to Claudia, to the entire community. I know it'll take hard work to repair all my relationships. I've recommitted to sobriety. I've returned to therapy. I'm ready to do whatever it takes to earn back your trust.

Astrid—you want to know what happened the week I was gone. All I can say is that while that lost week is significant, there's also immense pain I've struggled with for over five months, ever since I saw Mason murder a man with his bare hands. When I tried to stop it, Mason attacked me too. He almost killed me.

I couldn't—and I still can't—even *begin* to fathom that. I haven't been able to sleep. I keep seeing flashes of the baby shower. Of Mason's hands deep inside a corpse. What do you do when you realize the man you love has the capacity to kill another human? I don't think I'll ever heal from that day. The life I'd spent decades building instantly fell apart. Now I have trouble believing anything will last. I love this community we've created. But in my darkest moments, I believe everything in my life is doomed to collapse.

One week ago, I decided to drink again. I wanted to speed the implosion I viewed as inevitable. I wish I could point to some triggering moment that caused me to relapse, a simple explanation. But there wasn't. The dread that had been building inside me finally became intolerable.

So I booked a hotel room. Some shitty Best Western. I raided the minibar. Slammed back tiny bottles of vodka and bourbon and gin. I wanted to burn it all down. When I ran out of alcohol, I went to the hotel bar. I ordered drink after drink until the bartender gave me a dirty look and it was time to go. I went back to my room. And I hunted Mason down in virtual reality.

CLAUDIA: You . . . you contacted Mason?

YUNHO: I was so lonely. I just wanted to live our old life again. I wanted to feel that love. But he wanted nothing to do with me. He thought I was just a troll playing a cruel trick with a fake avatar. He blocked me. I wanted to die.

I got on Grindr. To scratch an old itch, that compulsion to get wasted and fuck anonymous guys until I couldn't remember my name or their names or who or where I was. Behavior I thought I'd abandoned forever resurfaced. And there I was, feeling twenty-four again, like I'd learned nothing, like I'd never matured or healed. I felt like a failure. The relapse brought this awful shame. And the shame made me drink more. It was a spiral I couldn't stop.

It went on for five days. I just drank and fucked random guys in my hotel room. I was constantly blacking out. There are stretches of time I'll never be able to account for.

But I'll never forget what happened on the sixth day.

A guy—white, thin, blond, sixteen, maybe seventeen— showed up at my door. I was shocked by his age. I didn't remember messaging with him on Grindr. But I didn't remember a lot of things. So I welcomed him in. Checked my phone. Sure enough, there were messages between us. He'd said he was twenty-two.

We didn't hook up. I accused him of lying about his age. He started crying. I felt bad. I told him he didn't have to leave; we could just talk. I asked him if this was his first time using Grindr. He said it was one of the first times. He rarely hooked up with guys because his family knew he was gay and hated him for it. Abused him. "My only friends are books," he said and laughed through his tears, and there was this brilliant sadness in his eyes, like he resented his own intelligence for illuminating the vile nature of his family.

I told him it would be okay. I held him as he wept in my arms. I felt sudden clarity. I needed to return to our community, where I was loved. Here was a boy breaking down in my arms because he lacked the type of love I had in abundance. I wanted to share that love. I wanted to bring this boy home with me. So I started telling him about the Ranch. That anyone was welcome here, especially queer people like himself. I said he could live with us. He said that sounded good. But he had to think about it. I walked the boy out of the hotel. Took the elevator with him. Walked him through the lobby. I realized I didn't know his name. So, I asked him.

"Tuck," he said.

"We're going to help you, Tuck," I promised. "Think about joining us on the Ranch."

"I will," he said. Then he left. I watched him walk through the doors and something about the way he walked—a sort of fake masculine strut—broke my heart. A boy performing manhood to survive the hate of people who were supposed to love him. His sad march into the parking lot lit a fire in me. I would help this boy. I would heal this boy.

But then I saw the hotel bar.

I would help this boy. I would heal this boy. But first I would have a drink. I could do it because I was gonna be sober again in the morning. Why not have one last blowout? I went up to the bar. The bartender knew me by now and eyed me warily but still gave me a gin and tonic. And another. And another. After two hours, I was wasted. Done. I asked for the check.

And then, someone grabbed my neck and slammed my head against the bar.

Something cold and metallic pressed against my back. A gun. A man whispered in my ear, told me he was making a militia arrest. He was a member of the local Anti-OL chapter. He said they killed one of our cows to send our community a message but apparently I didn't get it. He said I was a sexual predator, and that his son wanted to join my gay sex cult. He told me that would happen over *my* dead body.

The bartender polished glasses. Pretended not to see. No one wants trouble with a militia.

The man brought me out to his truck. He kept the gun at my back. Cuffed me. Threw me in the cargo bed. There was another man in the truck. He also had a gun. They drove me into the wilderness. The streetlights stopped. The road turned to dirt. The only illumination came from the truck's headlights. We pulled up to an old ranch house.

They brought me around the back. To a basement hatch. One of them pushed me down concrete steps. The basement was unfinished, with low ceilings and a dirt floor. There was a single light bulb suspended over a chair sinking into dark-red mud.

Standing behind the chair: Tuck. Tears and snot streamed down his face.

Tuck's father told his son not to cry, not to act like a fucking faggot. He said he was going to teach his son to be a real man. He demanded Tuck tie me up. The men aimed their guns at me and told me to sit. I followed orders. Tuck swallowed his sobs as he bound me to the chair.

Tuck's father demanded that I tell the "truth," and admit that our "sex cult" was working with Octo-Liberals in the U.S. government as a part of a conspiracy to abduct and molest our nation's children. And I admitted to all of it. Because Tuck held a gun to my head.

Then, the men went upstairs to watch a UFC fight. They told Tuck to monitor the hostage—another lesson. They needed to keep me alive because they wanted to bring me to the Anti-OL headquarters where the rest of the militia could continue their questioning.

Tuck agreed to watch me. The men left. We listened. Their footsteps shook the ceiling. We heard laughter. The blare of the television. I looked at Tuck. He aimed his gun at me. He had tears in his eyes. I said, "Tuck, you can't keep me here." And Tuck burst into sobs and said if he let me go, he was afraid his father would kill him. I told him that we could both run. That I would take him to safety. All he had to do was untie me.

He untied me. But instead of running, he collapsed on the ground and moaned. I grabbed his elbow and told him that I refused to let him stay here and risk his life for me. We were both getting out alive. He stood. A UFC cheer rattled the floorboards above us. We looked at each other. And ran.

We ran out of the basement and into a pitch-black field. He grabbed my arm and pulled me forward. He knew the way to the road, he said. We needed to get to the road.

A gunshot rang out. A floodlight blasted the field. There was nowhere to hide. We ran through the harsh glare. I saw a patch of trees at the edge of the field. A chain-link fence. Beyond it, I could make out snatches of road.

Another gunshot.

Tuck went down. I tried to help him up, tried to wrestle him into my arms.

I looked back. The two men charged toward us, guns in hand. "Run!" he screamed. "There's a hole in the fence!" I bolted. More shots. I'd almost reached the chain-link. I spotted the hole and squeezed through. Steel shredded my back. Then, I was in the forest. I found a hollow tree. It was charred. Fire had gutted its insides. I crawled inside the empty trunk. Burrowed in the dirt. Buried myself alive. Hid and waited for the gunshots to subside. For the shouts to cease.

I stayed awake all night. In the trunk of the tree.

At dawn, I wandered to the road. Walked back to town. Found the nearest bar. A shitty dive with a bartender who didn't blink twice when I walked in with my dirt-caked face and asked for a gin and tonic. "You got cash?" was all she asked. And I drank. And drank. And tried to forget. But there was no forgetting. I felt a desperate longing for this community. My home. I drank more. I blacked out. The next thing I remember was waking up on the floor of the Main Hall and seeing Astrid on the ground, holding her wrist. I'm . . . so sorry . . . [*Yunho weeps.*]

ASTRID: I . . . this is . . . a lot to process. This is the first we're hearing this story and—

CLAUDIA: Honestly, Yunho? Your actions have put us in *immense fucking danger.* I can't ev—

[*Nurse Grey runs into the room.*]

NURSE GREY: Everyone stop! We have an emergency—

[*End of transcript.*]

*

Gabriel had cried when Daniel said they couldn't go to the Community meeting. Gabriel didn't like going to the Nursery. They hated all the blocks and toys and kid stuff, hated being treated like a baby. Gabriel was almost five. Gabriel wanted to be with the grown-ups. With Yunho. It seemed like some people didn't love him anymore. *Of course, we still love him,* Daniel said that morning. *But sometimes loving people means being mad at them. And asking them to say sorry.*

Nurse Grey said it was time to play some dumb baby game. All the kids sat on the fluffy white carpet. The sun shined on their stupid faces. Gabriel didn't want to be on the floor with babies. So Gabriel played by themself in the corner of the room.

But then they heard a shout. They looked up and saw something strange through the window.

It was a man. Or boy. He was somewhere between a boy and a man. An Outsider. He was far down the dirt path. He was thin and white, and his skin was dirty, and he had blond hair that was clumped together like cold spaghetti. *Spaghetti head*, Gabriel thought and giggled.

The boy got closer. He was walking weird. Sort of hopping. He fell. Then he crawled. Crawled right through the dirt. Toward Gabriel. His lips moved. He was saying something, but he was too far away, and Gabriel couldn't hear. Bad butterflies flapped in Gabriel's tummy.

The boy crawled closer. He crawled until he was right outside the window where Gabriel stood. His head drooped like a dead flower. Gabriel couldn't see his face. But Gabriel could hear the boy crying. Gabriel wanted to ask why he was sad.

Gabriel tapped on the window. The boy looked up. Gabriel froze.

The boy had a hole instead of an eye. A wet red pocket. It pumped blood. Red gunk dripped down his cheeks. Dripped from his chin. White stuff hung from the hole like snot.

The boy slammed his hand against the window. Gabriel screamed.

FORTY-ONE

A nd here are your keys," his Realtor's avatar said on her way out the door. "Of course, they're just for aesthetic authenticity. To enter your home, you'll need to undergo an iOS Cerebrum Brain Scan."

"Thank you." A spell of dissociation sent Mason's consciousness spinning up toward rafters perfectly rendered by Cyclops Virtual Home Design to mimic the beams in his former Provincetown home, a home that, in reality, two months prior, had been walloped into kindling by Hurricane Marx, a storm that got its name from the anti-communist Republicans who'd taken over the National Oceanic and Atmospheric Administration. House arrest prevented Mason from traveling to assess the damage, but he'd been told it was terminal; the home where he spent so many gorgeous hours with the people he loved most had been demolished, razed, reduced to nothing more than a salty stretch of quicksand hungry for the detritus of his former life.

Now, here it was again. Restored. The details were uncanny, literally granular—a dusting of sand encircled the wicker beach basket by the screen door. A child's forgotten flip-flop broke his heart. History had been erased and Mason was back in Provincetown or, even better, back in the *idea* of Provincetown, but a Provincetown out of time, out of place, nowhere. A dreadful relief grew in his gut like a tumor; he could die happy here. Which was, of course, his plan.

Or, no, that wasn't quite right. He would die miserable but kill himself happily.

ATTENTION MASON DAUNT: YOU ARE UNDER HOUSE ARREST . . .
He shut his eyes and waited for the sirens to cease. When silence was restored, Mason prepared himself a negroni. Mason's psychotic tango with his Adderall prescription had progressively depleted him; he'd abused the amphetamine so much he'd become immune to its primary function, though, maddeningly, he was still vulnerable to its side effects. He was constantly jittery despite chronic exhaustion; the twitch in his left eye could be remedied only by a minimum of five cocktails. If he was blackout drunk, sometimes he could sleep through his Ankl alarm. Or at least not remember the times he woke up. Wasn't that almost the same as sleeping?

There was a clock in Mason's mind. Connected to his bank account. The only joy in Mason's life was now derived from virtual reality. His digital Provincetown "residence" cost $4,500 dollars a month. Meanwhile, he'd surrendered to his mother's demands and rented her a $10,000 a month Tudor in Hancock Park, a considerable expense on top of his own $7,000 a month condo, not to mention Skeletor's past-due legal fees. He had avoided paying the $73,000 he owed his lawyer; it would create a serious dent in the finite amount of cash that dictated the time he had left on Earth. Because he planned to leave his life when he could no longer afford it. Which—given the fact he had just $123,000 in savings—would be very soon. The clock would stop ticking when the money ran out and Mason would kill himself with the handgun he'd purchased from a militia supply site for the exorbitant sum of $5,500.

Unless.

Unless Yunho. Unless that really was his lover who had visited him at the Red Inn. And yet, all attempts to contact Yunho in the ensuing week had failed. It was possible it had just been some sick joke played by a random troll who'd decided to fuck with Mason by creating an avatar of his lost husband. But those tears. Yunho's sobs sounded real.

But why would Yunho deceive Mason like that? And for so many years? Mason's clandestine hunt for a canisexual dom began after he and Yunho decided to bring a child into the mess of humanity. At first, Mason bounced from sling to sling, unable to find a master strong enough to beat the guilt from his body. Then came Vex. Vex had a clairvoyant ability to summon Mason's anxieties in such specific detail it often unnerved Mason. But now, Mason realized Vex wasn't psychic. Vex was Yunho. And Yunho knew Mason's anxieties because he shared them and, apparently, also needed to sublimate them into the healing metaphors of a BDSM practice.

A spasm seized his left eye. Mason downed his negroni. A palpable emptiness bloomed in his gut. A hunger. For Yunho. The only man who could make things right. Yes, they'd finally talk about all those anxieties they'd annihilated in the dungeon, exhume them, examine them, and out of this honesty their love would grow anew, giving Mason what he lacked: a reason to live.

His face twitched in time to a virtual grandfather clock. Someone knocked at the door.

*

"Where have you been?"

"Montana. The Ranch."

"The phones were disconnected there."

"We've . . . changed a few things."

"We?"

"I . . . I don't know if it's worth getting into all that just yet."

"Getting into what?"

"You've still got your trial ahead of you . . ."

"*Getting into what?*"

". . . I think it's best if you focus on that for now."

"I'm running out of cash. I can't pay my lawyer."

"Then you have to be smarter about money—"

"*You sold our house!* Without telling me! You drained our *joint* bank accounts. And I let you because I love you and I feel this awful guilt about the baby shower, and I want us to be together again so desperately. But I think it would be *more* than fair if you gave me back some of *my own money.*"

"I don't have any money, Mason."

"You *spent* it all?"

"It belongs to our collective now. I don't have a personal account."

"Your 'collective'?"

"I want you to come join us. I miss you." Yunho stood by the CGI re-creation of his favorite feature of their Provincetown home: the bay windows overlooking the ocean. A simulacrum of sunshine cast a warm light across Yunho's face. A gull flew by, completing its programmed sunset loop. Mason watched it disappear in the distance, unsure if he was willing to surrender this lie. This world where their home was still standing, where he and Yunho could live forever, unwrinkled, immortal, two avatars outlasting their corporeal counterparts. "But there are things you need to know. About the way we're living out there."

"Who is 'we,' Yunho?"

FORTY-TWO

On May 2, 2044, the Canyon Fire hit Los Angeles County, starting as a small blaze at the tip of La Tuna Canyon. Nico got a call from AIG Wildfire Protection Unit at four A.M. Adrenaline kicked in. He crept into the bathroom to answer his phone, careful not to wake Blanca or Daisy. There was an unusual urgency to his boss's tone. Nico was informed he'd be fighting for a new client, an account that AIG had worked *very* hard to secure, which is why they were calling Nico, one of their best firefighters, for this job: to protect NuGrow Industrial.

Nico issued a grunt of affirmation. He hung up. Got ready. He kissed Daisy in her crib and Blanca in their bed. "I love you," Blanca said with the same fear in her voice that emerged every time he left to fight a fire. The fear that he might not come back.

Then he was on the road, driving AIG's fire truck. Sirens wailed as he tore through Burbank. To his surprise, they weren't defending the NuGrow factory off the northern stretch of Glenoaks Boulevard. Instead, they were headed to an off-site storage facility. *These fuckers have some nerve, demanding we risk our lives for a fucking storage unit*, Nico fumed as he drove. The facility was located deep in La Tuna Canyon Park, just one of the many public lands across the country that had been stripped of its protections and auctioned off to private companies by the current administration. Typically, federal leases were for oil and gas drilling, which is why

Nico found it odd that a company would obtain a federal lease for something as easily obtained as storage space. But he was not paid to have an opinion. He was paid to fight fire, to drive toward the billowing smoke, the burning horizon.

Fire brought, as it always did, memories of his mother. The last breakfast they'd shared. Pancakes, with chocolate chip eyes and a Reddi-wip smile. *You're so cute, you even make the pancakes smile,* she'd said, though Nico detected a trace of fear in her voice. She died later that day. Trapped at the hospital where she worked. Consumed by the fire that ravaged all of Paradise, California, back in 2018.

Now, at the wheel of the fire truck, speeding toward yet another blaze, Nico felt so fucking stupid. He'd fought countless fires in his lifetime, yet the hole his mother ripped in his heart when she died never got smaller. At the start of his career, Nico found solace in the fact that if he couldn't avenge his mother's death, he could at least save other families from similar devastation. But that was back when he worked in the public sector, before he'd joined a private firefighting firm. The privatization of U.S. fire operations had accelerated rapidly during the 2030s while funding was slashed for public fire protection programs. Nico believed all people had a right to be safe from disaster, not just people who could afford private insurance plans that included "supplemental response capability to fire emergencies." He hated that the poor were being left to burn. But after a round of budget cuts, Nico was fired from the public force, leaving him no choice but to join the major insurance company AIG's "Wildfire Protection Unit." Nico began to defend movie studios, banks, estates in Calabasas. His passion and purpose faded. The irony was painful; a man who became a firefighter to protect all families was being forced to abandon that dream to protect his own.

Nico steered the truck into the entrance to La Tuna Canyon Park. His team jumped into action, established base camp, then marched up a desiccated hillside. Sweat lined the interiors of their fire proximity suits. Scrubland gave way to a thick forest; they hiked until they reached the storage unit.

When Nico saw it, he wanted to scream. It stood nestled in a grove of redwoods. It was a rectangular building, about two thousand square feet, made of silver metal siding. No windows. He might never hear his daughter laugh again, all because of a two-thousand-square-foot storage facility.

Fury filled his heart for the next two days as they battled the worst blaze Nico had ever encountered. Day bled into night bled into day. The sun didn't stand a chance against the blanket of smoke in the sky. They shuttled back and forth to base camp for only the smallest moments of respite. Never more than an hour of sleep. Five minutes to shove a protein bar down your throat. The fire raged on, changing directions with the brutal wind. One minute it came from the west, then suddenly, impossibly, it blazed toward them from the north. Always circling, closing in. Nico and his force began to lose hope. The group lagged; they dreamed of escape, of returning to their terrified families.

Then, the tree fell. It was a massive redwood, burning like a torch. The men dropped their hoses and ran for safety. But Nico tripped over a patch of exposed roots. His ankle broke. He screamed in agony, but his team was too far ahead to hear. He looked back and saw the flaming tree smash down on the storage facility. It sliced through the center of the structure, chopping the building in half.

Suddenly: an explosion. Nico covered his head. A tsunami of heat washed over him. He looked back to the storage facility. There, rising from the charred remains of the building: a massive tower of smoke, already a hundred feet high, swelling exponentially, rising far above the blazing forest. The wind shifted. The cloud was on the move, headed straight for Burbank.

The smoke was bright pink.

*

"We lost the structure. Failed our mission. But we made it out alive. For that, I'm so grateful. I didn't lose a single man. But when we returned to

AIG's firehouse, a bunch of executives were waiting for us. They'd called an emergency meeting. I thought, 'Fuck, there goes my job.'

"They got us in the conference room. Then, they told us we were all getting one-hundred-thousand-dollar bonuses. I was shocked. We just failed miserably, and we were getting *rewarded*? It didn't make sense. But they were dead serious. They said we'd fought so hard out there and that even though we lost the storage facility, they wanted to acknowledge our backbreaking labor.

"There was just one thing they wanted us to sign before we got paid. A standard NDA. They said this mission had to remain confidential. They assured us this was just routine paperwork. Nothing to worry about. But we had to sign immediately if we wanted our bonuses. And I hate to admit it, but I signed right there. I mean, I had a family to feed. One hundred thousand dollars was more money than I ever got in my life at one time.

"But over the next few weeks, all this stuff started coming out about the pink smoke. About White Death. No one knew where this smoke came from. But I knew. And I got scared. I talked to the other guys who signed those NDAs. No one wanted to say anything. No one wanted to get sued by AIG or NuGrow. They could ruin our lives. But I knew where that pink smoke came from. And that information ate away at my conscience. I became a firefighter to protect *all* people, no matter how rich or poor. Now here I was, betraying my life's purpose, protecting a corporation that had released some deadly chemical into the air that was causing mass death and destruction. It made me so sick, so angry. My wife, Blanca, pulled me back from the edge so many times. Because this secret was destroying me. I had to tell someone. I worried I'd kill myself if I didn't. That's why I'm sitting here today . . ."

The TV flickered above the virtual re-creation of the fireplace in Mason's Provincetown home. Mason sat on the couch, rapt. The fake sun had set during the broadcast of Nico's interview with CNN; the screen was now the only light in the room. A blue glow illuminated Mason's weeping face. He wiped a tear and felt, for the first time since his baby shower, hope.

*

"This is *very* good for us, babe," Renata shouted over a chorus of screams that sounded like thirty children being slaughtered simultaneously. "Sorry, I'm at some stupid state fair chili cook-off thing? I don't know why anyone comes to Malibu now that the beaches are gone. And yet here I am, with my tedious nieces, waiting for them to dismount an ancient carnival ride that looks like it hasn't been safety-checked since 2016."

"Renata. I'm paying you four hundred and fifty dollars an hour."

"You're not, actually. There are numerous unpaid invoices—"

"The point is: I literally cannot afford to hear how your nieces are enjoying a chili cook-off in the ruins of Malibu."

"They're lessening your charges to voluntary manslaughter."

"That's good, right?"

"Well, I don't know if being charged with voluntary manslaughter is ever a '*good*' thing, but it's certainly better than first-degree murder."

"What's, like, the worst sentencing that could happen?"

"We could be looking at three years in prison . . ."

"Three *years* in prison?"

". . . or six, or eleven."

"Jesus, Renata. What about a deal?"

"I've tried. They don't want a deal. My theory is they don't want to look like they were wrong. They've invested so much time, money, and PR manpower into this case. They wanna mitigate the fallout. There's a precedent for the state winning manslaughter cases against people who've raised a White Death defense. So they think manslaughter charges are a safe bet. They want a win, even if it's not the guilty murder verdict they promised in their press conferences."

"But I mean, think about it. Who's *really* responsible for Patrick's death? Is it the chemical engineers who created whatever toxic substance exploded in that storage facility? Is it the top-ranking executives who oversaw this fiasco? Is it the state government for failing to regulate the production of this deadly chemical? Or is it the *federal* government for leasing public lands to NuGrow for the purpose of storing these chemicals? Or is it Patrick himself? The CEO who spearheaded this whole diabolical scheme? Considering recent revelations, couldn't we argue that Patrick essentially killed himself?"

"Sweetie, there's a video of you pummeling him to death with your bare hands."

"Renata, I'm not joking."

"Neither am I."

"I mean, this is not Fukushima, but it's also not *not* Fukushima. There are real questions here about the ethical entanglements of man-made disasters and who's truly responsible—"

"No, Tessa! You've already had *three* bowls of chili. I don't need you puking on the Death-Spinner!" Renata yelled nieceward before returning to the call. "Sorry, Mason. I'm just trying to be realistic. We'll *never* convince a jury that Patrick killed himself. But the CNN firefighter thing is good for us. I'll think about new strategies and get back to you."

Mason sighed. "Thanks."

"There's one more thing."

"Yes?"

"My invoices, Mason. I don't do pro bono, especially not for rich neoliberal gays who refuse to compromise their lifestyle while they ignore the pressing reality of a major criminal trial."

"I'm *not* a neoliberal."

"Whatever helps you sleep at night."

"Nothing helps me sleep at night. That's my problem."

"No, your problem is that you're not paying your high-powered, short-fused attorney. I'm beginning to worry that you're failing to fulfill your obligations under our representation agreement. I would hate to withdraw as your attorney but . . . ." She drifted off.

Mason downed a cold gulp of negroni. "I'll find the money."

"I'm on your side. And you want to *keep* me on your side. So pay up."

Another chorus of screams erupted in Mason's earpiece and then the line went dead. He downed his negroni and returned to the kitchen for a refill. Panic arrested him at the bar cart. He didn't have the money. He couldn't pay Renata. He threw his glass to the ground. It didn't shatter, of course. Things didn't break in virtual reality. The real world was a different story.

FORTY-THREE

Gabriel had never seen rain before. Sometimes they thought grown-ups made up rain like they made up Santa Claus. Because everyone knew that water came from the faucet. And hoses. And WeatherMod. It was crazy to think water could come from the sky. That was magic, and magic wasn't real. But then it *did* rain. It was the most amazing thing Gabriel ever saw.

Gabriel wanted to play in the rain. Astrid was lying in bed reading. Gabriel climbed up and grabbed her book. "Hey, you." She smiled. "I was reading that."

"Rain is magic."

Astrid laughed. "Yes, rain *is* magic. Or at least it feels that way, coming from L.A."

"I wanna play in the magic rain!"

"Okay, let's go play!"

"And Yunho can come too!"

Astrid frowned. Gabriel knew Yunho wasn't allowed around their Care Pod right now. Because he hurt Astrid. But Gabriel missed him. "Yunho can't play with us. Not right now."

"I want everyone to be friends with Yunho again!"

"We will." Astrid looked out the window. "But right now, we all need a little space."

*

Gabriel ran around the house and got all the kids and grown-ups to come out and play in the rain. Everyone gathered on the front lawn. The ground was muddy. Gabriel was sad because they had to wear boots. They wanted to feel the mud on their toes. "Can I take off my boots?"

"We don't want you to get all dirty."

"*Please, please.*"

"I guess it's a special occasion." Astrid smiled. Gabriel took off their boots and felt the cold ground between their toes. Across the lawn, Sophie looked up and opened her mouth and let the magic fall right in.

"Will we get magic powers if we drink the rain like Sophie?"

"Well, I'm not sure, but I guess we better try." Gabriel and Astrid opened their mouths and drank the rain. The water was warm; it didn't taste like anything. But when Gabriel swallowed, they felt the magic slide down into their body.

"I'm magic now!" Gabriel yelled and ran over to Sophie. "You're magic too. We're all magic!" Suddenly, Gabriel realized that Santa Claus might also be here at the Ranch. Because if the magic rain was real, then so was Santa. "I have to find Santa Claus!"

"He's here?" Sophie's eyes got big.

"Yes," Gabriel said. The grown-ups weren't paying attention. Gabriel grabbed Sophie's tiny, soft wrist. "You wanna come with me?"

*

"*Santa!*" Gabriel screamed Santa's name into the sky. "*Santa!*" They ran past the school. The main road wasn't dirt anymore; it was mud. Brown muck splashed the backs of their legs as they ran. Sophie had trouble keeping up. "*Santa!*"

Far down the road, Gabriel saw Yunho running with a jacket over his head. He ran into the funny yurt. The Infirmary. It was made with thick brown cloth that sagged in the rain. Gabriel wanted to tell Yunho about the magic rain. Gabriel knew Yunho was in a grown-up time-out and wasn't allowed to talk to their Care Pod, but Gabriel didn't care because they loved him.

"Stop!" Sophie yelled. Gabriel looked back. Sophie crossed her arms. "Santa isn't here. I'm going back!" She turned and stomped off.

Gabriel looked at the Infirmary. Maybe Santa wasn't on the Ranch. But Yunho was.

*

Gabriel stood outside the yurt. *You can't go to the Infirmary unless you're going for your visit with Dr. Cove,* Mahmood said yesterday. Gabriel wasn't supposed to be here because of the boy with the missing eye, the one who scared Gabriel. He was at the Infirmary. Getting better. His name was Tuck. The grown-ups thought he might be dangerous.

Gabriel grabbed the door flap to the yurt and peeked inside. The boy was on a bed, sleeping. A bandage covered the hole where his left eye used to be.

"How's he doing?" Yunho whispered. He stood in a corner with Daniel.

"Much better," Daniel whispered back.

"Look what his family did to him." Yunho shook his head. "We can't send him back."

"I don't disagree. But Claudia has valid concerns about bringing a militia member—"

"*Former* militia member—"

"—into our community."

"The militia gouged his eye out. I think that's pretty solid evidence that he's not exactly on speaking terms with them."

"Yunho, I get it. But I also share Claudia's concerns. Especially after what happened to Sally. And then you. Now this boy just shows up on our doorstep? It's hard to trust anyone with militia ties when the safety of our community is at stake."

"So, what—we just turn him away? Force him back into the arms of a family who gouged his eye out? I thought we welcomed everyone, Daniel."

"Can we save this for our next Community Meeting? I'm giving him medical care and—"

Bang! Gabriel slipped and fell on the yurt's wooden platform.

"Did you hear that?" Yunho asked.

Gabriel ran. They didn't want to get in trouble.

*

Gabriel was tired of searching for Santa but there was one place left that Santa might be: the road. Maybe Santa's sleigh couldn't fly when it rained, and he had to take the road. So Gabriel ran toward the fence at the edge of the property.

But then they saw something weird: a white van, parked just off the road. Its headlights were like lasers that sliced through the dark day and lit up the raindrops. Maybe that was Santa. Maybe Santa drove a van and the magic sleigh was made up. The van was big. You could fit a lot of presents in it. But Gabriel couldn't see if there were presents inside because there were no windows. Gabriel had an idea: rush to the van, open the doors. Find all the presents. So they ran. The rain came down harder. It almost hurt. The mud was cold. Gabriel's feet were numb. They got to the van. The driver's side window was black. Gabriel couldn't see inside.

The door opened.

A lady sat in the front seat. She wore pink high heels. "Why did I insist on wearing Stuart Weitzman slingbacks on the first day it decides to rain in Montana in over a year?" she said to someone in the passenger seat. She turned and screamed when she saw Gabriel. "*Oh, oh!*"

Gabriel stepped back. They couldn't figure out if this lady was nice or not. She was definitely not Santa. She wore a pink skirt and jacket and had shiny blonde hair. She wore a lot of makeup and red lipstick. She popped open an umbrella and stepped out of the van, smiling. "You scared me, cutie. Are you out here all by yourself?"

Gabriel shivered. "I was searching for Santa. He's here because of the magic rain."

The lady scrunched up her eyebrows, then turned to the man in the car. He was big and fat and wore a flannel shirt. "Told you they taught these kids some goofy shit," the man said.

He had something in his lap. Machine parts. He put them together. *Clunk, clunk.*

"Why are you so muddy?" the lady asked. "You're absolutely covered."

"I don't know." Gabriel shrugged and looked at the ground.

The back doors of the van opened. Another man popped out. He carried a big suitcase in his hands. Another man followed him. "Are your mommy and daddy around?"

"I don't have a mommy and daddy," Gabriel shrugged again.

"Right." The lady frowned. "Well, are there any grown-ups I can talk to?" Gabriel didn't say anything. "Or maybe I could talk to you for a little bit."

"What do you want?" Gabriel asked.

"I just want what's best for everyone."

The men crouched on the ground and popped open their suitcases. Gabriel started to cry.

FORTY-FOUR

A weeping child, covered in mud." The newscaster gestured to Gabriel, who sobbed in the rain, their face plastered with brown muck, clothes soaked through. *The bitch couldn't share her umbrella?* Mason wondered as he watched from virtual Provincetown. A headline scrolled across the screen: HOLLYWOOD ANARCHISTS FORM TERRORIST PREGNANCY CULT. "Gabriel is neglected, abused, and forced to reside in an anarchist pregnancy cult that has been established on Hollywood filmmaker Yunho Kim's Montana ranch, a fifty-eight-hundred-acre compound on the outskirts of a small town named Bridger. Claudia Jackson, a suspected domestic terrorist, is a cofounder of the group. These radicals attempt to recruit innocent civilians by luring them in with free meals, education, and healthcare. But once inside, members must devote themselves to the cult's terrorist mission to destroy the police, the militia, and the American family itself.

"Tensions with locals reached a boiling point this week, when Kim lured Tuck Wilson, a seventeen-year-old boy, into his clutches via the gay sex app Grindr. Kim brainwashed the child into joining the cult and disowning his family of patriotic militia members. Wilson's family says they'll stop at nothing to get their boy back—"

Mason shut off the TV. His mother had emailed him the video two days ago; it was their first communication since their fight about the price tag of her new rental home. She'd been attempting to repair their codependent bond by reanimating the idea of Yunho as a common enemy. But she should've known better than to think a video from the Anti-OL News Network (ANN) would convince her son of anything other than the fact of his mother's insanity.

Yet, to his surprise, in the wake of the ANN story, Mason noticed a proliferation of #KillTheKimCommune signs planted in the virtual lawns of his gay neighbors in Provincetown. This development could likely be attributed to ideas popularized by a centrist op-ed contributor to the *New York Times*, who eschewed the hyperbole of ANN, but still wondered why "these queer radicals are so determined to destroy the family and marriage—the institutions LGBTQ people are fighting to stay a part of despite so much anti-queer legislation." But those on the far left argued that the pyrrhic victory of gay marriage had always been an assimilationist fantasy, a bubble that had finally popped now that the true Christo-fascist nature of the American family was reasserting itself, and the only antidote was a community like the one on the Montana ranch. Those even *further* left argued this community was another example of the elite gentrification that had plagued Montana for decades, turning the state into a climate-safe playground for the rich, and forcing the working class into wage slavery that created deep resentment and led to increased militia violence. Others asserted that the anarchist commune was *fighting* gentrification through their efforts to provide *everyone* with free healthcare, food, and education, but the local working class was too racist and queerphobic to realize liberation had arrived in their backyard.

What to believe? Mason wanted to believe in the utopia Yunho described during their last discussion. Mason longed for real life again, life with Yunho, love with Yunho, a love stronger than anything except the love for their newborn.

A healthy baby, according to Yunho. A beautiful child.

Pound, pound, pound! Someone was knocking. Strange. Mason got up and opened his door.

The street was empty. A seagull waddled past Mason's white fence.

Pound, pound, pound! "FBI! Open up!"

The sound was coming from real life.

*

"I'm not saying anything without my lawyer present." Mason sat in his condo's breakfast nook, sweating. An FBI agent—tall, white, about thirty-five—paced Mason's kitchen. Agent Kilcher. A telltale swish betrayed homosexual leanings. Despite the dire circumstances, Mason found the agent garb a turn-on, especially when the muscle top wearing it clearly possessed a talent for inflicting punishment. Mason worried—was it problematic to be turned on by cops? Or could he get away with framing his attraction to them as a way of fetishizing a symbol of historical queer oppression to create a healing eroticism in which the sub/dom dynamic took on victim/cop drag and purged generational queer trauma inflicted by law enforcement?

"Of course you aren't." Kilcher gave Mason a wink, one small cruel gesture to communicate that Kilcher had caught Mason's cruising gaze. *How pathetic*, his tone suggested. *I'm here to destroy your life and you still can't hide your fucking boner.* "But is this the same lawyer you can't afford to pay? Who may drop your case before you go to trial?"

Mason had not been totally surprised to find an FBI agent at his front door. It was in keeping with the nightmare logic that governed his life; one could never predict the direction in which one's bad dreams turned, yet whatever path they took was certain to lead to a more dreadful fate than previously anticipated. It was with the haunted resignation of someone accustomed to living in a nightmare that Mason had welcomed Agent Kilcher, inevitable incubus, into his shitty seven-thousand-dollar-a-month condo-prison.

"I'm not speaking without my lawyer—"

"Here's the thing about that." Kilcher's tone spiked. "I *want* to help you. Believe it or not, it's my *job* to help you. But if we call your lawyer, that makes my job difficult. Because we can't have this conversation with your lawyer present. Because this conversation isn't happening. And how can we invite someone to something that isn't happening?"

Adrenaline flooded Mason's system. Surely, you couldn't tell an FBI agent to get out of your house? But shouldn't the agent have a warrant from the government or something? Mason knew nothing about what his rights were because, well, this type of thing didn't happen to people like Mason. "Do you have . . . uh, like, papers that . . . allow you to be here?" Mason stammered.

"Papers?" A smirk cracked Kilcher's unfortunately gorgeous face. "Oh yes, the *papers*! I forgot about the magic papers! I'll get my fucking fairy godfather to fly them in. Sound good?"

"N . . . no . . ." Tears threatened Mason's ducts.

"Now, let's talk. We've been surveilling you for months. You have no friends, you're hemorrhaging cash, you can't pay your lawyer, you can't sleep, and you drink like you're trying to kill yourself. Are you trying to kill yourself, Mason?" Silence. Mason bit his cheek. Blood pooled beneath his tongue. Kilcher slapped him. "I *said*, are you trying to *kill yourself*?"

"*No!*" Mason lied; Kilcher's palm print burned on his face.

"Well, then. I bet you're pretty concerned about these manslaughter charges. How many years in prison can you take? Six? Eleven? Or would just one *day* be too much?" Kilcher's words were interrupted by the sirens in Mason's mind. *ATTENTION MASON DAUNT, YOU ARE UNDER HOUSE ARREST* . . . Mason placed his head on the kitchen table, and gritted his teeth. His brain felt like it might burst. He fought the urge to punch the wall and punch the agent and burn his fucking condo to the ground. "I wouldn't be able to sleep either. If you go to prison, you'll never see your husband again, and *never* meet your child. Because do you really think they're gonna wait around for eleven years? After what *you* did? *No way.* They'll move on without you. They'll hate you more with every passing day. By the time you get out of prison, no one will be there to love you. You won't have a home. You won't have a family. You won't have a single soul on this Earth who thinks you're anything other than a *despicable piece of shit.*" Kilcher slapped him again. Mason choked back a sob. "But you're in luck! Because I can make this whole nightmare vanish."

"H . . . how?"

"Here at the FBI, we have friends in the California state government. And those friends are willing to work with us to drop the charges against you. Provided you do us a favor."

"I'm not saying anything without my lawyer present."

"Oh, you know what? I misspoke. It's not really a favor. It's more of a job. An easy job. With a salary. A *very nice* salary. Wouldn't you like an easy job with a nice salary?"

"Why should I believe you?" Mason wiped tears from his face.

"Because if you say 'yes' right now, I guarantee that tomorrow your lawyer will call to break the wonderful news that the state of California has let you off the hook."

Mason wanted his VR helmet, wanted to slap it on, to escape into virtual reality where he could get so blackout drunk that even the illusion of Provincetown would disappear and there would be nothing but the abyss of unconsciousness, a darkness unremembered, the temporary obliteration that did not require the courage it took to end your life. A coward's suicide.

"What's the job?" Mason asked.

FORTY-FIVE

D o you remember Uncle Mason, Gabriel?"

Gabriel looked up. They did remember Uncle Mason. But they didn't *want* to. They didn't *want* to remember how he punched a man's face until it turned to wet raw meat.

"I've known you since you were a baby," Mason said. "Can we be friends again?"

Everyone looked at Gabriel with big stupid smiles. Gabriel didn't want to be friends with Mason. But Gabriel also didn't want to upset the grown-ups. Gabriel had already upset them by talking to that mean lady from TV. Now everyone on the Outside hated the Ranch. Gabriel didn't want to make the grown-ups mad again, so they had lied and told Dr. Cove that they were happy Mason was coming back.

"Don't you wanna say 'hi'?" Astrid asked.

Gabriel stayed silent, jumped into Astrid's lap, and buried their head in her skirt.

"This is why I thought it was a bit early to reintroduce the kids to Mason," Claudia said.

"We talked with Dr. Cove, and they felt Gabriel was ready," Mahmood replied.

"I'm so sorry, guys." Mason bit his lip. "Maybe this was too soon."

"No, it's not your fault." Yunho rubbed Mason's back.

"Well . . ."

"Claudia, we have to work to *forgive* Mason if he's gonna be here," Yunho continued.

"No, no one has to forgive me. What I did is horrible and—"

"Yunho's right." Claudia sighed. "I promised I'd give you a chance, Mason. It's just hard to see you again. To be reminded . . ."

"Of course. And I didn't want to upset Gabriel—"

Gabriel popped their head up. They didn't like it when grown-ups talked about them like they weren't there. "I'm not disappeared," Gabriel said.

"We know that, sweetie," Yunho said. Gabriel was glad Yunho was allowed to be a part of their Care Pod again. They missed Yunho. But they never missed Uncle Mason.

"What do you say, can you give me a second chance?" Mason crouched down to look at Gabriel. Gabriel saw that Mason had tears in his eyes.

"Why are you crying?" Gabriel asked.

"I'm just so happy to be back here with everyone," he said.

But Uncle Mason didn't look happy.

FORTY-SIX

"What happened to our movie theater?" Gone were the velvet-upholstered seats, the elegant cocktail tables, the massive screen. The room was now lined with five cribs, three of them empty. A sea of children's toys occupied one corner. An adult bed—perfectly made, with white linens stretched across its surface—sat in the other. Grey, whom Yunho had referred to as one of the "Nurses," pressed their pregnant belly into the bars of a bassinet and cooed to the child within. A destabilizing realization spiraled in Mason's mind; he was standing in a room that no longer belonged to him, in a house seized by others, in a life from which he'd been erased so his successors could create a new existence, a new love, a new delusion, because what is love if not a shared delusion, a fantasy that feeds on faith, clap if you believe in fairies, and suddenly Mason felt like an emaciated Tinker Bell, starved for applause, left for dead in some pixie hospice while everyone he held dear found a new dream of love to believe in. "What happened to our . . . *stuff*?"

"We needed space for the Nursery," Yunho replied. "The screening room felt excessive."

Grey approached with a small, swaddled being, cradling it as gingerly as an undetonated grenade. "You want to hold them?"

The weight of the child in his arms brought Mason back down to Earth. He stared into the infant's eyes—perfect replicas of Yunho's. "Hello, beautiful." The child gurgled and yawned.

"I'll give you two a moment alone," Grey said as they retreated from the room.

"Fennel likes you," Yunho said.

This was his child. At last. He inhaled the scent of baby powder and shampoo and the sour ghost of some discarded dirty diaper. A bittersweet fragrance. Mason wanted to bottle it. Bathe in it. Drown in it. Die for it. Mason would martyr himself for this tender ball of flesh; each tiny toe, each chubby finger was a phenomenon worthy of worship. Fennel's heart fluttered against his own as he pressed this miracle to his chest. Yes, everyone thought of their child as a "miracle," but when Mason considered all he'd endured to get to this point, he felt that others were far too hasty to ascribe thaumaturgic import to the feckless humping that produced their own idiot spawn. Only *his* child was truly divine, born out of immense suffering and turmoil, yet imbued with the power to alleviate all that pain, to give anyone who looked in its eyes hope for the future despite the devastation of the past. "Yunho, this is . . . what we've always dreamed of."

"I know." A deep love emanated from Yunho's voice; maybe this child would be enough to repair their bond, to reconstruct their lives.

"Which is why I don't understand what you're doing here. Why are you allowing some near stranger to raise Fennel in the ruins of our former screening room?"

"Grey is one of our Nurses. Who are all wonderful and—"

"This baby is *ours*—"

"Children aren't *property*, Mason—"

"—and you're just pawning it off on someone else."

"Mason." Yunho took a deep breath. "We are attempting to separate the labor of biological reproduction from that of social reproduction."

"What the hell does that mean?"

"It means that the labor of gestating a baby is a job like any other on this Ranch. But a biological connection to a child does not automatically come with the responsibilities of parenthood. The duty to raise a child falls on our collective, rather than any individual."

"So no one has to take care of their babies?" Mason pouted.

"Nurses provide around-the-clock care for children during early childhood. But children also have meaningful contact with everyone in the community during this stage. Community Play is our 'getting to know you' time with babies and young toddlers. As the child gets older, the child will naturally gravitate toward members of a particular Care Pod. Between two and three, the child is given a choice as to which Care Pod they'd like to join. This Care Pod *isn't* a family. This Care Pod provides the child with consistent care providers who aid the child in their development, while the child also nurtures meaningful relationships with all community members. Care Pods don't necessarily exist along bloodlines, though in some cases children may be biologically related to Guardians within their Care Pod."

"Like Gabriel and Auden. They still live with Mahmood and Daniel."

"Yes. For children who arrived at the commune with preestablished parental relationships, we didn't want to disrupt those bonds. But Astrid, Claudia, and I have also joined their Care Pod as Guardians to Auden and Gabriel."

"So will Fennel be the first newborn to go through your system of child-rearing?"

Yunho hesitated. "Well . . . yes."

"Doesn't that make you even a *little* nervous?"

"It doesn't."

"You're lying. I can *tell* when you're bullshitting—"

"Okay, fine, I'm nervous! And that's completely reasonable, when one is considering the best way to raise another human being in a world that is totally fucked."

"Which is precisely why reinventing the wheel seems more than a little insane."

"Oh, because the wheel was working so well before?"

"Humanity has just, like, had families since the dawn of time!"

"Actually, the earliest humans lived in communal and polygamous matriarchies that were eventually overthrown by patriarchal class-based societies that favored a private family unit developed in order to hoard wealth and property and—"

"Oh, for fuck's sake, Yunho. I'm not talking about ancient societies; I'm talking about the *one we live in today.*"

"And do you think the nuclear family has been successful in modern society? No. It's a capitalist tool that subjugates the poor by privatizing their care units and forcing them to become wage slaves to purchase survival for their loved ones. Look at your own mother, brimming with rage because your family broke down, and she had to make so many sacrifices to support you."

"Don't bring my mother into this."

"But the very category of 'motherhood' is the point here. We've abolished 'motherhood,' abolished the family, and replaced it with a community where *everyone* is cared for equally."

"I just feel nervous about subjecting Fennel to some wild experiment."

"I feel nervous about *not* subjecting Fennel to this experiment. Our previous pursuit of traditional parenthood brought about ecological disaster, trauma to all our friends, and death. So, yes, I think it's worth trying something new."

"But do you have to take it so far? This is our home! It's overrun by strangers!"

"I fought *very* hard to convince our community to allow you to join." His gaze grew cold. "But you can leave right now if you want."

Fennel sneezed. The small contraction shook their entire body. This little being was so vulnerable. Mason felt an intense urge to protect this child, *his* child, no matter what. "No, I don't want to leave. I'm sorry." He cradled Fennel in one arm, while pulling Yunho into the other. Yunho's shoulders relaxed beneath Mason's palm. Mason kissed his lover—a tender assurance. Silence enveloped them like a hug. Father, father, child. Locked in a loving embrace. "I want to stay," he whispered.

What he failed to tell Yunho was that he couldn't leave, even if he wanted to.

Mason had a job to do.

*

They put Mason in the indoor shooting range. It was tucked into a forgotten corner of the lower level, adjacent to the small bowling alley Yunho had built as a tribute to the final scene in *There Will Be Blood*—one of his favorite films. The shooting range came with the house; this was Montana, after all, and the man who'd built the home (but never occupied it because he'd been thrown in prison for wire fraud) was an avid gun enthusiast. During renovations, Yunho had gone so over budget in his re-creation of Daniel Plainview's bowling alley that there was no money left to convert the shooting range into the bar their architect had designed. So the range stayed. Mason loathed the room, with its white concrete walls and rows of empty gun racks made from bright-blond oak. Two shooting booths stood at the far end of the space. Twin paper silhouettes hung downrange, beyond the firing lines. Targets. They hadn't removed them, initially due to neglect, though eventually the abandoned gun room became a kitschy part of the house tour. Yunho loved shocking dinner guests by taking them downstairs while the pastry chef assembled dessert. The lame joke was always the same: "This is where we take care of people with gluten allergies."

Yunho plugged in Mason's blow-up mattress. "Sorry, I know you hate the gun range."

"It's okay."

"It's just the only empty room we have these days."

"Right, because of . . ."

"The demands for space required by an evil anarchist pregnancy cult that's destroying the American family?" Yunho chuckled grimly and pressed the INFLATE button. The bed released a deafening whir. With a forlorn expression, Yunho watched the mattress rise.

Mason hesitated. "I'm sorry about all that awful press."

"It's not your fault." Yunho stretched a sheet over the bed.

"And I'm sorry about my freak-out in the Nursery. I just need some time to get used to all this." Mason dove onto the mattress, shoving a pillow beneath his head as he looked up at Yunho. "But I think that what you're doing here is beautiful."

"Thank you." Yunho lay next to Mason; the air mattress bounced from the impact. They bobbed like two buoys knocked by the same wave. "I'm glad you're here."

"I've missed you," Mason said as he slid into the nook of Yunho's left arm. It was a cuddle accomplished on autopilot; they'd done a version of this move every night and every morning for years, and even now, after six months apart, it came effortlessly.

"I wanted you to sleep in my bed, just so you know."

"I wish I could."

"It's just . . . Astrid and Claudia are nervous about you joining our Care Pod."

"I get it. Gabriel seemed so scared of me today. It broke my heart."

"Me too. I think it'll just take time to build up trust."

"Right."

"I could sleep down here tonight." There was fear in Yunho's voice, an apprehension Mason shared. Every moment they spent together was filled with the threat of existential catastrophe. Pieces of their fractured identities pressed against each other like tectonic plates; the smallest slip could create a seismic shock. Unanswered questions hung in the air like earthquake weather: *How have you been living while we've been apart? How has this shaped you? Who are you now? Are you a part of my future? Or a remnant from my past?* Mason knew the answers could only be obtained over time. And yet, he also hoped that one night could resolve it all, that the warmth of their bodies crushed together was the remedy they needed. Mason wanted to feel his heart beating in time to Yunho's, as if they shared the same vascular system, linked by a love so deep it transcended all their cerebral turmoil and left only the simple cadence of two bodies breathing as one.

"No, I don't want to take you from your Care Pod." Of course, that was precisely what Mason wanted to do. Take Yunho and Fennel away from this place that was no longer their home and create a new life somewhere far away. "Besides, this air mattress isn't meant for two."

"You're probably right." Yunho gave a sad small laugh.

"Hey." Mason kissed Yunho's tender frown. "I love you."

"I love you too."

Then Yunho was gone, leaving Mason alone among the empty gun racks. Mason waited for five minutes. Tension turned his shoulders to rock. He curled his toes. He clenched his jaw.

Then he opened his suitcase and got to work.

*

The moon was missing. Obscured by a cloud. The darkness was total. Mason walked deeper into the void. An unnerving sense of placelessness sent a dizzy rush through his skull. He stopped. There was nothing to grab onto, no surface to steady himself. He felt the weight of his backpack dragging him down. He took a deep breath. Pine. The air smelled of pine. The vertigo passed. He pressed onward. The only orientation he had: the road. He followed its outer contours with his feet, corrected course if he stumbled into the dirt shoulder. He gripped his flashlight, still afraid to use it, afraid someone back at the Ranch would wake in the middle of the night and stumble to the kitchen and pour themselves a glass of water and as they did, they'd look out the window above the sink and see an orb of light floating down the one-lane road and realize it was Mason. He'd be discovered, forced to confess the disgusting truth.

Which would almost be a relief. He longed to warn someone, to see the fury burn in their eyes as they banished him from the Ranch. But he was a coward. Too chickenshit to do the right thing. Instead, he crept along the dark road at two A.M. and prayed no one caught him. He looked over his shoulder. The Ranch loomed in the distance, a small glowing dot, a lone star in an empty galaxy. He pressed onward, turning with the road, until the dot vanished behind a thick row of pines.

He waited in the dark.

Headlights appeared on the horizon. Mason shielded his eyes. The twin beams grew brighter as the car approached. It stopped several feet in front of Mason, sending a harsh glare over mist-dappled asphalt. The whiteness flooded the surrounding wilderness, casting a tangle of shadows across the forest floor. Mason stepped closer, right up to the driver's side window.

It was empty, of course. An Uber on autopilot.

Mason opened the door, threw his backpack in the passenger seat. He sat behind the wheel. The engine purred. He closed his eyes and let the vehicle run on its own. The autopilot provided unexpected solace. It allowed Mason to pretend he had no control over this situation. He was simply fate's passenger, being driven to an inevitable end.

*

The car stopped half a mile from the fence. Kilcher had assured Mason that this location was out of security camera range. Mason looked to the right. His backpack slumped in the passenger seat like a surly child. Mason wanted to turn around, to race home through the starless Montana night, steal Fennel from their crib, and cradle the child until dawn, lost in a haze of love and relief.

But that was impossible. Mason had made a deal. *It's the easiest job ever.* Kilcher had promised. *It's a crime you're getting paid this much to do something so simple.*

Mason unzipped the backpack. He pulled out the ski mask and put it on. Then he grabbed the brick, felt its weight. A spider web of thin rope crisscrossed the surface. Beneath the binding: a crisp rectangle of folded white paper.

Mason double-checked the Uber app. His car was in "errand mode," ensuring the vehicle would wait while he finished his task. He clutched the brick. Took a breath. Opened his door.

Then, he was out on the road. He broke into a run, through the hushed dark. His shoes slapped the pavement. The brick chafed his palm. He thought of all those Los Angeles afternoons spent practicing his mission, struggling to launch the small projectile ten feet in the air. *You'll need that much height to clear the fence*, Kilcher had informed him. *Hope you've got a good arm.*

But this brick felt heavier than the one he'd practiced with; it was at least five pounds, maybe seven. His feet kept powering forward, even as his mind sabotaged his confidence. The brick seemed to gain more weight with every step; there was no way he'd clear the fence, no way he wouldn't trip the alarm system, no way this didn't end in his capture, torture, death. *This isn't a fucking easy job.* Panic seized Mason's chest. *This is a fucking death sentence.*

He turned a corner. A chain-link fence rose from a sea of prairie grass. It stretched for miles. Beyond it, an army of junipers stood sentinel. Their thick trunks twisted as if agonized by some invisible torturer. Floodlights cast a stark blue-white glow across the field.

He came to the spot where the fence met the road. The entrance to the compound was blocked by a solid iron gate. A row of metal blades fanged the top of the barrier. Adrenaline hammered Mason's temples. *Looks more like eleven feet. Maybe twelve.* He clutched the brick. Tensed his arm. His sweat soaked the rope, the paper beneath. He prayed the ink wouldn't bleed. That the message would remain clear. That he would never be forced to return.

He threw the brick. He held his breath. His lungs, still weak from White Death, threatened to spasm. But Mason fought the contraction. Watched as the brick soared upward. Six, seven feet in the air. Something like a prayer forced itself into Mason's thoughts. Eight feet, nine. His pulse pounded in his throat. Ten feet, eleven. The brick reached the row of security spikes.

Time stopped.

The brick cleared. Mason exhaled, dizzy with relief. He heard a faint thud from beyond the gate—the brick landing on the inside.

Then came the siren. A wail that pierced his eardrums. Emergency lights blasted Mason's retinas; his vision went white. He ran, despite the fact that he couldn't see. He blinked rapidly, desperate to clear the blinding afterimages from his gaze. Slowly the road appeared beneath him. Red light pulsed across the asphalt.

He looked back: nothing. No one followed.

He turned the corner. There, in the distance was his Uber. Waiting.

Suddenly: a loud crash. Like a car smashing into a brick wall.

He looked back over his shoulder. He screamed when he saw it. A massive machine sped toward him. It hurled forward on four steel legs. It moved with murderous grace; it had the stealth of a jaguar, though it was twice as large. Four hundred pounds. Steel armor encased its rectangular body. There was a click every time the robot contracted its metal limbs and leapt through the air, then a crash as the full weight of its body hit the ground again. *Click, crash.* The noise of its predation was rapid, relentless. *Click, crash.* The sound grew deafening as it closed in on Mason. *CLICK, CRASH.* It had no head, no neck, just a dark hole where a face should've been. *CLICK, CRASH.* A six-barrel machine gun emerged from the void.

FORTY-SEVEN

FBI COUNTERTERRORISM DIVISION—NATIONAL THREAT CENTER SECTION CLASSIFIED: SUSPICIOUS ACTIVITY REPORT—SEIZED EMAIL

From: Claudia Jackson <claudiajackson@gmail.com>

To: <DDS2044@gmail.com>

My dear sweet someone,

I've been baking. Astrid laughs each morning upon walking into the kitchen and discovering the day's bounty of muffins or coffee cake or scones. She'll take one and kiss my forehead and though she smiles, I can tell she's worried.

We're in more danger than ever before.

But baking . . .

Baking calms me. It's a meditation. A task to occupy my anxious mind. Baking is an exact science. You must pay attention to cups and teaspoons and techniques and time. When I'm baking, the hourly panic attacks cease and I'm nothing more than a vessel for this beautiful little project I can complete in one morning, a relief when my life is devoted to projects that never end. But this project *will* end, and I'll share it with everyone I love, and we'll come together and eat and laugh and I guess that's something I want to share with you, Fennel. This love of baking. This path toward peace, even if it's temporary.

I want you to have the recipe for my grandmother's corn bread drop biscuits. She'd make them every summer and serve them with ribs and corn salad and grilled peaches—and, oh, Fennel, you don't yet know the joy of grilled peaches, but rest assured you will. You will. But those drop biscuits—I'm stapling the recipe to this letter. And don't forget the final step: Take them out of the oven, drizzle them with honey, and eat them when they're so hot they burn the roof of your mouth.

Those biscuits meant the world to me. Those meals brought us all together, created community and joy and peace. I want that for you, Fennel, for us. I'm worried about our survival. Our mailbox bursts with death threats.

But we've also discovered newfound power. So many people have reached out, wanting to create their own communes modeled after ours. Ironically, the media coverage designed to eradicate our community has spread our message to people who would otherwise never receive it. I offer support, brainstorming with everyone about how they can adapt our organizational structure to suit their own needs.

I'm wondering if we should form a national coalition. To combine our disparate efforts. We could call it the United Commune Front. Because this is a movement. One I hope you'll continue when you're old enough.

I pray my efforts outlast me, though a part of me fears that everything we've worked for will soon be destroyed, that these letters will be the only proof we existed. Because we're in danger, Fennel. If, one day, you read these letters after I'm gone, in the ruins of our utopia, please know that I did everything in my power to protect you.

And make a batch of drop biscuits, just for me.

Yours forever,
Claudia

FORTY-EIGHT

H appy birthday to Gabriel, happy birthday to you," everyone sang
while Astrid carried in the cake. When it was your birthday, Chef
Alvaro would make any dessert you wanted. Gabriel asked for their
favorite—tres leches with blueberries. Now it was here, with five candles
on top. Gabriel took a deep breath. "Wait!" Astrid said. "What do you
wanna wish for?"

"I can't tell you." Gabriel shook their head. "Or it won't come true."

"Okay, then. Just blow out the candles!"

Gabriel took a breath and thought of their wish, which was many
different wishes rolled into one; they wished for life to go back to the way
it was when they first got to the Ranch, before Yunho disappeared, before
Sally got killed, before Mason came back. Gabriel blew the candles out.
They watched the smoke rise, imagining it would float up to the clouds
where the dragons lived. The dragons could read messages in birthday
smoke—*that's* how they knew what kids wished for. And the dragons would
make Gabriel's wishes come true.

"Good job, Gabriel!" Claudia wheeled up and began to cut the cake. The
party was on the stone patio in the backyard. All the kids sat around
the long concrete table. The field looked like a sea of yellow grass; the
wind made waves across the top. Behind it, there were mountains filled
with trees. When dragons got bored of living in the clouds, they'd come
down to the forest for vacation. Sometimes, dragons even wandered into

the fields. They'd walk up to Gabriel's window and check on them in the middle of the night to make sure Gabriel was safe. That's why they loved the dragons, and believed in dragons, even if the grown-ups didn't.

But Gabriel was worried that the dragons might get scared away by all the new people. The ones that lived in the fields. There were five big tents that had been set up past the edge of the patio. *We don't have enough space inside for all our new Community members,* Claudia had explained. *So they'll live outside while we build them housing.* Claudia said that since the Ranch was on TV, lots of people learned about their community. *Even though some people hate us, other people love us. Some even traveled from across the country to join us. And we've got love for everyone, remember?* But for the first time Gabriel was worried there wasn't enough love to go around. What if the new people were dangerous? What if they scared the dragons away?

"You get the first piece." Claudia gave Gabriel some cake.

But Gabriel didn't feel like eating. Gabriel felt worried. "Where's Uncle Mason?"

"He hasn't come upstairs yet," Astrid said. "He must be tired from all the traveling." Astrid seemed annoyed that Mason wasn't at the party. But Gabriel wasn't mad. Because one part of Gabriel's wish had come true: Mason was gone. And if that part came true, maybe the other parts would as well. Maybe they could all go back to the way it was before.

"Speak of the devil," Claudia said to someone behind Gabriel.

Gabriel turned to look. It was Uncle Mason. He was walking funny. Limping and holding his back. He wasn't disappeared. He was still there. Maybe the wish didn't work.

*

"He finally decides to join us," Yunho said, as Mason navigated a treacherous sea of screaming children. Beyond the stone perimeter of the patio stood the cluster of tents where the Ranch's newest denizens had established their Care Pod. Mason thanked the queer anarchist gods that his Entrance Application had been approved before these other newcomers. Though

Mason abhorred his blow-up mattress, the idea of *camping* was unfathomable. As required by the commune's by-laws, he'd invested his entire savings into the democratically run Community Trust (except for Kilcher's paychecks, which were squirreled into a secret bank account), and it was made explicitly clear that the amount one invested had no bearing on one's accommodations. These funds would be distributed across various line items in the Community Budget to ensure everyone had access to free healthcare, food, lodging, and education, and if there was a surplus, it would be funneled into the infrastructure fund, to support the expansion of their facilities. Still, Mason felt the $115,000 he'd surrendered entitled him to more than a flimsy fucking tent on the rocky Montana soil. "How'd you sleep?"

Mason winced as he ducked under a dragon-shaped piñata. "Not well. That air mattress fucked up my back," he lied. He'd almost vomited that morning when he'd looked over his shoulder, into the mirror, and saw the spiral of blue-black welts unfurling from his spinal column. He'd been lucky that Kilcher had provided him with the bullet-proof vest. He could still hear the machine gunfire, still feel where the bullets had battered his back.

"You should make an appointment with Daniel in the Infirmary." Grey approached, cradling Fennel. "He could give you something for the pain."

"No, no," Mason said quickly. "I'll do some stretches. That should straighten me out."

Fennel cooed and stretched their arms toward Mason. "I think Fennel wants to help you feel better. You want to hold them?"

The child was surprisingly warm; Mason pressed the bundle of heat against his chest and though his injured back twitched in response to the weight in his arms, the pain was alleviated by the dopamine flooding his brain. *You're my little hot potato,* Mason either thought or whispered; he was so enchanted he was unsure if he'd articulated his affection. But who needed words? Mason's heart beat against Fennel's fragile body; it was a rhythm more powerful than language.

Yes, he would spare Fennel. Yunho too. He looked toward his lover, beyond him. The party teemed with life. He wished he could save them all from the annihilation he'd set into motion. Claudia caught his gaze and smiled and gave him a sweet wave from across the crowd. Mason felt devastating regret; after a rocky start, he was on the verge of being accepted into this, well, not *family*, they were trying to abolish the family, and yet "queer anarchist gestational commune" felt too cold to describe the deep affection that radiated from this group. Mason *wanted* to join them, he realized. His skepticism had been eroded by the fact he'd never felt so much love in his life. Perhaps he was just vulnerable due to his exhaustion from battling a military-grade killing machine in the dark wilds of Montana last night, but for the first time since arriving at the Ranch he felt they were doing something right here. Maybe the type of love that had, for so long, been relegated to the nuclear family, needed to be shared by a larger collective. Maybe we all needed to take better care of one another. "I could get used to this," he whispered to Fennel. A sadness pulled at his heart. Because he meant it. And yet, he'd been sent to destroy the very community he was learning to love.

*

Gabriel looked to the sky. A dragon appeared. Far away. Just a small dark dot, flying in from the mountains. Getting closer. Their wish *had* come true. They ran to tell Astrid, who was talking to Yunho and Claudia. "A dragon is here for my birthday!"

"We're gonna do the dragon piñata in a minute, sweetie."

"No, a *real* dragon! It was my birthday wish and it came true—"

"Honey, I love your beautiful imagination, but I'm talking to grown-ups right now." Astrid patted Gabriel's head. "Sorry, Claudia—I think a national coalition is a fantastic idea."

"If we're going to face all this scrutiny in the press, we should have some sort of united front," Yunho agreed. "Strength in numbers sounds good right now."

Gabriel's face felt hot. They were mad. They marched off into the field. If no one would believe them about the dragon, they would bring the dragon back to *prove* it was real. They started running. A woman popped her head out of one of the tents. Keisha. She was new. She had long braids and soft cheeks. "Why are you running from your party?"

"There's a dragon coming!"

"Oh, wow! A real dragon?" She made her voice silly like she was playing. But Gabriel wasn't playing. They pointed. "Yes, it's right there."

Keisha followed Gabriel's finger. "What the hell is that?" It zipped toward them. It wasn't like any dragon Gabriel had ever seen in their picture books. It looked more like a helicopter. It had a square body and four propellers, and it just hung in the air. But it had a long neck like a dragon. And two big eyes that looked like video cameras.

"Let's go." Keisha grabbed Gabriel's hand. She was scared. "We gotta warn people."

"No! I wanna stay! It's my *birthday* and this was my *birthday* wish. And now it's come true because there's a dragon and you can't take me away from the dragon because you're new here and you didn't come with us from L.A. so you're not the boss of me." Gabriel was just about to cry, just about to scream, but then they looked up in the sky and saw something strange.

The dragon was peeing. A cloud of mist rained down on them. Gabriel felt a pain in their chest. Their eyes burned. Their throat got tight. They started choking. Keisha choked too and tripped and fell to the ground and then the mist was all around them. In the distance, everyone screamed.

FORTY-NINE

A package dropped from the drone. The white box was small and coffin-shaped, just large enough to bury a swallow. A tiny parachute carried it to the ground. It landed amidst the chaos, unnoticed. People were too concerned with the tear gas to detect the greater danger that had just arrived in their backyard.

*

The dining tables were cleared from the Main Hall, replaced by rows of chairs that faced the towering brick hearth. The entire community was present, save Keisha and Gabriel who were being treated by Daniel in the Infirmary for their exposure to the tear gas. Claudia sat in front of the fireplace, holding the drone-dropped package. She opened the lid and pulled out a tiny cylindrical device. It wriggled between her fingers like a worm. She shrieked in surprise and released the small machine. It clattered to the floor, sprouted six legs, and stopped moving. A hatch parted, revealing a pea-sized bulb. It flickered on, projecting a searing white light. An image materialized within the glow: a hulking white man, clad in army fatigues. A gray beard stretched from his chin to his chest. His eyes were small and mean, buried in sun-scorched cheeks.

Tuck gasped. "My dad."

A commotion erupted in the hall. Mason looked at Tuck. His panicked face was waxen, bloodless. Some secret terror played out behind the boy's one remaining eye.

"Does this sound familiar to any of you terrorist fucks?" The hologram of Tuck's father unfolded a piece of paper. "We got this sweet note from one of you last night: 'Dear Scum: We're winning this war. We have one of your own. Consider what happened with Tuck your warning. Our public message may be one of peace and love, but make no mistake, we possess an arsenal that has the power to destroy a hundred militias. We won't stop until you've been indoctrinated or eradicated. Our power will grow. Our might will be felt around the nation. Live in fear.'" He tossed the paper over his shoulder, then burst into violent hysterics. "That's pretty funny stuff. Especially coming from the scared little shit who hurled a brick with this message attached over our fence last night and then ran like a pussy bitch." A video appeared in the hologram, next to Tuck's father. A man in a ski mask threw a brick over a towering gate, then bolted. Mason's armpits turned to waterfalls as he watched himself in the hologram, praying the balaclava was enough to obscure his identity. "So here's our message in return: This pissing contest has gone on long enough. Return my son to his family. Or we will wipe you worthless fucks off the face of the Earth."

The hologram disappeared. The device exploded.

*

"I'm gonna ask a question I already know the answer to." Claudia surveyed the assembled. "Did anyone here write that ridiculously bogus letter?" Silence. Mason's lungs felt tight. Dark patches of sweat stained his shirt. "That's what I thought."

"But *who* would write it then?" Mahmood asked. "And why?"

"Maybe the militia wrote it themselves." Chef Alvaro spoke up from the kitchen, behind the rows of chairs, where he was preparing dinner. "To use it as an excuse to attack us."

"But they already had an excuse to attack us," Astrid insisted.

"What do you mean?"

Astrid hesitated. "Well, we have Tuck. The conservative press said we kidnapped him. The militia had all the justification they needed."

"They didn't give a fuck about me. You can just say it, Astrid," Tuck spat. "They told me—while my father held me down and my mother gouged my eye out—that if I wanted to live with you all and engage in a homosexual lifestyle, that I was dead to them. My dad doesn't give a shit about getting his son back. He's just pissed someone dared to provoke him. It wounded his pathetic little ego. He won't stand for that. Not when he's got a barn full of military-grade weapons supplied to him by the state through their Militia Grant Program."

"The letter was bait," Claudia said.

"But who would want to bait them?" Yunho asked.

"My guess is the FBI."

Mason's throat constricted. "But Claudia, don't you think you're being a bit paranoid?" he rasped, attempting to modulate the panic from his tone.

"Not at all. I think it's maybe the *only* logical explanation. This is FBI History 101, a move straight out of the COINTELPRO playbook. Stir up conflict and paranoia among rival radical groups with fake FBI-forged letters, which leads to internal discord and increased militarization. Ultimately, the groups either eradicate each other or implode internally."

"I doubt the FBI cares about our little community—"

"They've surveilled me for my entire adult life, Mason, and you *know* this, so the fact that you're doubting me here is wild. Were you not at Yunho's hearing before the Anti-American Speech Committee? Did you not see how Astrid and I were called out—"

"Yes, but they never *did* anything about it. I don't understand *why* you think they'd target our community *now*—"

"Because we represent a threat to the ruling ideology of the U.S.—"

"I don't need a refresher on our mission."

"It sounds like you do. And a refresher on the legacies of COINTELPRO and the Patriot Act and the FBI's continued effort—through violence, murder, surveillance, and manipulation—to eradicate all social justice movements that threaten the State."

"Okay, I'm sorry!"

"My theory is that they're using a fabricated letter to goad the local militia into attacking us. That way, the FBI wipes us out without getting their hands dirty."

"Well, what the fuck are we gonna do?" Terrance piped up. He was Keisha's partner; the two of them shared a tent. "Because we just got tear-gassed by a drone and then watched a hologram tell us we're gonna die. I didn't uproot my life just to get killed by white supremacists. If we can't do anything about the FBI, we *have* to do something about this militia."

"You're right," Claudia said. "We need to make peace."

"And how do we do that?"

FIFTY

T his isn't going to fix anything." Tuck picked at a seam on the fraying leather passenger seat of the commune's Tesla as it sped down an empty two-lane road. Sun sliced through the tall pines as they drove, smacking Tuck's face with intermittent beams of harsh white light. "They don't want me back. They just wanna fuck with you all."

"I know that, Tuck," Yunho murmured, eyes fixed to the road. "I wanted you to stay."

"Me too," Mason chimed in from the back seat.

"But everyone on the Ranch is scared," Yunho continued. "We don't know what to do—"

"All your talk about having love for everyone and you just throw me out like trash—"

"Hey—we're on your side—"

"Then why are you driving me back to the people who *gouged my fucking eye out*—"

"Your family—"

"*They're not my fucking family, don't you get that?* Your community is the only family I have. You're the only people who . . . love . . . me . . ." Tuck started sobbing. Heavy, wrenching cries.

Pain radiated from the galaxy of welts on Mason's back, inundating his nervous system with an agony so intense it almost, mercifully, stifled his guilty conscience. Mason tried to tell himself he was just Kilcher's puppet, a mindless marionette with timber hands tied to the federal government's strings. Yes, it was Kilcher who was responsible. Mason just threw a brick over a wall. But all Mason's attempts at mental exoneration were thwarted by an unpardonable feeling: He wanted this whole thing to explode. Because the longer it stretched on, the more work he'd have to do for Kilcher. And Mason couldn't handle it. His Ankl alarm had been silenced but he still couldn't sleep. Mason didn't want to send Tuck back; this kid seemed sweet, and Mason could only imagine the torturous homecoming Tuck's family had planned for their faggot son. But there was also the other reason: He needed to keep Tuck at the Ranch, so conflict would continue to build with the militia until the two radical entities wiped each other off the Earth. The sooner the FBI's vision was realized, the sooner Mason could stop living in this agonizing liminal space, suffering through the horror of not knowing how it would end, anticipating the moment his loved ones realized that he'd betrayed them.

"We don't have to send him back," Mason insisted.

"Don't make this harder," Yunho warned.

"*But he could be killed—*"

"*He's not going to be killed by his family.*"

"*I told you, they're not my fucking family.*" Tuck flung his door open. Asphalt blurred beneath the speeding vehicle.

"*What are you doing?*" Yunho slammed on the brakes.

Tuck ripped off his seat belt. "I'm walking home."

FIFTY-ONE

NO TOMORROW

Notes Against Futurity

By Tuck Wilson

Reproductive futurity and its consequences have been a disaster for the human race. All the moral posturing that accompanies the production of children is to cover up what everyone knows deep down: Death is the only truth. Children are an illusion to alleviate this reality, to access a fantasy of intergenerational immortality. But when you create children, all you really create is more death. More flesh bags to wander the planet, waste its resources, hoard wealth, start wars, rape, kill, and plunder, unaware their lives mean nothing, that they'll soon be a feast for worms, and all they'll have achieved is bringing humanity one step closer to annihilation. But instead of boring you with abstract theories, let me use my own abortion of a family to prove my point.

There's a vermin nest and it's filled with rats who are filled with shit, and I call it home sweet home. Let's start with my "mom." That cunt. Not a mother to me. I returned home yesterday. She was sitting on the porch with a PBR. She didn't even bat a crusty eyelash when she saw me marching up. Just sat there frowning and said, "Dad's in the barn. Go see him."

This is the woman who claimed she was so desperate to "save me" and bring me back to our family. Fuck family. THEY'RE the ones that kicked ME out. Right after they gouged out my eye. Dad held me down and my brother tied me to the bed and Mom went in with a fucking ice-cream scoop. Not even a knife. She popped my eye with the blunt force of the fucking scooper. It felt like my whole face exploded along with my eye and my vision went black as Mom bore deeper into my socket. Like she was digging in a stubborn pint of rocky road. CLICK. She clicked the scooper shut, ripped out my eye. I screamed. Dad said this is what I got for being a faggot and trying to join the Ranch. Said my grandaddy and great-grandaddy would be ashamed, they'd been leaders of the Klan, the Proud Boys, and here I was consorting with the enemy. After they ripped out my eye, Dad drove me to the Ranch, dropped me outside and said that if I wanted to go live with scum, then I could also die with scum.

My "extended family" are all just other dumb-fuck militia members. At a cookout in 2032, when I was five, some drunk idiot let the real dogs run alongside the AI quadrupedal robot dogs with assault weapons strapped to their backs. The SPURs. Special Purpose Unmanned Rifles. They hauled out one my grandaddy bought on the black market in 2023. But even though my dad said the

SPUR wasn't in attack mode—he lied—the thing opened fire on my aunt's Chihuahua. My aunt screamed while the SPUR shot the dog full of holes. But my dad laughed. Actually fucking laughed. And my "family" just joined in the hilarity, wheezing until tears rolled down their faces. And I thought: They aren't human. They're monsters.

I was terrified marching through our backyard yesterday. I choked back tears. Wished I was at the Ranch. What drives me crazy is that my stupid fucking family can't see that the Ranch is fighting to liberate ALL people. My family would BENEFIT from the universal income guaranteed to everyone on the Ranch, because my parents have battled poverty ever since labor automation decimated the job market. They'd BENEFIT from the abolition of the prison industrial complex that locked up Aunt Jean because she defended herself against a husband who beat her with a baseball bat. They'd BENEFIT from access to education when funding has been stripped from so many rural public schools.

But as I walked to meet my father in the barn—terrified of what he would do to me—I realized I disagreed with those Ranch fuckers who abandoned me. Their fairytale future is a ludicrous fantasy in which everyone is freed from capitalism. But even if the fairy tale comes true, my family doesn't deserve the liberation provided by the very people they're oppressing.

The only thing my family deserves is a mass grave.

My father swung the barn gates open. A rifle was strapped to his chest. To my surprise, he didn't aim it at me. Instead, he opened his arms. Started sobbing. "My baby boy is back."

I was numb. I felt nothing as he wrapped his arms around me. I looked over his shoulder. A fleet of

killing machines stood behind him. Six UDPs. Unmanned
Death Panthers. They made the clunky AI robot dogs from
the 2020s look like some kid's shitty science fair
project. Their steel bodies gleamed under harsh fluorescent lights. Racks of weaponry covered the walls.
Streaks of blood striped the concrete floor. Traces of
recent torture. Probably a poll worker. Dad made sure
the local ballot counts were "right." He was always
busy around election cycles.

My dad let me go. I stared at him through my one eye.
Now that half my vision is gone, I have no depth perception. My dad, the killing machines behind him—it all
flattened into a two-dimensional plane. Like a picture.
I felt dizzy. My adrenaline spiked. I couldn't gauge the
distance between me and my father. The room spun.

"Welcome back to the family. We love you so much."
Tears gleamed in my father's eyes. I imagined slicing
each one with an ice-cream scoop. I imagined laughing
at his screams.

I guess this is a memoir. Or a manifesto. Or a
suicide note.

I'm writing on some ancient word processor I found in
our basement, leaving no digital trace of my work, to
avoid being surveilled. I cannot afford to have anyone
stop my efforts. Because the story of my family isn't
finished, though it soon will be. I'm not yet sure of the
ending, though I know it will bring horror and tragedy
to many. It's an ending that I will write, fulfilling the
future's one true promise: death.

FIFTY-TWO

I have an exciting announcement," Claudia said to the classroom. Gabriel struggled to stay awake. They weren't sleeping at night—they kept having nightmares about the drone, dreams where tear gas rained down. They'd wake up coughing, screaming. They'd run into Daniel and Mahmood's room and climb into bed and stay awake until the sun came up.

Gabriel's eyes got heavy. They closed them. When they opened them again, Claudia was hovering next to their desk. "Are you okay, Gabriel?"

"I'm sleepy."

"It's okay. Let's just try to stay awake for class. I think you're gonna like the surprise I'm about to announce."

"What is it?" Sophie yelled.

Claudia wheeled back to her desk. "Next month we're going to host a very special party!"

"What kind of party?" Gabriel wasn't sure they liked parties anymore.

"Well, there are other communities like ours popping up all over the country. So we're gonna have a big meeting here at the Ranch, and people from these communities will come visit us. We'll get to laugh, eat food, and play. But we'll also talk about ways we can work together to make our communities stronger. We're calling it the United Commune Front. Doesn't that sound fun?" Everyone else in class seemed excited. But Gabriel felt afraid. "Now I know some of us got scared at Gabriel's birthday. But that's why we started Safety Drills. And that's another thing we'll talk about at the meeting: community safety! But you wanna know the most exciting part?"

"I do!" Sophie yelled out again.

"Kids will come to the big meeting too, so you'll make new friends from all over the country! You'll also form your very own Kids' Coalition, where you'll brainstorm how you'd like to see your communities change and grow." Claudia picked up a pile of thick white paper. "Now, I'm handing out watercolor paper. I want you to paint pictures about your lives. Later this month, when you have your Kids' Coalition meeting, you'll share your pictures and tell stories about your community." Claudia wheeled to Gabriel's desk. She handed them watercolor paper. But Gabriel felt too tired to paint. "I know what would cheer you up," she whispered.

"What?"

"How about a trip to the barn after class?"

*

The white canvas taunted him. Mason sat before the blankness, stumped. He'd purchased a mountain of art supplies in a manic spree, pointlessly debating which shades of paint to select for a project not yet conceived, tapping into the anesthetizing hypnosis of compulsive consumption. But relief dissipated when he clicked "purchase" on Amazon. Dread rushed back, and Mason realized he hadn't bested the mental labyrinth of his own making, where each thought led him deeper into an impossible maze of despair. He was still trapped, still hopelessly lost.

Mason needed to make art again.

But not art like the art he'd made recently: boring office installations, canvases painted by AI "assistants," corporate merchandise collaborations. He wanted to make art like the art he'd made at the start of his career, art that *meant* something. In college, he'd painted a series of photorealistic self-portraits, always with the same frame: his face against a flat black background. He could get lost for days in just one eye, obsessing over every brushstroke; he'd skip meals, stay in his studio to endlessly tweak; he'd dream of the eye; and so it went with every detail—each blemish, each hair, each centimeter of his full lips. Then came the portholes. Mason painted over sections of his face to give the illusion that whole swaths of skin were rotting off his skull, but instead of revealing his insides, these gaping wounds were portholes to an inner psychic space, windows containing sick tableaus—a panopticon stuffed with seal carcasses, a senator jerking his cock while getting face-fucked by a tank gun, a woman drowning in a sea of aborted fetuses. His classmates never liked these paintings, found them didactic and unsubtle, but Mason always felt that, well, the world was on fire so what was the point of being elliptical and academic? He wanted to create work that felt like a knife to the heart, and there was nothing subtle about a punctured aorta. Whenever he completed a self-portrait, Mason felt grounded; after being lost in a swirling cloud of dread, he'd paint himself back into the world, using nothing but his hands, a canvas, and acrylics. He'd find a way out of anxiety. An answer to unsolvable riddles. Or at least a reflection of the impossible questions posed by them.

He wanted to regain that youthful hope; the messianic delusion that he could heal himself *and* right the world with his art. But now, staring at the blank canvas only inspired terror. Paralysis. The sense that the world would never be right again, no matter how well he painted it.

An alarm sounded: a reminder. It was time to feed the calves.

*

The baby cows drank formula now because their mom was dead. Gabriel liked to comfort the babies by feeding them from the bottle. It also made Gabriel feel better. Claudia let them skip their after-school chores and go to the barn instead, as a treat. Hay scratched their ankles as they walked to the stall where Mason stood.

"Thank you for helping me with my job." Mason shoved a measuring cup into a bag of milk replacer. He put the powder into bottles and poured in hot water from the big metal sink. "You want to feed one of them?" He held out a bottle to Gabriel.

"Yes!" Gabriel took the bottle, held it out to a calf. The calf sniffed it, then jumped forward and started sucking. Gabriel almost dropped the bottle. It bobbed up and down while the cow drank. "How do you know how to take care of cows?"

"Well, I didn't when I got here. But I learned. Because I guess this is my job now." Mason laughed but seemed sad. "I used to be a famous artist. Now I feed cows. Not a trajectory I would recommend."

"Why aren't you a famous artist anymore?"

"Well, I guess I'm still somewhat famous. Though unfortunately for the wrong reasons."

"If you're still famous, why don't you also still be an artist?"

Mason looked surprised. "I guess I don't know what I would make art about."

"I made a painting in school today."

"What was it about?"

"My life."

"Well, that's a good subject. Time-tested." Suddenly, Mason's phone rang. He stared down at the screen and frowned. Something was wrong. "Hey, uh, I have to take a call. Be right back." He hurried toward the barn door.

"You should make a painting about *your* life," Gabriel called out.

"I would." Mason wiped a tear from his eye. "But I don't want to make something ugly."

FIFTY-THREE

Kilcher answered the door wearing a towel and nothing else. Of all the weapons of psychological warfare the FBI had unleashed on Mason, Kilcher's dewy post-shower six-pack was the most diabolical. Coming in second: the supernatural prominence of his ass, the upper summit of which was long and firm enough for two people to rest espresso cups comfortably. The towel was wrapped bandage-tight, hugging every contour of his haunches in a losing battle to stay put.

"What's up?" Kilcher stood in the doorframe, wincing as if Mason had busted into his hotel uninvited, instead of being summoned here urgently. "I just got out of the shower."

"You . . . asked me to come?" There was nowhere to look but Kilcher's almost-naked body.

"Wipe the drool off your chin." Kilcher retreated into his room—a weathered suite with stained carpet at a Montana motel deceitfully named the Quality Inn—and didn't bother to invite Mason inside. The door shut in Mason's face.

"Should I wait outside while you change—"

"Just come in for fuck's sake." Mason entered, shocked to discover Kilcher completely naked, leaning against a small writing desk that trembled under his titanic ass. Kilcher's dick drooped between his thighs, at least six inches soft, daring Mason to imagine anything other than how its veins might pulse when engorged. "Jesus, it's like you've never seen a naked man before."

"I'm, uh, sorry."

"I'm *pissed* at you. Do you think I *wanted* to be dragged to Siberian-Titty-Fuck, Montana, to babysit your flabby ass?" Mason blushed. His ass *was* flabby. "I have a husband at home. A *hot* husband. And two children we obtained through *very* expensive surrogacies."

"Congratulations?"

"Fuck you."

"I'm sorry, it just seemed like you were looking for validation or—"

"The only thing I'm *looking* for is an explanation as to why you are such a total failure."

"What do you mean? I did what you asked—"

"You '*did what I asked*'? Absolutely not. I asked you to stir discord among your commune while simultaneously ratcheting up tensions with local militia to eventually cause the two parties to neutralize each other or implode or both. Instead, you just sat there and watched while your commune *made peace* with the local militia by returning their son to them."

"*What am I supposed to do?*"

"*Your fucking job.*"

"*I tried! I failed! It's over! Please, can we just end this?*" Mason begged. "I wanna go back to a normal life. Back to Yunho. Start making art again."

"Oh, you want to start making *art* again? Then by all means, let's just drop this *wildly important mission* to save the American family." Kilcher shoved Mason onto the bed. He climbed on top of him and clamped his calloused hands around Mason's throat. "Do you realize how many people in D.C. are shitting their pants because of your crazy little anarchist friends? It's not just Republicans. Because if there's one issue that's bipartisan, it's the importance of the American family." Kilcher tightened his grip, pressed his naked body into Mason's. The marble-like heft of his statuesque thighs crushed the breath from Mason's body. "Because, as Whitney Houston said, 'The children are our *future*.' The future of *America*. To participate in the *future* of this country you must participate in the American *family*. It's what we homosexuals fought so desperately to join. And then we lost it with the fall of *Obergefell v. Hodges*. I want it back, Mason. *I need it.*" He shook Mason's neck, slammed his head against the bedframe. "For *my daughter*. For *my husband*. But your fucking freak friends are making it difficult for *normal* gays like me, gays with mortgages and kids and carpool duties, to regain our rightful place in American society." Mason clawed at Kilcher, fought for air, fought the strange eroticism festering in his skull, a force that sent blood rushing to his cock as Kilcher spat in his face. "If you destroy the American family, you destroy America. And we can't let that happen, can we?"

"No . . . we . . . can't," Mason choked out. "What . . . should I do?"

Kilcher slapped him. "Your." *Slap.* "Fucking." *Slap.* "Job." *Slap.* "Come up with some *ideas* to undermine your community, *you fucking idiot*." Kilcher punched Mason's chest. Throttled his airflow. Red spots obscured his vision. His cock stiffened. Kilcher's remained limp. "Give me some information I can use. Or I'll end your life in this Quality Inn." Kilcher let go.

Mason wheezed, desperate to fill his lungs. "They're . . . planning a meeting. Of communes around the country. A national coalition. October twentieth. I'll give you all the details."

Finally, and to Mason's surprise, Kilcher's cock hardened.

*

Tears streamed down Mason's face as Kilcher fucked his throat. He gagged, flinched backward, but Kilcher caught his skull and held it in place. He fucked Mason's mouth harder. Mason wretched again, reeled back, fell to the floor, and gasped on the stained carpet.

Then, something strange happened. The fibers of the carpet turned green. Grew from the floor like grass. No, they *were* grass. He was on someone's lawn. Mason looked up. It was *his* lawn. In Los Angeles. At the old Los Feliz place. But how had he gotten here? Kilcher stood above him, grinning. Mason's estate loomed in the background. He squinted at the structure—it was filled with his friends. A flock of synchronized swimmers bottlenecked at the entrance. Patrick was there. And Yunho. Everyone watched him.

His baby shower. He'd traveled back in time to his baby shower.

He looked up at Kilcher, who stood before him, his hard-on extending with Pinnochian rapidity. His penis became a yardstick, a spear. Finally, a machine gun. The crowd looked on expectantly. They wanted Mason to choke on it. To die. Mason opened wide. But before he could swallow Kilcher's bullets, Kilcher disappeared. *Poof.* He left a puff of smoke in his wake.

Pink smoke.

Mason inhaled. His vision went white. He screamed.

He awoke sweating on his air mattress. Just another nightmare. They always ended the same. With White Death. But the replication of the real-life incident with Kilcher had been a new addition. *How kind of my subconscious to find fresh ways to torture me*, Mason thought. He got up, flipped on a light, and winced under the fluorescents of the shooting range. The empty gun racks had a ghostly quality, radiating with the spectral brutality of a latent curse. He passed them on his way to take a piss. But he paused at the bathroom door, arrested by the sight of a blank canvas wrapped in plastic, like a cadaver at a crime scene. All that savage potentiality, as violent as the unkept promise of the room around him.

Suddenly, Mason knew what to paint.

He didn't stop to piss, some adrenal force lifted the pressure of the fluids against his urethra and instead of pissing he slashed the plastic that sealed the canvas and grabbed a box of acrylics. He began painting to figure out who he'd be once this terror no longer defined his life, because maybe it was over, maybe the information he'd given Kilcher was enough to propel this situation to its awful conclusion. *October twentieth*—two magic words to conjure the evil force that would destroy them all. Except Mason. He'd be free, free to walk, to run, to do, well, what exactly? Yes, he'd be spared whatever fate he inflicted upon the commune, but he'd still be forced to live with a lethal guilt that would work its way through his system like a slow-moving poison, and it was this poison Mason was attempting to purge when he first slapped the blank canvas with a wet brush.

He started with white. Plain white. Primer. He didn't dilute the acrylics. He wanted the paint to feel thick, layered, sculptural. He waited for a coat of white to dry, then painted another thick white coat on top of it until the painting became three-dimensional, until it looked like a square cutout of a white cloud. Then came the red. He painted two long crimson streaks across the white. Each streak looked like a gash from a stab wound, like someone had slashed a cumulonimbus and discovered its vaporous body contained a network of veins and arteries.

He knew the painting was done when it looked like a bleeding cloud. He knew the painting was done when it transported him back to the moment his soul died. He knew the painting was done when he was looking at an exact representation of White Death.

FIFTY-FOUR

"October twentieth. Look toward that date in fear." The voice was a perfect match of timbre and tone. "We're assembling a national force of anarchist soldiers." We all sat in the barn, watching the hologram of Claudia. Seeing her face again brought back an agony I thought I'd deadened. Not only did I feel that agony again (the pain of being abandoned by the only people who loved me), but there was also the disconcerting realization that I'd been feeling that agony ever since I returned "home"—it was just lurking beneath the dulled and disso-ciated surface of my consciousness.

Only it wasn't Claudia. Sure, the hologram looked like Claudia. But there was a glitch with her eyes—a deadness that didn't match the determination perpetually burning in her pupils. I've always doubted "Soul-Detectors," those who claim they can detect a VoidFake due to the dead eyes of its subject. The entire endeavor is too psychic-adjacent to be a legit form of forensics, like when the police employ mediums, as if they need any more help bringing "criminals" to "justice" based on no real evidence. But looking at Claudia's hologram, I began to think Soul-Detectors were on to something. The AI used to create digitally faked holograms has surpassed the technology to detect those same fakes, but nothing can duplicate the intimacy of looking into someone's eyes and recognizing the contours of their humanity.

And Claudia's eyes were dead. Twin lacunas. "We'll attack, and we won't relent until every piece of scum in your pathetic hidey-hole is obliterated." This movie villain dialogue wasn't her; she'd never say something like that. But there was something appealing about Void-Fake Claudia. Her dead eyes matched my own. I often feel like a VoidFake of myself. A hologram with no connection to a soul. I'm dying here, trapped with my vile family. I need an outlet. To purge my fury. The direction of the violence doesn't matter. What matters is the blood.

"We're going after them," my dad bellowed to the assembled idiots. "This shit has got to stop. On October twentieth, we attack."

"Are you stupid, Dad?" I asked.

"Don't you fucking talk to me like that, boy."

"The enemy has given us a specific date on which to attack them. Doesn't that strike you as suspicious? Like maybe they're setting a trap?" The crowd wavered, seeing my point. I don't, of course, believe that Claudia has set a trap for us. Because I don't believe she made this hologram. Who did? The FBI, maybe? She had her suspicions about them. Regardless, this trap isn't one I want to walk into. If there's violence in my future, I want to control it. "Well, Dad?"

My dad said nothing, unwilling to admit he was wrong. But his silence was the permission everyone needed to turn toward me, their new leader.

"What do you think we should do?" some rifle-wielding fuckwit asked.

A plan, subconsciously sculpted, concretized in my mind. Like my agony, I had been unaware of it until the moment it revealed itself to me, fully realized. I had the answer. A release for my rage. "We strike sooner. An ambush. We take no prisoners."

Everyone applauded, stomped, hollered.

Of course, that's not my real plan. If they knew my real plan, they'd shut the fuck up. Cower in their seats. Scream in terror. But for now, they'll have to live in ignorance, their favorite state, a territory so blissfully vast one can never see the reckoning on the horizon.

FIFTY-FIVE

H i, uh, Mason?"

"Yes, this is Mason."

"Nell Ponce. Listen, babe—I'm running to another meeting, so I've gotta be quick. Sorry I was such a cryptic little diva in my email. But I always prefer a phone chat. It's so dangerous to discuss anything over email these days."

"Right . . ."

"Or to use a phone for that matter. Your phone isn't tapped, is it?"

"Honestly, I can't guarantee—"

"Ah, fuck it. I'm not saying anything incriminating."

"Well, that's . . . good . . . I guess?"

"I wanted to discuss your representation. I heard you were dropped by your gallery after all the, uh . . . *hullabaloo* surrounding your baby shower."

"Correct. Mahmood's fathers no longer wanted to represent me after the . . . hullabaloo. Can we not call it that?"

"Of course, honey."

"Honestly, Mahmood is also in a rough patch with his dads. They've cut him off. They don't understand what we're doing out here in Montana—"

"And I *really* don't wanna know what you're doing. Just in case the phones *are* tapped."

"What *did* you want, Nell?"

"Well, now that the hullabaloo—*sorry*—is over it seems like Mason Daunt could be due for a victorious comeback to the art scene. You emerge from the wreckage of your life with a brave new body of work that earns us twin dump trucks filled with money."

"You're funny."

"I'm *serious*. When I reached out and you mentioned you were working on a new series of paintings I thought: 'Kismet!' Then, when I saw the pictures of those canvases, I was stunned. So beautiful. So simple. So devoid of meaning."

"They're *not* meaningless—"

"Stop right there, Mason. I'm sure these paintings have all sorts of personal resonance for you. But that's between you and . . . yourself. I don't *want* to know what these paintings mean to you. Especially if these phones *are* tapped. Okay? I don't want to be dragged up before the Anti-American Speech Committee to testify that you confided in me that your work has secret anarchist undertones or overtones or highlights or lowlights or blow-outs or bangs. Got it?"

"Got it."

"Repeat after me: My work means nothing."

"My work means nothing."

"Beautiful. Besides, your presence alone is enough to stir up all sorts of controversy. But the good kind of controversy. The kind that pays the bills and doesn't get us indicted."

"Okay . . ."

"Now, down to business. I have a rather sudden opening at my Hudson Yards gallery."

"Oh, yes. I think I saw something in the news?"

"A tragedy. Poor Maggie Shotwell. I mean, I totally get the *impulse* to set yourself on fire to protest the corporate greed accelerating climate change, but to actually do it? That's nuts."

"Right. Now I'm remembering."

"So sad. And to not document it seems like a waste of a suicide and frankly against the self-mythologizing impulse of every artist I know. If you're going to kill yourself to become an artistic climate martyr, at least have the curatorial foresight to make sure someone takes a picture."

"Uh, well . . . maybe her art show wasn't exactly her priority?"

"You're telling me. Anyway, I have nothing to exhibit. But maybe that's the point. Maybe Maggie intended this suicide to negate her career, and function as a statement against the type of bourgeoise art production in which she was engaged, i.e., a problematic entanglement with wealthy patrons who paid her with funds gained through the very climate-disaster-inducing acts she protested through her art. Maybe her death was the first honest work she produced."

"Nell, don't you have another appointment—"

"Still, I wish she'd left me more than a four-by-six patch of burnt floor and bone dust. As it turns out, Maggie was generating no new work. And I'm *supposed* to host an opening in two weeks. So there's space. For your canvases, Mason. For your comeback. What do you say?"

"I say yes."

"Fantastic. Now just promise you won't kill yourself."

"Is that a joke—"

"Yes, yes, of course. But also promise you won't kill yourself."

"I won't kill myself."

"You won't kill yourself."

"I won't kill myself."

"This is all very exciting. I'll be in touch soon!"

*

I won't kill myself. The phrase stuck in Mason's head like a bad pop song, a noxious yet irresistible melody he couldn't purge from his thoughts. *I won't kill myself.* It appeared without fail, whenever he had moments of calm. Which, in the two weeks following Nell Ponce's call, were mercifully few. It was not uncommon to book a gallery show a year in advance, so the crunched timeline of two weeks left Mason scrambling to fulfill press obligations and coordinate with art handlers to transport to his work to New York, not to mention the most important task: finishing the additional five paintings he promised Nell. Mason was also still obligated to perform his Ranch duties, namely caring for the baby calves, one of whom decided the high-pressure lead-up to Mason's comeback was a perfect time to get a deadly case of neonatal calf diarrhea, which required him to constantly nurse the sick calf, feeding it medicine and oral electrolytes while consoling an apoplectic Gabriel who was terrified their "baby" would meet the same fate as its poor dead mom, Sally.

No, there wasn't a lot of downtime. But whenever his mind had a moment to rest, the same phrase came rushing in: *I won't kill myself.* Late-night baths at two A.M. were essential to maintaining his sanity; it was the only time his favorite bathroom with the claw-foot tub was not dominated by Care Pod activity, the relentless pissing and shitting and toothbrushing and face washing. Yet the minute he slipped into bathwater, the minute his thoughts began to drift, he discovered that phrase waiting for him, like a sniper who'd been staked out all day: *I won't kill myself.* Or it hit him during the nights Yunho snuck down to the shooting range to cuddle with Mason on the blow-up mattress. He loved curling up in Yunho's embrace, smelling his musk, an aroma that erased Mason's mounting anxiety until, seconds later, the phrase returned to rob him of sleep: *I won't kill myself.* He tried meditating, but it visited him then too: *I won't kill myself.* Some days, the words lost their meaning through repetition, and this obsessive loop felt like a tic, an empty compulsive behavior that served as a container for unprocessed dread. Yet there were other times the meaning hit him with such sickening urgency that he feared he might do the opposite; he might slit his throat. *I won't kill myself.* Why would anyone insist they *wouldn't* kill themselves unless it had occurred to them that they *would*?

*

Mason boarded the plane. *I won't kill myself.* It was a hard promise to keep when confronted with the indignity of basic economy. The commune had voted to pay for his flight using the Flex Fund, as this trip would bring the Ranch a financial windfall should Mason sell his work, because any income earned by community members was routed back to the Community Trust.

But unfortunately, his compatriots had vehemently denied him first class. Mason looked over his shoulder. Yunho trudged up the aisle behind him. "How will we survive this flight?"

Yunho laughed. "You will manage, my love." Mason fought the urge to weep. Those two words—*my love*—issued so casually. Like they were just another couple trapped on a shitty flight. As if their entire world was not on the verge of obliteration. *You will manage, my love.* And as they stumbled into their seats, Mason felt that he *could* manage. With Yunho by his side, they would make it through.

"I love you." Mason kissed Yunho. Turbulence shook the aircraft as it hurtled skyward. Then, the cabin settled. Mason closed his eyes. He expected the familiar suicidal phrase to surface. It never did. Instead, an ambient optimism hummed inside him, warm and comforting.

Mason drifted to sleep. He woke up when the plane hit the runway. Was it just him, or did light hit differently in New York? The city radiated with possibility; it was a glowing metropolis untainted by their history. Without a past, the future could be anything. The sun illuminated floating dust motes; they danced in front of Yunho's sleeping face.

"We're here," Mason whispered. For one beautiful moment, he thought he might get to love his life again.

FIFTY-SIX

A rts and crafts period. Astrid was in charge. She didn't usually teach at school, but Claudia was busy getting ready for the United Commune Front. Also, Astrid was an artist, so she could help them with their paintings for the Kids' Coalition. Astrid stood in front of the class, working on her own piece: a portrait of Gabriel. It was large, almost as tall as Gabriel in real life. Astrid said it would hang in the Main Hall during the UCF meetings. Gabriel had agreed to be in the portrait because it made them feel special. But looking at it now, they felt strange. Their eyes were missing. Astrid hadn't painted them yet. Gabriel thought of Sally's eyes for some reason, filling the empty space. Sally's dead eyes in Gabriel's sockets. They raised their hand.

"Yes, Gabriel?"

"Can I come up and look at your painting?"

"Of course! Can I look at your painting too?"

"Okay." Gabriel grabbed their watercolor and walked up to Astrid. "Why didn't you paint my eyes yet?" They grabbed Astrid's long skirt.

"Well, because the eyes are the most important part. And you have such big, beautiful eyes. I want to make sure I get them right. I'm gonna make everyone fall in love with you."

"What does it say?" There were big block letters above Gabriel's head.

"Do you wanna try to read it? Sound it out?"

"Okay." Gabriel squinted at the letters. "H . . . O . . . P . . . E. Hope?"

"Yes, that's right . . ."

". . . is . . . a . . ."

"Yes, you've got it."

"I don't know that word."

"'Discipline.'"

"Hope . . . is a . . . discipline."

"Yes! It's a quote from Mariame Kaba."

"What's a 'discipline'?"

"It's something you have to do every day and work hard at."

"Why is hope hard work?"

"Well, sometimes it's difficult to have hope. Like, at your birthday party. You were really upset, right?"

"Yeah, because those mean people sent their drones."

"Right. We were all sad after that happened. But we didn't give up. Because we're doing something good. Something we love. So we keep hope alive. But that can be hard work when bad things happen."

"Do I still have hope?"

"You tell me."

"Yeah, I think so."

"Well, good! That's why you're in my painting. Because people will look at your picture and know you have hope. Now can I see what *you're* painting?" Gabriel showed their painting to Astrid. She frowned. "What is it?"

"A map. I'm showing them where the dragons live in the woods."

"We know that dragons aren't real though, right?"

"Dragons *are* real. They're gonna breathe fire on the bad guys that try to kill us."

"No one's going to try to kill us, sweetie. I'm worried that your map might confuse the other kids. We can't have people running off to the woods in search of dragons, okay?"

"But the dragons will *protect us*."

"No, Gabriel. There are no dragons. Now give me this." Astrid snatched Gabriel's drawing. Gabriel didn't let go. The map ripped into two pieces.

"You *ruined* my map!"

"Gabriel, you are *not* going to throw a tantrum—"

"It was gonna keep the kids safe but now we're all gonna die—"

"Stop it!" Astrid yelled. The class looked scared. *"No one's gonna die."*

*

Faces. The Unmanned Death Panthers consume faces. They don't devour actual flesh-and-blood countenances like their animal-kingdom brethren, but rather images of faces. I've taken the responsibility of programming our UDP for our upcoming raid. At my instruction, our UDP has ingested photos of each target, creating comprehensive "mental" portraits of these people. The UDP will then kill its targets during our mission. The UDP also shares a database with all other unmanned AI-powered weaponry. This database creates an algorithm that identifies the type of person most likely to be a target. This is supposed to help "prevent" crime but, of course, it only concretizes law enforcement biases and creates robots just as prejudiced as their programmers. I realize the problems inherent in contributing to this murderous database, but these problems don't concern me. These are problems for someone who believes in the future. I no longer do.

The UDP also consumes satellite images of Earth that allow it to anticipate the challenges presented by any landscape it is charged with raiding. I'm currently staring at a satellite image of the Ranch. It looks so small on my screen. Like a map a child would draw, a simplistic rendering of their space in the world, designed to give them some sense of meaning. I imagine I have a big eraser. I imagine scrubbing that little

```
map until there's nothing left. No place, no people, no
future, nothing.
    We attack tonight.
```

*

Gabriel waited until everyone was asleep, then snuck down their bunk bed ladder. They tiptoed through the hallway past Astrid's bedroom. Gabriel's ears burned when they thought of her. The way she ripped up Gabriel's map. The one that showed where the dragons lived, the beautiful beasts that would protect them all from death. But Astrid wouldn't listen. *No one* would listen, no one *believed* Gabriel, everyone just treated them like *some little kid* with an "overactive imagination." But Gabriel wouldn't scream anymore, They wouldn't cry.

Gabriel would run away.

They came to the stairway, grabbed the banister, and let their eyes adjust to the dark. They stepped onto the first step. They were scared. They wanted to turn around. But they kept going. Hope is a discipline. Hard work. Gabriel was leaving to find the dragons. And the dragons would protect them.

Gabriel reached the bottom step. The Great Hall was filled with people in sleeping bags, people from communes around the country. They were the ones here for the big meeting who couldn't afford a hotel. All of them were bundled in their bags like caterpillars. They sighed and snored. Gabriel snuck past. Their breath brushed Gabriel's bare feet. The painting of Gabriel hung above the fireplace. The eyes were finished. Gabriel-in-the-Painting watched over the sleeping people. But the real Gabriel was leaving forever.

"Where are you going, sweetie?"

Gabriel turned and saw an old woman with long gray hair. She was curled up in her sleeping bag. Her eyes were barely open. "Nowhere," Gabriel whispered.

"Stay here . . ." she said softly as her eyelids drooped and closed. "Stay here . . ."

Then she was asleep again.

Gabriel rushed to the door. Turned the knob. Slipped into the warm, dark night.

*

I held the Leash. That's what we call the UDP's manual controller. Of course, the UDP didn't need anyone directing its movements. It had a clear mission it would complete without human assistance. The Leash was for emergencies, should the UDP go rogue and attack the wrong people. This was a rare occurrence, but there had been a situation recently where a UDP accidentally ingested photos of two police officers instead of their criminal targets. This UDP murdered not only those two cops, but seven others, because the UDP database had criminally profiled police officers in general. This UDP became the first to be "put down," i.e., incinerated for its malfunction. It also led to increased usage of the Leash, a safety feature that could stop any UDP in its tracks. Whoever held the Leash, held the power.

Tonight, it was me. I've become our de facto leader.

The Leash was strapped to my wrist. Its small display was about one square inch. The car was silent. My dad sat shotgun, body tensed for battle, gripping an Uzi. His beer gut strained against his camo jacket. Mom was in the back—I caught her balaclava-framed gaze in the rearview. My brother sat to her left, rifle in his lap, his stare fixed on the dark wilderness outside. Behind us, we lugged a trailer. It held our dormant UDP. We led a train of vehicles. Three trucks followed us down the empty road.

I brought our car to a stop at the agreed-upon location. I turned off my engine. The trucks behind us did the same. Our headlights went dark. The moon cast a pale glow over the asphalt.

I opened my door. My family followed suit. We filed out, just like we'd done in our drills. I waved to the men behind us, who unloaded weapons from their trucks. I walked to the trailer, opened its doors. The UDP was hunched in a corner, steel haunches folded beneath its sleek body. Powered down. Conserving energy for the attack. I pressed the Leash on my wrist; its screen glowed. I toggled between settings, then landed on the proper mode: HUNT.

The UDP stirred to life, then emerged onto the moonlit highway. Its silver exterior caught what little lunar brilliance it could, gleaming defiantly in the near-black night. There was something sensual about the feline contours of its smooth body. Our infantry stopped its work to watch the UDP awaken. There was a strange respect reserved for this stunning beast created to do what its human inventors could not: Kill without culpability.

We began our march.

*

Gabriel wished they'd brought a flashlight. Or a friend. It was dark. They felt scared. They looked over their shoulder. The house was far away. Gabriel was close to the woods, close to the dragons. But they weren't brave enough to go out there alone.

Gabriel passed the barn and got an idea: They would bring a baby cow to the dragons. Then, they wouldn't feel so scared or alone. Because Gabriel loved the little calves like family.

Gabriel walked up to the barn, pulled on the big wooden door, and entered.

It smelled like poop and hay like always. It was dark inside. They stood on their tiptoes and flipped on the light switch. The brightness woke all the calves. They wobbled up from beds of hay. Gabriel approached their favorite and stuck their hand through the slats of the baby's stall. "Do you wanna visit the dragons?" The little cow licked their hand with its scratchy tongue. Gabriel giggled and unlatched the stall.

But then they heard a noise outside. Footsteps. Gabriel froze.

A whisper came from the other side of the barn door. "Are you sure this is right?"

It wasn't a voice Gabriel knew.

"Yes," someone else said.

Gabriel ducked into the stall with the calf and latched the door closed.

"It doesn't seem right," the first person said.

Gabriel burrowed under a pile of hay. The little cow moaned.

"Well, that's because you're a fucking idiot. Now, let's go," the other person said.

Suddenly, Gabriel recognized the second voice: It was Tuck.

The barn door opened.

FIFTY-SEVEN

The room seethed with money. Not literal currency—bills did not bubble forth from a molten fissure in the gallery floor. Rather, the rancid atmosphere teemed with a nearly tangible greed—the moisture from sweaty handshakes, the heat from fake hugs, the sprays of spittle riding empty laughter and conspiratorial whispers and news of this hedge fund's downfall and bets about that IPO and tips for manipulating autocrats and complaints concerning contractor delays on third and fourth homes. People entered the room, but no one seemed to leave. The warmth became unbearable. The windows fogged. Everyone was boxed in by white walls. White floors. White faces. Mason stood at the center of the sour human broth, boiling in an old Margiela suit, worrying about his worth, which was the primary concern of all assembled.

What *was* Mason's worth? The answer to this question was being decided in real time. Mason dissociated as the voices in the room echoed in his mind until he could no longer differentiate between his thoughts and the bitchy snatches of dialogue slapping his eardrums. Everyone wondered the same thing: *Would the market—aka the people in this room— take to Mason again?*

From that one question, a thousand others sprung: *Would anyone buy a painting? Would anyone publicly support this controversial figure? Would the show sell out? And if so, what effect would that have on Mason's overall market value? Would his old work have a resurgence in the secondary market?*

Was it time to pull your dusty Mason Daunt painting out of the Geneva freeport warehouse where it had been stashed for a decade, untaxed, untraced, unseen along with so many other pieces of art that functioned solely as receptacles to hide wealth, waiting for a moment like this, when you could toss the old art to Christie's for an auction and make a considerable return on your initial investment? Or was this gallery show merely a stunt? A way for Ponce to conduct a concert of free publicity, tuned to the twin cacophonies created by Maggie Shotwell's suicide and Mason's murderous past? Was it all bullshit? Even if it was, did that matter? The paintings were weird, but beautiful. White. Neutral enough to fit with most interior design schemes. Inoffensive. The paintings didn't seem to be about anything. But didn't someone say they were about White Death? Or climate change? Or clouds? No? Well, does anyone really care? Wouldn't that piece look amazing over our credenza? In the Hamptons estate? In the Bel-Air compound? Then again, there was the stigma. Wasn't Mason an anarchist? Or a terrorist? Shouldn't we wait to see how that Montana situation pans out before coughing up sixty thousand dollars for a painting? I mean, that's a bargain basement price, but still. No one wants to form an alliance with an anarchist, not in this climate. Did you want to talk to Ponce about a piece? No? Where should we get dinner? The new Italian place on Tenth?

"Mason?" Ponce stared at him strangely.

"Honey, are you okay?" Yunho asked.

I won't kill myself. The compulsive refrain had returned. *I won't kill myself.* The denial felt more tenuous than ever. "I'm fine. Just a little overheated."

"Did you still want to say a few words?" Ponce nervously clenched a plastic wineglass.

"Yes, of course." *I won't kill myself.* It felt like a lie.

Ponce clapped his hands to quiet the crowd.

*

Mason fingered the knife in his pocket.

"White Death tore my world apart," he insisted. "From the moment I inhaled that toxic chemical compound at my baby shower, life has been a series of interlocking disasters I've been unable to escape. Or, perhaps, I've been unwilling to escape them. If you look hard enough at any societal ill, there exists at its core one central problem: whiteness. It's the foundation upon which all other evils are built. The idea of whiteness was an invention—not a discovery. When enslaved Africans were first forced to Virginia in 1619, there were no 'white people' in colonial records. The invention of a superior 'white race' was utilized in the construction of the American state as a method of social control that kept 'white' lower classes (formerly oppressed under European feudalism) under the illusion that settler colonialism gave them new privilege, namely 'white' privilege to oppress an underclass of slaves and Indigenous people. Poor whites foolishly abandoned opportunities to join Black and Native uprisings and instead allied themselves with their own elite oppressors, paving the way for a capitalist white supremacist state supported by a lower class of 'white' people it exploited. Since then, whiteness has been exported globally, deployed as an excuse to pursue imperialist, capitalist, colonialist, and fascist imperatives."

Mason sank the tip of the blade into his thumb. Just a little. Not enough to draw blood.

"I was finally, brutally, forced to confront my complicity with whiteness when I killed my benefactor Patrick Sullivan—a generous donor to Republicans determined to uphold our white supremacist authoritarian state (a fact I ignored to garner capital to sustain my lifestyle and the lifestyle I imagined for my then-unborn child). I was driven to murder by White Death, a psychotic reaction to the toxic chemical byproduct of the illegal means of production Patrick utilized to create fire-retardant crops as a part of NuGrow's global effort to exploit climate change for billions in profit. While I never could've predicted the advent of White Death, I knew Patrick's money-making methods would result in disaster for a great many people. I assumed that, by being friends with him, I would be protected. I was so, so wrong.

"Whether or not you view this as poetic justice depends upon your definitions of poetry and justice. After my confrontation with White Death, I considered art a dead end, I considered poetry an ineffective way of pursuing justice, a self-indulgent waste, a cynical way of 'addressing' interlocking systems of oppression that comprised modern statehood. But still, something inside me needed to be purged. There was an impulse that hadn't died: the drive to make meaning of chaos. To make meaning of my life. I thought maybe, if I was able to re-create exactly what I saw during my psychotic bout with White Death, I could define the contours of the problem we all face: the fatal threat whiteness poses to humanity. So I painted the canvases in this room. I realize now: how embarrassing. The hubris. The hypocrisy."

His thumb was a little balloon, ready to pop. Pressure built at the knifepoint.

"So you know my intention with my work. Now what? You purchase a canvas to hang in your home and feel good about your self-awareness of your whiteness without actually interrogating it beyond a simple glance at my painting as you walk through your seventeen-million-dollar Hudson Yards penthouse purchased with wealth garnered through, let's say, modern slave labor that's been exported overseas to spare you and your company any uncomfortable confrontation with your exploitative methods of procuring a morally abhorrent surplus of capital. Or maybe your home is only two-point-three million dollars, and you aren't filthy rich; maybe you're just regular rich and you've done 'the work' and you buy my painting and you're committed to examining your own whiteness and my piece becomes central to that idea of yourself. You've invested sixty thousand dollars in a painting that reminds you of your complicity in the centuries of oppression that sprung from the invention of the white race, money that could be used elsewhere but, let's be real, aren't we all allowed a little luxury? So this piece hangs above your dining table and you invite friends over for dinner, friends who are majority white or maybe they're not, maybe you've got an erudite and integrated friend group, and you eat dinner and talk about my painting, and everyone goes home and feels good about themselves or bad about themselves for having unpacked the difficult issue of whiteness. But even in the best-case scenario there is still the problem of the *beauty* of my painting. The way it refuses to disrupt your bourgeois trappings. The days pass, and the painting blends into your home's design scheme. Soon, all your friends have seen it and discussed it and it just hangs on the wall, drained of meaning, reduced to a beautiful object in your beautiful home. A nice white painting. And therefore, it has failed. In my attempt to reflect the true ugliness of whiteness I have stupidly underestimated whiteness's self-protecting ability to insist upon its superior beauty. My work fails on an aesthetic level, which leads to total conceptual failure. The piece of art I've intended as a destruction of whiteness—a photorealistic reflection of the unsubtly named phenomenon of White Death—becomes an endorsement of the very thing it aims to destroy.

"I am at the center of this failure, benefiting financially from my own abysmal flop, the pathetic spectacle of my bungled attempts to untangle the Gordian knot of my own whiteness. Yet for all my self-indulgent yammering now, for all the invocations of complexity, there was a very simple aesthetic solution to my problem that I failed to see: render whiteness as hideous."

A gentle pop. His thumb. The skin broke. The blood flowed. It seeped into his pocket.

"But there's hope for hideousness yet. One option to remind you that whiteness spares no one in the end." Mason pulled the knife from his suit jacket. Slit his throat. The crowd screamed. Blood geysered from his neck. He crumpled to his knees like a marionette cut from its strings. Rivers of red stained his white shirt. He coughed and coughed; blood spewed from his mouth, from the gash his neck, splashing white walls, white floors, white skin, and white paintings.

*

Of course, Mason didn't kill himself. That was just a fantasy he'd rehearsed in his mind. In reality, he mumbled a few obfuscating words to the crowd, eschewing any controversial subject matter that could cause trouble with the Anti-American Speech Committee. The bored mob dispersed shortly thereafter, leaving mountains of plastic wine cups piled in trash cans.

"Hey." Yunho approached Mason as the crowd filtered out. "It was a great show."

"So great that no one bought anything?"

Before Yunho could reply with some platitude about patience, Ponce approached with a severe redhead. She wore a crisp black skirt suit and projected the expensive corporate blankness characteristic of people who work with other people's money. "Mason—meet Lydia Lash, an art adviser to Edgar Millet, one of my favorite collectors."

"The show was excellent," she intoned with perfunctory hollowness. "My client was unable to attend in person, but he did make the VR simul-viewing. He believes there's an enticing investment opportunity here."

"Well, I love to hear that," Mason said. "Which painting are you interested in?"

"My client isn't interested in just one piece," she insisted as joy—that long forgotten feeling—swelled within Mason's heart. "He'd like to purchase them all."

FIFTY-EIGHT

G abriel could count to twenty-one.
One, two, three, four, five people came into the barn. They wore dark camouflage.

Gabriel stayed still as a statue, hidden underneath the hay in the stall.

Six, seven, eight, nine people. They carried guns.

Counting made Gabriel feel better, like they had control over what was happening, like they could put these people together like a math problem.

Ten, eleven, twelve. The people looked around the barn. Confused.

Sweat dripped down Gabriel's face. Thirteen, fourteen, fifteen. The hay scratched their skin. Their arms itched. But Gabriel was too afraid to scratch. Even when the itch got worse. Even when it felt like fire. Even when they wanted to scream. Sixteen, seventeen, eighteen, nineteen. Gabriel counted instead of screaming. Twenty. They couldn't breathe. Why couldn't they breathe? Twenty-one. More people came in. But Gabriel didn't know any more numbers.

*

I was the last human to enter the barn. Our UDP followed. I closed the door behind us. I faced our militia, a clown car's worth of amped-up bozos with military-grade weapons. Rage burned in my father's eyes. "What the hell are we doing in a barn with a bunch of fucking cows?"

"This is a part of my plan."

"You didn't tell us about this part," Dad fumed.

"I wanted a place to hold us all, before we attacked," I insisted.

"But why?" A member of our militia burped.

A swarm of bullets ripped through his face. It was just one of the faces I'd fed to the UDP during my programming session, imagining this very end. His spine snapped; his neck bent at ninety degrees. He fell to the ground. Dead. Chaos ensued. Our militia ran in circles, like ants when a rock is lifted, and the shadow of a boot descends.

"The fucking thing is going AWOL!" my mother screamed. She dove into one of the stalls. Blocked her body with a moaning calf. "Tuck—use the Leash!"

I did nothing but stand next to the UDP. It obstructed the exit. I allowed the robot to finish the mission I'd programmed. The shower of bullets continued unabated. The floor became a mess of dead bodies. Blood seeped from their corpses and mixed with hay and cow shit. Silence descended. The UDP ceased its assault and retracted its weapon.

My mother emerged from a stall. Her hiding place. My father appeared from behind a beam. My brother descended from the hay loft, gently tiptoeing down the stairs.

They converged in front of me, terrified. The fact that my family was alive was no accident. I'd spared them. I wanted them to see everyone they loved murdered before their eyes.

"What the fuck happened?" My father slammed my body against the barn door.

"Let him go," Mom begged. "We gotta get outta here—"

"WHAT THE FUCK HAPPENED?"

But if my father wanted a response, there was no way I could offer one. His hands were too tight around my throat. I struggled for air as he strangled me. Dizziness overwhelmed my senses. I slammed the Leash against the barn door. The UDP stirred. Spat bullets.

My father's head exploded. His warm brains slapped my face. He crumpled to the ground. Bullets C-sectioned his white belly; intestines burst out, like he was giving birth to pale-pink snakes.

My mother was next. Mascara hemorrhaged from her weeping eyes, mixing with the blood coating her face. She cowered in her stall, using the calf as a shield. The UDP marched forward as she screamed. Its bullets tore through the calf. She dropped the dead animal and threw herself prostrate before the killing machine. "Tuck, spare me—" But she was interrupted by the final, fatal shot—straight through her left eye and up into her worthless brain.

My brother pissed his pants. Like a fucking toddler. A stain spread across his crotch. He started bawling. Drool dripped from his pale-blond beard. "You're . . . fucking sick. Kill me. Go ahead. Just know that God is watching. He'll judge you in the end."

I laughed in his face. The UDP was out of bullets. It retracted its machine gun. In its place, it produced a massive metal blade. All it took was one swift chop. My brother's head went flying. My mission was almost complete.

*

Something heavy landed on Gabriel. Something wet and warm. Gabriel hid at the bottom of a pile of hay. All they could see was the golden dried grass above them. Then came the red. Something thick dripped into the straw, stained it almost-black. Blood. Just a little at first. Then it flowed faster. It covered their neck and face, pooled in their nostrils. Gabriel wanted to scream but couldn't. So, they closed their eyes. But they could still hear people dying—the moans, the burps, the gurgles.

Then it was quiet. Maybe everyone was gone. Or dead. Maybe it was safe to come out. Gabriel opened their eyes and made a peephole in the pile of hay. Bodies, bodies everywhere. On the ground. Piled high. The floor was shiny. Slick. Red.

"Gone, gone, gone." It was Tuck, talking to himself. "All of you erased. Rubbed out. Rub-a-dub-dub. Little rubber duckies. Fucky-ducky-dead." Tuck sat on the floor, his back to Gabriel. Rocking back and forth. "Little dead ducks." He pulled a pen from his pocket. A piece of paper. He started scribbling. Writing something. "Who's my next duck to die?"

A strand of hay tickled Gabriel's cheek. They fought, fought, fought a sneeze.

"Tuck the fucking duck killer. Tuck-a-duck. Fuck-a-duck."

Gabriel squirmed. The object on top of them rolled off and fell in front of the peephole. It was a man's head. Gabriel gasped. The hay scratched their face. The itch was unstoppable.

Gabriel sneezed.

Tuck froze. He stopped writing and shoved the paper into his pocket. "Did I miss a little duckling?" Tuck stood. He walked toward Gabriel. The metal monster followed. Tuck took a shiny belt out of his backpack. Only it wasn't a belt. It was bullets, all strung together. Tuck held it out to the monster. A door opened on the side of its body and a metal arm stretched out and grabbed the bullets and snapped them back inside.

Gabriel began to shake. Sobs bubbled up from their belly. They stayed under the hay even though they couldn't hide now—Tuck had found them. Gabriel looked through the peephole and saw Tuck, but it was almost like it wasn't Tuck. Because of Tuck's eye. His one eye. It seemed lifeless. Dead.

Tuck kicked his brother's head out of his way. The monster stomped on it, crushed it like a rotten grape. Tuck bent over Gabriel. He tossed the hay aside. Gabriel stayed curled up on the ground. Sobbing. Screaming. Tuck crouched down next to Gabriel, looking right at them. But something was different.

Tuck's eye was back to normal. Alive again. "*Gabriel*," he gasped.

Gabriel tried to say something, but they couldn't speak. It was like they forgot how.

"Gabriel." Tuck hugged Gabriel. "I'm so sorry." The metal monster loomed. A machine gun appeared from the hole where its head should've been. Gabriel opened their mouth, but nothing came out. Tuck pressed a pile of paper into their small, shaking hands. "Please, give this to Claudia."

Gabriel stared down at the words on the page, then looked up again.

Tuck dropped to his knees.

The sound of gunfire filled the barn.

FIFTY-NINE

They splurged on a bottle of Moët. Or rather, Mason splurged as Yunho reminded him that alcohol was poison and "isn't it an incredible testament to the powers of capitalist propaganda that we've been convinced to spend mountains of money on a lethal substance that sates no essential human need? And while I'm happy to watch you pour death down your throat, I encourage you to take it a *bit* easy because we have a flight tomorrow."

"Oh honey, *relax*." Mason downed the champagne from his glass. He was thirsty for more; he remembered this feeling of being drunk on victory, the feeling when art and commerce collide, and your bank account swells, and the money feels like proof of your worth. Pride emanated from his lover's gaze, and he was reminded that money impressed Yunho as well. Mason was transported back to the heady days of their early successes, back when the world had endless rewards for them both. He reclined on their murderously uncomfortable mattress, ignoring the bleachy itch of his threadbare hotel robe, or *motel* robe, really, he'd been surprised their budget lodging in Queens even *had* robes. Yes, he'd chat with everyone back in Montana about this, surely the Flex Fund could be a bit more *flexible* in terms of funding livable travel accommodations, especially for someone who'd secured the community a much-needed infusion of cash. "I just made three hundred thousand dollars on my show. I don't want to discuss capitalism and the death drive."

"They go hand in hand, sweetie," Yunho said, with a condescending smirk.

"Oh my god, *stop*." Mason tackled his lover playfully, pinning him to the mattress.

"Okay!" Yunho laughed. "Enjoy your champagne. After all your hard work, you deserve to be poisoned."

"Shut the fuck up"—Mason nuzzled Yunho—"and kiss your horrifically compromised drunk capitalist husband." Yunho rolled his eyes and gave Mason a playful peck, which quickly turned into something deeper, something urgent, a kiss to remind them of the past, to revive their hope for the future. They broke apart and a manic optimism swelled within Mason. "Make all the jokes you want, but we can do a lot with three hundred thousand dollars. The Ranch is wildly overcrowded. People are living in tents. This cash could build us additional housing."

"You're right. Plus, Daniel has been desperate for more equipment in the Infirmary."

"Not to mention the school supplies Claudia needs."

"And think about the future. More art shows for you. I could get back into filmmaking. The money we make could have a profound impact on the commune. We could really change the lives of all the people we love."

Mason felt a nascent passion, felt it as they lay there together on the shitty motel mattress, limbs and dreams intertwined, felt it radiating from Yunho, as tangible as the heat emanating from their braided legs, as comforting as the gentle scratch of Yunho's stubble against his cheek, as real as the truth that revealed itself with a power that overwhelmed all the hurt and pain and trauma they'd endured since they first decided to have a child: They still loved each other.

What a relief.

Suddenly, Mason's iOS Cerebrum rang: *Claudia*. Strange, for her to be calling this late.

SIXTY

My mother ripped out my eye with an ice-cream scoop. I realize I've harped on that point in these letters (letters I'm leaving to the commune as an explanation, or an apology, or a suicide note), but if the woman who gave birth to you ever did something so comically brutal, you might also obsessively search for meaning in such a senseless act of violence. Yet, I've ultimately failed. The only truth I can find is in the ungodly pain I felt in that moment. The agony that gave way to oblivion. Unconsciousness. So close to death.

Death feels more honest to me than the lie of the future, the fight for the world our children will inherit. The fight my family fought. The fight the commune is fighting. Sure, the two groups possess wildly different goals. But the reason they fight, the animating force fixed in their imaginations is the same: the Child.

But what's so great about children? We keep churning them out because of some insistence that the future will be better, that we must make it better for them. As sung by noted child molester Michael Jackson in his Save the Children propaganda song, we need to "heal the

world, make it a better place, for you and for me and
the entire human race." But has producing children
ever inspired humanity to make the world a better
place?

No. This insistence on reproductive futurity is
precisely what's killing the Earth. Don't believe me?
Look around. Look at our own present, the "better
future" previous generations fought to create for us.
And it's shit. The present, which was formerly the
future, is absolute shit. Let's be honest for one
second: The bad guys won.

So I killed off some bad guys. Seems like the least
I could do.

But I also stopped believing in your commune's hopes
for the future. Because things only get worse. For
every victory over oppression, another sector of people
is exploited in the opposite corner of the globe, like
some game of neoliberal whack-a-prole in which the
working class is enslaved to create more money for
fewer people. Yet, we—and the "we" here is limited to
those holding on to the illusion of some brighter
destiny for humankind—persist with this blind optimism
that the future is a better place we're building for
our children.

And so, while I admire your commune's attempts to
form a reproductive colony aimed at being "anti-family,"
how can you truly be anti-family if you insist on
birthing children, thereby subscribing to the heterosexual fantasy of reproductive futurity, no matter how
queer the methods of reproduction may be?

You're playing a losing game. As evidence, I'm leaving
this mess in your barn. This pile of bodies is proof
that the future is nothing, that investing in it only

breeds death. It was a mistake for you to take me in. I created nothing but trouble. You would've been better off if you never believed in me, never wanted to build a better future for someone so wretched, so tainted by the sins of his parents. It would've been better if I never existed.

If you're finding this letter, you're finding it next to my dead body. Don't bury me. I don't deserve a grave. Let me be forgotten. Let me be erased from history. Free me from the future.

SIXTY-ONE

It wasn't cold. But Gabriel couldn't stop shaking. Bright lights lit up the lawn. They were attached to big stands that stood in a circle around the barn door. They shined on the ground; the dirt was wet with blood. People, so many people. Walking, running, standing, crying. Members of the commune. Visitors for the conference. The police. One police officer shoved a pole in the ground; another followed with a roll of yellow tape. Gabriel shook harder. They couldn't feel their body. It was like they were watching their body from outside their body, almost like a movie, yes, they were watching a movie of their own life as their body shook harder and someone put a blanket over them. Gabriel looked up.

It was Mahmood. Bullets flew into his pregnant belly. It burst like a water balloon filled with blood.

Gabriel screamed and shut their eyes, but when they opened their eyes again Mahmood was fine, everything was fine and Mahmood said, *Gabriel, sweetie, stay with me, okay?* and Gabriel watched the movie of themself and felt nothing even though Movie Gabriel cried and screamed, *They're all dead, I saw them die!* Mahmood hugged Movie Gabriel so tight they couldn't breathe, and Mahmood said, *Gabriel, you're scaring me,* and then Astrid was in the movie too. She gave Movie Gabriel a kiss and said, *No one can hurt you anymore because we're here,* and Gabriel knew that was a lie but Movie Gabriel nodded and said, *Okay,* to make the grown-ups feel better. Then Daniel came, then Claudia, and Movie Gabriel asked, *Where's Yunho?*

and Claudia said, *He's in New York, but he and Mason will be on the first plane back tomorrow*, and then Astrid and Claudia were fighting and Astrid said, *I can't believe you of all people called the police*, and Claudia said, *There's a pile of dead bodies on our property. Was I supposed to wait and hope the cops never noticed fifteen of their white supremacist BFFs were lying dead in our barn? I didn't want it to look like we were hiding something*, and they kept fighting and Claudia started crying but Gabriel felt nothing and then a policeman walked up and asked, *Who is the parent of the child here?* and Astrid said, *We share parenting duties among groups called Care Pods*, and the policeman said, *I don't care about your hippie bullshit—who's the legal guardian?* and Mahmood said, *I am*, and the policeman said, *Okay, we're going to take your child to the station for questioning*, and Mahmood said, *No, Gabriel's been traumatized enough, they don't need to go to a police station*, and the policeman said, *May I remind you that it's in your best interest to cooperate with this investigation?* and Mahmood said, *Don't you need my permission to question my child?*

And all the voices in the movie started to mix together in Gabriel's mind until they became one loud drone voice and Gabriel couldn't follow the movie anymore so they shut their eyes and listened to the one voice that was lots of voices mixed together and it said, *Yes, we need your permission to question your child Then I don't grant you permission Well, I suggest you reconsider because your child is the only witness to a mass murder that happened on your property But you read Tuck's note, the one he gave to Gabriel, Tuck was acting on his own, no one on the Ranch was involved All I know is this is an open investigation with many possible outcomes and if you deny us this interview with your child we could come to the conclusion that you're protecting someone who had something to do with this and if that's the case and there's a murderer living among you, Child Protective Services would be forced to remove the child from your custody You can't take Gabriel we've done nothing wrong Well you may be charged with obstructing a police investigation if you prevent us from interviewing the sole witness to this crime so I encourage you to cooperate so this doesn't get uglier than it has to and—*

And then it stopped. The voice stopped. Silence. Gabriel kept their eyes shut. They felt like they were floating in water. Black water. Numb. Nothing. No arms. No legs. They were just a mind. Without a body. Floating in black. Beauty. Nothing.

Then, another voice. A new voice. This voice didn't come from the movie outside. This voice came from the black. Came from nothing. Came from inside Gabriel's mind. This voice was real. Nothing else was. *Gabriel*, the voice said. *It's almost time.*

Who are you? Why can't I see you?

You must find me first.

But where should I look?

Follow the fire, my sweet child.

SIXTY-TWO

And now, our ANN top story of the evening. We turn our discussion toward a new development regarding the tragic massacre of patriotic militia members that took place on the property of the terrorist pregnancy cult in Montana. Just minutes ago, disturbing security camera footage of the massacre surfaced. The video shows Tuck Wilson—the boy abducted by the extremist cult before being surrendered back into the loving arms of his family—guiding a UDP to kill his own militia in a barn on the ranch property of the anarchist group. Here to chat with me about the video is White House press secretary Mark Hall. Mark, what are your thoughts here?"

"Well, as we all know, Rick, VoidFakes are a huge problem these days. We can't trust video footage when it's so easy to create an undetectable fake with AI. And we know that leftist extremists are constantly using fake videos to whip up a frenzy over fake police brutality, fake suppression of protests, fake militia violence against poll workers, etc. We can't trust the videos we see circulating online, especially when they're coming from the left."

"So you're saying this video is a VoidFake?"

"There's no doubt in my mind. I guarantee the *real* video footage shows the terrorist cult—led by Claudia Jackson—luring this innocent militia into an evil trap, then murdering them one by one. This whole VoidFake has been whipped up by this anarchist terrorist cell to evade responsibility for massacring a group of innocent patriots."

"Terrifying. But what would you say to those who don't buy that this is a VoidFake?"

"'Wake up and smell the terrorism!' But let's say, devil's advocate, the video is real. And Tuck Wilson really did massacre his family. Well, remember that Tuck was *brainwashed by this cult while being held hostage.* So even though they returned Tuck to his family, who's to say that the cult didn't stay in secret contact with him and orchestrate this entire thing? They could have been using Tuck as a double agent to take down the militia from within. Any way you slice it, this thing stinks like terrorism."

"Let's look to the future. What danger do these terrorists pose to the nation at large?"

"They're the biggest threat to American freedom we've ever seen. But now, we've got the smoking gun on these guys. We gotta take 'em down. Thankfully, we have a great justice system here in America. So, we bring these terrorists in, charge them with everything we've got, and get them to confess using whatever means necessary."

"What do you mean by 'whatever means necessary'?"

"I mean torture. Filmed and broadcast for the nation to see. And, in some cases, public execution. If that sounds harsh, think about it: These people aren't people. They're monsters. Because what do these terrorists want?"

"To destroy the American family."

"Exactly. And God's not gonna let that happen. This is a holy war to save our children."

"One last question, Mark. An estimated two hundred thousand Americans are now living in terrorist cells modeled after the cult in Montana. A recent poll showed that forty-three percent of Democrats supported the 'right' of these terrorist cells to exist. What do we do about the proliferation of terrorists who are holding increasing sway over the minds of our nation's citizens?"

"We round them up."

"And then?"

"You've got such an amazing imagination, Rick. Use it."

SIXTY-THREE

The room was white. And cold. The bright lights made Gabriel squint. They sat at a tall table. In a big chair. Their feet dangled. They shivered. *Be brave*, the voice said. The voice was always with Gabriel now. In their mind. In their heart. *I'll protect you no matter what.*

Mahmood sat next to Gabriel. *Don't tell him about me.* Gabriel squeezed Mahmood's hand. *He loves you but he won't understand.* A lawyer sat next to them. She was on their side. She was tall and Black and had a nice laugh, but Gabriel was still scared of her because she was new. *And we don't know if we trust her yet.*

The police officer came into the room. Gabriel's heart pounded. They wanted to go back to feeling nothing and watching the movie of their life, but the voice said, *No, Gabriel, stay here, you can't disappear, you have to be strong.* "Hey guys, sorry to make you wait."

"We've been sitting here for an hour, this is completely unreasonable," the lawyer said.

"I *said* I was sorry to make you wait. But we are just a *little* busy right now." The policeman threw a pack of M&M's onto the table. *Bang!* "Brought a treat for our little guy here. I know it's been a tough day." Gabriel didn't touch the candy.

Don't worry, Gabriel, we'll add him to the list, the voice said.

What's the list?

Don't pretend you don't know.

The door opened. Another woman walked in. She was old and thin with messy gray hair. She wore thick glasses that made her brown eyes tiny, like raisins had dried in her sockets.

"This is Celia Nelson. She's a Child Protection Specialist from the Montana Child and Family Services Division."

"What is CPS doing here?" Mahmood asked.

"The safety of your child is our utmost concern. Celia has years of experience interviewing traumatized children. We're conducting a joint investigation with Montana CPS—"

"You are *not* taking my child away—"

"No one is taking your child away, Mahmood—"

"This is *bullshit*, I—"

"Let's just calm down," the lawyer said. "Mahmood—we prepared for this possibility, remember? It's in your best interest to cooperate here."

The policeman grabbed the M&M's he bought for Gabriel, opened them, and threw a bunch in his mouth. "Listen to your lawyer. We don't want Celia getting the wrong impression of you, do we, Mahmood? That could lead to an outcome no one wants . . ."

"It's *reasonable* for me to be upset if I'm being threatened—"

"Mahmood, please," the lawyer said. "No one is threatening anything, is that correct?"

"We're just trying to figure out what happened in that barn," the policeman continued. "Celia—you ready?"

Celia looked up from a notepad. She squinted and her raisins got smaller. Meaner. *She's evil, Gabriel. A witch.* "Do you mind answering a few questions for us, Gabriel?" She scribbled something on her pad. "We want to know about your home. About your family."

"We've got love for everyone," Gabriel murmured into the floor.

"I'm sure you do," Celia said. "But sometimes even the people we love can hurt us."

She's first on the list, Gabriel.

But why?

Because that's where the cunts go.

*

Silence. The voice was gone. The car was stuck. They were surrounded by bodies. People jumped on the hood, pounded the windshield. Dirty hands smeared the glass. They slammed their signs against the car. *SLAM*. They pushed. *SLAM*. The car rocked. *SLAM*. Gabriel's tummy flipped. The people lifted Gabriel's side of the car. Up, up, up it went. Then: *CRASH*. It came back down. Screams. Laughter. The other side of the car tilted up, up, up. Mahmood rose higher and higher. "*Fucking put us down.*" *CRASH*. More screams. More laughter. A kid smashed his face against Gabriel's window. He dragged his tongue across the glass.

"*Let us through!*" Mahmood screamed.

The car started rising again. Gabriel's side. Up, up, up. It got so high that Gabriel could see over the people, over their heads and hats and signs. And right there, just past the gates: the Ranch. They were so close. Up, up, up. Trapped in a cage. Up, up, up. Gabriel grabbed their seat belt. The fabric cut their hands. The car kept going up, up, up, and it didn't stop until it went down, down, down in one big rush, but it fell the wrong way, upside down, and then *crash*.

Glass exploded in Gabriel's face.

The people cheered. The whole car was upside down. Gabriel's seat belt kept them hanging in place. They looked at Mahmood. His eyes were shut. His pregnant stomach pushed against the airbag. His hair was wet. Something dark. Almost black. Blood. He looked asleep. They felt dizzy. Gabriel wanted to sleep too. Their eyelids felt heavy, like two thick blankets.

Gabriel looked out the broken windshield. Upside-down shoes. Attached to upside-down legs. A kid dropped to his belly and stuck his tongue out. He held a sign. On it, there was a picture. "Look! It's you, stupid!" the kid shouted. And it *was* Gabriel. A picture of Gabriel, on the sign. Gabriel was upside down. On the sign, but in real life too. Gabriel was crying. On the sign, but in real life too. Gabriel was screaming. On the sign, but in real life too.

The sign had words on it. It said: SAVE OUR CHILDREN.

SIXTY-FOUR

A squad of soldiers surrounded the tank in the driveway. Though its gun was aimed at the swarm of protestors beyond the Ranch gates, the accompanying servicemen directed their hostility toward Mason and Yunho as they passed. One spat in Yunho's path. *They're here to keep the peace*, Astrid had warned the couple. But peace seemed impossible in the shadow of a tank; its presence was proof of war.

They were home, but it didn't feel like it.

The Main Hall was in chaos. Abandoned sleeping bags littered the floor like a tangle of deflated cocoons, the aftermath of some mass eclosion; flitting strangers infested the space, winging past Mason on gusts of anxious energy. He took a gulp of the perspiratory miasma; it felt impossible to *breathe*—one could only *swallow* mouthfuls of thick wet air. Debates about whether to stay for the remainder of the UCF meetings rumbled across the humid crucible and mixed with the relentless drone of news helicopters and menacing chants from protestors outside. Post-massacre, their commune had become, according to Fox News, "The Battleground for the Soul of America," while ANN preferred "The Cult of Satanic Murder-Anarchists," but regardless of which state-endorsed media outlet one believed, it was clear the Ranch occupied a dangerous place in the imaginations of those who operated the machinery of American power.

A small explosion rattled the windows. Everyone quieted. Froze in place. Waited.

Nothing happened. It was just some protestor's homemade pipe bomb, detonated at a safe distance behind police lines. Someone in the crowd laughed; it sounded involuntary, instinctual, a mirthless release of internal pressure.

They're all dead, Claudia had hyperventilated over the phone just fourteen hours prior. Those three words had triggered in Mason a sensation of falling so tangible that it obliterated the reality of the motel bed beneath him, and he shut his eyes and plummeted through a mineshaft; the heat intensified as he hurtled, his skin itched with sweat, his blood boiled; then, from somewhere miles above, on the Earth's cool surface, he heard his lover's voice. *Who's dead, Claudia?* She replied: *Tuck. His whole militia.* Yunho coaxed the truth out of her—everyone they loved was safe—and Mason opened his eyes and rode a wave of relief back to reality. Then, a realization regulated his temperature, lowered his blood pressure: He had three hundred thousand dollars. A plan formulated in his mind. No one else had to get hurt. No one else had to die. He could save them all. *We're coming on the first flight out.*

"I need to find Claudia," he said now, turning toward Yunho. "You coming?"

"I want to check on Gabriel first. They're in the Infirmary with Daniel."

"Yunho, wait."

"Yes?"

"I know things are bad." Mason hesitated. "But they'll be better soon. I promise."

*

He found Claudia outside, contemplating the mountain range that loomed in the distance. There was something comforting about its immensity, its ancientness. It was a portion of the Earth's crust exposed, vaulted, vulnerable; and yet it stood sentinel, as it had for millions of years, withstanding erosion, never yielding to oblivion. Humans were a glitch in the eternity these mountains knew—just yesterday they'd suffered dinosaurs. If there was such a thing as mountain consciousness—and assessing the mysterious depth of shadow between its peaks, this idea didn't seem absurd—then surely this big purple beauty was unimpressed by the petty squabbles of the tiny pests who squirmed at its base as if anything they did mattered. *So there's something I'd like to confess*, Mason planned to say. *But before I do, just remember that these mountains will witness our extinction, so the fact I was an FBI informant really isn't important, and besides, it's over now, I found a solution to save us all.* But when he opened his mouth, he only had the courage to mutter, "We're back."

Claudia grabbed her hand-rims and turned toward Mason. "Good," was her curt reply.

Mason swallowed. Reconsidered. He didn't need to tell Claudia the truth. He just needed to convince her that the dream had died, that it was time to dissolve the group and run. Sure, they had love for everyone, but love wasn't enough when the National Guard was parked in your driveway. After all, Kilcher's goal was to neutralize the commune. He never said they had to die. What if they simply disbanded? One press conference could end it all: *We surrender, no more anarchy, we pledge allegiance to the flag, and to the evil for which it stands.*

"Is Gabriel okay?"

"Their arm's broken but they'll be fine."

"And Mahmood?"

"We . . . we think so. His baby survived. But his head trauma was too severe for Daniel to treat in the Infirmary. He's at the hospital . . ."

"Claudia. I've been thinking. And I'm wondering if we should disband—"

"Don't tell me you wanna let *fascists* seize what we've worked *so* hard to build here."

"Hear me out. If we publicly announce that we're dissolving the commune—"

"Some people are leaving. That's their right. You can leave too."

"But you can come with me. We can bring our whole Care Pod. Move someplace new. Far away. I have three hundred thousand dollars from my show. *That money can save us—*"

"You think disbanding is going to solve our problems? We have targets on our backs. We're official state-sponsored villains. If you really believe you can just sashay off this property and go back to some 'normal' life you're stupider than I thought. *They'll kill us no matter what.*"

"*So what the fuck are we supposed to do?*"

"*Defend ourselves!*"

Their shouts echoed between indifferent mountain peaks. Silence swelled between them.

"And how do we do that?" Mason asked, quieter.

"We ask our community. In an emergency forum."

"I have a right to suggest my strategy. That we publicly disband. Flee the Ranch."

"Of course you do."

"And I hope you come around. We can leave before war arrives at our doorstep."

"This is America." Weariness deadened Claudia's features. "War isn't coming. It's been here all along."

SIXTY-FIVE

FBI COUNTERTERRORISM DIVISION——NATIONAL THREAT CENTER SECTION CLASSIFIED: **SUSPICIOUS ACTIVITY REPORT——SEIZED EMAIL**

From: Claudia Jackson <claudiajackson@gmail.com>

To: <DSS2044@gmail.com>

My dear sweet someone,

I dream of you, Fennel. Every night it's the same: I dream that you're bundled tight, crying in my arms. Somehow I can walk again, I can run, a miraculous strength has found its way to my legs and they're flying across a dead field. You're screaming now; I hold you tighter against my chest as I run toward something I can't discern. A blur on the horizon. My arms ache, my legs burn. Then, I see it: an army. They hold bayonets. Bayonets? I feel out of time.

Out of place. I stare down the murderous fleet. Blood drips from each knife. At their feet: bodies. The carcasses of everyone I love. Only the two of us are left alive.

And I wake up. *Fennel*, I gasp. Astrid is next to me. In bed. Already caressing my forehead. *Fennel's asleep in the nursery, safe*, she says. Astrid hasn't slept in days. This is us, now. This is what our nights bring. Astrid draws me into her arms. My forearms cramp. The pain pulses up my limbs. My muscles are perpetually tense. Ready to run. Or fight. But I'm not ready. We're not ready. My body is warning me. Astrid massages my hands, my wrists, my arms. She kisses me. I remind myself to cherish the sweet tang of her sweat, and the soft folds of her skin, and the knowledge that you, my dear Fennel, are safe and sleeping. To cherish it all, because soon . . .

I can't bring myself to finish that sentence.

The presidential elections have been deferred. Indefinitely.

The president's speech filled me with horror. He says our "domestic terrorist cell" poses "the biggest threat to national security in history." This is why our dictator in chief launched the Save America Superforce, "a tactical squad of real-life superheroes who will take to the streets and wipe out every last terrorist on American soil."

When I watched this speech, my arms cramped, then my neck, then my back; it was as if there was a torture device inside my body. It felt like my muscles were wrapped around a gear twisting in my gut, and as my muscles tangled in its spokes, my body shrunk into itself. The sinew in my neck felt ready to snap. The president declared a national emergency. He was so sure of an impending coup that he saw no choice but to remain in the oval office until every last anarchist was imprisoned or executed, even if it took decades.

Which means he'll never cede power. This is what happens when you spend decades flirting with authoritarianism: Eventually you get fucked by a dictator. But I didn't predict the way this news would impact my body, how the gear in my gut would twist my muscles into a deadly helix. Each limb feels so tightly wound, seething with unrealized violence. Eventually—when they come to kill me, to kill us all—the gear will release, and I'll spring forward, and defend myself.

But I know that the more I defend myself the more I will be attacked because my self-defense will be viewed as an act of aggression, a justification for murdering me and everyone I love, because the script is already written and it's an old one, used for centuries against the colonized, against Black and brown people, against queers, against any oppressed being who summons the courage to insist they deserve better than state-sponsored murder.

The love I feel for you, Fennel, is killing me in a different way. It reminds me of my humanity when sometimes it feels like it would be easier to allow the state to erase it and execute me. But when faced with the warmth of your delicate body, the innocence of your laughter, the sense of wonder that radiates from your beautiful brown eyes—I'm reminded that life is worth living, love is alive, and hope is a discipline.

I've not given up. I'm writing you this letter, Fennel. I pray you can be the answer to our awful problem, that the hope you've always inspired can give me the strength to survive whatever violence comes our way. But that feels naive. I'm not sure I'll see you grow up. I'm not sure any of us will survive. I don't want to say goodbye. But maybe I will, just in case.

Goodbye, my dear sweet someone.

Yours forever,
Claudia

SIXTY-SIX

Mason stared out at the blinding Manhattan skyline; the too brightly rendered sun sent an uncanny shimmer rippling across virtual buildings. The edifice that shined with the greatest luminescence: the World Trade Center. The twin surprises of these ghostly anachronisms conjured up a nebulous dread in Mason, one that mixed with the more identifiable apprehension he felt regarding his imminent meeting with Edgar Millet.

As he waited, Mason contemplated strategies for saving the commune, to put forth in their upcoming emergency forum. He hoped that if they publicly denounced their anarchist mission, the government would be forced to choose new boogeymen. Then, the commune could disappear. But where would they go? Foreign democracies were unlikely to offer asylum; that was an invitation to war. But surely, somewhere among the commune's supporters, there existed an off-the-grid sympathizer with bunkers big enough to hide them all. They'd escape into the night, hire helicopters or human traffickers, money was no object, or at least it wouldn't be after Mason met with Millet, the collector who'd purchased every canvas at Mason's opening.

Mason was assured by Ponce that the meeting was a formality, that Millet simply wished to share a few laughs before he forked over three hundred thousand of his mysteriously earned dollars. Having been caught in the problematic crosshairs of global capital before, Mason was apprehensive. He knew nothing about Millet, other than the fact that Ponce insisted he was a "wonderful collector," which translated to "he's rich as fuck, so don't overthink this."

But overthinking was all Mason could do as he waited in Millet's lavish virtual office. Black marble floors stretched on for thousands of square feet before ending at floor-to-ceiling windows. Each piece of furniture possessed a digital Stamp of Authentication from its designer; the Wassily™ Chair in which he sat, with its elegant Bauhaus lines, carried the seal of the Knoll Virtual Showroom. It stood opposite a black marble desk, similarly authenticated. Behind the desk rose a dark monolith reminiscent of those in *2001: A Space Odyssey*; the only departure in design was the fireplace at its foundation, home to an inferno that blazed with prehistoric gusto, like it might leap from its marble prison, set the wealthy on fire, and restore civilization to its ancient anarchist glory. Or maybe he was just projecting.

CLICK. The sound of a door opening echoed across the cavernous space. Mason looked over his shoulder. The door remained slightly ajar, though no one walked through. "Hello?" he called out. Nothing. "Edgar—er, uh, Mr. Millet, is that you?"

A small cloud floated into the room. It hovered three feet in the air. White, fluffy, circular. It looked like a floating pancake made of marshmallows. Four feet in diameter, it asserted an aggressive cuteness incongruent with the chic severity of its surroundings. But even the anomaly of the cloud could not prepare Mason for the surprise that emerged from the door next: Hello Kitty.

Yes, *the* Hello Kitty marched into the room on her stumpy legs. She was two-dimensional, aesthetically dissonant with her hyperrealistic virtual surroundings. Her form was delineated by a thick black outline. She wore a pink dress. A matching bow sat at the base of her pointy left ear. Three whiskers drooped from each cheek. Her nose was a tiny yellow button. Her eyes, dead black dots. She had no mouth.

She giggled. A high-pitched squeal, more pig than cat. Her paws— really, just circular stubs—moved over her face as if to cover a smile, though she was incapable of smiling, as she had no lips or teeth, just blank white space at the bottom of her flat visage. She closed her eyes; the twin dots became crescent moons. Another pig squeal emanated from her mouthless head.

Sweat collected above Mason's trembling lip. "Mr. . . . Mr. Millet?"

"*Bad boy.*" Hello Kitty grabbed the edge of her floating cloud, mumbling to herself as she climbed on board. "*Bad, bad.*" When she spoke, the sound simply resonated from her face.

"I . . . I don't understand—"

"*You get killed!*" Her cloud jolted forward with violent speed, careening toward Mason. Her two eyes became one furious flat line, a fatal EKG.

"*Stop! Don't hurt me!*" Mason dove beneath the desk and curled into a fetal ball, his hands wrapped around his head. He waited, frozen on the floor.

"*Ha, ha, ha.*" Hello Kitty floated above him on her cloud, laughing and clutching her empty cartoon stomach. "I don't kill you. My daddy kill you."

"Your . . . daddy." A belated realization. This was a child. A girl who had chosen Hello Kitty as her virtual reality avatar and had somehow snuck into Daddy's office. Relief washed over Mason. He crawled from beneath the desk, and reclaimed his former seat, not wanting his benefactor to find him prostrate before a cartoon. "Where's your daddy?"

"He's right here." The sound of this familiar voice sent oxygen and blood rushing from Mason's head. The room spun and his vision blurred, as he turned to face the shocking truth: It was Kilcher. "Don't tell me you're surprised that me and Edgar Millet are the same person."

"I . . . I . . ."

"Calm down. You'll get your money. I just have one request regarding how you use it."

Hello Kitty laughed and laughed and laughed.

SIXTY-SEVEN

I'm sorry, Claudia, he'd said that morning. *You're right, we need to defend ourselves.* She'd accepted his apology because *internal discord will just make us weaker and right now, we need to preserve our strength, close ranks*, and she *was* correct; there was no other option than to stay and fight. Whatever delusions Mason had about public apologies and fleeing in the night were obliterated by the realities that came to light during his meeting with Kilcher. The FBI would not rest until the commune was eradicated. *Eradicated*, yes, that was the euphemism Mason would use to gloss over the fact they were all, except for Mason (who'd been promised immunity), barreling toward death, much like how Mason was barreling across dry grasslands right now, his truck's wheels slicing twin crop trails in the desiccated straw. Finally, the dirt path appeared, the road Mason had been promised, a small track of exposed soil that vanished intermittently, untraced by GPS, encroached upon by tall blond blades.

The sun shone, having no alternative, on the nothing new. Mason thought of Beckett's opening line in *Murphy* as he slammed down the truck's visor to shield his eyes from harsh noon rays that bounced off the infinite yellow pasture. There was nothing new about Mason's plight, nothing surprising about the intersecting systems of corruption and money and power and the slippery slope of moral compromise that led him to this very dirt road, a path that would, finally, guide him out of liminal misery and into whatever guilt-ridden hell awaited him on the other side of his unforgivable betrayal of everyone he loved. But if nothing was new and humans were powerless against history's repeating cycles, then did any of it matter? When it came time to write history, Mason would—provided the government's control over U.S. textbooks remained ironclad—be cast as a hero. Wasn't it easier to accept his role? If not him, someone else would dutifully play the part of informant, sabotaging the revolution from within, colluding with the elite to ensure power structures remained intact. Why resist his fate as a cog in the system? Why not take comfort in the soothing hum of machinery operating as it always did?

He pounded the truck's steering wheel and screamed. He wanted to believe in his loved ones, wanted to believe something new was possible, that the sun had yet to see the radically magnificent societies that would emerge from the imaginations within the United Commune Front, the autonomous self-sustaining anarchies free from authoritarian global order.

But Kilcher had ensured the UCF would never realize their vision. He'd revealed his perfect plan to Mason during their meeting. The gallery show had been a trap. It appealed to Mason's vanity, so he'd been happy to ignore the suspicious nature of Ponce's convenient offer of a solo show. Unbeknownst to Mason, Ponce had been interrogated by the FBI because his gallery represented artists on the government's list of extremists. Ponce made a deal to secretly cooperate with the FBI in apprehending subversive figures to avoid prison himself. (Mason now wondered if there was a more sinister explanation for Maggie Shotwell's "suicide.") Kilcher's ruse was perfect. The art adviser to "Edgar Millet" presented Mason with an offer he couldn't refuse. But when Mason learned Kilcher was behind the purchase, refusing was the *only* thing Mason wanted to do. Because Kilcher had terrifying plans for that three hundred thousand dollars. Of course, there was no way for Mason to reject the money. The FBI held the trump card of federal prison should he refuse to cooperate. But even if Mason had gathered the courage to refuse "Millet's" offer, it would've caused Yunho to ask unanswerable questions about why Mason would decline three hundred thousand dollars when their community needed cash so badly. He couldn't fathom telling Yunho the truth. Which is how he arrived here, winding through backroads, on his final mission.

Mason made a sharp turn, past a cluster of lanky ponderosas. A small shack appeared in the distance. He accelerated. The building's aluminum siding looked new. The metal gleamed in the sun; the roof was covered with solar paneling. There were no windows. Gravel popped under Mason's tires as he pulled into a driveway. He killed the engine and got out of the truck. The shack door swung open. A man burst out. Gaunt, white, short, no older than twenty-three. He aimed a machine gun straight at Mason who threw his arms in the air. "It's Mason! We were connected by your, uh, colleague earlier?"

*

"The serials on these are obliterated." The man motioned to a glass display case loaded with weaponry—AR-15s, AK-47s, machine guns, handguns, bombs. "There's *no way* anybody's tracking these puppies. We also got ghost guns I made with my 3D printer."

"Got it." Mason assessed the artillery in the glass case. It was surreal that it had come to this. After his apology to Claudia that morning, they conducted their emergency community forum. The decision was unanimous: Militarization was necessary. And Claudia was right. The commune *did* need to defend itself. An attack was imminent. But—and this is why Kilcher had given Mason money for weapons—if the commune was militarized, they could be classified as even more of a threat. What the FBI, the president, and nearly all of Washington wanted was a massacre. A simple CPS raid, a bloodless seizure of the children—that wouldn't be enough, not when the president had painted the Ranch as a diabolical terrorist cell fighting to overthrow the U.S. government. No, what the president needed was genocide, but to justify tomorrow's slaughter and his new dictatorship, he needed proof—*real* proof, in the form of shiny mountains of artillery—that the Ranch was teeming with foaming-at-the-mouth, coup-hungry bogeythems.

The newscast wrote itself: *A raid of the queer anarchist commune revealed stockpiles of deadly weapons, confirming the government's fears that these extremists intended to violently overthrow our democracy.* All state-controlled media would broadcast footage of the lethal weapons Mason was purchasing today, and this footage would be used to explain the *other* footage on those same newscasts, the footage of dead bodies, *A violent but justified end to this commune's reign of terror. However, it's not yet time for America to rest easy—there are still many other terrorist cells around the country. The presidential election will remain deferred indefinitely, until this threat has been eradicated from American soil.*

But for any of this to happen, Kilcher needed Mason to supply the commune with guns. Which meant Mason had one last sliver of leverage over the FBI. And he knew exactly how he planned to use it.

Mason could see it all as clearly as his reflection in the glass weapons case before him. He stared at his double, through it. Below, an AK-47 glistened on a bed of green velvet. It radiated with the oracular luminescence of a crystal ball. Mason looked deep into its gleaming surface. The future shined back.

SIXTY-EIGHT

Gabriel wasn't supposed to be in the shooting range, but Mason was outside taking a phone call. So Gabriel snuck down to Mason's room to see what the grown-ups were worried about.

Don't feel guilty. You belong here. The voice was back. *And I'll be with you until the end.* But the voice wouldn't tell Gabriel what the end was. Or how it ended. Or when it ended. They felt sick. *I'll protect you. Don't be afraid.* The guns were in their cases on the walls, lit up. They floated behind glass, glowing like angels. *The guns won't hurt you.* Gabriel stepped closer to the case. *Not while I'm around.* They lifted the latch. *Go ahead.* The door opened. *Grab the little one.* Gabriel reached for a baby at the bottom of the case. It was silver. With a white handle. *You've almost got it.* Then it was in their hand.

"I'm scared shitless about tomorrow, Kilcher." Mason's voice. He was coming down the stairs. "And I *don't* think it's too much to ask you to *fucking promise me this one thing*—" Mason stopped when he saw Gabriel. They got that floaty feeling again, the feeling they were outside their body. They pointed the gun at Mason. "Gabriel." Mason's voice sounded far away, a TV underwater. "Put that down." Gabriel's fingers were slippery, sweaty. "And I won't tell on you." The gun was heavy. "This can be our secret. Just hand me the gun."

It's not time yet, the voice said. *Wait until tomorrow.*

SIXTY-NINE

Y ou sure you don't mind?" Grey asked. The Main Hall rumbled with morning activity. The protestors outside continued their relentless chants. It was the last day of the conference. The crowd had thinned; the UCF had lost many participants, people who flew home in fear.

"Of course not," Mason insisted. "Claudia put you in the Nursery for the whole conference. It's not fair."

"True." Grey issued a bitter snort.

"Let Yunho and I give you a break. You can help Claudia with her live broadcast."

"I thought Yunho was going to film it—"

"But you're just as capable. Didn't you shoot the documentary about LOMAX!!!?"

"You're right. Sometimes I think Claudia forgets I'm a former member of her seminal queer noise band and not just a babysitting android."

Mason laughed. "Seriously, Yunho and I can take the reins for one day."

"Okay! I'll give you the Kids' Coalition curriculum. They're just sharing art projects."

"Great."

"Thank you." Grey threw their arms around Mason, lavishing him with affection he didn't deserve. As Mason guiltily withdrew himself from the embrace, he startled at the sight of something that shouldn't have surprised him. It was what they'd planned as a community the previous evening: Keisha guarded the front door, gripping an AK-47. She made a shit soldier—she was still human, not yet a machine, still in touch with reason, empathy, her own mortality.

They didn't stand a chance.

*

I'm here, Gabriel.

Where?

I'll reveal myself soon enough.

But how will I know it's time?

You'll see fire in the sky.

Gabriel's arm itched inside their cast. They wanted to rip it off, but Daniel said it had to stay on longer. That made them want to scream. "Sweetie, let's put on your shoes," Daniel said. "You have to go to the Kids' Coalition."

Don't go there. It's not safe. "No! You can't make me!"

"Gabriel! We don't have time to—"

"I want *Dad* to put on my shoes."

"You know Mahmood is in the hospital, and we call him 'Guardian'—"

"*I want my DAD!*"

"*Just stop it!*" Daniel started crying and seeing him cry made Gabriel cry too and then they were both weeping on the bottom bunk of Gabriel's bed as Daniel threw the shoes on the floor and pushed his hands into his eyes like he was trying to pop them because if he didn't have eyes then he wouldn't have to cry. "I'm sorry." He pulled Gabriel into a hug and whispered into their hair. "There's just . . . a lot going on . . ."

Gabriel, ask him. "Can . . . I come with you?"

Daniel sighed. "So *that's* what this is about."

"I wanna go with the grown-ups."

"But the grown-ups are just gonna do boring stuff."

"I don't care! *Please, please, please,* can I go with you?"

"Fine. But you have to be quiet. And you have to put on your shoes."

"Okay! We can put them on." Daniel put on the shoes. He tied them too tight, but Gabriel didn't care, because Gabriel was doing everything the voice said, and if Gabriel followed the voice's instructions, then Gabriel would be safe, they'd all be safe. But Gabriel was scared. They still had a question: *What happens after the fire in the sky?*

Ash will rain down.

And then?

I'll emerge to fulfill my promise.

*

"I promise you, it's what she said," Mason lied.

"I just can't believe Claudia wants Grey to shoot the live broadcast instead of me." Yunho pushed a pile of floor cushions into the center of the Nursery. One by one, he placed them in a circle. "And I've been relegated to *childcare*."

"You say that like childcare isn't a valid form of labor deserving of respect." Mason gazed into Fennel's crib, battling the panic he felt staring at the infant's fragile fat limbs; how easily they could be ripped apart, like segments of a warm cinnamon roll.

"Oh my god." Yunho rolled his eyes. "I'm allowed to feel hurt. How many cushions do we need?"

"Twenty-six. Which is why I want you here. I can't handle twenty-six kids on my own."

"I should go talk to Claudia." Yunho tossed a cushion to the ground and made his way to the door. "To make sure she's feeling good about the switch—"

Fennel's flesh was warm between Mason's thumb and index finger. His nails were poised like a scorpion's pincer. He crushed the infant's hand. Bone slid beneath the skin. The child screamed. Mason released his grip and donned a mask of surprise. "Yunho, wait. Fennel . . ." Yunho stopped. Rushed back. Swooped the child into his arms. Pushed up against Mason. The warmth of Yunho's body reminded Mason why he was doing this: love.

"Shhh, it's okay, sweetie." Fennel quieted in Yunho's arms.

"Stay here with us," Mason whispered. "Fennel needs their father."

*

"Where's Yunho?" Claudia sat in the shooting range, with a machine gun strapped to the back of her wheelchair. Behind her: a wooden case filled with floating guns. In front of her: a camera. Bright lights shined on her. They made the whole room hot. Gabriel felt like they had a fever. Everyone huddled together to watch the broadcast. They all had guns.

"He's in the nursery with Mason," Grey said. "They're watching the kids for me."

"This isn't the plan."

"Just trust me, Claudia. I've been your friend and collaborator for over eleven years—"

"*I just want to talk to him—*"

"We go live in *one minute*," Daniel interrupted. "Do we really need him? The lighting is set up. We have our shot. All Grey needs to do is press record."

Everyone was quiet. "Okay." Claudia sighed. "Let's just roll."

"Grey will do a great job." Astrid stood by the door. Guarding it with a rifle.

Gabriel, offer to help.

But I'm scared.

Don't be. I'm coming, remember?

"I wanna help you, Claudia."

"Sweetie, this is a grown-up thing," Daniel said. "We don't need—"

"Actually, I could use your help, Gabriel." Claudia smiled and stretched out her arms.

*

Yunho's face lit up when he talked to the kids. His cheeks rose on the tide of his smile, like two goofy buoys. His joy was enough to keep everyone afloat. Yunho sat on the floor, in a circle of children. "Today we're going to share our paintings." There was something horrifically naive about his earnest commitment to the lesson, as if he would get to finish, uninterrupted by tragedy. But Yunho had no way of knowing what would happen. Mason, on the other hand, could literally see the future. It appeared behind Yunho, in the Nursery's picture-book window: an army, far in the distance, yet as clear as the bright Montana day through which it marched.

*

It's almost time.

Gabriel sat in Claudia's lap. Her body was warm. It made Gabriel feel warm too. Safe. Claudia talked to the camera. "State-controlled media outlets have been forbidden from airing anything sympathetic to our mission. So I'm taking to our own social media channels for this live broadcast, to address the nation and clear up confusion." Claudia smiled down at Gabriel. "And Gabriel here is gonna help me. Because we've got what?"

"Love for everyone!"

She doesn't know what's coming, Gabriel. No one does.

"Yes! We've got love for everyone, and that's all we need. Which is why I think it's funny when people ask what we 'demand' from the government. We demand nothing from a State beyond repair. In our lifetime, we've witnessed a murderous authoritarian reclamation of America by the Christian white supremacist capitalist patriarchy. Their actions are not, as some feckless Puppet Democrats insist, 'against everything America stands for.' Rather, this is *precisely* what America stands for. America has *always* been evil, ever since its genocidal founding. We've never been a direct democracy, the founders created a *republic*, with elected representatives—aka elite, propertied white men—barring the public from truly participating in decisions impacting their lives. Alexander Hamilton called pure democracy a 'disease' that would result in an 'ungovernable mob.' James Madison was fiercely concerned with protecting the private property of the wealthy and believed democracy to be at odds with this goal. Many conservatives have pointed to facts like these as evidence that America was never meant to be a democracy. This is the only instance in which I'll agree with Repub-licans. Their actions are in keeping with our founding fathers' intentions to allow a cabal of elite, propertied white men to run our nation like we're living in the eighteenth fucking century."

Do you feel that, Gabriel? Just a small vibration.

"Well, I don't live in the eighteenth fucking century. Instead of looking to the past, I look to the future. I wonder where life can thrive, where love can live. And let me tell you, it's not America. Which is why we've built a community that exists apart from America, inside its borders yet outside its ideology. So, what are our 'demands'? We only have one: Leave us alone. So we can build an egalitarian future for this world, one in which every human being is valued, and obedient to love alone. For those of you who think love is not a stable foundation upon which to build a society, I would ask you to look at how we've succeeded within our Montana community and in so many other communities across the country. Besides, how *stable* is America? An authoritarian state in which the majority are furious at the minority elite who govern through draconian measures to ensure that hope is beaten from a populace large enough to overthrow its rulers. They're scared of us. Of our collective power. They should be."

When they arrive, you'll be ready.

*

Mason watched through the window. They moved stealthily, in concert, approaching the door to the Main Hall. Their jackets billowed and snapped in the wind; the official logos emblazoned across their backs bounced nonsensically, like letters in a sentence that refused to fall into place: FBI, MPD, CPS, SAS. Mason froze, desperate to cling to these final moments of peace. Yunho babbled on, unaware of the annihilating swarm at his back. "That's a pretty picture of your school, Auden. Can you tell me what your favorite subject is?"

Auden didn't answer; he stood and pointed at the window. "Who are they?"

Yunho turned. Horror warped his face. He stammered, unable to speak. Fennel writhed in their crib. Mason scooped the infant into his arms, ran to his lover, and pulled his family toward the door.

*

Do you hear that, Gabriel? Footsteps. On the ceiling above.

"This is why those in power fear our community. We have one weapon money cannot buy: love. Politicians and their propaganda machines try to use old anti-anarchist tropes to paint us as agents of havoc. But anarchy isn't chaos. Anarchy is organization. Anarchy is mutual aid. Anarchy is abolition. Anarchy is love. A powerful love that scares the State so much that the president himself has threatened to destroy us. Because he knows that hate is no match for love. And the only thing the State has to offer is hatred. And violence. And fear."

Louder footsteps. People are looking up. They wonder what's coming.

"We're not stupid. We know that fear, when weaponized by a ruthless state with massive capital, is an incredibly powerful force. We don't want to use violence; it is anathema to our community. We're peaceful. We wish to remain that way. But if you bring war to our doorstep, we will have no choice but to defend ourselves."

Yes, that's a gunshot. Upstairs. It's almost time.

*

"*What the fuck is going on?*" Yunho screamed as Mason dragged him to the door and flung it open. Police officers rushed down the hallway toward the nursery. Their uniforms were wet. Dark splatters soaked their blue shirts. *Keisha. The gunshot was for Keisha.* Mason froze in terror. Yunho slammed the door shut, locking them inside the Nursery. The children began to cry.

*

Don't be scared, Gabriel. The door burst open. A gang of men. Black jackets. Yellow lettering. White faces. FBI. They yelled. Blocked the stairway. *We'll put them on the list.* They aimed their guns into the room. "Put your hands in the air!" one man screamed. Claudia followed orders. So did Gabriel. *They'll be sorry they ever came here.* Everyone had their arms up. Fingers shook in the air like leaves, like they were a whole garden, shivering in the breeze.

"Please, don't shoot." Astrid was the closest to the men. "We're cooperating—"

"I'll be the judge of that," the agent replied.

"Just . . . just tell us what you want—"

"We're here for the children."

Run, Gabriel.

*

They were locked in the Nursery. Yunho obstructed the door with his body. But children clawed at his legs, climbed his torso. "*Let us out!*" a small redhead screamed and leapt onto Yunho with such force that he crumpled to the floor. "*I want my mommy!*" A mess of children swarmed Yunho, a violent amoeba of flailing arms and legs and hair and teeth. The children wanted out. Mason stepped forward and—still cradling his baby in one arm—slapped their freckled leader. The child fell to the ground. The mob quieted, terrified.

"Mason, you can't *hit* a child—"

A pounding. "*Police. Open up.*"

"We're gonna be okay." Mason felt sick. "We're gonna be okay."

"*Open this door or we'll knock it down.*" POUND. POUND.

"We have to get out of here." Yunho scanned the room for other possible exits. His gaze landed on the picture-book window. It was fixed; there was no way to open it.

POUND. "*We're gonna be okay.*"

POUND. "*Stop fucking SAYING that.*" Yunho rushed toward Fennel's empty crib. Grabbed it. Launched it at the window. The glass pane exploded. Then, an opening. A jagged portal, framed by shards of splintered glass.

Dead grassland beckoned. Freedom. Yunho turned to the crying children. "*Let's go, kids. Out the window.*" POUND. "*Mason—fucking help me.*"

This wasn't the plan. It couldn't happen like this. POUND. Mason clutched Fennel tighter. POUND. He backed away from the window. POUND. He grasped the doorknob. POUND. Cold metal shocked his fist. POUND. He turned the lock and opened the door.

*

Run, Gabriel. The men with guns rushed through the crowd. "We have a court order from the state of Montana authorizing an emergency removal of all children on the premises." *Run, run, run.* "Resist us, and we will use force." One man walked up to Gabriel. He crouched down in front of their face. "Come with me, son." *Run, run, run.* But Gabriel's legs were stones. The man grabbed their arm. Gabriel looked up at Claudia. Another man held a gun to her back. She stared ahead. Crying. "*Let's go, kid!*" the man shouted. He pulled so hard that Gabriel fell out of Claudia's lap. He dragged Gabriel across the floor by one arm. *Run, run, run.*

"*Don't touch them!*" Astrid screamed. The man stopped and let go of Gabriel.

A bullet hit Astrid in her chest.

Run, run, run. Finally, Gabriel obeyed the voice.

*

A grizzled woman stood in the doorframe. Five men stood behind her, carrying guns. They all wore jackets emblazoned with the same terrible letters: CPS.

"What the fuck is this?" Yunho stepped forward, placing himself between the children and the CPS agents in the door. He whipped his head toward Mason. "Did you . . . *let them in?*"

"Yunho, let's just cooperate here—"

"These people are attempting to *steal* our *children*—"

"*Yunho, stop!*" Mason screamed. The room fell silent. He turned to the woman from CPS, cradling Fennel in his arms. "My name is Mason Daunt . . ."

"Mason, what . . . why are you—"

"This is Yunho Kim." Tears fell down Mason's cheeks.

"*Mason—*"

"And this—" Mason choked out a sob. "—is our child, Fennel."

"*What the fuck is happening?*"

"And Agent Kilcher has assured me that we'll be spared: me, Yunho, and our child."

"Yes, we spoke with Kilcher." The woman frowned. "The three of you can have a seat." She motioned to her men, who corralled the howling children. "We won't be long."

*

Run, run, run. Gunshots rang out. Everyone kept their hands in the air. The police fired anyway. *Run, run, run.* People fell. Blood sprayed onto Gabriel's face and clothing. *Run, run, run.* Then, they stopped. Astrid's body lay on the floor. They had to help her. *There's not enough time, Gabriel.* But Gabriel didn't care. They tried to wake her up. They pushed wet hair out of her face. Pulled at her eyelids and saw the whites underneath. "*Wake up,*" they whispered. "I saved you."

Her mouth opened. Blood poured from her lips. Gabriel screamed.

Claudia wheeled over from across the room. She shouted something Gabriel couldn't hear. A police officer ran toward her and aimed his gun. Another came at her from behind. He grabbed her arms and cuffed them.

You must leave her, Gabriel.

*

Yunho's eyes burned with a hatred Mason would never forget. Mason stepped forward, cradling Fennel. He presented the child like a peace offering, struggling to speak between sobs. "I . . . I . . ." But he was interrupted by a sonic roar so loud it rattled the walls. The velocity and arc of the sound implied something fast, airborne, deadly. An explosion shattered the remaining windows in the Nursery. Glass shards rained down on the children. Shocked silence soon gave way to delayed response; spittle erupted from each small mouth as it screamed. A brown-haired boy clutched his eyes. Blood seeped through his fingers. A girl scraped glass from her cheeks. The lead CPS officer hunched under the makeshift carapace of her jacket; she popped her head out like some deranged turtle. "Let's go, boys!" she shouted to her crew, shaken yet undeterred. They rounded up mutilated toddlers with clinical detachment.

Mason had thrown himself over Yunho to shield his lover from harm; shards of glass dug into his back like nettles. Beneath them both, protected, screaming in the space between their bodies: Fennel. Yunho grabbed the baby in one swift, instinctual movement, like an animal protecting its young. Mason attempted to caress his lover. Yunho lurched backward. "I know it doesn't look like it now," Mason cried. "But I . . . I did this for us."

"No, you didn't." Yunho spat in his face.

*

Gabriel lay on the floor. Their head hurt. They hit it in the fall. The explosion had knocked everyone to the ground.

The stairs, Gabriel. Take the stairs.

Gabriel ran. Up the stairs. Into the Main Hall. Toward the door. Past Keisha's body. *Don't look, Gabriel. There's no time to mourn.* Gabriel rushed outside. A row of police cars lined the gravel drive. Men aimed their guns at Gabriel, shouting.

The earth shook. Gabriel fell. Another explosion. Where did it come from? They looked to the forest. For a sign. For hope. Then, it appeared: *fire in the sky.*

Come find me, Gabriel.

SEVENTY

S now in the sky. Impossible. And yet, the flakes fell. Danced on the hot breeze. Gabriel looked up as they ran through the dead field, toward the forest. They pumped their legs harder. Every muscle burned. Fire. They smelled smoke. They looked up at the snow. Some flakes were gray. Some were black. It wasn't snow.

Ash will rain down. A promise kept. *Fire in the sky.*

Gabriel ran through ash toward the burning treetops. *Yes, Gabriel. You're almost there.* Gabriel looked over their shoulder. A man chugged behind. Black jacket. Yellow letters. He pumped his arms. In his fist: a gun. "Hey, kid!" the man yelled. "Stop! I just wanna help you."

Gabriel knew the man was lying. Gabriel kept running until they reached the tree line. They ran into the forest. The air grew hotter. *You'll feel the heat from the flames.* Gabriel was close. Sweat soaked their shirt. Dead nettles crunched underfoot. The air grew thick with smoke. They sucked it into their lungs. They coughed and it hurt. But it was a good hurt. The smoke was a sign. Gabriel was on the right path. They turned a corner. Saw a wall of fire. Gabriel wasn't scared. They had hoped for this. Proof. *Fire in the sky.*

"*Stop!*" the man screamed. But Gabriel didn't look back.

The fire was warm. Like a blanket. Gabriel looked up at the burning canopy. Treetops turned to ash, vanished. Like magic. Magic that would save everyone they loved.

It was the dragons.

"Get away from me!" Gabriel screamed. "*Or my dragon will kill you!*"

"*Are you crazy, kid?*" the man screamed.

Hot. So hot. Gabriel's blood boiled inside their veins. Their skin burned. But they went deeper. Into the heat, into the burning pines. They looked over their shoulder. A giant tree groaned as it fell to the forest floor, right on top of the man. "*FUCK!*" He howled as the fiery trunk pinned him to the ground. "*HELP ME!*" Gabriel watched him scream, watched his face bubble like a raw pancake on a skillet. His right eye popped. The left one too. Red jam pooled in his sockets. He stopped moving. The man wasn't a man anymore. He was just a body. Almost a skeleton. Almost ash, almost light enough to rise on a wave of heat, and dance deeper into the forest.

Gabriel turned. Fire on their left side. On their right. A circle of fire and Gabriel was in the center. Tears streamed down their face. Happy tears. The dragon was coming. They took a big, beautiful breath of smoke. They felt dizzy. They fell. Their face landed on a patch of warm moss. So soft, like a pillow. Right in front of their eyes was a family of mushrooms. One by one, the caps caught fire. It was so hot. Their body ached. Their lungs hurt. But Gabriel held on to hope. They closed their eyes. For just a minute, they swam in the dark, safe in the black.

Gabriel heard a snap.

They opened their eyes. In the distance, something slithered behind a wall of fire. A tree toppled, creating an opening in a thicket of scorched forest. What they saw amazed them: a patchwork of blue-green scales. Firelight shimmered off the surface. It was a tail. A mane of white hair lined the top; the matted ringlets were stained brown in spots, black in others—consequences of a life spent wrestling earth and fire. The tail curled in on itself; its scales clattered like wind chimes. They made music. A strange melody drifted through burnt trunks. It was unlike any music Gabriel had ever heard, yet they knew it was the perfect expression of something they'd always felt but had never been able to name, harmonies that lived within, waiting for someone else to sing them first, to give voice to the life inside Gabriel.

The tail tightened into a spiral. Then, it unfurled, landing with an impact that shook the earth. The forest floor rippled like a lake. Trees fell. A path opened.

Gabriel stood to face the dragon. They weren't afraid. They'd been waiting for this moment. The dragon was bigger than four cows put together. Its torso shimmered, like an ocean at sunset. Its scales chimed as it heaved its massive haunches forward; every stride was a new song. Each step a little earthquake. The dragon's head swooped earthward, riding on the muscular swell of its serpentine neck. Its mouth stopped inches from Gabriel's face. It opened wide; stalactite fangs hung from wet black gums; its scarlet tongue flopped like a skinned seal. Its maw was cavernous. A flame flickered deep within its esophagus, lighting a throat spotted with cysts that erupted in volcanic bursts of thick white pus. Streams of curdled discharge slid down into the beast's larynx-fire, sizzling and baking as they fell.

The dragon snapped its jaw shut. Smoke puffed from scabrous nostrils. *You found me, Gabriel.*

Can I hug you? Gabriel asked. The dragon blinked. Thick eyelashes brushed Gabriel's body. The lashes felt like horsehair, coarse but comforting. Gabriel looked into the dragon's black eyes. They failed to reflect Gabriel's image, failed to reflect any light at all, like two black holes, twin stretches of space-time where nothing escapes, and gravity consumes all.

Yes, you can hug me, the dragon replied. Gabriel threw their arms around the dragon's neck. The scales were hot, but Gabriel didn't care. The heat felt good. It warmed Gabriel's heart, their lungs, their guts, their insides. Yes, their insides were burning. Their whole body was burning.

Do you want to climb onto my back?

Yes, please. Gabriel straddled the dragon's neck and gripped its knotty mane. Their stomach flipped as the dragon raised its head. They felt a gust of wind. Gabriel looked behind them; the dragon had spread its wings. The undersides were dark green, a mottled leather that stretched between a bat-like network of bone. Slowly, the beast climbed through the atmosphere; but as they flew higher, Gabriel felt a searing heat in their body, and an intense pressure in their skull, like their brain might burst, and the pain grew so great it blinded Gabriel.

Their vision went black.

Then, a flash. Something red. Another flash. Something green. Gabriel's vision was returning. They didn't have to open their eyes to see. Movies played out on the backs of their eyelids. Was this dreaming? Another flash. A fuzzy image. Another flash. It was a house. Another flash. It was the Ranch.

Gabriel gripped the dragon's mane tighter. It felt like grass.

Another flash. Men stood outside the Ranch. Policemen.

The world would be a better place without some people, wouldn't it, Gabriel?

Yes. Let's get rid of them.

Another flash. Fire burst from the dragon's mouth. The policemen evaporated, their screams swallowed by the roar of the flame. Another flash. Bone segments flew—a chunk of femur, a slice of skull, a nubby patella coated with blackened meat.

Another flash. A woman. CPS on her jacket. The woman who had questioned Gabriel at the police station. She pushed children into a white van.

Another flash. The woman was on the ground now. Screaming. Pinned by a dragon claw. A talon sliced her stomach. Shit frothed inside, mixed with her mangled guts.

Another flash. Everyone Gabriel loved was watching. Grateful. Gabriel had saved them all. Another flash. The people surrounded Gabriel. They hugged Gabriel. But it was too hot. All the bodies—too hot. Gabriel wanted to escape. Wanted to scream. But they couldn't. They couldn't move. They couldn't breathe. It got hotter and hotter.

Gabriel's vision went black.

*

Gabriel woke up alone, lying on a bed of blackened nettles. The stench of burnt pine stung their nostrils. Had it just been a dream? A nightmare?

There wasn't much hope left in Gabriel's heart. There was even less love. But something ached in their chest, something like dragon fire, something that told Gabriel to rise from the dirt, and face the awful dawn.

There was work to do.

DEATH

2134

SEVENTY-ONE

A dull ache throbbed beneath his closed eyelids. He opened them and stared out the tank porthole at the landscape that had caused his decrepit tear ducts to seize. The Amazon stretched out before him, its scorched plains nothing like the wilds he remembered. But the mountains. Their awesome silhouettes remained the same, their dominance over the horizon went unchallenged even if their forests had been decimated, reduced to little more than rock and dirt, precarious cliffsides that would avalanche at the slightest hint of rain, which was now a once-in-a-decade occurrence. Still, this mountainous promise of destruction loomed over the desolate wilderness, the perennial threat of a landslide just one of nature's merciless assurances that soon—despite whatever belated technological interventions Imperialists employed to provide their Earth-bound slaves with protection—the planet would be completely hostile to human life and Imperialists would be forced to relinquish small portions of their respective Martian settlements to create new slave habitats in order to preserve the proper ratio of surplus labor essential to maintaining the royal lifestyle to which they'd become accustomed. The Imperialists didn't like sharing.

But there was something about those mountains. Their silhouette had the sentimental power of an old song that could reduce one to a blubbering mess. For Mason, that song had long been "California" by Joni Mitchell, until the years passed, and the fires raged, and California fell into such ruin that no corporate sponsor was interested in leasing the state. Mason gradually forgot what he'd found so bittersweet about Joni's yearning melody. No, "California" no longer did it for him. But, to his surprise, these mountains did.

Mason's eyes spasmed in a failed attempt to produce tears. He'd delayed a tear duct transplant to make the arduous interplanetary trip, just one of four LyfeHack surgeries—including colon replacement, kidney transplant, and eardrum transplant—that Peter had gifted him for the occasion of Mason's 125th birthday. Peter hadn't approved of Mason's sudden decision to forgo the surgeries and accompanying LyfeHack treatments—essential to his survival—to make a hasty and ill-advised return to Earth.

But this was an emergency.

If Mason failed to make this trip, it would be a decision he'd regret for the rest of his possibly eternal life. And that sort of regret could calcify into something deadly, just ask Jessica Hinterland. The fact that the founder of LyfeHack (the startup that won the decades-long race to "disrupt death" by treating wealthy clients to a revolutionary biohacking regimen) had committed suicide was an irony lost on every Imperialist except Mason.

The tank continued its predetermined course toward the DMZ. Mason's claustrophobia mounted. Despite his heated leather seat and the "welcome glass" of champagne he'd guzzled upon entering the armored vehicle, he couldn't get comfortable. The chamber was oppressively small—all luxury tanks had been rented months prior due to the Amazon Terrestrial Solutions Conference taking place in Butte, which meant Mason had been stuck with a mini "tankette." Yet another reason Peter objected to the trip. Not enough protection.

Mason stared out the small window that sat above a console beeping in service of some artificially intelligent system he had zero idea how to operate. Shards of morning light sliced through clouds of smoke that gathered around his beloved mountaintops. Below them were miles of windowless steel structures. Amazon's new Labor Storage Bins. A piercing whistle blew. Guards marched through the rows of metal cages. One by one, the guards unlocked them, and Laborers marched out, their emaciated faces drained of life. They shuffled toward the Fulfillment Center that stood at the mountain's base. The building was a giant concrete block, out of which a river of armored delivery trucks streamed.

Mason made eye contact with a Laborer. Her face trembled with some awful hope. Suddenly, she broke rank and ran toward him. Dread blossomed in his gut. The tank console flashed. The woman's body appeared on screen, rendered in stark colors of infrared imaging. Mason screamed, but she couldn't hear. She wouldn't have stopped regardless. This was suicide.

A small whir shook the tank. Bullets deployed. The woman fell to the ground. She rolled over to face the sky. A horrible smile cracked her face. Blood trickled through her lips.

The tank stopped. They'd reached the DMZ.

*

"You've reached a Save America Superforce checkpoint, on the border of Demilitarized Zone Thirteen-A. Drop your weapons and exit your vehicle."

Mason climbed out of the tank's hatch and jumped onto the armored skirt that covered the vehicle's road wheels. Adrenaline pulsed in his skull; he peered up at the towering gate that stood between him and the most dangerous of all demilitarized zones in the United Corporate Colonies of America. The border wall stretched for miles, a series of towering thirty-foot concrete slabs fanged with barbed wire and AI-powered sniper-bots. Unmanned Death Panthers stalked the barrier's perimeter in programmed circles; each paced its own small patch of land like a zoo-deranged lion driven mad by its carceral habitat.

"No one may pass the Military Demarcation Line without clearance from the president of the UCCA or, alternatively, the Imperialist Order. Prepare to identify yourself." The voice blasted from speakers mounted on a cylindrical lookout tower lined with dead-eyed soldiers deficient in the esprit de corps of their progenitors, those bushy-tailed fascists who'd signed up for the Save America Superforce in its infancy, prior to Civil War II. "Dismount your vehicle."

Mason's mortal terror was suddenly replaced by a more quotidian fear, inspired by the patch of tank-churned earth into which he was expected to leap while wearing new cowhide loafers. The shoes had been a birthday present from Peter. They were wildly expensive because they'd been imported from Earth due to the absence of real cowhide on Mars caused by a fatal brucellosis outbreak among their biodome's cattle population. Imperialists had been so afraid of contracting the illness nicknamed "contagious abortion" that they'd herded even uninfected cows out of the biodome's controlled climate and put them out to Martian pasture, aka let them stumble through an atmosphere so pressurized that their organs burst inside their bodies. The idea of stepping just one hundred-thousand-dollar heel in the muck beneath his tank caused panic to balloon in his chest and made Mason wonder if he should order a lung transplant upon his return to Mars.

An SAS officer ran toward the tank, flanked by two UDPs that glinted in the sun as they bounded behind their keeper. Mason leapt to the earth, hands in the air. "I'm cooperating."

"Present your body for scanning."

Mason spread his legs, keeping his arms aloft. The officer produced a large scanner from his backpack. The device caressed Mason's body with a red beam. The officer's eyes widened in fear as he assessed the scanner's screen. *At last*, Mason thought, *the respect I deserve.*

"Gr . . . greetings Imperial Leader Daunt," the idiot stammered. "It's an honor."

"Am I cleared to pass?"

"Of course, sir." The soldier hesitated. "Though I'm not sure why someone like you wants to go . . . there." He pointed toward the barren sweep of the DMZ.

"I guess that's not any of your fucking business. Now, can you open the gates?"

"I'm sorry, sir, but first I have to read you our standard warning." The soldier looked down at his scanner; a script appeared on screen. "'Those who pass beyond our God-blessed borders of the United Corporate Colonies of America do so at their own risk. Leaving our hallowed nation means abandoning all claims to the one great American guarantee: freedom. Each of the fifteen Autonomous Anarchist Republics that blight our nation's soil is a horrific threat to that freedom. You are one of the rare few granted permission to cross into these evil havens of corruption, violence, and death. Beyond this border, the Save America Superforce can offer no protection. In the years since Civil War Two, all diplomatic relations attempted with AARs have failed. Enter at your own risk, with the knowledge you may perish at the hands of merciless anarchists who are sated by nothing less than the smell of blood and the warm sensation of freshly harvested American organs beating in their diabolical, devil-worshipping fists.'"

"Is that it?"

The soldier blinked dumbly. "Uh, um, yeah."

"Wonderful. I accept the warning."

"Then you're cleared to go, sir. Have a great day!"

Mason climbed into his tankette. Panic itched up his spine. Sweat pooled beneath him. The gates parted. Beyond them, the wilds of the demilitarized zone unfurled. He had no idea what horrors awaited, only that he'd received an invitation he couldn't decline.

*

The DMZ stretched for 631 miles across the width of the state formerly known as Montana, yet it was only 2 miles deep. The land had become an informal wildlife sanctuary, one of the rare habitats in the United Corporate Colonies of America that hadn't been raped to death by the Imperialist Order. That's not to say it was an impressive or verdant landscape; it was remarkable only in that it was untouched by human hands. Much of the DMZ was the dried bed of what had once been the Milk River. Mason's tank churned through red clay as it crossed toward the opposite border. A rusty steel fence appeared in his dirt-crusted windshield.

The tank stopped suddenly. A coyote dashed in front of the vehicle; he was emaciated, a skeleton wrapped in fur. The animal galloped toward its pack, an assemblage of similarly starved mongrels. They snapped at one another, desperate for a mouthful of the rotted carcass around which they clustered. A battle escalated between two coyotes; they lunged, became one savage hurricane that carried them away from the corpse. Mason caught a glimpse of the dead thing—it was human. Or, it had been. Now it was a rotted place for flies to lay their larvae. Maggots fed on the decaying flesh, growing stronger, larger—soon they'd repopulate the dying Earth.

The two battling coyotes ended their skirmish; the victor stood growling above the defeated other, who lay on the earth with its mud-caked belly in the air. The dead-eyed dominance that glinted in the triumphant dog's gaze and the submissive posture of its vanquished partner conjured a memory for Mason: Vex. Which, of course, reminded him of Yunho.

First the mountains, now these memories; a sentimental swell heaved in his throat—still, his tear ducts refused him release. But there was no time to surrender to some maudlin spell, not when he was just feet away from the AAR checkpoint and its own coterie of armed guards. This barrier was far less imposing than its UCCA counterpart; corroded steel bars stretched a mere eight feet in the air. A small hut with a patchwork iron siding leaned next to the entry, pathetically ramshackle. So why did fear rack Mason's body? This wasn't unfamiliar territory; Mason had once lived with the AAR's founders. But that was years ago, in a time of great conflict but relative peace, before the savage realities of domestic bloodshed warped the spirit of the country and drove humans to evil ends they never imagined possible. No one—not Mason, not the Imperialists, not the UCCA's puppet government—knew what horrors lay beyond the gates of the AAR, or how indignation had blistered the hearts of its inhabitants.

The tank approached the gate. "Present yourself for identification!" a voice echoed across the DMZ. An ancient UDP, possibly from as early as the 2040s, limped from behind the hut; its weary machine gun head shuddered to life. Guards swarmed Mason's vehicle, aiming firearms at the tank's hatch.

Mason emerged with his hands in the air. "Please, don't shoot." The guards kept their guns raised. Mason saw a flash of movement in the rusted hut.

Slowly, an elderly figure emerged from the structure and into the brutal sun. The person shuffled toward the tank with painful effort; each step seemed more labored than the last. They squinted, held one hand in the air to block the blinding daylight; a handprint shadow fell across their pruned face. The figure grew closer; bags drooped under dull and milky eyes; sallow skin cascaded from severe cheekbones and collected in bags of flesh around the chin; a galaxy of dark moles dotted the furrows of their peeling brow; a long mane of tangled white hair flowed down their back, its curls saturated with so much dirt they were nearly dreadlocked.

The person stopped behind the row of guards. "No need to scan him. I recognize him."

"I'm sorry, do I know you?"

"Yes, you do, Mason." Their mouth twisted into a bitter grin. "It's Gabriel."

SEVENTY-TWO

*Y*ou've changed!" Mason shouted. Gabriel didn't respond, only gripped the steering wheel harder. Their knuckles whitened. The golf cart lurched down a crumbling road that stretched across the dead grassland of the AAR. Mason looked over his shoulder in fear—his tank was now just a speck in the distance, soon to be swallowed by the horizon's vanishing point. The dying roar of the golf cart's engine was awful, like a furious mechanical beast was being tortured beneath the hood. Perhaps Gabriel hadn't heard him. "*I said, you've changed!*"

"*You haven't!*" Gabriel shouted back, over the screaming motor.

"*LyfeHack!*" Mason shrugged, embarrassed by his wealth. Gabriel's apocalyptically cratered skin led Mason to surmise that they couldn't afford the biohacking regimen he so thoughtlessly consumed back in the comfort of his Martian biodome. Guilt struck his heart. "*I could get you a discount.*" Mason offered feebly. "*Eternal life is worth the splurge.*"

"*I would rather die!*" Gabriel yelled as disgust warped their features. Before Mason could reply, a shocking sight robbed him of breath: a miles-long biodome rose from the sun scorched clay, not unlike the Martian biodome that housed Mason, Peter, the Palantir staff, and all their Volunteers.

"*It's . . . it's just like our biodome!*" Mason shouted. "*On Mars!*"

"*No, it's better.* The hemispherical structure was made from massive triangles of high-performance glass held together by white steel framing.

A verdant forest canopy pressed against moisture-fogged panes. The golf cart stopped in the biodome's shadow, directly in front of the entrance. A steel hatch opened, revealing a hangar filled with vehicles and aircrafts—some armored, some not. They drove through the fleet, arriving at a smaller hatch at the opposite end of the hangar. The entrance to the biodome. "Ready?" Gabriel turned to Mason with a forlorn expression. It was a sadness Mason recognized; suddenly, the cherubic toddler from ninety years prior surfaced in Gabriel's visage. A tenderness swelled within Mason.

"It's good to see you, Gabriel." Mason caressed Gabriel's back.

They averted their eyes. "I didn't want you to come."

"Then why am I here?" The gate shuddered open.

"It wasn't up to me." Gabriel turned the ignition; the engine screamed for mercy.

*

An apple orchard. A whole fucking orchard. Not just a few scraggly trees with tiny bitter fruit and aphid-infested trunks, like the specimens they'd struggled to grow back on Mars, which were the pathetic efforts of crackpot scientists with an easily corrupted grasp on their field, the only type of scientist approved for interplanetary travel, the only type of scientist that hadn't been imprisoned for crimes of "treason," crimes that amounted to simply looking out the window at the literally burning Earth and announcing the obvious: Everyone was going to die. Many wondered what happened to the rare legitimate scientists who'd escaped the UCCA for the terrifying plight of living as a refugee in an AAR. But now, as Mason surveyed rows of fecund apple trees sagging with fruit, he realized that fears about the fates of refugee scientists were unnecessary—they were thriving as architects of artificial biomes in the AARs.

A team of harvesters marched along grassy footpaths between rows of apple trees. They wore matching sun hats to shield against the bright rays that filtered through the mile-high glass ceiling. One worker laughed at something another said and threw their head back so hard their sun hat flopped onto the road. Gabriel stopped the golf cart as the person plucked their hat from the asphalt. "Javi! How's the harvest?" Gabriel said, suddenly seeming nervous.

"It's our most gorgeous yet." Javi looked at Mason with wide eyes. "And who's *this*?"

"Just a friend," Gabriel replied. When that answer elicited a suspicious squint from Javi—clearly new people did not just casually cross the deadly expanse of the DMZ for a quick catch-up with friends—Mason was surprised to hear Gabriel lie. "A refugee from the UCCA."

Javi's face fell into an expression of genuine sympathy. "Welcome. I can only imagine the journey you've endured." They offered Mason a glistening apple from the basket they held in their arms. "Here, take one."

Mason felt the apple in his palm; it was weighty and firm. "Thank you."

"See you later, Javi!" Gabriel hit the gas, propelling the golf cart forward.

"Why did you lie?" Mason asked, when they were out of earshot.

Gabriel frowned. "Every decision made within the AAR is made democratically, but in a fashion that will sound foreign to you. We don't believe in a government composed of a ruling elite; we believe in organizing society from the 'ground up.' Each industry within our biodome—whether it be farming, healthcare, gestational labor, etc.—is organized into a collective advocacy group not dissimilar to what was formerly called a union. Within these 'unions,' members advocate for their needs within our biodome's society. There are delegates that represent each 'union' at meetings where important decisions are made regarding life in our bubble. But these delegates carry no greater power and possess no greater wealth than anyone else. We are all paid equally according to our Fixed Universal Income, we all have access to free housing and healthcare. There are no official 'leaders' in the way you're accustomed to, having grown up within American 'democracy.'" Gabriel took a theatrically laborious breath. "*So.* I feared your visitation to the AAR would almost definitely cause an uproar and sometimes when dealing with our anarcho-socialist consensus process—which to be clear, I believe to be a major advancement in human evolution—arriving at a unanimous decision about controversial measures can be nearly impossible. To avoid endless and maddening debate, I lied and said you were a refugee rather than admit that you're the legendarily loathed Judas who nearly destroyed the utopia we've upheld throughout many years of horrifically deadly warfare triggered in part by your actions."

Mason knew when to shut up. "Thank you for smuggling me in."

"Again, don't thank me."

"Right." Mason bit his apple. "Beautiful," he murmured as juice dripped down his chin.

"What?"

"This apple. But it's not just the apple, it's . . . everything. There's so much beauty here."

"You can thank your former husband for that."

"What do you mean?"

"Yunho kept things running underground while Claudia and the other survivors of the Ranch Police Raid were in prison. He took me in, hid me from CPS. It was just the two of us for a while."

"I was the one who saved Yunho." Mason felt the sudden need for Gabriel's forgiveness. "I got him immunity. I . . . I'm part of the reason why this is all here too."

Gabriel gave him a look of crushing pity. "Can you really be that deluded?"

But Mason couldn't answer—he was crying. Tears, at last, flowed down his cheeks and mixed with the sweet juice drying on his chin. He wiped his mouth. He felt invigorated. Being back here awakened something within him, he was no longer simply subsisting, eating lab-grown steaks in his gorgeous, boring Martian dining room and killing time between organ transplants. After all, to commit to the project of eternal life means that one is daily aware of its fatal negation; if such a thing as a soul existed, Mason could affirm that the LyfeHack process whittled it down to nothing. But with one bite of an apple, his spirit was restored. After years of merely living, Mason finally felt *alive*.

Suddenly, the golf cart turned. They emerged from the orchard. Mason dropped his apple when he saw the building at the end of the road: the Ranch, just as he remembered it.

SEVENTY-THREE

This was a terrible mistake. An amorphous foreboding overwhelmed Gabriel as they watched Mason's face fail to express shock at the sight of the Ranch; after years of LyfeHack facial augmentations, Mason's features were too white, too unblemished, too smooth—akin to a rubber Halloween mask. Gabriel couldn't shake the feeling that something terrible lay beneath the plastic veneer. Mason's eyes gleamed uncannily from atop twin peaks of cheek filler, shining so brightly Gabriel questioned if they were even his *original* eyes. Gabriel remembered Mason having blue eyes, not these sparkling brown orbs. "Shall we go inside?"

"Please," Mason said, his voice conveying emotion his face could not.

Yes, a terrible mistake. Yet Gabriel had been unable to deny their lover's dying wish; they couldn't look into the fading eyes of a person who'd been their best friend for over seventy years and refuse them the one thing they wanted desperately before they passed. To deny this request would have been to deny the many beautiful years they'd shared together, to deny those halcyon days after the war and during the Construction Era, when they'd tilled the soil of what would become the orchard by hand, two teens joking to pass the time as they dug shovels into the earth, relieved they hadn't been selected to hang from the mile-high steel framing and install plates of greenhouse glass above. It would have been to deny the tender moment when their friendship deepened into something aching and urgent, the evening they sat on the cold rocks that lined the tank of the coral reef biome, dangling their feet into the water, tentatively pressing their goose-pimpled arms together, until finally Gabriel summoned the courage for a kiss. It would have been to deny the Care Pod they formed with all their beloved friends and sometimes sexual partners in the Equal Housing Unit they'd so carefully made their home, with its handcrafted furniture from the Carpenter Collective, and its cozy kitchen where they cooked an abundance of meals and tended to their six houseplants, the maximum number allowed by the Botanist Collective. (Biodome denizens had an urgent connection to every plant, each carbon emission mattered, it was essential to maintain the balance of carbon dioxide and oxygen.) It would be to deny their work within the Crop Collective, all the grueling hours they spent farming; it would be to deny the theater they founded, the stage they built, how it became an institution with an ambitious dramaturgical agenda, staging classic plays as well as new works reflecting the world around them. It would've been to deny the deaths of everyone they held dear, everyone they'd watched in their Care Pod succumb to disease, to old age, until they were the only two surviving members, partners until the very end, blessed to still love each other after a rich existence spent inventing a new way of living on the dying planet.

No, Gabriel could not deny the life they had built with Fennel.

Especially now when Fennel was slipping away. And so, Gabriel had worked to grant Fennel's impossible wish. To bring back the man who had raised Fennel until they were thirteen years old. They needed to see Mason one last time, to settle something unresolved.

*

Elon Musk's recent effort to make time travel a reality had been an abject failure, despite the attempts of his publicists to put a positive spin on the disaster of his aborted TimeTourist launch. But as Mason stood in the Main Hall of the Ranch, he felt for a brief manic moment that he'd traversed the space-time continuum to arrive here, in his own past, to repair his severed relationships with people he'd loved more than anyone before or since. The towering fireplace. The ten-foot ceilings. The exposed beams. Context collapsed. Reality faded.

Mason turned. There stood Yunho.

A small cry escaped Mason's lips. Yunho was just as Mason remembered him, just as Mason left him on that awful day, the day of the Great Ranch Massacre, when Mason had run from the Nursery with Fennel in his arms, escorted by FBI agents, screaming, begging Yunho to join his rightful family as they fled to the armored truck that would whisk them to safety. But Yunho refused to abandon everyone he held dear. He'd stood sentinel on the nursery floor, as screaming children ran from CPS agents. His face had projected fury and hatred. It was an expression that would haunt Mason for decades to come.

"Pretty lifelike, huh?" Gabriel's voice startled Mason out of his trance. "It's our Founder's Memorial."

Mason looked beyond Yunho. Sure enough, he was just one of many statues that stood in the Great Hall. Behind him: Claudia in her wheelchair, Astrid with a basket of vegetables, Daniel in a physician's smock, Mahmood crouched by a calf, Grey cradling a baby. "I was there too, you know," Mason insisted, angry at the exclusion. "At the beginning."

Gabriel pointedly ignored Mason, walking further into the Great Hall. Mason hung back, not willing to part with Yunho. He imagined the sculpture coming to life. The embrace they'd share. The musk of Yunho's sweat, the warmth of his body. He felt the pang of bittersweet relief, as if Yunho had forgiven him, as if time travel was real and history was just a canvas you could paint over, should the first figuration lack the proper resonance. "I love you," he whispered, like an idiot, to the inanimate object before him.

*

"Housing units have been constructed around the freshwater lake in our grassland biome. That way we could renovate this main house to operate as our healthcare facility." Gabriel guided Mason through the converted halls. The hardwood corridors were lined with examination rooms.

Comforting murmurs and soft cries emanated from behind closed doors. "We treat all residents of the AAR, as well as refugees injured by whatever horrific expedition they endured to arrive here. We take them in, tend to their wounds, and orient them to the systems of our AAR."

"Don't you worry about overpopulation?"

"Frankly, we need refugees. For our survival. Many Care Pods have decided not to raise children. As a result, demand for infants from our Gestator Union has declined. Production of new life has slowed to a trickle, and we depend on refugees to sustain our society."

"But why don't people want to have children?"

Gabriel issued a weary sigh. How to explain the strange utopic claustrophobia unique to their society? How to explain that the thrill of the Construction Era had long since disappeared now that it was no longer possible to sneak across the Canadian border to smuggle supplies or board a flight and travel the world to collect environmental specimens from every biome on Earth? The construction of their closed ecological system had been successful; it was a ten-mile triumph, a re-creation of every habitat soon to be wiped off the planet. But how to explain that the afterglow of that victory had faded, that sometimes life in a ten-mile bubble felt maddeningly confined? How to explain the fatigue caused by the physical labor required to ensure that the crops survived and that the CO_2 levels remained sustainable so everyone could breathe? How to explain the depression that set in when Gabriel realized they would never again pass beyond the borders of the DMZ? How to explain the exhaustion Gabriel felt after decades of living under threat of siege, where a distant rumble of an aircraft could jolt them from the deepest sleep and into a fierce panic that didn't cease until it was confirmed their fragile ecosystem had not been bombed, raided, or overwhelmed by enemy tanks? How to explain that utopia could never really be utopia as long as humans roamed the Earth or Mars, that no matter how egalitarian a life one could construct, there would always be someone who wanted to destroy it?

It was not a surprise that fewer and fewer residents of the AAR felt the desire to reproduce. They knew the uncertain future that would face their offspring, the possibility of invasion, occupation, enslavement, and death, the mortal threat that lay on the other side of the DMZ. Gabriel and Fennel had started the anti-natalism trend among AAR Care Pods, quietly declining to put their names in the Birthing Lottery year after year, watching as other Care Pods began to do the same, until the Gestators Union noticed a decreased demand for their product. The Gestators argued this did not bode well for the future of the AAR. Gabriel and Fennel and the others countered that this was precisely the point; the future was doomed. Still, the Gestators asserted, there was the present to worry about. Refugees could fill the labor ranks more immediately than children, the anti-natalists argued. But what about pregnant refugees? What would happen to their children? It was an unanswered question. One that fueled the few Care Pods who refused to jump on the anti-natalist bandwagon.

"It's a long story," Gabriel muttered. "Suffice to say that hope is in short supply."

"But you've created the most incredible community."

"Our presence on Earth is tenuous at best, under constant threat from the UCCA."

"*But—*"

"Mason. We've abolished incarceration and execution, but I'm sure we could make an exception for you. So please, shut up." Gabriel stopped outside Room Fifteen. "We're here."

*

Fennel lay sleeping on their hospital bed, curled into fetal position. Their body was so still Mason momentarily feared he was too late. Evidence of a fitful slumber manifested in the mess of the bed sheets beneath their skeletal frame; hospital corners had been torn from their folds; a green blanket hung off the side of the bed. Fennel dozed atop the cotton wreckage; their hospital gown fluttered in an HVAC blast. Sweaty tangles of gray hair shrouded their face; their head rested beneath a dark halo of perspiration stained into the pillowcase.

Mason and Gabriel stood over the bed in silent contemplation. Terror, grief, and affection fought for dominance over Gabriel's features as they considered their lover's dying body.

"Should we come back later?" Mason whispered. Before Gabriel could reply, Fennel gasped awake, inhaling a lock of hair. They gagged, pulled wet strands from their mouth. "Fennel." Mason grasped Fennel's brittle hand. "I'm here."

"Mason." Fennel recoiled but stopped short of withdrawing their hand from Mason's.

"I'm . . . I'm sorry." It felt like such a stupid and underwhelming and pointless thing to say. Mason waited for Fennel to respond, but they only lay there, catching their breath. He nervously rambled, anxious to fill the silence. "I know words mean nothing after what we've been through. So let me make this up to you somehow. I can get a LyfeHack team across the DMZ, I don't care what kind of bureaucratic red tape I'll have to slash through. Maybe they can reverse whatever's happening here, extend your life by a year, a decade, or—"

"*Mason, stop!*" Fennel shouted, wincing in pain. "I don't want to live forever."

"But—"

"I *want* to die. Have you ever wondered why people with the greatest stains on their conscience are the ones who've chosen to pursue eternal life?"

"I . . . guess I haven't."

"Because they know it'll be impossible for them to rest in peace."

Uncertainty swelled in a painful silence. "Why did you ask me to come?"

Fennel faltered. "I . . . I don't know." Some nebulous terror gathered like a storm behind their pupils. "I guess I wanted . . . to say goodbye."

Fennel's face. It was like staring at an optical illusion the moment one realizes it's a reversible figure containing two images. From one vantage point, it was Fennel staring up at him, the aged version of the child he'd abducted with the help of the federal government eighty-nine years prior, the child he'd raised with a guilty lament in his bitter heart, the child who'd received the finest luxuries the money of a civil war hero could buy, and yet still, Fennel grew to resent Mason once they discovered the disgusting truth about the coward who called himself "father," and that resentment swelled into rage. Mason had denied Fennel the life they'd been meant to live, a life among a loving community instead of a coterie of disgusting kleptocrats who eventually became Mason's friends and clients. So, at just thirteen years old, Fennel did the unthinkable: They fled across enemy lines, across the DMZ, in search of their true home.

But when viewed from a different vantage, Fennel's face became that of their biological father's, the resemblance as clear as an echo across a placid lake. Suddenly it was Yunho who lay dying in front of Mason, as real as the day they first decided to have a child, all those decades ago, in Daniel and Mahmood's backyard, crouched in the sandbox with three-year-old Gabriel. Gabriel's imagination had been boundless; the child's mind was a place where dragons were real and love reigned, an antidote to the cynicism of American life at the time. In that sandbox, Mason and Yunho decided to bear a child of their own, a child that would represent what every child represented: the promise of the future. Surely, they'd be forced to keep this promise when they were responsible for another small being; they wanted their child to live a better life than they had. Mason and Yunho would have no choice but to take greater responsibility for the dying planet, no choice but to put a stop to greed and the global decline of compassion. As they sat with Gabriel that day, they made a decision so many parents had made before them: the decision to bet on love.

"Can you ever forgive me?" Mason asked.

Fennel paused and stared directly into Mason's eyes, searching for something in his gaze. "No," they said finally. "I can't."

A heat rose within Mason, a love like lava, a force so hot and propulsive that he couldn't stop the eruption of warm fluid that spilled from his nostrils, his mouth, even his dehydrated tear ducts, but the fluid didn't feel like mucus, it felt like body-magma, bits of internal history dislodged and melted down by the furnace of his feelings. "Please," Mason begged. "*Please.*"

Fennel said nothing, just fixed their cold stare on Mason's heaving body. He buried his face in his hands and wept in the devastating silence, his desperation intensified by Fennel's denial. But no, this wasn't the end, it couldn't be, he refused to accept this punishment. They could find healing. Mason wiped the tears and snot from his face, and lifted his head, and stared at Fennel's dying face, which seemed, at the same time, like Yunho's dying face.

Suddenly, he was struck with an idea. A path to forgiveness. But Mason remained silent; he didn't know how to voice this epiphany in a way that didn't sound delusional or grandiose or like something a movie president might say when confronted with an asteroid aimed at Earth. Because Mason had a plan—he was going to save the world.

SEVENTY-FOUR

I cannot *believe* that Jeff hasn't RSVP'd to our baby shower." Mason sat upright in bed, furiously scanning the retinal projection of their invite list that hovered in front of his face.

"Honey, I think it's safe to assume he's not coming." Peter ripped the intravenous line out of his arm with a wince and rose from their bed, a tufted expanse that stretched in front of the massive window-wall currently framing another stunning sunrise over the jagged western lip of the Jezero Crater. Peter pushed the IV pole out of his way and sent the equipment clattering onto the marble floor. He flinched in surprise; he was still unaccustomed to the newfound strength that accompanied his pectoral implants. "Wow, I thought my new tits would be purely aesthetic."

"Are you sure you're okay to rip out your IV like that, sweetie?" Mason rolled his eyes back into his skull to cease the retinal projection and turned his gaze toward Peter's falsely sinewed naked body. "Shouldn't we get the doctor to check—"

"Mason, this is my ninety-sixth surgery over eight decades of LyfeHack surgeries. I know when it's safe to take out my fucking IV drip."

"Jesus."

Peter softened. "Sorry, I didn't mean to snap. It's the stress of this baby shower." He vanished into the blazing glow of their theatrically lit walk-in closet, itself bigger than any of the shed-sized Volunteer living quarters that annexed the main Palantir biodome in which Mason, Peter, and other members of the Palantir sector of the Imperialist Class lived. "And Jeff *can* go fuck himself for skipping ours," Peter called from within the closet. "He expects us to attend *his* baby shower every year and suffer through the same lab-grown steak sliders when you *know* that bitch can afford real Earth-imported beef."

"I mean, we could *all* abandon the expensive pageantry of these things if we *wanted* to, but we don't!" Mason yelled back. "But Jeff doesn't give a fuck, he just holes up in his penthouse in the Amazon biodome, puts the *least* amount of effort into *his* baby showers, and then skips every other Imperialist baby shower."

"Exactly." Peter emerged from the closet wearing his new tuxedo. He attempted a smile; his frozen cheeks rose slightly, his green eyes (the third pair he'd implanted in two years; he always got bored of his iris color) glistened with mischief. "But I have something more important to discuss." Peter presented a small black box, tied with a red ribbon.

"What is this?"

"A push present. You do such a wonderful job of overseeing the Crop every year."

"Well, I have a lot of help. A whole staff—"

"Still, you're the best daddy that our children could ever ask for."

Mason took the box and pulled at the ribbon. He gasped when he saw the contents. "Oh, Peter you shouldn't have."

"Do you like it?"

"Like it? I *love* it." There in the box, glistening on a bed of cryo-ICE: a tongue. Still pink with life, pulsing slightly. It was fresh. Tears, beautiful tears, flowed from Mason's new tear ducts. The delayed LyfeHack surgeries had been the first thing Peter insisted Mason take care of upon returning to Mars. But this tongue was a luxury, an elective their doctor suggested as a decadent possibility, because though Mason's current tongue could technically function for at least another decade, his sense of taste would deteriorate exponentially over those years. "Is it . . . ?"

"Real human? Of course. I'd never saddle you with some cheap lab-grown knockoff."

"How much did this cost?"

"It doesn't matter; what's important is that I love you. I missed you so much while you were on Earth."

Mason looked down at the tongue. The mention of Mason's Earth trip combined with the extravagant gift elicited a guilty churn in Mason's gut. His plan to save the world (and thereby secure Fennel's forgiveness) had become waylaid upon his return to the luxurious confines of his Martian estate. Mason kept mentally rehearsing different ways to broach the subject with Peter, but every practice run only increased his anxiety. After weeks of agonizing, fear won out; it was easier to enjoy the comfort of his home rather than suggest a wildly ambitious plan to disrupt the life of every Martian citizen; his resolve faded along with the memory of his dying child's cold and accusatory stare. But now, Mason's guilt revived his need for exoneration with sudden urgency. "Honey, I wanna talk to you about something." Mason's voice wavered. "I need your help."

SEVENTY-FIVE

The Honored Volunteers stumbled through the ballroom in a skittish pack, their swollen bellies straining the seams of ill-fitting gala attire loaned to them for this occasion only. They sipped seltzer from wineglasses and picked at sliders made from real Earth-imported Wagyu beef. As was typical of these events, the Imperialist crowd regarded the Honored Volunteers with exasperated smiles, as if acknowledging their humanity was an arduous task that required great sacrifice. This display of "kindness" was so poisoned by resentment that it was impossible for the Honored Volunteers to forget that the minute their pregnancies concluded, they'd be stripped of their vaunted status.

Mason watched the crowd from his throne on the ballroom stage and swallowed the bilious surge of self-loathing that had followed a Wagyu belch. How had this become his life? It wasn't as if he'd just woken up one day to discover he was the well-kept house husband of one of the richest men in the galaxy, and yet suddenly Mason felt this was *precisely* what had happened; a strange existential amnesia wiped his memory and triggered a terrifying dissociation. Mason struggled to recall a single moment from his 125 years of living that had brought him here, to the surreal nightmare of an eternal life that he'd never have the courage to end.

"You okay, sweetie?" Peter squeezed Mason's hand. Mason looked toward his lover, who sat on the neighboring throne. Both royal seats were made of gold-plated iron, but Peter's was larger than Mason's. *You're the queen, my love,* Peter had teased when the furniture was first installed. *You need a daintier throne than the king.*

"Yeah, just a bit of indigestion."

"How many times have I told you that your stomach is not equipped for those sliders?"

"I think I'm just nervous about my speech."

"Don't be. Your plan is going to be very well received." Peter turned his gaze to their crowded ballroom. "If you show them as much passion as you showed me in our discussion this morning, you'll have no trouble convincing this room full of idiots to get on board with your big, beautiful idea. Okay?"

"Okay."

"Now let's get this baby shower over with." Peter turned to the hulking security guard that stood next to his throne. "Round up the Honored Volunteers."

Mason suppressed his dread as he watched the guard wrangle the scared huddle of Honored Volunteers. From the early planning stages of the Mars Colonies, Mason had objected to the concept of the Volunteer but had been powerless to change the foundational structure of Martian society, as he was only the spouse of an Imperialist Leader, and therefore not taken seriously by the Founding Parents who comprised the Martian Constitutional Convention. When first designing their society, the Founding Parents were confronted with a problem: They needed cheap labor to build luxury biodomes, but the hundreds of impoverished humans who would be transported to Mars to create this workforce would never be able to pay the wildly expensive price that accompanied interplanetary space travel. The solution: They could repay their debt through indentured servitude. It was brilliant; there was no shortage of desperate people who would gladly trade miserable Earthbound poverty for a chance to reside among the galaxy's wealthiest individuals and possibly advance within their society. For this was another promise the early colonizers of Mars included in their pitch to would-be members of the inaugural underclass: the opportunity to climb into the upper tiers of Martian aristocracy. Travis Kalanick, during initial meetings with fellow Imperialists, suggested they call this underclass "slaves." His argument was that they were resurrecting the ancient Roman model of slavery, which was fundamentally different than its more recent American iteration; like the Roman slaves, Martian slaves would have the ability to eventually (after logging enough hours of unremunerative work to reduce their debt to zero) earn money for their labor and pay their owners the requisite fee to free themselves. Once free, former slaves would be granted citizenship; they'd be allowed to pursue paid employment at any Mars-based industry and could even own slaves themselves if they wished to start their own businesses. Each slave would be instilled with a Martian Dream nearly impossible to attain, yet even more tantalizing for the rarity of its realization. But ultimately it was decided by the Founding Parents that *slave* was a word with too much stigma attached, that people wouldn't understand the historical *nuance* they intended. After lengthy debate, *Volunteer* was settled upon for the term to describe the underclass that created the surplus of free labor that kept Martian society running.

"Welcome, friends," Peter addressed the Honored Volunteers as they lurched their pregnant bodies onto the stage. There were twenty-five in total, varying in ethnicity, gender, and sexuality, in keeping with the Constitution's Diversity and Inclusion Amendment that ensured *all* humans had equal opportunity to serve as Volunteers. "Is everyone ready to begin?"

Some Honored Volunteers nodded catatonically; others stared dead-eyed into the crowd. Already, the assembled Imperialists were murmuring among themselves, hushing their voices in anticipation. Peter crossed to Mason's throne and whispered into his ear, "Let me finish the ceremony, then I'll cue you up for your speech, okay?"

"Okay."

An announcer's voice boomed from the sound system. "Ladies and Gentlemen, please give a warm round of applause for the Imperial Leader of the Palantir Martian Settlement, Peter Thiel!" Despite the encouragement of the announcer, the temperature of the ensuing applause was chilly at best. Mason stared at the bored faces of Imperialists who'd seen hundreds of these baby showers in their artificially extended lifetimes.

"Thank you." Peter quieted the room. "I'm happy to commence this beloved ritual that all our Martian Settlements perform every year. Baby showers are an opportunity for us to reflect on our beautiful cycle of life and pay tribute to the Honored Volunteers who offer up their bodies in service of keeping each Martian Settlement healthy, productive, and strong!"

Golf claps rose from the stultified crowd. Jeff Bezos yawned, in attendance despite his lack of an RSVP. *So* rude. The Honored Volunteers fidgeted under the stage lighting. Suddenly, one pregnant man grabbed another and burst into sobs.

Peter winced, gritted his teeth, and continued. "We're so grateful these Volunteers chose this year to mate and provide our big Martian family with beautiful new babies that will grow up to become productive Volunteers within our society, just like their mommies and daddies." Sweat pooled beneath Mason, soaking his throne cushion. This part of their yearly shower always filled him with extreme revulsion. The guard handed Mason a metal bucket, just in case.

"But as we welcome new life, we must consider the limited amount of oxygen we share and the levels of carbon dioxide in our biosphere." A screen lowered from the ceiling, unfurling above Mason's throne. A scream emanated from within the Honored Volunteer huddle. "Which is why it's with profound respect that I introduce you to this year's Class of Retirees." A live video flickered onto the screen. A wide shot, filmed from a ceiling corner. Rows and rows of sparkling steel tables. Strapped to each: a body. "The twenty-five beautiful souls you see on this screen have worked tirelessly to sustain the utopia we all enjoy here on Mars, no matter which Settlement we reside in. Though none of these individuals managed to pay off their Original Debt within the time limit outlined in their contracts and rise out of the Volunteer class, that doesn't make them any less important. But now we must say goodbye and make room for the new life growing inside each of our Honored Volunteers . . ."

Mason looked out at the crowd, half of whom looked as though they might fall asleep standing up. The other half anxiously hailed the un-honored Volunteers handing out buckets.

"Now, let's begin the Harvest."

The crowd watched the screen.

Silence. Then, a whirring followed by a chorus of rapid-fire clicks, like hundreds of little claws scampering across linoleum. Slowly, from underneath each table, a Reap Spider emerged. They were an army, moving in unison. They scuttled to the left of their respective tables, clattering across the floor on jointed steel legs. They all stopped at once. Their massive glass abdomens, made of translucent bulletproof glass and big enough to hold a wild boar, glistened under harsh fluorescent lighting. They were empty. They were ready.

Each Reap Spider possessed a cluster of lenses—aka "eyes"—mounted on a titanium thorax. Each assessed the distance between the floor and its table. Each flexed its razor-sharp chelicerae; the unison clicks of fifty mouthparts coalesced into one metallic thunderclap.

Then, they leapt. Flying effortlessly, they landed on their prey. Shrieks rose from the restrained Retirees as they faced the hypodermic fangs of the Reap Spiders. Each AI-arachnid sunk its needled chelicerae into the neck of its prey, pumping tranquilizer into carotid arteries. No matter how loud the Retirees screamed, no matter how much they thrashed against the leather restraints keeping them splayed on cold steel tables, the shot never failed to quiet them within seconds.

Once the Retirees had wilted, the Reap Spiders began their work. The room was silent, except for the sounds of bodies being carved. The robotic clicks of razored claws. Flesh being sliced. Ribs cracking. The wet slurp of jostled organs. Each Reap Spider worked in the same methodical fashion as it harvested the body beneath. For every heart, lung, and wildly valuable kidney it was the same; the Spider would remove the organ from the carcass, sprout a fresh needle from its chelicerae, flush the organ with preservation solution, and wrap it in ReapSilk, the hypothermic silver gauze that protected the organ until it could be properly stored in the LyfeHack Lab. The Spider then opened the hatch on its glass abdomen and deposited the organ inside. Over time, each Spider amassed a mountain of human parts inside its bulletproof belly.

"Finally, I'd like to thank our corporate partners at LyfeHack," Peter continued his monologue, though most audience members were hunched over their metal bucket, vomiting prodigiously. "I know I speak for every citizen across Mars when I say we treasure our relationship with *the* corporate leader in the life extension space." Those who weren't regurgitating sliders into their slop pails clapped.

Nausea swept Mason's senses, but he repressed the urge to join the vomitous tsunami ripping through the ballroom. He had to remain strong. He had to put an end to the tyranny of the quadrillionaire class. He had to abolish the horrific ritual of the Martian baby shower, a bogus propagandic party to "honor" pregnant Volunteers while murdering others and selling them to LyfeHack BioLabs for luxury body parts, a fate the Volunteer babies being feted in Mason's ballroom would almost certainly share if they reached the contractually lethal age of forty and failed to accomplish the nearly impossible task of rising above their station. There was a wretched pragmatism to this population control; the Martian biodomes could only support a finite amount of life due to the necessity of maintaining a balance of oxygen and CO_2; thus aging, "obsolete" Volunteers had to be sacrificed (sending them back to Earth would be too expensive) before new beings could breathe the urgently monitored air supply. Plus, LyfeHack needed a regular supply of body parts to ensure all Imperialists had plenty of organs to utilize in their respective quests for eternal life.

Mason looked at the crowd with disgust. Extending your life did not necessarily deepen it; in fact, Mason had experienced a *flattening* in the years beyond his hundredth birthday, time crushed his spirit, steamrolled his sense of self. He felt like a one-dimensional character in an ancient video game, an Atari avatar doomed to forever walk the same course, confront the same undying villains. Yes, Mason would stop this madness. Peter would help. Mason looked to his husband. "You're up, sweetie," Peter said, gesturing for Mason to stand. "Knock 'em dead."

*

Mason knew his audience well. To appeal to someone's sense of morality, that person must first possess a sense of morality. An impassioned speech wherein Mason argued for a restructuring of Martian society and its earthly colonies to emulate the AAR utopias and free humanity from economic exploitation would fail to stir a single cold, dead, technocratic soul in the room. So Mason pitched them something they *could* understand—optimization. If he could convince his audience that industry *functioned* better when people lived equally, when everyone had enough resources to thrive, then there was hope. As Mason spoke, he peppered his pitch with personal anecdotes of the overwhelming resurgence of love he experienced visiting the AAR. Love, yes love, was still alive in the AARs, a love that unified everyone and made society run better than any politician or executive ever could, "a sense of love and equality that creates a near-perfect community model we can export to our own planet. Let's invest in the AARs, let's free our Labor down on Earth, let them run the factories, let them build their own biodomes. Let's liberate humanity from the shackles of interplanetary colonization." Mason's pulse accelerated; his words gained velocity. He felt the audience shifting; with a little more convincing, he could change history. "Please, look within your hearts. We have a chance to—"

Eight sharp spikes sunk into Mason's shoulders. He screamed, looked down; waterfalls of blood burst from wounds inflicted by multi-jointed steel legs. He screamed again, looked up: a Reap Spider perched on his shoulders. Its empty abdomen glistened.

"*Peter!*" Mason howled. "*Peter, help!*"

But Peter wasn't looking at Mason, he was looking out at the audience. "As everyone in this room knows, we here on Mars have a zero-tolerance policy for sedition. It brings me great pain that the traitor among us is my own husband."

Three more Reap Spiders skittered onto the stage. They lunged at Mason, slammed into his torso, and knocked him to the ground. They pinned him to the stage, one spider for each wrist, one for each ankle. "*Peter—don't do this to me!*" Mason screamed.

"I felt it important that you all hear his horrific insurrectionist ideas before his public execution. This is a teachable moment. To remind us of the consequences for attempting to undermine the perfect societal structure we've obtained here on Mars."

"Please . . ." Mason was losing blood, losing consciousness. "I'll . . . take it back. Please."

"Our Reap Spiders have been reprogrammed to forgo the tranquilizer we offer our beloved Retirees. We want Mason to feel every organ as it's ripped from his body."

A fifth Reap Spider crawled onto Mason's torso. Its eye-cluster assessed his body. Machinery whirred as it planned Mason's vivisection. It raised one daggered leg, then plunged the knife point into Mason's gut. Mason howled as the blade sliced his abdomen. Steam rose from his insides. A gust of air tickled his open heart. The last thing he heard was applause.

SEVENTY-SIX

There is a commonly held belief that revenge is a base and deplorable human impulse, that an eye for an eye leaves the whole world blind, but there lies an ableist prejudice at the heart of that sentiment, the idea that happiness is impossible to achieve without sight. If this were true, how would one explain the twinkle in Fennel's milky white irises, or the smile on their face as they sat in their wheelchair in the apple orchard, barely conscious, barely breathing, baking in sunlight beating down through greenhouse glass, next to a tall tree, heavy with clusters of red fruit? How would one explain the relief they expressed through slow and deliberate gasps of air, struggling to hold on to life, yet determined to thank Gabriel for summoning Mason to Earth? The visit gave Fennel such peace, such joy, and the healing satisfaction of withholding forgiveness, the relief of being confronted with the person who had caused so much harm and realizing that if someone doesn't deserve mercy, you don't have to give it to them. But revenge alone is not enough to sustain a life. It can motivate you, yes, but once it's achieved there is nothing left.

Which is why you need love.

"Did you . . . bring them?" Fennel grabbed their lover's hand. Gabriel felt a sickening lurch in their heart, which triggered dissociation, and their consciousness floated high above the orchard. They closed their eyes, and imagined they were speeding toward space, into nothing, because that is what life without Fennel would be: nothing, not worth living, because how could they continue without love? Wouldn't suicide be a relief, revenge against the pain of living? Gabriel was glad Fennel was going first. They could spare Fennel the anguish of waking up alone, that daily reminder that life was worthless because love had left this Earth.

"Yes, I have them here." Gabriel took out the letters given to Fennel upon their return to the AAR, a gift from Claudia that filled Fennel with gratitude and passion and a profound appreciation for every soul in their strange, beautiful community. "Just stay with me," Gabriel said, and though Fennel was slipping away, certain to depart before the end of the letter, Gabriel read the text aloud, holding on to each word like it was scripture, something holy, though it wasn't, it was simply one woman's message to a child, amidst the agony of war.

*

June 17, 2045—Montana Women's Prison
Monitored Electronic Message

My dear sweet someone,

The day of the police raid, an officer hauled me into his vehicle. As we sped toward the station, a searing white heat ripped at my heart and I remembered Astrid, the way she'd been shot down. I screamed out and the cop screamed back, told me to shut up or he'd shoot me. Shock took over. My mind shut down. I was no longer human; they whittled my soul into almost nothing. But then I remembered you, Fennel, and the idea of you filled me with light.

On my worst days here in prison, you keep me alive. I've been here for months now, and I don't know what's happened to you, or any of the children from our community, but the goal of finding you, saving you, ensuring you carry on our work of building utopia, this fills me with a longing so powerful it overwhelms my desire for death, the temptation of the end.

I've never believed in endings. My work, my life, has been a radical rejection of all end points; how can any honest revolution ever conclude? True anarchism asserts that there is only ever a beginning. Because there will always be something else, *someone* else, residing just past your idea of an ending; there could be whole oppressed populations waiting beyond your definition of justice. We have no idea what realities we'll be forced to confront once this civil war is over; we must be flexible, imaginative, and committed to the creative promise inherent in destruction, to the idea that abolition is an infinite beginning, to the endless experiment of creating a liberated, egalitarian, and ever-new society.

I'm happy our world burned, Fennel. All we're left with is a charred and beautiful and blackened foundation. We can build anything. Together. I'm hopeful about the prisoner swap. Though they've denied me direct contact with Yunho, I've watched in admiration as he's negotiated with the U.S. government and brought the concerns of the United Commune Front to the fore. I'm hopeful that not only I, but everyone apprehended by the SAS during this civil war will be released. I hear rumors that armored trucks will transport us through the newly established DMZ. That we will be deposited in front of the gates to the AAR.

Fennel—will you wait for me there, just beyond the borders we long to abolish? Will you be cradled in Yunho's embrace? Can we commit to a project of eternal liberation and love? A love more powerful than any state apparatus that attempts to destroy it? A love more powerful than any god because it doesn't live in the sky, it lives within each of us, you and me and everyone we know, everyone we love but also everyone we hate? A love available to anyone, always? A love that will live on in the endless beginnings that follow our brief experiment on this planet?

If all these questions are too overwhelming to answer, just let me hold you in my arms. We don't need words; we'll know that this is the start of something unbounded, ungovernable, something limitless and soaring and lyric, an irreligious hymn, a song with no coda, a melody anyone can learn, a love powerful enough to fill every heart on Earth.

Because it's not the end of the world. It's only the beginning.

Yours forever,
Claudia

ACKNOWLEDGMENTS

Thank you to PJ Mark—I am forever grateful for your guidance, fearlessness, humor, care, and friendship. This book would not be the same without your brilliant perspective. Also, thank you to Madeline Ticknor and Kerry-Ann Bentley, who read early drafts of the novel and provided support along the way.

Mo Crist—I could not have asked for a better editor. Thank you for your endless curiosity, wonderful sense of humor, wise suggestions, and beautiful collaborative spirit. From the very beginning, you understood my vision and worked tirelessly to support it.

To everyone at Bloomsbury—thank you for shepherding this book into the world with boldness and brilliance. I'm grateful to my production editor Barbara Darko, copy editor Logan Hill, art director Patti Ratchford, marketer Katie Vaughn, and publicist Amanda Dissinger. Also, Lauren Peters-Collaer—your cover absolutely stunned me from the start.

To the many friends, some of whom read early drafts, others who provided emotional support along the way, I am so grateful for your continued support: Karley Sciortino, Coco Mellors, Henry Slavens, Kate Brody, Will Lippincott, Taymour Soomro, Kelsey Miller, Chrissy Angliker, Jason Yamas, Kyle Dillon Hertz, and Jeremy Atherton Lin.

To all the readers who embraced my debut, *Yes, Daddy*, with such passion—I am forever grateful to you.

To my family—I love you all.

And finally, to Ryan O'Connell—words fail to express the depth of my love for you. You give me life, strength, joy, and laughter, so much laughter.

A NOTE ON THE AUTHOR

JONATHAN PARKS-RAMAGE is a Los Angeles–based novelist, playwright, screenwriter, and journalist. His critically acclaimed debut novel, *Yes, Daddy* (HarperCollins), was named one of the best queer books of 2021 by *Entertainment Weekly*, NBC News, *The Advocate*, Lambda Literary, *Bustle*, Goodreads, and more. His writing has been widely published in such outlets as *Vice, Slate, Out, W, Electric Literature*, Atlas Obscura, Literary Hub, and *Elle*. He is also the co-creator of the Off-Broadway musical comedy *The Big Gay Jamboree*.